Atlantis Rey, single mom to Verruca Rey, wakes from her cry-ogenic sleep pod 105 years in the future to find out things have not gone to plan. Vega, the ship's AI, explains that the vampire clean-up did not go as scheduled and that she and the 249 other passengers, are the last known living humans.

Vega appoints Atlantis as the leader of the awakees, and they all look to her for the answers to how to survive their new lives. Knowing their best chance is to return to Earth, she has to find the right place to settle them before space or malicious awakees foil her plans.

Yet amidst this chaos, Atlantis and Verruca manage to find lovers and a new family to surround themselves with.

Treacherous Heavens
Copyright © 2023 Michell Burgan
ISBN: 978-1-4874-3750-3
Cover art by Martine Jardin

Published by eXtasy Books Inc

Look for us online at:
www.eXtasybooks.com

Treacherous Heavens
A New World Tale 1

By

Michell Burgan

DEDICATION

To my daughter, who is why I do everything. To my angel in heaven, we miss you every day. To all my friends who have believed in me from the beginning, Thank You.

CHAPTER ONE: THE WAKING

I opened my eyes but quickly jerked my head to the side and slammed them shut against the blinding light. I tried to bring my hands to my face to wipe away the tears from my eyes, but they banged into something metallic. My heartbeat picked up a notch as I tried opening my eyes again, but this time only a sliver. I barely made out a small glass window in what looked like a sheet of metal. My breathing quickened, coming in short explosive intakes of air. I lifted my head slowly to look at this metal thing I was lying in and slammed my forehead into the top of it. My head instantly dropped back down from the pain of impact. I couldn't really see much from where I lay because there was no room to move. A sense of claustrophobia began to set in. My mind raced in a million different directions with the dread of lying in a metal sarcophagus.

Doing my best not to completely panic, my fuzzy brain began trying to remember where I was, with just flashes of memories breaking through. I willed my arms to rise again, barely feeling them through a vibrating burn a hundred times worse than when limbs fall asleep, and I pushed on the metal with the glass window. It didn't budge. I tried several more times with no luck. My heartbeat picked up again as I searched the edges for a button, a lever, or anything that would make it open before the panic threatening my control took over. I even tried kicking it, but that sent shocking pain through my foot.

I was breathing through the agony when the top part of the

1

tube started making a clicking and hissing noise. Then I felt a sharp jab, like little claws were releasing their grip on my neck. My instinct was to reach for my neck, but I still couldn't get my hands that far up. I sucked in a sharp breath from a sudden slithering sensation that zinged from my lower back all the way up my spine to where I had felt the sting in my neck. It felt like wire was being pulled from my body.

The top portion of the lid slid down over the bottom half. The whole thing lifted about two inches on some kind of metal arms, then slid down a few inches before turning toward the floor. Then the top half rose again like a shield standing at the end of my pod. The sounds of clicking and popping came from my right, and I turned my head as the side slid down out of the way.

After the metal tube quit making noise, I quickly sat up, sucking in the cool air. I leaned my forehead into my hands, taking deep breaths. I paused my freaking out when I realized the air was stale, like a house that had been shut up for a long time. Not knowing what to make of that, I took a moment to let my fuzzy brain painstakingly piece together the flashes of memory. After a few minutes of fitting pieces together like a puzzle, I began to slowly make sense of everything and opened my eyes.

Carefully and clumsily, I swung one leg at a time over the edge, letting them dangle. My legs now experienced the same burning, tingling feeling as my arms. After a few minutes, my limbs started to feel normal, and the flashes of memories began to make a little more sense.

Memories of the end of 2032 came rushing back. My daughter and I had volunteered for the first Cryogenic Sleep Program due to the volatile situation in the world. I was forty-one, and my daughter was twenty when we had been placed into our pods. We were supposed to sleep for two years. Had it been two years already?

I sat staring at my feet and shook my head slightly, needing a few more moments to clear the cobwebs cluttering my thoughts. My whole body ached from being unused for so long. I slowly rolled my head from side to side, stretching the muscles, waking them up, and felt the tightness gradually ease. After a few more deep breaths, I felt ready to look up and take in where I was.

I slowly lifted my heavy, still slightly fuzzy head and looked around. The bright lights still made me squint, but I could tell this was not a warehouse, which was where we were supposed to be stored. The walls of the room were a dark gun-metal gray and appeared metallic. Exposed octagon-shaped girders ran from floor to ceiling on one side of the room, then across and back down to the floor on the opposite wall. Three sets of girders were in the room, one at each end and one in the middle. Two rows of pods lined the walls between the girders with a wide walkway down the center of the room. The floor was covered in a very short light-gray carpet. Blue lights glowed along the edges of the ceiling, and about midway up the walls was a medium orange stripe that ran around the whole room at the same height.

They were definitely not colors I would have put together, but I didn't have a say in the color palette.

I was positive I was on some sort of vessel. I could feel a soft vibration, like the engines of a plane or a boat. I tried to look out the large octagon-shaped window above my pod but couldn't see much. All I could see was pitch black with white speckles and wispy, smoky-looking patches, which made no sense to my slowly working brain. My gaze dropped to the monitor mounted on the wall above my pod. It showed a picture of the moon and the stars surrounding it.

Needing a better view out the window, I prepared to stand, but I wasn't sure my legs could hold me. I wiggled my toes and rolled my ankles, which caused the muscles to burn and joints to pop. Still slightly apprehensive about standing, I swung my legs back and forth to see if they would listen to the command. The tingling sensation made my limbs feel disconnected from my body, as if the signal from my brain was delayed. They felt heavy and moved clumsily. After a few minutes, I slid off the side of the pod and set my feet on the floor to see if I could stand. The pressure of my weight on my legs made the lower half of my body tingle even more. I breathed deeply and wrinkled my nose, still not used to the stuffy air. I pushed myself somewhat upright and tried a few steps. I stumbled but quickly caught myself on the cryo-pod. I gently put one foot in front of the other until I was walking, albeit slowly, but I was still walking. I kept hold of the pod next to mine to keep my balance.

I paused to give my muscles a break. My fingers absently began to rub the metal of the pod. The color was a burnished silvery gray, and the finish was rough. At the foot of the tubes were the initials *CGSV* stamped into the metal. I ran my fingers over them, wondering what they meant, but shrugged it off. My gaze traveled up the lid and saw a logo stamped in the center that looked like a phaser gun, similar in shape to a scan gun at a grocery store checkout. Encircling the phaser image was the company name, Phaser Cryogenics.

I began walking back and forth along the pod, my balance getting better with each step I took, but my shoulders felt like my muscles were tied up in knots. I kept trying to straighten up that last little bit, but every time I did, my muscles tightened, and a sharp pain shot through my upper back. Leaning my hip against the pod, I lifted my arms slowly over my head and stretched from side to side. It was helping a little, even though it hurt with each pull on my muscles. I dropped my chin to my chest, and with a soft grunt, I forced myself to roll my head from side to side. After several times of doing this, my muscles finally released and relaxed enough for me to stand up straight.

I walked unaided up the path in the center of the room, gaining strength with each movement, looking at pod after pod lining the walls on each side. Monitors were attached to the top of each unit that displayed images of stars and swirling galaxies. I continued walking slowly down the path, trying to take everything in. I could now see recessed lighting in the ceiling above each pod, creating soft lighting in the room. Well, not when I first woke up, it seemed blinding then. Now, combined with the blue lighting, it spread a soft, warm glow throughout the room.

I paused for a moment to catch my breath. As I took in more details around me, I noticed that each pod sat on a pedestal with a long oval base on the floor and a central supporting arm holding a platform on which the pods sat. The more I looked at the shape, the more it resembled a phaser gun. Leave it to a company to get their logo worked into every aspect of their design.

Feeling ready to move again, I headed toward the end of the room with a large glass door. From what I could see, it led into a corridor with multiple hallways jutting off it.

It suddenly dawned on me that I was the only one awake, and terror engulfed me. My heartbeat raced out of control. My breathing became erratic, and my whole body trembled from a spike of adrenaline. I thought I had panicked before, but it was nothing like what I now felt, the fear that my daughter was not here.

Turning to the closest pod, I frantically began checking the faces through the window in the top of the pods. The first one was a young man, and the second was another man. I crossed the room, and the first pod I investigated was also a man. Feeling bile rise in my throat, I ran to the next one. When I peered inside, I saw my daughter's beautiful face as she lay there. Relief flooded me, and I dropped my head onto the top of Verruca's pod, taking several deep breaths to steady myself. I didn't know how any of this equipment worked. I needed to figure out how to open the pods and wake someone up.

Afraid to mess up anything, I went back to the first guy's pod. I knew it might seem cruel, but I just couldn't experiment on my daughter's pod. I would never forgive myself if something went wrong.

Taking a chance, I tapped the screen above the guy's pod. The image of the moon disappeared, replaced with a blueprint of a strange-looking triangular ship, and underneath the ship's outline were the words *Moon Viper*. I guess it was the name of the vessel or the company that made it. Anyway, it didn't matter. I tapped the screen again, but nothing happened. I double-tapped, and still nothing happened. Not sure how to get the screen to come on, I looked for buttons or a mouse but could not find anything. Frustrated, I grabbed each side of the monitor and shook it. *Stop, stop, you will figure it out. Slow down and think.*

Taking a deep breath and staring at the monitor, I tried to remember other ways a person could open a locked screen. My first thought was face recognition. I grabbed each side of the monitor and faced it toward me so it could scan my face, but nothing happened. With both hands still on the monitor, I tried to think of another way. I loosened my grip, and my thumb slid down the side of the screen, which made something flash. Excited, I swiped down the screen. Again nothing. I swiped up. Nothing. Then I swiped to the right, and the locked screen slid away.

Another screen popped up with rows of generic-looking app icons that were simple and easy to understand. The first image was a red square with a white cross, clearly a medical alert symbol. Pausing just before I touched it, I pondered if it would harm the guy in the pod. I didn't want to hurt anyone, but I needed to know what was going on. Biting my lower lip, I tapped the icon.

Up popped a screen with a picture of the guy in the pod and a brief physical description. He was six foot five inches, two hundred and fifty pounds, with black curly shoulder-length hair. Looking back at him, I could see streaks of red and caramel, like he spent a lot of time in the sun. Upon closer examination, I noticed a cable connected to the back of his neck and instinctively reached for the back of my neck. I grimaced when I felt a ball just under the skin, not knowing what it was used for.

I looked at the profile picture again. The guy had dark tanned skin, slightly almond-shaped tawny eyes, a broad nose, and full lips. I looked back at him and saw a swirling tribal-looking tattoo on his chest. I gazed at his face again, studying his features. From what I could see, he looked to be Samoan.

At the bottom of the monitor was a blinking line running across the screen like light trails in a photo, showing a steady heartbeat. In the corner was a blinking heart with large numbers under it. I assumed it was his pulse oxygen level. I remember looking at screens like this when I had to sit in the emergency room with my dad during bad asthma attacks. Dealing with his severe asthma condition my whole life is one of the reasons I don't panic under pressure.

Another section toward the bottom of the screen showed bobbing lines. I was not sure what it was monitoring, but it had several lines moving up and down, making a graph like an EKG or a polygraph readout. I continued to watch the little bobbing line. Something about it held my attention. Then it clicked, it was monitoring his brain waves.

I continued to look over the page and saw that next to his name, which was Ryo Kekoa, was a blue profile link. After deciding I didn't have time to read a long profile on the guy,

I swiped to the left and got back to the home screen.

A green icon that had a tree on it caught my attention. Again, I paused due to that feeling of messing something up, but I hadn't caused any catastrophes by touching the other one. Mentally I thanked Dad again for my calm under pressure. He had always left me to run the house while he was working, but he also lost his shit anytime someone was hurt, me especially. Between running a household by the time I was eight and being forced to be the rational one when the shit hit the fan, I had learned my skills of remaining calm at a young age. And now was not the time for me to panic or lose my confidence. Again, I dropped my finger and tapped the icon.

A new screen came up with tabs at the top that said things like *Air Quality, Air Scrubbers,* and *Natural Filters.* I clicked the tab labeled *Air Quality,* and the screen switched to a bar graph. Four colored columns in the chart were slightly moving up and down. After a minute of scanning the information on the screen, I realized each column displayed air elements and levels. The first column was green with the word *Oxygen* above it, and to the left, it read *100 percent.* The yellow column was labeled *Nitrogen* and showed the level at *78 percent.* The last two columns read *Carbon Dioxide* for the red bar and *Carbon Monoxide* for the pink bar. Both showed *0 percent,* which I was glad to see. The last thing I needed was to have an issue with breathable air on the ship. According to this page, it seemed that we had plenty of breathable air. Of course, I might not totally understand what I was looking at, but I hoped I was correct.

I clicked on the next tab labeled *Air Scrubbers.* The screen displayed four squares with a circle in the center of each one. Inside the circles were spinning fans. Some basic info about the scrubbers showed at the bottom of the squares, and all the squares' backgrounds were green. I assumed that meant they were all working correctly.

The next tab was labeled *Natural Filters,* and when I opened it, there was a list of plants. I clicked on a blue link that said, *Layout.* A blueprint of the ship came up, identifying certain sections of the interior. I selected the one labeled *Communal Area Blue Deck.* It showed plants in tiered planters with pipes coming out of the side and running up to the ceiling. The back row said *Bamboo Palms.* The next tier listed *mother-in-law's tongues* and *dragon tail plants,* and the last layer had *aloes* and *peace lilies.* I scanned through all the communal areas on each deck, and all had the same tiered plants.

I checked out the cabin section of the blueprints, and each cabin had *ivies* and *spider plants* attached to the kitchen walls. Then there were more spider plants running the length of the halls, hanging close to the ceiling. The ship was evidently using the plants to help filter the air and generate oxygen. It was a cool concept. Personally, I have always liked the peace and calm plants brought into a living space.

Looking over the map made me realize the ship was much larger than this room. There were five decks and a round disk-shaped deck on top, which looked like a wheel room or cockpit. The shape of the ship looked like a slice of cheese or cake but with two large holes at the back.

One tab, in particular, piqued my interest. I clicked on this tab to see how much water we had aboard. The first screen showed two large bars, one blue and the other brown. Next to the blue one, it read a hundred percent, and under it said *Clean Water.* On the side of the brown one, it read ten percent, and under it said *Dirty Water.* There were two sub-tabs, one labeled *Recycle* and the other *Hydroponics.* The first sub-tab walked me through how the water was recycled on the ship.

At the bottom of the screen was the word *Backup* in bright blue letters. I paused for a minute, scared about what the backup plan would be. I hoped it was not instructions on how to boil and filter your pee or something like that. I took a deep breath and tapped the link. To my relief, it was instructions for an ice-collecting system. Several pages of instructions walked me through how to deploy two pieces of wide fine mesh material that would blanket each side of the ship. The mesh collected and trapped ice from the surrounding area and transferred it to collection tanks. As the ice melted, a special filtering system would separate the water from other elements, purify it, then send it to the clean water tanks.

The second tab talked about the hybrid hydroponics system in which the plants were grown. The hybrid system used soil and a highly nutrient-rich water solution.

This ship was almost a completely self-sustaining environment. My mind was spinning from what I had just read. I didn't even know we had technology like that.

I continued going through the other icons, checking our levels to make sure we could survive on this ship. We were going to need time to figure out what to do and where we were.

Once I was done with my review, I pulled up Ryo's chart and left it there. Seeing his heartbeat move across the screen was strangely calming. I watched the blips skip across the screen while my mind tried to think of my next steps. I wasn't sure if I wanted to wake Verruca and Ryo now or hold off until I knew more about what was going on. I flipped back and forth between the two ideas but finally decided to wait.

I turned from the pod and walked to the door. Placing my hands on the frame, I pushed hard, but it didn't open. Trying to slide it open didn't work either. Heading to the wall on the left, I ran my fingers around the edges, searching for a panel or a button but found nothing. Moving to the right side, I repeated the action to no avail. Frustrated, I tried waving my hands around, hoping it was motion-activated like the doors at the grocery store, but again it didn't open.

I stood staring at the door, tapping my index finger on my

chin, trying to think of something that might make it open. Then it hit me. Maybe it was voice-activated.

"Hello," I said, but nothing happened.

"On." Still nothing.

I was getting angrier by the minute when I yelled, "Ship!"

Still, nothing happened. I was about to try kicking the door when a deep, dark, seductive male voice answered me.

"Ms. Atlantis, how can I help you?" The voice sounded like it came from the ceiling.

Bouncing up and down, I said, "Yes, can you open the door?"

The smooth male voice answered, "Yes, I can."

I began rambling, turning in a circle and looking at the ceiling. "Where am I? I need food. Can you show me where it is? How many of us are on this ship? What year is it?" I paused to take in a deep breath.

"Yes, I can help with all of those questions, but one thing at a time," the male voice interrupted with a stern tone.

A sudden ripple in the air in front of me manifested into a tall man, at least six-foot-seven, wearing dark blue jeans and a light-blue collared sweater. The sweater and his eyes were almost the same color, though his eyes were slightly lighter. His skin was a warm chestnut, and his hair was a strange mix of mahogany brown and blond.

"Who are you?" I asked, staring at the apparition.

"I am Vega, Ms. Atlantis." The male turned his head to the side slightly as if studying me.

Then I noticed he was slightly transparent around the edges of his shape. So he wasn't real, just a holographic image.

A click and whoosh came from the direction of the door. I turned, and it was open. I walked out into the corridor, looking at all the hallways, not knowing which one to go down.

"We will follow the lighted blue arrows. They will show us

where to go." Vega pointed to his left.

Blue arrows appeared on the hallway floor, so I followed them. I looked around, trying to take in everything as I passed. I looked back toward where I had come from and noticed the arrows disappearing behind me. This concerned me a little, which must have shown on my face.

"Don't worry, the arrows will appear as long as you need them," Vega assured.

Vega stayed by my side as we followed the arrows for about another ten minutes, and then they turned to the left. We continued down another hallway, and I looked left and right. There were empty rooms down most of this hallway, each of them with one table and a couple chairs around the table. I looked through the last door on the left and saw two large washers and two large dryers. I paused and gave the room a thorough look then turned to look back down the hallway. I began moving my index finger in a steady beat as I counted the doors down the hallway so I could remember how far down the hall the laundry room was located.

"You can relax, Ms. Atlantis. I will help you until you know the ship."

"In this form?"

"In whatever form you would like."

I was about to respond when we came to a large doorway at the end of the hall. As I stepped into the room, I could see that it was a large cafeteria.

"Okay, well, how do I find food, and can you also start answering the other questions I asked?" I probably sounded slightly impatient, but Vega hadn't said much to this point.

Vega didn't respond right away, so I walked across the room toward the far wall, where I saw tiers of plants like I'd seen on the computer. Now that I was closer, I could tell they were vegetables and could also see the hydroponics system. Each tier was a long clear box. The bottom six inches of the boxes contained water that the roots of the plants were growing in. Then above that was a thin black something covered with a few inches of dirt that the tops of the plants sprouted from. It was an interesting-looking system.

"Vega," I said, "can you please start telling me what's going on?"

"I am Vega, the ship's AI and your assistant. There are two hundred and fifty people on this ship, including you. It is star date twenty-one thirty-seven. I have videos that will explain how you got here and what you are to do now."

I raised an eyebrow at his tone and stopped my inspection of the plants. I turned to look at him. "Okay, Vega, please show me how to get food. My stomach began growling halfway here, and now it feels like it's trying to eat me from the inside out."

"Let's follow the arrows to the back of the dining room."

I followed him and walked into a large commercial kitchen.

"You will find meat in the freezer. The ship was stocked with enough food to feed all two hundred and fifty occupants for thirty months. The developers figured by the end of thirty months, the occupants of the ship would have animals born and old enough to reproduce."

"Wait what do you mean? Animals born?"

"I can guide you to the labs later and explain everything. First, let's get you fed. As I mentioned, the meat is in the freezer. Vegetables are on the plants you have already seen, and the cooking utensils are hanging in the kitchen area," Vega explained with a nonchalant wave of his hand.

"Thank you, Vega."

I stood in the doorway facing into the kitchen space, looking around while a million different possibilities clouded my thoughts. The what-ifs were turning so fast that I had to literally shake my head to clear my thoughts. A bevy of pots and pans hung on racks attached to the ceiling. Chef's knives clung to magnetic strips on the wall, and other utensils were standing in different containers on the stainless-steel counters that lined the walls. I walked from the doorway to where several stainless-steel tables ran down the middle of the kitchen like islands with the cooktop embedded into the center table. I looked around the kitchen for ovens and found a double-wall oven on my right.

Then I headed to the back toward a large metal door. As I got closer, I realized the handles looked similar to those found on a walk-in freezer. Grasping it, I pulled with a little bit of force, because if it was like the previous ones I'd dealt with, the door would be stuck. It opened easier than I expected, and I stumbled slightly. Stepping forward, I moved the plastic flaps out of the way and saw stacks of bins along the walls, each containing piles of plastic packages with labels on them.

Reaching into the first bin, I pulled out a package labeled *Steak*. Walking out of the freezer, I inspected the packaging in the brighter light of the kitchen. I could tell that the meat had been freeze-dried or preserved in some way I had never seen before. The meat looked like I was picking up a fresh package at my local grocery store. It was still a nice red color, and I could see the texture of the meat. It really looked great. I closed the freezer, still turning the package over in my hands. It may look nice, but how it tasted would be another story.

"Vega, how was this food preserved?"

"Phaser had scientists working on a new preservation process. It combines high-pressure food preservation with vacuum-sealed packaging and electronic pulses added to the freezer system."

"Electrical pulses?"

"Yes, it kills any organism that might have survived the high-pressure preservation process and keeps cells in the food from aging and breaking down."

"Wow, I knew about high pressure and vacuum sealing to preserve food, but I would have never thought of using electrical pulses. Wait, I was just in there, and I didn't feel any electric pulses."

"That's because the pulses only occur once an hour on the hour for ten minutes, and the freezer automatically locks until the process is done," Vega explained.

I nodded and returned my attention to making food. I put the steak under some running hot water in the sink, then turned to find a pan. I picked a skillet from the rack and sat it on the counter next to the stove. I then realized I would need a side dish to go with the steak. I walked back into the main dining area where the plants were growing, looking around at the choices available. That's when I noticed squash vines on a trellis in the back. Tiptoeing to reach them, I pulled two from the vines. Back in the kitchen, I retrieved a second skillet from the racks overhead and placed it on a burner. I looked around for some oil and seasonings but didn't see any. I turned to Vega, who was still standing in the same place, watching me, tilting his head side to side like a puppy.

"Vega, do we have oil and seasonings?"

"Yes, in the cabinet on the back wall to the left of the dishwasher."

I opened the cabinet and found a vast selection of seasonings, oils, mixes, and condiments of all kinds. The first shelf had large containers of garlic, pepper, salt, chili powder, paprika, and many more spices, while the next one held gallons of oils of all kinds. The shelf under that had gravy mixes, ranch mixes, packs of sour cream powder, ketchup, mustard, and just about every condiment you could think of. The bottom two shelves were filled with containers to hold smaller portions of all the items above. I pulled out what I needed, then went back to the stove.

I turned the burner on low, poured the oil in, and retrieved the steak from the sink. Once I removed the packaging, I placed it in the pan and seasoned it. While it was cooking, it was time to prepare my side dish. I walked over to the knives and scanned the options. There were so many different kinds I didn't know which to choose. Spotting a good chopping knife, I pulled it from the wall and returned to what I was doing. I sliced the squash into thin round pieces, threw them into the skillet, then sprinkled salt, pepper, and some garlic onto them. After grabbing the smooth metal fork from the cutting board, I used it to reach over and flip my steak. Smells of seared meat with hints of garlic were wafting up from the skillet, which made my stomach growl even louder.

After everything was cooked, I plated it and walked back out to find a table. The room was set up a lot like a large school cafeteria with rows of cafeteria-style tables, the ones with attached seats or benches. Large walkways lined each side of the room and a main pathway down the middle. On my right were the vegetable planters, and on my left was the doorway I'd first walked through.

I sat at the first table I came to. I only got a few bites of squash before my mind began to race about what the ship said. Replaying Vega's words in my head, I took another bite of squash, and then it hit me. He said the year was 2137.

Speaking with a mouth half-full of food, I called out, "Vega, what year is it again?" I turned to look for him.

"It is star date twenty-one thirty-seven."

I turned to face the direction his voice came from just as he popped into view. "What time of day is it even?" I blurted, almost cutting him off.

"It is two in the morning, Earth time," Vega answered with just a hint of annoyance in his tone.

"Wait, are you sure about the date? It was twenty-thirty-two when my daughter and I were placed into our cryo-pods. We were only supposed to be asleep for two years, not a hundred years." I almost choked, trying to swallow the food in my mouth.

Still trying to clear my throat so I could ask more questions, I looked around, chastising myself for not getting something to drink when I prepared my food.

Vega gestured toward the kitchen, accurately guessing my dilemma. "In the cabinets to the right of the doorway is where all the glasses and cups are stored."

I walked back into the kitchen and got a glass of water. I gulped the contents while standing at the sink and refilled it before returning to the dining area.

"It has been a century since twenty-thirty-seven, Ms. Atlantis. As I said, I have videos that will explain what happened, but you should finish your meal first."

I sat back down, cut into my steak hungrily, then shoved a large piece into my mouth. Chewing such a large piece was difficult after sleeping for so long, but I continued while waiting for Vega to say something. I paused my slight mental breakdown from learning I'd been asleep for a hundred years and realized the steak tasted exceptionally good. I hadn't expected that from food that had been preserved with an experiential process.

"Originally, the pod system was supposed to wake the people aboard this ship after eighty years," Vega continued. "But there was so much chaos at the end, somehow it was mis-programmed. I initiated the ship-wide systems six months ago, then programmed the droid to plant vegetables here and flowering plants on each level. The other plants, like the bamboo palms, mother-in-law's tongue, and dragon tails, have been on the ship since it launched and maintained with the self-regulating hydroponics system."

I swallowed my current mouthful of food before I tried to speak. "Vega, what sea are we currently adrift in? Are we close to America, or are we overseas somewhere?"

After a long pause and a puzzled look, Vega finally responded. "We are not at sea, Ms. Atlantis, we are in space."

I froze in shock with a fork full of squash midway to my mouth. I slowly placed my fork on the plate. After staring at my plate for a long minute to process what he said, I took a deep breath and asked, "What do you mean we are in space? Like outer space, with stars and planets?"

"Yes." Vega's simple response made me pause.

Not knowing what else to ask, I just sat there eating and thinking, continuing bite after bite in a daze, staring at the table but not actually seeing anything. All possible reasons we could be on a ship in space raced through my mind—everything from a vampire-ridden world to the annihilation of the human race and everything in between. What could have happened that would have driven them to shoot us into space instead of putting us in the warehouse?

"Can you wake anyone I want?"

"Would you like for me to wake your daughter?"

"Yes, I do, but not yet. I have no answers for her." I sat there for a minute, then asked, "How did you know who I was?"

"I know the names and info for everyone onboard this ship." Vega paused, looking to the side like he was reading something. "You are Atlantis Rey from Houston, Texas. You are a single mom to one daughter, Verruca Rey, who is twenty years old. You had one son who passed away. You are an artist and photographer, and you love anything creative. Your daughter is a hair and makeup artist."

"Why did you wake me first?"

"You seemed to be someone that could keep calm under pressure. I actually have much more info on you than what I just mentioned. I also know your work history, that you were raised by a single father, and that in most sports and clubs you were part of, you were a leader. I also know you're a Leo, and they are natural leaders. Or at least that is what the info I have read on Leos says."

"Wait, how do you know all these things? I don't remember giving them that much info."

"When the last of the scientists decided to send as many people as this ship could hold into space, they did in-depth research on each of you. They pulled up everything they could find about each person, including education records, birth records, court documents . . . anything your name was attached to. They uploaded all the information into my mainframe. One of the scientists programmed my systems to gather thoughts and dreams while you all slept. We didn't know if it would work. The Dream Wave Program was in final development at the time of launch, but it has mostly worked. It hasn't been completely reliable. Sometimes I cannot make sense of what some people are dreaming or the thoughts flashing through their minds, but overall, the program works."

"Wow. Well, don't hold all my thoughts or dreams against me. I can be blunt and extremely truthful sometimes. It usually rubs people the wrong way."

"I will not, but that is also part of the reason I chose to wake you first. I saw that you have handled some of the toughest moments a person could have and stayed strong. You continued to do what needed to be done and never fell apart. I assume that was mostly because you had your daughter to raise, but that would not have been good enough for most people."

I was shocked that the ship knew so much about me, let alone anyone else on this ship. I sat there in silence, eating, just letting everything process through my muddled brain.

After what seemed like an hour, Vega spoke again. "I have the videos ready for your review if you are ready."

I took a deep breath and said, "I am as ready as I am going to be."

CHAPTER TWO: FINDING OUT WHAT HAPPENED TO EARTH

Beams of light from a black bar in the ceiling appeared above my table, forming images.

"Ms. Atlantis, these videos may scare you, but it is the truth about what happened and why you are on this ship," Vega said just before he vanished.

"I understand, Vega. I just need to know, because I'll have to help everyone else understand what is going on."

With a flicker of more light, the videos began. The first was info on the Cryogenic Sleep Program that my daughter and I had volunteered for. The narrator was the same guy who took us on our tour of the labs and guided us through all the steps. The video opened with the man standing in front of the company headquarters, introducing himself, the company, and the program. He flung the front doors open wide, and the camera followed him as he walked through the building, talking about the program.

"Phaser Cryogenics has finally and successfully created the first cryogenic sleep program. Their scientists developed the first pods, computer programs, and solutions that allow people to sleep, not age, and stay alive over long periods. Phaser Cryogenics worked on the technology for two decades before coming close to a working formula. Then, with the advancements in technology and science in the last five years, they made the breakthrough they had been looking for. After many successful lab trials, Phaser was granted approval to test on humans.

"Phaser called for volunteers from the public at large for the trials. They offered a safe way to sleep through the cleanup of the vampire virus and a compensation of seventy-five thousand dollars to each volunteer for the two-year trial."

The video jumped into some boring details on how the program worked and then ended.

The money offered was one of the reasons my daughter and I decided to join the trials. But seeing the end of the video, it appeared lots of people had showed up to volunteer.

The second video's narrator was also male, sitting at a desk like a news broadcaster. Pictures flashed on a screen behind him as he spoke.

"The vampire virus has caused widespread havoc. Elixir, one of the largest pharmaceutical companies in the world, created *The Fountain of Youth* vaccine, which is now known as the vampire virus. The company had asked for volunteers to try their new youth vaccine to see if it truly slowed down the aging process. The shot was supposed to slow the human body's aging process to the point that a person's body would barely age, resulting in a person's life expanding exponentially. Hence the nickname, *vampire virus*. Their first round of human test subjects had extremely limited and mild side effects. Seeing such impressive results in test group A, the company asked for more volunteers."

The narrator droned on as I watched the pictures of people getting needles filled with a pale purple liquid shoved into their arms and them waiting for side effects before being sent home. As more images of people flashed by, I noticed that all of them were in what looked like an emergency room, writhing in their beds with tubes hanging from their arms. I tuned back in to what the narrator was saying.

"The side effects of the larger study group were not what they had expected. After they were allowed to go home, some people went crazy, and others claimed they had become actual vampires.

"The crazy ones, now known as *fang wraiths*, became rabid, wandering the streets, confused, not knowing who they were or where they were. The worst part was their sudden bursts of anger, blindly attacking any person, animal, or object that came close to them."

The images flashing on the screen showed thin, human-looking creatures walking along the streets of a city. They didn't have much clothing on and were snarling at each other. Then several started attacking things close to them. One creature was biting, scratching, and yanking on a signpost, foaming at the mouth throughout its blind attack. The video switched to a different city, where the fang wraiths were attacking each other. Their attention switched to chasing a dog that turned a corner, unknowingly walking into danger. The images continued switching from city to city, all showing similar violence.

"The other group declaring themselves actual vampires claimed they craved blood and could not control their cravings or actions until the hunger had been quenched. It didn't matter what kind of blood, but a substantial portion of them seemed to prefer human to animal. According to a report released today from the CDC it takes only one bite from an infected vampire to change a human. Please stay away from these creatures, they can transmit the virus if they bite you and if you see them report the location to your local authorities." The narrator added a few more warnings before the video ended.

After watching the second video, a lot of my memories became clearer. I remembered that the chaos in the streets was another reason we had decided to volunteer for the Cryogenic Sleep Program. During orientation, we were told we would wake in two years and that there would be a chest at the end of each pod with clothes and instructions on how to assimilate to the new world. We would be rejoining the world late in the vampire virus cleanup phase, able to move forward into a new world with a new life. Evidently, something had gone wrong, because now we were in space.

Video three had a female narrator sitting at what looked like the same desk the male used in the last video. She, on the other hand, looked tired and worn out with bags under her eyes, no make-up, and her clothes were mismatched. Just like in the last video, pictures flashed on a screen behind her as she began talking.

"Vampires have spread and are now trying to take over the world. Elixir's reversal vaccine has not worked on most of the infected subjects. Originally, the vampires had been separated into two classes, known as the vampires and the fang wraiths."

Pictures of the two types of vampires flashed across the screen. The fang wraiths looked even more gaunt and sallow than in the last video, but the others appeared healthy and strong.

"The vampire class sectioned themselves into three levels of rank. The Jades are at the top of the hierarchy. They got their name due to their jade-colored eyes. They are the healthiest but not always the strongest of vampires. They use the next levels to do their fighting. They are considered the elite and have become immensely powerful and rich almost overnight.

"The Drakes are the next level in the hierarchy, easily identified by their blue eyes. They make up the officers of the vampire army. They are stronger than the Jades but are prone to health issues, and they can take longer to heal when wounded.

"The Embers are the lowest level of functioning hierarchy. They have unique, amber-colored eyes and are faster and even stronger than the other two levels. Embers will not heal when wounded, no matter how much blood they consume. A study shows it's because they barely transformed into full vampires. Therefore, the two levels above them see them as expendable. They are the soldiers of the vampire army. The Jades have been using their armies to take over the world.

"The fang wraiths, those who did not make the transition into vampirism, are still considered highly dangerous to humans. When they reach the end stage of this disease, they are called fang rots since they start falling apart because the disease has done so much damage to their bodies. In this final stage, they lose their teeth and fangs first. Hence the name *fang rots*."

I continued watching in horror as the images of these creatures flashed across the screen. The virus had ravaged their bodies to the point they looked more like fast-moving zombies than vampires. Instead of clothing hanging from their bodies, most now had only skin or body parts dangling.

The video flickered and then continued with a male narrator.

"The world's governments are working to create a plan as the vampires gain numbers and strength. Fang rots and vampires are running wild worldwide, forcing humans to hide to survive. Humans have created compounds to hide in, and governments have also opened their underground bunkers to the public."

Pictures of schools and military bases flashed across the screen behind him. They looked like prisons with armed guards walking the grounds. Large guns sat every few feet along fence lines like sentries guarding the compounds and the people they enclosed. This was crazy. How could our governments have let things get this bad?

"The vampires have at least one fortress in each country. World governments tried various forms of extermination with little success. Efforts were doubled when one of the vampire armies in the US gained access to a nuclear base. The vampires threatened to use nuclear weapons on the world if humans did not back down and bow to them. Instead of surrender, the governments decided to coordinate a simultaneous nuclear attack on the vampire fortresses in every country."

That video ended, and a new one began.

The narrator of this one was again female, but she was wearing a lab coat and looking more tired than any of the others.

"When Phaser learned of the nuclear attacks, they took as many volunteers as they could from the Cryogenic Sleep Program and placed them on a ship. The ship had been a prototype for a manned mission to Mars, but they knew if humanity had any chance of survival, they needed to make the ship work without the government's knowledge. They did just that. A ship with two hundred and fifty sleeping humans was launched into space the day before the attack on the vampires. On May twenty-fifth, twenty-thirty-three, governments across the globe launched nuclear weapons at each of the fifty fortresses around the world. The results were devastating."

The narrator started crying.

Images of nuclear fallout flicked by as I continued to watch in horror. People dead, lying scattered across cities and landscapes. Others wandered through the streets with large sores and burns across most of their bodies. Unable to turn away, I continued watching as the narrator went on.

"Phaser labs were able to hold some people for a brief time, and we monitored what we could by using satellites still in orbit. The cities not directly hit still had working cameras, electrical grids, internet, and communications. Unfortunately, drinking water or food that was not contaminated was in short supply."

Images continued to move across the screen, showing the complete devastation caused by the bombs. Then the video of the female broadcaster cut off, and a large man with tan skin, almond-shaped eyes, and short black hair appeared.

"I am the last person left in the labs. This might be the last of the transmissions from the Earth that the ship receives. I am trying to hold on, but I have had to do things that no person should have to do to stay alive this long." The look in the man's eyes was wild and unfocused. He kept turning his head side to side between sentences like he was waiting for something to attack him.

"I will set the system to continue transmission feeds to the ship every five hours, but if I die, I do not know how long the system will keep running. I hope that everyone on Moon Viper will awaken, see these videos, and make the decision to return to Earth. The planet will need clean DNA lines to restart the human race."

The video ended, and I sat staring at the area where the images had appeared. I wasn't sure what to say or do. Then my survival instincts kicked in. I stood up quickly and began to pace, muttering to myself, letting all I'd seen and heard process through my muddled brain.

"Ms. Atlantis, are you okay? Would you like me to wake someone now to help you?"

"No, Vega. Where are the other videos from this guy?"

"Most of the videos didn't really have any information on them, mostly just movement in the room. The last one from this man didn't make sense. He seemed to be ranting incoherently."

I continued pacing as the last part of the video replayed in my head. It suddenly hit me that I had no clue where in space we were.

"Vega, exactly where are we in space?" I sat back down on the bench.

"We are orbiting the moon and currently on the dark side."

"Vega, can we see the Earth from our orbit? Can we change position to orbit the Earth? I began looking around the room for a window, discovering that all the windows were in the ceiling.

"Yes, we can see the Earth as we orbit on the light side of the moon. And yes, I can change the ship's position."

"Vega, other than my daughter, who else do we have on board with us?"

"There are two hundred and forty-eight people besides you and your daughter. I can go through each person if you would like?"

"No, that is too many people to filter through." I took a minute to think of how best to filter the list for people who would be most helpful. "Vega, do we have people aboard that could be relevant to running this ship? Like mechanics, pilots, or scientists?"

I got up to head back to the pod room. When I got to the dining room doorway, I was thankful for the blue arrows illuminating the way. I glanced into one of the empty rooms and saw a human-looking droid that stood at about five foot-five and appeared very gender-neutral. It went about its chores, not even acknowledging I had paused to look at it. I continued just as Vega reported his findings.

"Within the two hundred fifty people aboard this ship, we have many different professions represented. We have commercial pilots, several mechanics, weapons specialists, several teachers, nurses, and doctors. Construction managers, two restaurant owners, two lawyers, and a martial arts teacher, to name a few."

I made it back to the pod room, and the doors opened automatically with a quiet swoosh, allowing us to enter. I walked up to the first pod I had checked before, Ryo Kekoa's. I looked at him through the little window, taking in the features of his tanned face.

"Vega, what does Ryo do?"

"He is a commercial pilot, according to his profile."

"Okay, wake him and my daughter up first, please."

Vega disappeared, leaving me standing in the center of the walkway, watching both pods as he began the waking process. I could hear hissing and groaning noises coming from each pod as the process progressed. After about fifteen minutes, there was a loud hiss and a click, then the tops of each pod slid down.

Verruca sat up first, looking around confused, then she saw me. "Mom!"

She started climbing out of her pod, but taking only one painful-looking step, she stumbled and fell to one knee.

"What's going on, Mom? Why can't I walk or move correctly?"

"Calm down, take a minute. Stretch your muscles some, and then try again."

She nodded, then pushed up into a standing position, placing her hand on her pod to keep her balance. She stretched and shook her legs. After standing still for a few seconds, she tried to take a step. When she wobbled, she threw her arms to her sides to steady herself. I jerked forward, attempting to catch her, but I was too far away.

While I was watching Verruca, Ryo had also climbed out of his pod. He was also having a tough time making his body move the way he wanted it to.

"Ryo, try stretching your leg muscles a little. It seems to help," I said.

Ryo nodded and tried stretching. He also used his pod to help maintain his balance as he maneuvered his legs. After that, he was able to control his limbs better. He tried to speak, which startled me because his voice cracked a few times and made a wheezing sound.

He coughed several times to clear his throat. His words became clearer, but his voice was not much louder than a whisper. "Who are you? Where are we?"

I put my hand up to signal him to hold on a moment, then turned back to Verruca, who was only a few steps away. I reached out my hands to her, and she grabbed them. I caught her as she stumbled, kissed the top of her head, hugged her tight, and swayed side to side for a long minute.

Still hugging Verruca, I looked over at Ryo. "I am Atlantis Rey. This is my daughter, Verruca Rey, and we are on a spaceship called the *Moon Viper*."

Verruca pulled out of my hug, causing my attention to snap back to her. She looked at me as if I was an alien. Ryo was giving me the same look when I glanced at him.

"I will explain everything, but I want to wake up a few more people before I go into the long explanation and show you the videos."

Verruca and Ryo both looked confused but nodded.

"Vega, can you wake the weapons specialist, the mechanics, the martial arts teacher, and two of the other teachers you talked about?"

I looked for somewhere for Ryo and Verruca to sit. On the left side of the glass door was a bench sticking out from the wall. I ushered them to it, making them sit down.

"We have several mechanics. Which ones would you like me to wake?" Vega asked.

"Can you tell me their names and what kind of mechanics they are?"

"Night Blue is a commercial airplane mechanic. Jax Kelean is a car and motorbike mechanic. Then there is a heavy truck mechanic, a small engine mechanic, and a heating and air conditioning mechanic."

That made it a lot easier. I thought about it for a minute, then made my decision. "Vega, please wake up Night Blue and Jax Kelean in addition to the others I requested."

Without a verbal response, I began hearing the waking process for more pods. I looked around for the other people, but they were missing.

"Vega, we are missing people. Didn't their pods open correctly?"

Vega informed me that the weapons specialist was in the second pod room and two others were coming from the third pod room both located on the other side of the kitchen area. He explained that this deck, deck five or the black deck, had three pod rooms. Two contained eighty-three people and the third contained eighty four.

"Vega, can you guide the others to this pod room, please?"

"Yes, Ms. Atlantis."

I sat down on the floor in front of the glass doors, waiting for the others to follow the arrows to us. They entered the room with a wide-eyed look of confusion, clearly still having a hard time moving. I glanced at the whole group and figured we would all need stretching exercises to work out our stiff muscles.

CHAPTER THREE: FIRST LOOK AT EARTH

Everyone looked scared and unsure of what was going on. Now that the last one was in the room, I stood up to address the group. "Hello, everyone. I know y'all are confused and have questions. We will get all those questions answered, but first, I would like everyone to introduce themselves. I'll go first.

"I am Atlantis Rey, originally from a small town in South Texas, but most recently I resided in Houston Texas. I am an artist, photographer, and writer. I like anything creative. I am also a single mom, and my daughter is here with us." I pointed at Verruca.

She stood up, looked out at the group, and waved slightly. "My name is Verruca. I am a hair and make-up artist, and as my mom already said, I am her daughter."

The group looked us over, some seeming puzzled. Maybe they were confused about how I could have a daughter Verruca's age or because her hair and eye colors were different to mine. I have blue hair—normally blonde—green eyes, and light skin even though I am half Hispanic. Whereas Verruca has dark hair with purple ends, dark eyes, and medium-tanned skin. Being half-African American gave Verruca her darker hair, eyes, and skin tone. Other than that, we looked like twins.

After a few minutes, Ryo got up. He nodded to me, then turned back to the group. "Hi, I am Ryo Kekoa." His voice cracked and squeaked on the last part of his name, so he cleared his throat before speaking again. "I am twenty-five

31

years old and a pilot for a private airline. My *ohana*, I mean my family, well, some of my family went into this program with me, but I am not sure if they are here." He looked back at me and shrugged.

Ryo was just about to sit back down when another male walked in. Ryo froze for a moment, then ran to the man and threw his arms around him. "Ronan! Oh my god, I am so glad you are here, *brah*. I don't know what I would have done without you."

Ryo pulled out of the hug and looked the other man over to make sure he was whole.

Ronan patted Ryo on the shoulder. "*Lolo*. I am fine. You're embarrassing us, *brah*." The guy chuckled.

I waved at Ronan to come to the front and introduce himself. As the two approached side by side, I took in their features. Both were about six and a half feet tall with broad shoulders, dark hair, and similar features. Ronan had dark eyes, and Ryo was a little thicker around the waist, but they could pass as brothers. Ronan was well-toned with shorter hair than Ryo, and he had a red dragon tattoo that ran down his left shoulder to his rib cage. The details were easy to see since we had not been dressed in much when placed into the pods. Males wore only a pair of shorts, and females a sports bra and shorts. It didn't leave much to the imagination. And looking at these two well-built, attractive men side by side had me imagining plenty of things.

Ronan began speaking, and his voice snapped me out of my scrutiny. "Hi, I am Ronan. I'm Ryo's older, smarter, and better-looking brother." He looked at his little brother lovingly.

Ryo elbowed Ronan in the ribs, and they laughed. I smiled at having guessed correctly about them being brothers.

Ronan went on. "I am thirty-nine years old, and we are from Maui, Hawaii. I teach martial arts. We had more family that volunteered with us, and I'd like to find out if they are here."

The next man to stand was taller than Vega, probably closer to seven feet, with warm beige skin, short dark blond hair, and blue eyes. I didn't see any tattoos. He looked to be around my age.

"I'm Kilian Ryan. I am forty-one years old from Portland, Oregon, and I don't know how I got here. The last thing I remember was being on assignment for the company I worked for."

Now my mind was racing. Did some of the people aboard not even sign up for the program? They might not take things very well. That was something I would have to watch out for.

A female walked up to the front of the group. She was average height for a woman, thin, light skin, with brown hair and eyes.

She cleared her throat, but her voice cracked when she tried to speak, so she cleared it again. "My name's Juniper Lovelace, and I am twenty-five years old. I taught science to high school kids in San Antonio, Texas. I don't know how I got wherever we are. This doesn't look like a warehouse, and I would love to know what is going on."

Another male stood but didn't move to the front. "Name's Night Blue, forty years old. I am a Native American from a small town in New Mexico. As far as work goes, I was an airplane mechanic before I volunteered to do the Cryogenic sleep trials, and now I am here."

I looked him over as he stood staring at me. He appeared to be a bit over six and a half feet tall with shoulder-length black hair, very tanned skin, hazel eyes, and a well-toned body. He had several tribal-looking tattoos on his body, along with a crow on his left rib cage and a wolf on the right. When he turned to sit back down, I saw a tattoo of an eagle with its wings spread across his shoulders.

The next man stood and walked to the front of the group. One corner of his mouth was turned up in a crooked smile like he was up to no good. As I scrutinized him, I thought to myself that he might be trouble. He stood a little over six feet with blond hair that hung just past his ears, brown eyes, tattoos everywhere, a short beard, and a warm honey complexion. He had his right eyebrow pierced and several piercings in his ears, none of which had jewelry in them. When he opened his mouth to speak, I could see a tongue ring.

"I am Jax Kelean. I am thirty-five years old. I was a mechanic and specialized in motorcycles before I volunteered for the Cryogenic sleep trials. I am from Austin, Texas, where I was part of an MC. I'm an only child. The last of my family line." The man looked down at his feet and took a deep breath before glancing at the group again, nodding, then returning to his seat.

The last male stood up, looking very much out of his comfort zone. He stood at about six feet, with brown hair, green eyes, pale skin, medium build, and one tattoo of a treble cleft on his shoulder.

He stood in place and began his introduction. "I am Cash Lee, thirty-three years old. I'm from Corpus Christi, Texas, and I taught music at a local high school. I am not sure where we are. Like Juniper mentioned, I was told I would wake up in a warehouse."

After Cash was done speaking, everyone started talking among themselves. I let it go on for a while because I had no idea how to start telling them about the videos Vega had shown me. After about ten minutes, I decided to use food as the next distraction so I could get my thoughts together on how to proceed.

"So, who's hungry?"

Several voices in the group cried out excitedly.

"Yes."

"Most definitely."

"I could eat."

I beckoned them to follow me and led them to the dining and kitchen area. Once everyone was seated, I told them about the food options and let them decide what they wanted me to cook for them. Most didn't really care what I made as long as it was edible. I went to the kitchen and decided the best way to inform them of what was going on was to just jump in headfirst with the videos. Once I was out of earshot of the rest, I asked Vega to show them the videos while I was cooking.

Vega began by introducing himself before appearing in his visible form. I smiled at the surprised reactions, since I had experienced the same thing. Once Vega had everyone's attention, he briefly explained what he was about to show them. As the videos began, I went to the vegetable vines and picked some more squash. When I spotted tomatoes and cucumbers, I added them to my collection.

I carried everything back to the kitchen as the group watched the ending of the first video. I was a little nervous about how they were going to react to the news the others showed.

As I planned and started preparations for our meal, I kept glancing through the door, trying to discern how they were responding to the videos. Wanting to check on them, I took some glasses and a pitcher of tea out to the table. Like a lot of the food on the ship, the tea was instant, but something was better than nothing.

When I approached the table, I glanced at as many faces as I could. Jax, Ronan, and Ryo appeared dumbfounded after the second video ended. I noticed Ryo and Ronan had their arms on the table, touching as if making sure the other was still there. Night was staring blankly at the area the video had just been playing. I heard a slight sob from the opposite side of the table and saw Juniper crying softly and Cash reaching across the table to hold her hand. Verruca, sitting next to Juniper, had a stern and determined look on her face, which I knew was her freaked-out expression.

I set the tea and glasses down on the table. As I turned to head back to the kitchen, I saw Kilian drop his face into his hands. I felt bad for everyone, but nothing I could do would ease their shock. They needed to watch the rest of the videos.

When I returned to the kitchen, the pork chops I'd left in the skillet were done, but the potatoes and chicken in the oven weren't quite ready. I took the skillet off the burner and placed a lid over the chops to keep them warm. I started working on the vegetables for the meal when I heard everyone talking, some louder than others.

"Vega, are the videos finished? Please only answer where I can hear you." I kept my voice low so the others wouldn't overhear.

"Yes, the videos are done playing. Everyone is talking about what they saw and what could be going on with the Earth now. And just to let you know, for me to speak only to you is called privacy mode."

"Thank you, Vega,"

I finished cutting up the squash, placed them on a sheet pan, and slid it into the oven to cook.

"Vega, all the condiments are in the cabinet, right?"

"Yes, but a few are located in this pantry." He appeared in front of the cabinet he was indicating.

I walked across the kitchen to the large cabinet and flung open the doors. I pulled out the ones I needed and read the instructions. Vega moved to the end of the table. I looked up at him to see he was intently watching what I was doing.

I mixed everything in separate bowls. Then I read the instructions for the ranch and found that I needed to mix up another round of sour cream first. I went back to the cabinet for another pack of the sour cream mix, then completed the batch of ranch dressing. Afterward, I looked up to find Vega was gone.

Finishing off all the food took another thirty minutes, and when I walked out to the table holding trays of food, everyone got excited. I set everything out on a separate table like a buffet, then backed up and let them have at it.

Kilian spoke as he took a seat. "So, what do we do about our situation?"

I held up my hand to indicate hold on, while I chewed my food. "Vega informed me that we are currently on the dark side of the moon. In a few hours, we will reach the light side, where we will be able to see the Earth. He hasn't told me what it looks like, but after what we just watched, I'm sure it's not going to be pretty."

Ryo asked with a hint of alarm in his tone. "Can we even get back to Earth, or are we stuck in space forever?"

In a soothing tone I tried to reassure him. "Yes, we can move to orbit Earth to better see what is going on. Then when we are ready and find the right spot to land, we will be able to. Vega assured me he knows how to do all of that."

Everyone returned to silence as they continued to eat. I knew this was a lot to process, but we all would have to face our reality soon. I began to think about all the things we needed to know about the ship, about each other, and the Earth. As my mind swirled with info, bits of a plan began to form.

We needed to limit the number of people we woke until we returned to Earth. Everyone should have an assigned job. If we woke only a small group of people, we had a better chance of controlling the situation and helping people adjust to our new life easier. Once I was sure I had this tiny part of the plan straight in my mind, I wanted to share it with the group.

Clearing my throat, I got everyone's attention. "I think, for now, just us nine should explore the ship and learn as much as we can over the next week or so before we decide to wake more people. I believe if we wake too many people without more answers, we will have chaos on our hands, and nothing will be accomplished."

No one spoke for several minutes, then Ryo broke the silence. "I think you are right. If we cannot assure them that we can survive here or on Earth, everyone will be scared, and nothing good can come of that."

Kilian spoke next. "I also think we should establish leaders and roles for everyone. We need to have leaders who can assure people that they are working on making us safe. The people we awaken will need jobs to keep them busy and to make them feel like they are contributing to our survival."

I sat there for a few minutes, waiting for someone else to chime in on anything. I was glad to see they were on the same page as me.

Since no one else spoke, I chimed in. "I agree with you, Kilian. I think everyone in this room should oversee distinct functions on this ship. Then the next group we wake can fall under each leader to contribute the best they can according to their skills. I also have a few ideas about some of the other things we need, but I want to get my thoughts together before I go into too many details."

Apparently, Night wanted to keep the discussion going because he asked me to elaborate.

I hesitated for a moment. "Well, my thoughts are not really formed into a solid plan, but I can give y'all the basics. I think we will need a security team. I haven't figured out which one of y'all should be in charge of that. We need people knowledgeable on the different areas of the ship, such as engineering and navigation. I am sure there are other areas I have not thought of yet. I take that back. I have thought about leadership.

"I think we should have a council that helps the leader to make the best decisions for everyone on the ship. Then we need training for the different jobs. We will need education for any children on board. Wait, do we have children on board?" I asked, more to myself than anyone. "Vega, do we have children on board?"

"Yes, Ms. Atlantis, we have ten children on board ranging from five to fourteen."

"Okay, so we will need schooling for them at some point. I also think we should take this time to learn some self-defense, how to shoot a gun, or any survival skills that will help us live on this ship and will also help us once we're back on the ground.

"And I think we should be strategic in who we wake. Some people aboard have more needed skills than others, such as doctors, nurses, chefs, and lawyers, to handle disputes. These are the basics for a structure we can build on, then we can adjust as we need to. Let me know if y'all agree." I looked over the group of people, trying to read their expressions.

Everyone began talking to each other and discussing the plan. I took the opportunity to explain to Verruca that I wanted to be the leader because I wanted to oversee the over-all mission. I just didn't trust anyone else to get us back to Earth in one piece. Nor did I want anyone else controlling our future because then no one would keep us from getting back to Earth where Verruca and I could build our home and have security.

Night interrupted me by calling my name. "I agree that we should make up the council. The main decision is who is going to be the leader."

"I think Ms. Atlantis should be Iksen," Vega interjected as he manifested behind me.

Everyone looked at him, confused. I glanced at everyone, not saying a word, trying to gauge their reactions.

"What is Iksen?" I asked Vega.

"It is the word for leader in my database."

"Where is it from?"

"It doesn't say. It just lists the word and its meaning in my mainframe. It's a nice word for leader, and I like it."

"I agree," Night said. "Atlantis should be the leader or Iksen."

"Me too," Verruca said, quickly seconding the motion.

Then the rest of the group began nodding and agreeing.

"Okay, then it's official. You will be Iksen," Kilian said as he stared at me strangely.

"None of y'all want to be Iksen?" I waited for someone else to pipe up, but no one did. Surprised, I went on. "Okay, thank you for the chance to lead y'all. I'll do my best to keep us all safe and get us back to Earth."

Verruca leaned over and whispered in my ear. "I think Vega was listening to us."

I just shrugged my shoulders and smiled at her. I didn't know if he heard us talking or if he had it planned. Either way, I got what I wanted.

Juniper asked, "So, what now?"

"Who wants to explore the rest of the decks?" I asked as I stood up.

Everyone stood up, ready to go.

"Vega, can you guide us through our exploration?"

Vega started by projecting a 3D image of the ship into the air above the table. Verruca and I let the shorter people stand in front of us so they could see better. Looking at the overall layout, it appeared every room had at least one very large octagonal window to view outside. The bottom level also showed several large doors on each side, which I assumed were hangar doors. Vega tapped the bottom level, causing it to light up and enlarge, and he began to describe each deck.

"Deck five, which is the one we're on, is the very bottom of the ship and is called the black deck. It contains three pod rooms, the cafeteria, two hangars for drone storage, a weapons storage, and three hangars equipped to hold animals. Several large non-designated rooms are currently empty and could be used for anything. Between hangars A and B is a flight room for programming and launching the drones.

"Last but not least, on the far end of this deck, on the right side of this projection, is the engine room. The engine room takes up most of the back end of this deck and houses the nuclear core of the ship. The core is housed in a protective case and should never be entered unless properly clothed." Vega tapped the next level, lighting it up so we could see the different sections.

"The fourth deck, or the gold deck, holds laboratories on the back end. The rest of the empty rooms moving toward the front of the ship can be set up for any workspace needed. In the front section of this deck, you will find family housing, a large common area, and plants that help filter the air for this deck.

"The third deck is the silver deck and is all living quarters for the people of this ship. There are mostly large suites for families. Although the front section of this deck has two-bedroom cabins. The decor within the accommodations is mixed, so people can pick what they like. You can find warm tones and cool tones. There are large common areas in the front and rear of this deck.

"The second deck is the green deck and is comprised mostly of two-bedroom cabins. All the rooms on this floor are decorated in earth tones. Like the third deck, this one has large common areas in the front and the rear. All decks have air-filtering plants located in the common rooms and hallways.

"The first deck is the blue deck and is all living quarters. This one has two- and one-bedroom cabins, which are all decorated in cool colors. Like decks two, three, and four, there are large common areas in the front and back.

"The oval-shaped disk on top is the bridge, which houses all flight, communications, and navigation controls," The blueprint disappeared when Vega stopped talking.

It took a minute, but we decided we wanted to start in the laboratories. The group wanted to see what had been set up in there for us to figure out. Vega showed us the way to the elevator that we rode to the next level up. When the doors opened, we all spilled out into the hall. The people in the front of the group paused, looking nervous about moving forward.

I pushed my way to the front of the group, explaining the blue arrows and following them to the door of the first lab. I didn't even have to ask this time, the doors opened automatically. The lights began flickering to life as we walked into the room. Along each side of the entrance were several lighted glass cabinets against the walls, creating a walkway down the center. Every cabinet was filled with vials and rows of glass petri dishes. I stepped out of the walkway into a long rectangular room with multiple long metal tables spread out to create evenly spaced work areas. Across each surface were microscopes of assorted styles, large machines that looked like overgrown printers, and large monitors.

On each side of the room, a span of the walls was set back, creating large nooks. I noticed large silver containers standing within each space. The containers looked like oversized round kilns that you fire ceramics in. I walked up to the one on my left and opened it. The lid opened partially, hissing like the sleep pods and allowing cold, smoky air to escape. I lifted the lid completely and looked inside. There were four odd-shaped canisters with handles attached to the tops. I reached in, pulled on a handle, and up slid a long rack of vials. I propped the rack against the top edge of the container and pulled a vial from its holder. The label on it read *Female*

Holstein Embryos, with a red number four in the right corner above the word, *embryos*.

I placed the vial back into the clips that held it and looked at the rest of the labels. I found three more vials of female cow embryos, and four vials of male embryos that matched. I continued my inspection, the rack contained many bovine breeds with matching male and female embryos. About mid-way down the rack, it changed from cows to deer species. I paused reading labels and turned the rack examining it. Each circular row was two vials deep and with a quick count it appeared there were twenty-five rows. That was a lot of embryos for us to . . . well I wasn't sure what we needed to do with them.

The rack clicked into place and I pulled up the next holder. The first four rows were all small wild animals, each species contained matching females and male embryos.

As I moved down the second rack it moved into larger wild animals such as bears and big cats. The third rack was more farm animals. *Sheep* and *horses* were the labels I glanced at before I slid it back in place. The fourth rack was extra mixed vials of the farm and wild animals, each with a matching pair.

I made sure all the racks were replaced correctly and resealed the main container. I walked to the other side of the room where the other container stood. Ryo and Verruca already had it open.

Verruca looked up at me. "These are all water animals, fresh and salt. There are several females and matching males."

I nodded. "The other side is all land animals of different kinds with matching pairs."

"Y'all, look at this. It's instructions on how to grow those embryos," Jax called out, looking through pages on a computer screen.

As we browsed through the documents on the screen, we came across pictures of large bags containing half-oval, red fleshy-looking things. The caption at the bottom of the images said, *Artificial Wombs.*

"What the hell?" I blurted, turning and looking around the room for cabinets matching the pictures but didn't find any. "Vega, where are the other labs on this deck?"

"To the right of this room is a lab for growing plants, and to the left is the birthing lab, Ms. Atlantis. The one you are in is called the embryo lab."

I walked back down the corridor, out of the lab, and turned to the left. As I approached the door, it swished open, and I stepped inside. The lights began to turn on, and I saw large cabinets with frosted glass doors lining every wall. I walked to the closest one and tried to open it but could not.

"Vega, why can I not open this door?"

Vega shimmered into view. "Ms. Atlantis, we cannot open these doors until we are ready to try to grow embryos. They must stay in a sterile environment until that moment. Once the embryos are placed in the artificial wombs, the cabinet will be sealed again and the air sterilized." Vega explained to me like he was talking to a skittish animal.

He must have caught my harsh tone.

I turned to try and peer through the glass. "I would like to see what these artificial wombs look like." I glanced at Vega over my shoulder expectantly.

I looked back at the cabinet, waiting for something to happen. Then the glass on the door cleared, revealing bags of various sizes hanging in racks. I tried to read the labels, but none were clearly visible from where I stood. Several other people walked in, joining me to observe the wombs.

Kilian read out several small wild animal names from the wombs he was inspecting.

Verruca called for me from another room.

I stepped back into the hallway and yelled for her.

She answered from the other lab we had not explored.

When I walked in, she, Ryo, Ronan, Jax, and Night were looking through drawers of small packets.

Verruca looked up with surprise written across her face. "It's seeds, millions of seeds. There are flowers, trees, bushes, and vegetables."

I looked around the room. The drawers of seed lined the length of the wall on my right, from ceiling to floor. The opposite wall was lined with what looked like large dispensers, standing side by side for the length of the room. I walked up to the closest one and pulled the lever. Soft, dark, damp soil fell out of the dispenser into my hand, smelling strongly of manure and other fertilizers. The back wall of the room was lined with metal tables, and on one end was a monitor and microscope. The rest of the tables had stacks of small pots and planting tools.

I stood in the center of the room, taking it all in. "It appears that whoever put us on this ship wanted us to be prepared to restart life if we needed to."

Everyone else nodded in agreement as they also looked around the room. After taking in all of what the labs had to offer, we headed to the silver, green, and blue decks. We walked through the diverse types of rooms available on each floor to check out the accommodations and then headed up to the bridge.

When the elevator door opened, my mouth fell open at the view that greeted us. Millions of stars, asteroids, and the moon stared back at us. It was beautiful and amazing to look at, yet a little nerve-racking at the same time.

As we entered the bridge, I noticed we were surrounded by almost 360 degrees of windows with workstations evenly spaced beneath them. Just to the left side of the elevator was a casual sitting or meeting area with two couches facing each other and three swivel chairs at each end. To the right was a large glass-top table standing on a raised section of the floor.

In the middle of the bridge, on another raised platform, sat three chairs, each with small screens attached to one side. In front of those chairs was a large, curved control center with several workstations and a line of clear glass panels. As we moved closer to this station, the two center windows in the front of the room turned into screens, showing different parts of the ship.

Vega materialized in front of them. "Each of these windows can be used as screens to monitor anything on the ship. Each station also has personal screens set into the station's control panels. Now, if you look to your left, the Earth will be coming into view shortly."

Collectively, the group immediately moved to the windows on the left. I held my breath until just a sliver of the Earth became visible. With my heart pounding, I began trying to discern what I was seeing. As more of the planet became visible, the first thing I noticed was almost the complete lack of clouds. Only thin wispy patches where visible from our position. The oceans appear to have receded a good distance out from land causing the Continents to appear larger. Places that I remembered being green in past pictures looked beige now. I was positive the drastic changes I could make out from here were nothing compared to the what the earth actually looked like.

My stomach fell to my feet, and my mind began to race about the possibility of not being able to go back to Earth. I tried not to let my fear show on my face as I looked at the others. I felt my heart break when I saw my fears reflected in each person's eyes. I turned and blinked my eyes a few times to clear the tears trying to escape. I took a deep breath and exhaled, fixing my expression.

"I know it seems early in the day, with it only being eleven in the morning, but I think we should all find a place to stay. Everyone needs to get some rest before we try to wrap our minds around all of this."

Everyone snapped out of their stupor, turning to look at me, then one at a time, they began to nod. We all exited the bridge together, and when the elevator stopped on the first floor, about half of us got off. The rest continued to the decks below.

CHAPTER FOUR: HARD CHOICES

I woke from a deep sleep to Vega calling out to me.
"Ms. Atlantis, are you okay?"

"Yes, why?" My voice cracked because of a really dry throat. I must have been snoring.

"You have been asleep for more than twelve hours. I just wanted to make sure you were okay."

"My sleep schedule is messed up. That or the little I did after waking up was too much for me. Anyway, I'm up. Did you need something?"

"Not particularly. I just wanted to inform you that almost everyone else is awake."

"Thank you. What time is it?"

"By the ship's clock, it is just past midnight. Would you like me to set the ship's time to Earth time?"

"Yes. Do you know what month it is or the day of the week?"

"No, but I'll research it and see what I can figure out."

"Thank you. Wait, did you say midnight?"

"Yes. Midnight is the reset of the twenty-four-hour timeframe established at the time of launch. Isn't that the restart of your day?"

"No, Vega, most people on Earth start their day when the sun comes up, which is somewhere between six-thirty and seven-thirty in the morning, not the middle of the night."

"That makes no sense. Why would time reset in the middle of the night?"

"That's a good question." I got up because, while I was

48

talking to Vega, my stomach began to growl viciously, but I needed a shower before I could do anything.

I had claimed a one-bedroom suite on the blue deck but hadn't explored it before crashing on the bed. The walls throughout each room were light gray, and the floor was covered with dark gray carpet. The furniture colors were varied shades of blue, with some white and purple thrown in as accents. The bathroom walls were covered in black, silver, and cobalt blue glass tile from floor to ceiling, even in the shower. The countertop and sink were one unit made of stainless steel. The toilet was also stainless steel, which I'd have to get used to. All the fixtures were brushed nickel, and the shower was enclosed with transparent glass.

White towels hung on the towel bar, with more stacked in the round metal cubby on the wall. They looked like bottles of wine in a rack. Under the towels was a shelf with necessary bathroom supplies such as toothbrushes, toothpaste, hairbrush, rubber bands, and other personal hygiene items. Under the shelves was a cabinet that had more bathroom supplies.

Once I had pilfered the items I wanted, I moved to the shower only to find more supplies for both men and women. After rearranging the shower supplies, I decided to explore my accommodation again. I was discovering new things and wanted to see what I had missed in the rest of the cabin. I made my way through the bedroom and into the front room area.

I was feeling the fabric of the couch and pillows when I noticed that the wall behind it was more a slate blue than gray with a 3D wave pattern going across it. I stepped back to see the effect, which was very cool. Each wave dipped and weaved together, making it look very futuristic.

The kitchen opened onto the living area with a small table and two chairs at the far end close to the door. Above the table, running the length of that section of the wall, was a clear pipe with ivy and spider plants growing out of it. Both had long runners hanging down the wall.

A countertop took up the opposite wall, with a cooktop at one end, a sink in the middle, and a narrow French door-styled fridge at the other end. Above and below the counter were rows of cabinets. There was no oven that I noticed, but there was a microwave.

I walked over and pulled open the fridge, finding only bottles of water, no food. I would have to stock it with food from the main kitchen.

After looking around once more, I was satisfied with my space and decided to go next door to check out Verruca's place.

I knocked on the door and heard Verruca call out, "Open."

The door slid back, allowing me to walk in. I could immediately see that Verruca's apartment was almost identical to mine, but her color scheme was purple and gray. On the wall where I had waves, she had small, perfectly square blocks sticking out at different depths, some even stacked on top of each other. It was painted a smoky purple that blended well with the rest of the color scheme. I glanced at her kitchen space, which had a layout identical to mine, plants and all.

She called out to me from the bedroom area.

When I entered, I found her standing in front of the wall to the right of the door.

She looked at me and smiled. "It's a closet with clothes for men and women."

I stepped over to where she was standing, and sure enough, clothes of different sizes were hanging there. I examined the opened door and noticed the outer side looked just like the wall. That must have been why I didn't see it in my room.

"How did you find it?" I asked.

"I was running my hands along the wall feeling the textures. I felt the lines of the door and asked Vega how to open it."

She turned to the dresser and opened a drawer, revealing underclothes for both men and women. We both smiled and began pulling out and checking the items. There were bras in several assorted sizes, including ours. We sorted through the other underclothes finding our sizes among them. We returned to the closet and went through the clothes, discovering two pairs of pants and two shirts for each size. Surprised at what we found, I could only guess every room was like this.

After finding out clean clothes were available, I headed back to take that shower I'd been distracted from. Verruca wanted to do the same. We agreed to meet in the dining room once we were done. On my way out, I ran into Kilian in the hall. He smiled impishly as he sauntered his way toward me.

"I see you figured out the room and that there are clothes?" I said.

He laughed and patted his shirt. "I did. It took me a while to figure it out, but I finally did."

"Ahh, a clean shirt, I see. It looks good on you." And it did look good stretched across his chest, leaving very little to the imagination.

He smiled widely, noticing me looking him up and down. "I am going to make some food. Do you want to join me? Or I can make you something and bring it back."

"No, I need a shower before I think about food. I'll come down to find something when I am clean and dressed."

"Are you sure? I really don't mind," Kilian called out before stepping into the elevator.

"I'm sure," I replied as the door to my apartment opened. I smiled, waved at him, then stepped into my cabin.

As soon as the door closed behind me, I stripped my clothes off as I made my way through the apartment until I was standing naked in the shower. I turned around, looking for the knob to turn the water on but didn't find one.

Then it clicked . . . voice command. "Shower on."

Water fell from the ceiling in warm rivulets that felt so good running down my body, but it wasn't hot enough. I asked for a warmer temperature and got it. After repeating the command several more times, the water was finally the right temperature. I leaned my head back, letting the water flow from the top of my head to the tips of my toes. I just stood there for a long time, willing the water to drown out the craziness of our new reality. I allowed a few tears to escape before I washed them away. I turned, reading the bottles in the shower to find what I needed when Vega spoke. I jumped and flung my arms around my body to cover the important parts.

"*Chingoa!* Vega! Wait, can you see me?" When startled, I naturally reverted to my Tex Mex and swore in Spanish.

"No, Ms. Atlantis. I didn't mean to startle you. I just wanted to let you know I have the information from the scans you asked me to run."

"Okay, I'll come to the bridge later. Right now, I want a shower and then food."

"Yes, Ms. Atlantis."

I took a deep breath and resumed my shower, washing the soap from my body. I turned to rinse the conditioner from my hair, running my fingers through it, making sure I removed the excess conditioner. Whoever had overseen hygiene products had chosen well. This conditioner did an awesome job, leaving my hair feeling silky. I turned to look at the additional bottles sitting on the built-in shelf of the shower. I read each bottle and tube, finding more body wash and face cleanser, some beard wash, and the last tube was face scrub. "Yes." I snatched the tube, flipped the cap open, and squeezed some into the palm of my hand. I scrubbed my face, relishing the feel of the little, tiny granules scouring the dead skin away.

After rinsing my face, the grimy feeling was gone, and all I felt was smooth skin.

I was beginning to feel renewed and clean as I stood under the rainfall of hot water.

"Hot water will run out in five minutes," I heard a disembodied voice say from somewhere above me.

"Figures," I hissed with a few extra s's at the end for dramatic effect. Turning my body under the hot water, I made sure to rinse the last of the soap and cleansers from my skin before growling, "Water off."

The shower turned off, and I stepped out, snatching a towel from the rack. I wrapped it around my body and pulled another one from the cubby. I bent over, flinging my hair over my head and wrapping the second towel around it. I stood back upright and moved to the shelf with the toothbrushes, choosing a blue one. I also picked up a black paddle hairbrush and a thick rubber band, then grabbed the toothpaste before turning to the sink.

Keeping the brush in hand, I laid everything else on the counter, then removed the towel from my hair before glancing at my reflection in the mirror. For the first time since I woke up, I really looked at myself. Turning my head from side to side, I inspected what my face looked like after sleeping for over a hundred years. Leaning closer to the mirror, I could still see the small laugh lines around my eyes and mouth but nothing different from the last time I'd looked at myself. Leaning back, I undid the towel wrapped around me and let it fall to the floor. I stared at my reflection again. Turning side to side, I examined the lines of my figure. I was still plus size, but I had lost some weight and muscle tone. Other than that, I still looked the same. My freckles, moles, and tattoos were all still in the same places. Some of the skin sagged a little more, like under my arms, but none of the differences were dramatic.

It seemed crazy to look in the mirror after all this time and see exactly the same me as I did the day I entered the program. Several tears rolled down my cheek as the absurdity and amazement of it sank in. I knew I was being silly, so I wiped away the tears, squirted toothpaste on my toothbrush, and began brushing my teeth.

If you fall apart now, you may never pick up the pieces. Keep it together. You are the only one stubborn enough to get everyone back to Earth. Then you and Verruca can set out on y'alls own if need be.

I shook my head to clear away my pick-me-up speech. I cleaned the toothbrush and laid it on the side of the sink before rinsing my mouth. Then I brushed my hair back into a ponytail and soothed moisturizer over my face. I finished by applying the deodorant I'd found on the shelf.

I opened the top left drawer of the dresser and found the underwear size I needed, then opened the right drawer and retrieved a bra. I laid the items on the bed and looked around for some lotion. I was about to give up when I thought to check the nightstand on the far side of the bed. Voila . . . Not sure why it was in the drawer, but I was grateful to find it. I slathered it all over my body and then put on my underclothes. I had to give kudos to whoever had stocked this ship since I had found everything I needed so far.

Next, I stepped up to the closet and ran my hand all along it, like Verruca said she'd done, but nothing happened. I commanded the door to open, but it didn't. I asked two more times before it finally opened. Frustrated, I ordered Vega to find the issue and fix it.

I pulled out a pair of black pants made of a smooth stretchy material like workout pants and chose a blue, short-sleeved t-shirt. The other shirt in my size was a long-sleeved black t-shirt. I looked all around for shoes but didn't see any. I went back to the dresser to see if they had put flat shoes in one of the drawers. There weren't any, but there were socks.

"Vega, do we have shoes?"

"Yes, Ms. Atlantis. They are located in the storage space at the bottom of the closet."

I went back to the closet and looked at the bottom. There wasn't any storage space or shoes. I moved the clothes aside and still didn't see anything on the floor. Sighing and about to ask Vega for help again, I heard a soft whir. The bottom of the closet raised in the gap between the clothes, becoming a rack with numerous pairs of what looked like work boots or hiking boots sitting in separate little cubbies. I chose my size and sat on the bed to put them on. I slid my feet in, stood up, and fell in love. It felt like I was standing on clouds.

I made my way to the dining room, where Kilian, Night, Verruca, Ryo, and Jax were sitting at a table, eating and talking. I sat down between Verruca and Kilian, practically drooling over the food in the center of the table. I then grabbed a plate and placed several different items on it.

"I thought you were going to meet me," Verruca said.

"I was, but the water felt amazing, and then I had a few hiccups with the closet. But you could have just let yourself into my place like always."

Kilian looked over at me and smiled. "I cooked most of the food with a little help from these other three guys."

I smirked. "I'm sure that Vega helped as well."

Night started chuckling on the other side of Verruca. I ignored him and dug into my food. The guys had made chorizo and eggs, bacon, and ham. For food that had been preserved for as long as this had, it tasted exceptionally good, or maybe it was just because I was so hungry. One of the guys had even made tortillas, and I was dying to know which one knew how to do that.

I listened to everyone talk as I finished my food and drank some tea. I was impressed with how well the men did with making breakfast. Dinner? Midnight snack? It didn't really matter — it was good, and I was starving. I drifted in and out of the group's conversation, but they were sharing more about themselves from before the sleep program. Night began telling his story when I truly started paying attention to the conversation. I turned to look at Night and noticed that Cash and Juniper had joined us.

"I own, well owned, a small ranch, just outside of the reservation I grew up on," Night said. "I am part of the Mescalero Apache tribe of New Mexico and grew up on the reservation until I decided to go to a mechanic's school.

"My mom still lives, well, lived on the reservation, along with two of her sisters. I was an only child. My dad passed away when I was in high school."

"I'm sorry to hear that." I smiled sympathetically at him.

"Thanks, but I knew I had to do something where I could make enough money to take care of myself and my mom. I chose an aviation mechanic's program at Eastern New Mexico University in Roswell. I went to work for a major airline right out of school and lived with my mom until I saved up enough money to buy my little ranch.

"I recently moved to another company, with a big pay increase, as a floor supervisor. I still got to work on engines but mostly oversaw the other mechanics, making sure they had all the needed supplies. In my spare time I was incredibly involved with the tribe and played the drums at all our ceremonies." He opened his mouth a few times before any words came out. "At least that was me before all of this."

I reached around Verruca and ran a hand down Night's arm to offer comfort. He smiled at me.

Kilian piped in with his story. "Well, I was born and raised in Portland, Oregon. I was the older of three. I had a brother, a year younger than me, and a sister two years younger. My sister lived at home with our parents. My dad had been having health problems.

"As for my career, I went into the Navy right out of high

school and became a weapons specialist after about two years. I took college classes at each base where I was stationed and eventually got a degree in engineering. It helped me when I retired from the military because I went to work for a private weapons design company.

"I was actually out on assignment for that company, we were testing a new laser guided handgun. I remember us getting pinned down in a fire fight, but after that everything is blank until we woke up here. I wish I knew why I was put on this ship. "

He took his seat next to me, and I patted his shoulder and smiled. We had been chatting among ourselves for a few moments when Ryo stood up.

Ryo smiled at the group. "I grew up with my three brothers and two sisters. Our parents passed away when I was a teenager. My older siblings raised my youngest sister and me until we were out of high school. I didn't know what I wanted to do for a long time, but finally decided to get my pilot's license. Once I got that I went to work for a private company, flying charters for rich people. I also helped Ronan teach judo and aikido classes at his dojo. The rest of my family was supposed to volunteer with Ronan and me, but I don't know if they are here."

"Get Vega to check the manifest, Ryo," I suggested.

He nodded and sat back down.

We all had gone back to our conversations until we were interrupted when Jax stood up. He glanced around at the group and then cleared his throat. He opened his mouth but then closed it. I was a little surprised because he didn't look like the shy type.

Finally, Jax cleared his throat again and took a deep breath. "I'm from Austin, Texas and I was a mechanic. I can fix anything, but I preferred working on motorcycles. I was ten when my parents died in a car accident. Since I had no family that I could live with I was put into foster care. Foster care was not easy because I bounced from family to family until I aged out. Then, I joined the motorcycle club when I was twenty-two. I had been part of the MC for five years before I volunteered. The MC had chosen five of us to volunteer for this program to make sure the club would survive. So that's how I got here."

I was about to stand up when Verruca stood up and began speaking.

"Well, I am from Houston, Texas. Well actually I claim my hometown as Portland Oregon, because that's where I grew up before we came back to Texas and settled in Houston. Besides being an instructor of cosmetology, I had just opened my salon, and my mom helped me run it. It was just starting to really gain popularity, and our customer base was growing fast. Then we started seeing news segments on the vampire virus mutating. The outbreak caused all our customers to dry up just as quickly as they came. Losing my business is one reason I decided to volunteer. "

Verruca sat back down and leaned her head on my shoulder.

I leaned my head on top of hers to let her know I was there.

Cash spoke up from where he was sitting. "Well, I taught band, gave private lessons, and all the other stuff that goes with being a band director. I was an only child and was raised by a single mom. Out of everyone, I want to know what happened to her the most. I had a distant cousin that I talked to once in a while. Mostly it was me, my mom, and my students. I led a calm and slow life."

I looked at Juniper, but she just sat there looking at the table. She looked sad, so I wasn't going to push her into speaking. I wanted her to share on her own terms.

Night looked at me and waggled his eyebrows, "So what about you, Atlantis, want to tell us a little more about yourself?"

"I guess. I used to be a Loss Prevention Manager, before I started helping Verruca and pursuing my art more. I was a single mom her whole life." I shrugged. "Ahh, I grew up in South Texas and was raised by a single dad. Umm, he left me to take care of everything. Either he worked all the time, or he wasn't working and slept all the time. He was Hispanic but he half assed it. Or at least that's what my grandma would say." I chuckled. "But I learned all my Spanish curse words from him. He taught me how to make some of my favorite Mexican foods. He also taught me how to be extremely strong and how to take care of everything on my own. But that was more from his lack of knowing how to be an adult than him actually teaching me those things. I don't know. I'm not that interesting."

Night snorted and eyed me up and down. It was like he was saying *yeah right*. I just winked at him and smiled slyly.

We sat there for a while in silence, and my mind rehashed what everyone had said.

Then Kilian broke the silence. "Let's take some time right now to go through who will be team leads for each department and what it entails. If we have time we could even go through who we should wake next."

"I agree with you," I said. "Vega, can you call Ronan to the dining room."

"Yes, Ms. Atlantis."

We all chatted and ate more while we waited for Ronan. When he entered the cafeteria, he made a plate of food and sat down next to Ryo.

"I hope you all don't mind, but I'm going eat while you talk," he said with a taco halfway to his mouth.

"I'll get us started while you eat." I smiled at Ronan, then turned my attention to the rest of the group. "I have been working on a list in my head. Let me run y'all through it.

"First, we need to understand the ship and how it runs. Second, I think the council should have ten people. With eight spots taken already, we need to decide on the last two. Third, go through the list of people still sleeping and see who would be best to wake up.

"As for our roles, this is what I was thinking. Kilian could be our sergeant at arms. His experience with weapons and the Navy makes him a great choice for the job. Night and Jax should take on the roles of the ship's engineers since their experience makes them the most suitable for the position. Ryo should be our pilot, of course. Ronan, I would like you to work with Kilian and do some fight training with willing people to prepare us for the ground. Cash and Juniper, we will eventually need schooling, but until then, three things. One, can you work with everyone on some training materials for each department. Two, create a life-on-the-ship type video. Three, can y'all work with Verruca to help where extra hands are needed?"

Cash nodded when I looked at him, and so did Juniper. No one said anything right away, apparently processing all the info I'd just dumped. I poured myself some more tea and was midway through the glass when the silence was broken.

Night cleared his throat. "Atlantis is right about what she said. We need to go to the bridge and start looking through the systems. We need to know what this ship can do, learn how it works, and start thinking about what other talents we will need. As for us" —he looked around the room— "I think we should learn as much as we can about all operations of this ship. If we are to be the leaders, we will have to be the experts on how things work."

We all agreed it was a good starting point. As soon as everyone was done eating, we headed for the elevator to go to the bridge.

As soon as the doors closed Verruca spoke. "I know

everyone has extra clothes in the closets of their rooms. I think we should take the ones that don't fit from each person and create a common closet in one of the extra rooms on the black deck. We should also collect the extra hygiene product. We cannot afford to waste any of these additional items. I volunteer to collect everything if someone can organize them."

Juniper raised her hand. "I can help with that."

Everyone filed out of the elevator, stepping onto the bridge. Our entrance caused all the screens to light up. The main windows cleared, and the void of space was now visible. Kilian, Night, and Ryo walked up to the consoles and began tapping screens.

Kilian pointed toward the screen and asked, "Vega, can you put my screen up on the main viewing screen?"

Without a word, the center windows darkened, and a menu screen appeared. I knew what the screen was because I had already looked at these sections when I first woke up, but the rest of the team did not.

I stepped forward. "This screen allows us to access some of the systems on the ship and view profiles of everyone onboard."

I tapped the red and white cross icon. The medical chart for Gage Delgado came up.

"In this section, we can look at the vitals of everyone still in a pod. It shows a live reading of their current condition and all variances. As you can see, there's a picture and a brief profile of the person."

I swiped back to the previous screen and tapped the tree icon. "This is the air and filter section. The first page shows us our oxygen levels, along with other gas levels. The next section is manufactured filters. It has subsections for air filters and air scrubbers. The last section covers natural air filters and shows you the locations of all the plants on the ship. I think Night and Jax need to get familiar with the air scrubbers and filters. Learn what they do and how they do it."

Not remembering any instructions on how to take care of the plants, I asked, "Vega, who takes care of the plants?"

"The hybrid hydroponics system does most of the work independently. The android and I monitor it for efficiency."

"Okay." I was surprised it was so sophisticated.

Kilian backed out of that screen and went back to the home screen before I could do it. He clicked on the next icon that looked like a lightning bolt. When the section opened, it was divided into nuclear and solar. I tapped on the nuclear tab. Besides showing a blueprint of the core and its housing, the screen listed instructions for troubleshooting issues, entering the core, and several for general maintenance.

"Kilian, Night, Ryo, and Jax, I think the four of you should learn this information. Not only so more than one person knows it, but so y'all can also break it down for the rest of us."

They agreed, and then Kilian tapped the tab that said solar. When the section opened, a blueprint of the ship's exterior came up. It showed large panels that could be extended to catch the sun's rays. It was good to know we had solar as a backup power source. We might need it back on Earth.

Kilian went through the rest of the icons. The food icon gave us a list of the food supplies available on the ship, and the water icon showed us our water supply. A sub-screen walked us through how the water was recycled and cleaned. One icon showed us an inventory of cleaning supplies, dry goods, and other supplies used for maintenance on the ship.

We broke into groups and began poring through the rest of the information. Cash suggested we make notes about anything we might want a training manual for. Ryo got up and started looking around, checking all the consoles and pulling on handles.

"What are you looking for?" I asked.

Ryo closed the cabinet. "I am looking for something to take

notes on."

"Vega, do we have pens and paper or something we can use to write notes?"

"Yes, Ms. Atlantis. There are tablets in the storage cabinet in the wall behind the seating area."

I walked over to the wall behind the couch and found the outline of a smooth panel. I pushed on it and felt it move, but it didn't open. I tried the left corner, and it still didn't open. So I poked on the bottom right side and heard a click. I let the pressure off, and a door opened. Inside the cabinet were rows and rows of thin sheets of glass with attached pens, each sitting in charging docks. I started handing them out to everyone.

"We have a closed network aboard this ship," Vega said as he rippled into view next to the chair. "You can create a direct messaging profile under the message in a bottle icon. You can have private messaging with people, but you can also set up group messaging. There is the last version of several word processing programs, a notepad program, along with several other presentation programs. There are voice command and dictation capabilities as well. These are just a few of the features the tablets and our network has available." By the time he was done explaining, he had walked around the whole group.

Everyone was taking notes and working on learning the different sections of the ship. Vega stood around and watched us for a while, then disappeared.

I partnered with Verruca and began making notes as we discussed possible landing sites, items needed for our survival, and things we needed to know about Earth. Our next list was what the ship could do for us now and once we were on the ground. The more we talked, the more our ideas turned into a structured checklist, and pieces of a plan came together. I turned to the group to see what everyone was working on and saw Kilian heading toward Verruca and me.

"What are y'all working on?" he asked as he stared me directly in the eyes.

I passed him my tablet because I was a little thrown off by his intense gaze. Then I looked over at Verruca with both my eyebrows raised in a what-the-hell look. She just shrugged. Kilian had been doing things like that all day. He would hold my gaze or stare me dead in the face from across the room. It was a little unnerving.

He passed my tablet back and stepped closer. "I think that you and Verruca should work on that list." He gazed at me intensely.

Then he suddenly turned to face the group. "I think Ronan and I should go to the black deck and begin going through our inventory of other gear stored down there. I would also like to see if we have any type of weapons stored down there. Once we know what we have for protection, we can come up with a safety plan and what type of defense training will be needed."

When I nodded my agreement, Kilian waved for Ronan to follow him, and they left the bridge.

I stared after the two until the elevator closed, and a voice interrupted my daze.

"Jax and I need to continue going through the systems and making notes," Night stated. "We're going to the engine room to check out what's down there. Afterward, we will sit down and come up with a training plan for others. I'm also going to go through the ship's other passengers to see who we can use as team members."

Liking the direction Night described, I agreed they should continue. Ryo claimed he was staying on the bridge to figure out the flight controls while the rest of us got onto the elevator to go work on our own things.

When the doors closed, I checked with Cash and Juniper

on their plans. "Verruca and I are heading to a common room on blue deck to work on our checklist. Do y'all have something to get started with?"

"Yes," Juniper replied. "Cash and I are looking through the programs on the network so we can find the easiest one to create training presentations when we get the input."

"Good. Can y'all create an introductory presentation about living on the ship or a video to help people understand where we are and what is going on? I think the video should be shown to the newly awake when they see the other videos. You can keep it to the basics if you want. I don't want to scare them after just waking up."

Juniper nodded as she wrote down a quick note. "The tablets have a camera we can use to capture images and actions."

As Verruca and I exited the elevator, I waved over my shoulder. "That works for me!"

Verruca and I continued to the common room near our cabins. When we reached the sitting area, I flopped down into a large round gray leather chair. Verruca sprawled across a matching sofa. I pulled up a blank document in the word processing program and began asking questions about Earth.

"Vega, it's been a hundred and five years since we were on Earth. Do you know what the climate is like down there now?"

Vega shimmered into view. "I only recently started monitoring the climate regularly. In the last year, the climate has been leveling out. Previously, I only took readings every three months, and the climate was volatile. It would be hot and sunny in a normally cold region, then a tornado would suddenly spawn. All this would happen in a matter of hours. Over the last year, the climate has settled, and the storms are beginning to set into predictable patterns."

"Okay, what else is going on? What about people or animals that have survived? Have you seen any evidence of that?"

Vega moved closer. "I have seen evidence of animal-like creatures. I have a camera that can zoom in far enough to view close images of the land. While scanning the surface, I captured a few pictures of these creatures. A few of the photos showed humanoid-looking shapes, but I am not sure they are people as you knew them."

"I would like to see those pictures. Can you send them to my tablet? Can we use that camera to see the Earth and scout potential places to live? Do we have the capabilities to take samples and measure the air and water for contaminants?"

"I will send the pictures to your tablet, but I suggest we don't show them to everyone."

"Why?"

"The pictures could upset some people. It might be best to ease them into the appearance of the creatures."

"Ahh, I understand. It could create panic. I will limit who I show until everyone is more settled."

Vega moved in front of me. "As for your other questions. There are four drones in hangar A capable of obtaining the samples you are requesting. We will need to bring the ship closer to Earth before we can launch them. Once the drones are on Earth they cannot travel more than five miles from their drop site before our control over them becomes spotty due to the distance between them and our location in space. Also, their battery life is twelve hours, but it requires a great deal of battery power to drop to Earth and then return to the ship. Leaving us with a very short time frame to gather samples and have them return to the ship."

"Awesome. When can we start bringing the ship into Earth orbit?"

"I can set a course for Earth when we return to the light side of the moon."

"Yes, do it. How long will that be from now?"

"It will be about four hours from now."

"Okay, please send over all the pictures of the Earth. I want to see everything you have."

"Yes, Ms. Atlantis. They are already sent."

Verruca got up and came over to sit on the arm of my chair.

I pulled up the first image, which showed land masses. Shocked at what I was seeing, I decided to share with the council even though Vega had warned against it. The image was heartbreaking. There were damaged buildings with vegetation growing all over them. Another picture showed rusted streetlights, stop lights barely hanging from their wires, and faded store fronts with broken windows. I could not keep this information from them. They had a right to know what Earth looked like now.

I messaged the rest of the group via the tablets, asking them to return to the bridge, adding that I wanted them to see something.

Verruca was apparently getting tired, so I pulled her by both hands to get her off the couch. I laughed at her silliness as we began our trip back to the bridge.

When Verruca and I entered the bridge, most of the group was already present. They gathered around me at the main screen, and when Cash and Juniper joined us, I displayed the first image.

"These are pictures of Earth that Vega has taken over the years we've been in space. He doesn't have many from the beginning, but what is here will give us an idea of what happened down there. There are more images from the past year because that's when he started monitoring Earth more closely."

Kilian pulled up the manifest. "Okay, so let's go through them."

We began scrolling through the pictures and talking about what we were looking at. As we got closer to the current images, we decided to make a map out of them.

"Vega, can we print these pictures to create a map?" Kilian asked.

"You can't print them, but you can use the table to the right of the elevator."

The tabletop lit up when we all approached it. As we stepped up on the platform, the pictures began popping up on the tabletop. They were smaller in size, running along the left and right sides of the screen. The center of the screen had just an outline of a map of the United States.

"Would you like me to place the pictures on the map for you," Vega asked as he approached the end of the table.

"No, I would like to do it," I answered.

I have never been one to let others do stuff for me especially something so simple. But I think I would like the process of doing it myself. It feels like I have a little control over something. I know that sounds weird but considering what little control we do have is balanced precariously and is subject to space and this ship, I'll take every bit of control I can get.

We started piecing a map together using the pictures. We had pictures in place that gave us an overall idea of the conditions for all of Texas, Louisiana, Alabama, Georgia, and Florida. On the other side of Texas, we had laid pictures in place for all of New Mexico to Nevada and the southern half of California. As we moved up the west coast, we pieced together an overall picture of Oregon and Washington. It was bits and pieces from there until we made it to the East Coast. The pictures covered all of New York State down to North Carolina. We had no images of anything above New York State, and everything below North Carolina was just one or two pictures. The center of the map followed the same pattern.

Observing the layout of the pictures emphasized the drastic changes the Earth had undergone, which hurt my heart. Even though the visual created by the map was a bit shocking, it would be a good way to organize all new images going forward.

"Let us go through the pictures of the creatures and add them to the map. This can help us decide where to investigate for our landing."

"Okay, I like that idea. This can be a living document, and we can make changes as needed," Ronan said. "Vega, please bring up the pictures of the creatures and where the images were taken. Include only the ones from the past year."

Vega complied, and pictures of creatures began appearing on the screen with their locations. The first image looked like an exceptionally large black panther. It had hairless black skin, and its tail had white-colored objects protruding from it every few inches. Its paws were slightly larger than proportionately correct for its size, with long thick claws coming out of each toe that looked more raptor-like. Upon closer review, it appeared they didn't retract. The picture was taken in central Texas, so we dropped it into that general location on the map.

The next animal looked like a polar bear. It had white fur on most of its body with some bald spots. Ronan enlarged the picture, and we saw that the bald areas were extremely translucent patches of skin, allowing a clear view of the creature's bones and internal organs. This creature's picture was taken in south Texas, of all places. Shaking my head at the pure craziness, or maybe the pure sadness of it all, I dropped the picture in South Texas.

The next one was a dog creature larger than a Great Dane and built like a wolf with a mohawk of silvery gray fur running from the top of his head down to the tip of his tail. The rest of his body was covered in black leathery-looking skin. According to the location, the picture was taken in Oklahoma.

Then there was another dog-like creature about a foot taller than the last one that looked more like a hyena. It had orange-colored fur with spots and stripes. It also had a greenish-colored drool dripping from its mouth. Its picture was taken in Louisiana.

We continued to drop pictures onto the map until we had all the creatures in their locations. I stood back, studying the map, and began wondering how we could easily identify the different species. I stared for a while longer, just trying to wrap my head around everything I saw.

"What do we call all these animals?" I asked the group.

Night began to speak but paused, "That's a good question."

Ronan snapped his fingers. "The bear creature we could call *bea*. It's Hawaiian for bear."

I nodded. "Okay, that sounds good. What about the cat?"

Kilian enlarged the picture. "They look like they have razor blades down their tails."

Verruca exclaimed with a shiver, "Yeah, I think it's their vertebrae,"

I stared at the image of the creature, sifting through different names, trying to find something that fit what I was looking at. Then it hit me, "Razor cat."

Night thought about it for a second. "I like that name."

Verruca snapped her fingers at me, " How about a grimm dog for the overgrown black wolf? It reminds me of a creature from a book I read."

"I've got the last one's name, venom dog," Jax said, shrugging his shoulders. "It's obvious. Venom is dripping from its mouth."

We all looked at him, confused because he said it like we were supposed to understand.

"Come on . . . every movie ever. If the creature has something green dripping from its mouth, it's always poisonous or toxic, so it only makes sense."

"I like the name, so venom dogs it is," Verruca said.

We all kind of chuckled and agreed on the names selected.

I was tired, and my eyes were burning because I didn't have my glasses. Whoever packed us up remembered everything else but those. I suggested we all get some food, take a break from all of this, and then go through Night's list of people still sleeping. We needed to decide on which ones from his list to wake next.

"I need to go back to the engine room to check on some reports I have running," Jax said. "Can y'all send me a message when the food is ready?"

"Yes, we can. Too bad we don't have hand radios. It would make it a lot easier to communicate," Verruca said.

Before I could even ask about radios, Vega spoke.

"Ms. Atlantis, if you would like a personal communicator, they are in the cabinet next to where the tablets were located."

"Absolutely, thank you Vega."

I walked over to the wall and pushed on the lower section in a few different spots before the door opened. In the cabinet sat what looked like watches. I took one out and tapped the screen. A logo of a transparent human figure shimmered onto a black screen with the words *Black Holo Communication Devices* in a silvery-colored font scrolling across the bottom. Then different icons popped up.

I tapped the one shaped like a speaker, and a soundwave bar appeared across the center. "Hello?" I heard my voice echo through the ship-wide system.

I then swiped the screen to the right, and it went back to the main screen. I tapped the person icon, and instructions appeared on personalizing the device and adding other communicators to the contact list. All you had to do was tap the devices against each other, and their name was added to your list. I swiped back to the main menu and tapped on one that looked like a projection coming from a box labeled *holo*. A blank screen appeared, floating above a tiny pinprick in the top center of my communicator.

Verruca reached into the cabinet and pulled out several devices, tossing them to the group until everyone had one. They put on their communicators and took a few minutes to explore them. We all tapped each other's devices before leaving the bridge.

In the elevator, Ronan reminded us about food, so I pushed the button for the black deck. I went into the kitchen and gathered enough food to feed everyone. While I pulled down pots and pans, the guys foraged through the leftovers from breakfast and began snacking.

"What are y'all doing? I am making food." Damn, I sounded like a mom scolding her teenage sons.

"Hello, we are guys." Night grinned from ear to ear. "We can snack on this and still eat what you cook. Besides, we got a lot of making up to do."

Kilian snorted and then said, "Yeah, like a hundred years of making up."

"Fine, get out so I can cook. Go on, shoo." I used both hands to wave them out of the kitchen. They left, each holding a taco, and I returned to pulling out the rest of the supplies to make our meal.

I was well into cooking when Night came into the kitchen. He leaned against the metal table next to me.

"So, what do you think about all this?"

I looked up at him and stared for a few seconds. "Honestly, I have no idea. I am not even sure I know what I'm doing."

"It's cool. I'm not sure I know what I'm doing or what we should be doing either. I just wanted to see how you were handling overseeing all of it."

"Handling tough situations is my specialty. I'm used to being the one to hold everything together."

"You are not alone. You don't have to hold us all together by yourself. I can help. If you let me."

I shrugged. "I'm used to it. My dad always left me to handle everything. It's what I have done my whole life. I wouldn't even know how to accept help from someone else."

"I'm here. You just have to trust me to have your back."

Not looking at him, I rolled my eyes. I had heard that line so many times it was ridiculous.

Night hoisted himself upright and stepped closer, invading my space. "I see that doubt in your eyes. I also see the worry."

"Mind your own business. I know how to take care of myself."

"It's okay to be freaking out. I mean, who in their right mind has a post-apocalyptic plan to save the last of humanity stored in their brain for a just-in-case situation?"

"Me." I snorted. "Didn't you know all women have a plan for everything stored in their head?"

Now he snorted with laughter, which made me chuckle more.

I shook my head. "For real, though, I just want to make the right decisions for all of us until we get back to Earth. Then I figured we can all go our separate ways if we need."

We were both silent for a moment, just staring at each other. Not sure what else to say, I started checking on all the food. I bent over to inspect some bread warming in the oven, and when I stood up, two large arms snaked around my waist from behind. Startled, I twitched slightly.

"I have wanted to do this from the moment I saw you," Night whispered into my ear.

Shocked, I kept my eyes straight ahead, watching everyone else in the dining room. Luckily, they were engaged in conversation, and no one was paying attention.

Night started running his nose up the length of my neck, sending chills down my back and a sweet tingle shooting straight to my clit. I set the spatula on the counter and placed my hands on his arms. He began kissing and nipping my neck, and without any thought, my hand automatically went to his head. I slid my fingers through his hair, and a husky sigh escaped my lips.

With his lips at my ear, he moaned softly. "You are the right choice to lead us. I know you will make the right decision to protect everyone. If not, the council is here to temper your decisions. Besides, I'll always take your side because I want you." He finished with a kiss on my neck that sent electricity shooting through my body.

I had not even thought about sex since waking up. My mind had been stuck on how to keep everyone alive and make it back to Earth. But now, my mind was swirling with how good Night might be in bed. Completely distracted from the task at hand, I watched him as he walked out the door. He sat down at the table, quickly joining the conversation.

I shook off the tingles and got back to cooking, but the thought of Night in my bed kept playing at the back of my mind. I put the next round of potatoes in the skillet and checked the chicken in the oven. The chicken still needed time, but I had to snatch the bread out before it burned. I'd totally forgotten about it. I looked up and scowled at Night, but then images of him towering over me in bed flashed through my mind. My scowl faded quickly.

I looked down in the direction of my clit. *You need to stop. A few kisses on the neck are all it takes for you now? You better go back to sleep. I don't have time for this right now.* As if it was telling me to fuck off, another slight tingle spread outward, warming my insides. I huffed, shaking my head, and went back to cooking.

I cut open the packages of pork chops, then pulled down another skillet. I poured a little oil into the skillet, then added two of the chops. I was seasoning the meat when my daughter came into the kitchen.

"Hey, Mom." Verruca hugged me. "So, what do you think

of all this crazy bullshit?"

I couldn't help but laugh and shake my head. "I really don't know what to think. I haven't really had time to figure out how to feel. I just know I don't want you and me getting the short end of anything."

"Yeah, me either." Verruca was silent for a few minutes. "I saw Night come in here to talk to you. What did he want?"

I tried not to smile. "He just wanted to see how I was doing with all of this. He wanted to let me know that he supported me as leader and thought I would do a great job."

"And! I see that smile you are trying to hide."

"There was nothing else. That's all he said."

"So, that's what he said when he wrapped his arms around your waist?"

"You don't miss much, do you? He said he wanted me, then kissed my neck and walked out."

"I knew it! I knew he was your type but wasn't sure if you were his."

"That is the last thing on my mind right now. We have too much to do."

"You can do both. He's hot. Take advantage. Hell, take advantage of them all. I plan to."

When I glanced at her, she was smiling wide. "La, la, la . . . too much info, daughter." I shut my eyes tight and waved her out of the way. "I do not need to know those things. Just like you don't need to know those things about me."

With a smirk and an eye roll, she grabbed the long, flat pan full of fried potatoes and headed for the table.

Laughing, I grabbed the pan with the corn and the salad bowl and followed her. She elbowed me in the ribs as I stopped next to her to set down the food. I poked her in the ribs and turned to go grab the meat from the kitchen. It felt nice that we could fall into our usual routine of teasing each other in the middle of this craziness.

Everyone was placing food on their plates when I returned with the meat. Night handed me a dish that already had salad, corn, and potatoes on it. Just as I took it from his hand, Kilian slapped a pork chop on it like a caveman and smiled at me.

I shook my head and rolled my eyes as I sat between the two men. Not that they gave me much choice. Verruca looked over at me and smiled knowingly. I glared at her with one eyebrow raised and a crooked smirk on my lips as I cut into my pork chop.

Everyone was silent for a while, and then slowly, softly spoken conversations began around the table. I heard Ryo and Ronan talking about starting up martial arts classes for fight training. Jax and Night were talking about motorcycles. Verruca and Cash were talking about music and hair styling. I was watching everyone chattering, amazed at how well they were all handling our situation, when Kilian nudged me with his elbow.

I turned to look at him. "What was that for?"

"You were looking waaay too serious."

"Oh. I was just marveling at how well everyone is doing with our situation. If this group continues to take things this well, we will be able to handle anything." I held his gaze, hoping that maybe if I boldly returned his stare, he would stop doing it all the time.

He smiled wide and squeezed my thigh. The contact electrified my skin under his hand, but I smiled back.

What the hell? My body has not reacted to a man's touch like this in a long time. Now I might have to choose between Kilian and Night. No, this is not going to happen right now. We have too much other shit to worry about. Another shot of electricity sizzled across my thigh as he rubbed his hand along it. It was enough to snap me out of my inner thoughts and realize he was talking to me.

"Wait, back up. What did you say?"

"I was saying, I think everyone feels this relaxed because

you are not freaking out. You are calm and decisive and have kept everyone busy planning. Keeping busy helps them from overly focusing on the situation." He took a bite of potatoes.

I barely looked at him from the corner of my eye. Then I just smiled and picked up my corn. I caught Verruca staring as I took a bite.

She smirked at me and mouthed, "Him too?"

I shrugged my shoulders and continued eating.

After I had finished my meal, I returned to the kitchen to do some cleaning. I looked around at the mess and knew right away I needed some motivation.

"Vega, can you play music? Rock or grunge if you got it."

"Yes, Ms. Atlantis. I have a variety of music. What is your favorite song?"

"War Pigs by Black Sabbath." After a few seconds, I heard the familiar guitar of one of my favorite songs and started dancing and singing away. I was putting leftovers into storage bowls and pans into the dishwasher, when a body suddenly pressed against my back, pinning my hips to the counter.

Surprised, I snapped my head to the side to see Kilian. "What are you doing?"

"I wanted to say thank you for dinner," he almost growled in my ear, "then I saw you dancing while you sang a great song, and all I could do was picture you shaking that ass naked for me."

"So, I guess everyone's hormones are starting to revive after being suppressed for a hundred years."

"Mine were working just fine the moment I climbed out of that tube."

I felt his cock grow harder between us. Intrigued by what I could feel so far, I turned to face him. My gaze roamed over every feature of his face. He leaned in a little closer, so close I could see the flecks of gray in his eyes. It was unusual but added depth to the blue color. I realized he was appraising me as well. He placed a hand on my shoulder and slid it up the side of my neck to my nape. Then he pulled me in for a kiss. He devoured my mouth, and my body melted into his as I returned the kiss. After a few seconds of bliss, I snapped back to reality.

I pushed him back and caught my breath. "We can't do that here. As great as it felt, I am not an exhibitionist."

"Fine, let's take it to my place."

"I still need to clean up in here."

"The cook shouldn't clean and do the dishes, too."

"Oh, I'm not doing the dishes. That is someone else's job. I cooked, put the food away, and now I'll wipe down the counters, but I refuse to do the dishes. Besides, it's not hard. The ship is equipped with a professional dishwasher." I pointed toward the back corner, where a large shiny silver square machine stood.

"Then come to my cabin, and we can finish this."

I wanted to scream *yes* and drag him off to his cabin, but I knew we needed to be discreet about things. So, I decided not to take him up on his offer.

"I can't right now. I must be careful. I am Iksen, and you know everyone will be watching me."

"Okay, I get that." He took a step back. "But I want you, and I don't plan on waiting long to have you."

Then he walked out of the kitchen, and I turned, placed my hands on the counter, and took a deep breath. *Son of a motherless goat, what is going on today? Did everyone's hormones turn back on in full force?* My body was on fire from his being pressed against mine. Oh, my God, it took more strength than I knew I had to stop. I shook my head to clear the lust from it, took another deep breath, held it for a few seconds, and then let it out. Grabbing the towel from the edge of the sink, I sprayed the countertops with cleaner and wiped them all down.

CHAPTER FIVE: FINDING A LOVER OR TWO

I sat down on the couch in my cabin. "Vega, what kind of entertainment do we have?"

"Well, we have music, I can download books to your tablet, and we have movies and TV series."

"Really! What movies do we have?"

Vega pulled up the list of movies stored in the ship's mainframe. As he scrolled through them page by page, my mind could not stop thinking about our next steps. My thoughts jumped from one half-formed idea to another, making my mind a complete and total mess. Somehow my mind latched on to the title of one of my favorite sci-fi movies as it scrolled by, which snapped me out of the tornado forming in my head.

"Vega, play the *Star Trek* movie."

Vega started the movie, the image appearing in the air from a strange-looking projector sitting on the sideboard. The device sat on a square base with a narrow foot-long black bar on top, each end curved slightly upward. Tiny lights ran along the top of the curved bar and were what created the 3D image in the air. It was awesome. The image span was easily the same as a fifty-five-inch flat-screen TV. I continued to watch the movie in amusement when I realized that the picture frame behind it completely enclosed the image. The totally blank white surface within the frame allowed the colors of the 3D image to be bright and vivid. I was in love with my new entertainment system.

I refocused on the movie and settled in to relax. About twenty minutes later, I heard a knock at the door. I looked all around for a clock but didn't see one.

"Vega?"

Knock.

"What time is it?"

Knock. Knock.

"It's six in the morning, Ms. Atlantis."

I walked closer to the door and called out, "Who is it?"

"It's Night."

Confused as to why he was at my door this late, well early since our day had been ass-backward, my curiosity was piqued. "Open."

Night stood there smiling brightly as the door slid back.

"Yes?" I was still not sure what to expect.

"Well, let me in at least."

"Why, what do you need? You know it's six in the morning, right?"

"Yes." He pushed past me into my cabin. "I wanted to see what you were doing. Maybe hang out for a little while. Since our day was flip-flopped, I had a hard time falling asleep. I thought maybe you were having the same problem."

I squinted one eye in suspicion. Even though he was right. I wasn't sleepy yet, having slept a lot yesterday into today. "Fine, I was watching a movie. You like *Star Trek?*"

"Wait, we have movies?"

"Yeah, and a really cool way to watch it." I pointed toward my projector.

"What! That is freaking awesome. Play it, I want to see."

"Resume movie."

The movie started again, and Night watched in amazement. After a few seconds, he sat down, leaned back, and got comfortable next to me. He then patted his thigh as he snatched a throw pillow from the opposite corner of the couch. He placed the pillow on his thigh and pulled me down to lay my head on it.

I allowed it and then tuned back into the movie.

He began running a hand through my hair as we watched the movie. After a few minutes, it no longer distracted me. By the time the movie ended, his hand had found its way to resting on my hip.

"I hadn't seen that movie in forever," Night said, stretching his arms above his head.

"Yeah, in like a hundred years." I rolled onto my back and winked at him.

"Ha, ha. You're not funny, smart ass."

I smiled innocently back at him. Dark smoldering lust filled his eyes as he slid a hand under my head. He leaned down, lifting me and bringing our lips together in a kiss. I was a bit apprehensive for a split second before I relaxed into his embrace. I don't know if it was because I wanted the kiss as badly as him or if he was just that good, but my body lit up. Each nerve ending tingled, making each of his touches feel like fire.

I reached up and ran my fingers through his long thick black hair. I grabbed a handful when I got to the nape of his neck and pulled his head closer, turning it to the side so I could kiss and graze my teeth along the pulse in his neck. My action solicited a soft moan from Night. Then without warning, I bit him. He growled, and the hand gliding up and down my side suddenly gripped my hip tightly. He stopped me and just breathed for a second. After gaining his composure, he pushed me into a sitting position and stood up.

"I don't want to do this here. Can you give me a minute?" He looked at me expectantly.

"Okay, sure." Now I was really confused.

He turned and went into my room. He was in there for maybe five minutes. Then he came back and reached his hand out to me. "Come with me."

Not sure what he was up to, I carefully placed my hand in his and let him lead me to the bedroom.

When I walked in, the lighting was a deep soothing blue.

"What? How did you do this?"

The lights changed to purple.

"I figured it out by accident. I needed the lights on in my room, and when I asked for them, the ship asked if I wanted regular light, mood light, or . . . He gave me a long list of specific types of lighting available."

"This is cool. Who would have thought we had mood lighting?" I shook my head in disbelief. "Of all the things to think of for a ship carrying the last of humanity."

After giving me a second to admire the room, Night spun me into his arms and kissed me. He splayed one hand in the center of my back and held me snugly against him. His other hand slid up my nape and wrapped into my hair, then angled my head the way he wanted to deepen the kiss. His tongue plunged into my mouth and tangled with mine. A soft groan escaped him when my tongue mimicked his enthusiasm.

He explored every inch of my mouth and controlled every movement of my head. As hot as his dominance was, I needed him to know I wouldn't be easy to control. I caught his lower lip between my teeth. I slowly pulled out of the kiss, dragging my teeth across his skin until his lip was almost free, and then I bit down. Not enough to draw blood but enough to sting.

A growling groan of approval rumbled out of him. "Mmm, a little pain with our pleasure?"

"That was to let you know you are not the only dominant one in the room."

His hand moved from my back and began gathering my shirt. In one swift move, he whipped it up and over my head, dropping it to the floor. I used the moment of him not holding me in place to divest him of his shirt. I then reached for his waistband to get rid of the pants keeping me from what I really wanted, but he stopped me. He moved my hand and reached for my pants, sliding my pants over my hips and down my thighs, letting them pool to the floor. I stepped out of them and stood up straight. Night's gaze roamed over every inch of my body, taking in each dip, curve, and imperfection.

I let him stare. *I know who I am and what I look like, and I'm good with how I appear.*

He must have liked what he saw because he held my hands out to the side, still staring, and whispered, "Beautiful."

Then he pulled me into another intense kiss. His hands began to roam my body, touching every inch he could. After several long minutes, he reached around to my back and unhooked my bra, slowly sliding the straps from my shoulders. I reached up and pulled it from between us, letting it fall into the pile of clothes already on the floor.

The feel of his smooth, hard chest pressing against my breasts made my nipples hard. It also made me impatient. I decided to take control of the situation and maneuver him toward the bed. He would not move. I tried to push him onto the bed from where we were standing, but that didn't work cither. All this foreplay was driving me crazy. I wanted to get to the main event.

"Patience," he murmured near my ear.

"I'm not a patient person."

Night chuckled softly and glided his hands down my body to my panties. He slid them down my legs as he held my stare. His hands slid back up my body until he reached my shoulders, his gaze never leaving mine. Then without warning, he shoved me onto the bed. I hadn't even noticed he had maneuvered me toward it. He followed me down, towering over me with our bodies pressed together. He kissed me once more, devastating my mouth completely before he made his way to my neck. His teeth grazed my skin, kissed, licked, and bit it. My moans deepened as each section of my nerves ignited like lights being systematically turned on in a house. My entire body hummed with pleasure, making me ache to have his cock filling me.

I need you inside me came out in a whimper from the need starting to build.

He didn't answer. He just kissed and nipped his way down to my left breast. Each nibble sent little sparks that made their way south to my clit, which in return started warm tendrils to pool in my core. I relished the sensations flooding my body. Then Night sucked my nipple into his mouth, hard and fast. I gasped at the new pleasure and arched into him.

I placed a hand on the back of his head, holding him in place as I managed to moan, "Harder."

Night obliged and grazed my nipple with his teeth. I moaned in approval. His hand roughly grabbed my free breast, squeezing, molding, and pinching the nipple. Different sensations shot through my body as he lavished attention on my breasts. Once he had bitten, plucked, and swirled his tongue around one nipple, he moved his mouth to the other one and repeated the torture. Wrapped up in the pleasure he created, I writhed under him, uttering soft, breathy moans.

Once done with my breasts, Night's mouth began to move south, kissing, nipping, and licking my bare skin until he reached my pussy. He slowly slid his tongue between my folds and circled my clit.

My hips jerked, and I moaned, "Fuuuck."

"Did you like that?" His warm breath sent shudders through me since he barely lifted his mouth enough to speak.

"Yesssss!" hissed out of me as he circled my clit again.

"Mmmm, you taste so good," he rumbled in a deep husky tone, then licked again. "I knew you would."

Night returned to licking, sucking, and biting my clit. I contorted under him, needing more pleasure and more of him. Then my body bowed, and I sucked in a sharp breath when

Night roughly sank two fingers into me. I let my breath out in a long moan of pleasure. He began finger fucking me, rough and hard.

"You are so tight and hot."

My only response was another deep moan. Night returned his tongue to my clit, spreading pure pleasure throughout my body. Sparks of electricity set every inch of me alight with overwhelming sensations. I reached down and threaded my fingers into his hair, making sure I had a way to control his movements. It felt so good my hips began moving in small circular motions of their own accord. A deep gravelly groan rumbled up his chest. I didn't know if it was in approval or admonishment, but I didn't care. I just didn't want this raw pleasure to stop.

Then I felt it. That all-telling sign that my orgasm was starting to build. Hot liquid rapture began to pool deep in my core, and all I wanted was for him to keep doing what he was doing until I could fall over that edge into pure delight. Usually, oral sex never got me this close to an orgasm. He was either very skilled or the hundred-plus years my body had gone without had me primed and ready. My inner walls began to ripple and flutter around his fingers.

"No, no. You can't come yet. I want to be inside you before that happens." Night chided and nipped my inner thigh.

"Then you better hurry up and put your dick in me."

"When I am done tasting you, I will. Until then, you will wait."

"We will see."

Night slapped my clit. I raised up on my elbows and glared at him. He returned his mouth to my clit and held my gaze as he sucked hard, nibbled, and flicked my clit with his tongue. I didn't want to be the first to look away, but the surge of ecstasy made me fall back on the bed. Deep moans escaped my lips as each movement added to the need building inside. My inner walls began to flutter again.

"No," Night growled around a mouth full of my pussy.

His growls didn't help his objection. The vibrations just added to the multitudes of sensations spreading through my body. I gripped the sheets tight, unsure if I could hold out much longer, and damn sure didn't want to. I was so close to the edge, wanting nothing more than to fall into that oblivion. To let my body and mind float in the bliss where nothing existed but pure pleasure.

"Night?"

Night didn't answer. He continued his assault on my body, which didn't calm my rippling inner walls. I was so ready to let the floodgates open.

In my most demanding tone, I issued a warning. "Night, I need to come."

Still, Night made no move to put his cock in me, so I decided not to wait. I fully relaxed into the pleasure and let my orgasm build to its peak. I was just about to fall headfirst into the mind-bending rapture of ecstasy when Night stopped.

"I told you to wait."

"I don't want to. "

"Hmm."

Night went right back to lapping and sipping at my clit, which sent me right back to teetering on that edge. Then the bastard curved his fingers inside me and rubbed against my g-spot. I moaned loudly from the intense sensation that shot through me and straight to my core. He almost threw me over the edge but not quite. It would only take a few more minutes with what he was doing, and I would swan dive right over that edge into my orgasm.

"Night, please let me come. I cannot hold out any longer. And if you even think of bringing me down again, I'll send you to your cabin."

Night didn't answer, didn't move, he just continued what

he was doing.

Frustrated and getting more irritated by the minute, I changed tactics. Growling between clenched teeth, I pleaded, "Night, please."

That must have been what he wanted to hear because he replaced his mouth with his cock and slammed home. The bit of pain from being stretched and filled completely was more than enough to send me over that edge. I shattered around his cock with a loud, deep, soul-reaching groan of pure ecstasy as my orgasm hit so hard I saw spots. My inner walls rippled and squeezed his thick cock while intense waves of pleasure rolled through my body.

Then Night began to move slowly but steadily, prolonging the extreme pleasure and dragging out my orgasm. The sensations became so intense that I had to reach out and still Night so I could catch my breath. He paused with his cock buried deep inside me, but the pause let me calm down some. My body was still quivering slightly, but my breathing had slowed. Night took my even breaths as a sign to begin rocking in and out of me again.

He leaned down so that our mouths were almost touching. "Damn, that was a hard one. I don't think I have ever had a woman come that hard for me."

"Well, don't get used to it. It won't always be that easy."

He stopped moving . . . again. "You don't think I can make you come like that every time?"

"It's not always that easy for me. The closer the rounds of sex, the harder it is for me to orgasm. Plus, all the right combination of things must happen at the same time for me to reach my peak."

"We will see. I'm a fast learner. I'll figure out how to make it happen every time."

"Stop talking and get to work then."

Night began moving again, keeping a leisurely pace,

making my body loosen and relax again. It didn't take long for my body to become ready for more.

Night suddenly flipped me onto my stomach and pushed my legs together. He straddled my thighs and shoved his cock deep inside me, the crown reaching my cervix. He made several shallow thrusts, making contact over and over, which sparked another build of hot liquid in my core.

"Oh, my God!"

My inner walls began fluttering again as hot sparks reignited all my nerve endings. Night reached up and collared my throat. Not impressed—well, maybe slightly impressed—with his dominant move, I raised up on my elbows with a growl. With his lips at my ear, I felt them curve into a smile. He leaned over me, pressing his chest to my back and moving his free arm to prop himself on his elbow. Then he opened his fist and grabbed a handful of my breast. He pinched the nipple, rolling it between his fingers and sending electric zings straight to my clit. He began biting the bare skin of my shoulder, making my whole body quiver and shudder. Deep low moans rumbled up my throat that spurred Night on. His thrusts turned deep and hard, causing my orgasm to crawl the steep climb to the edge of blinding rapture.

Between low throaty grunts, he growled into my ear, "I want your ass."

"I haven't done that in a long time. It won't be easy."

"I want your ass, and you will give it to me."

I grunted at his command, and he chuckled. His grip around my throat tightened as he pulled out of me. Then the head of his cock tapped the entrance of my ass. Taking a deep breath, I relaxed as he pushed in slowly, an inch at a time, with groans and words of approval.

I thought his cock had made my pussy feel full, but this sensation was amazing. It felt like too much and not enough all at the same time. I was being stretched more than ever in the past, but the pain and pleasure mixing together felt so good that I didn't want him to stop.

After he sank in a few more inches, I slowly began to move into his thrusts, making him go deeper. The sensation of being so filled had my whole body overloaded and hanging on the edge by a fingernail. Night returned to nibbling my neck where it met my shoulder. The sensations assaulting my nerves made pure molten pleasure explode throughout my body. I wanted to rip away that last finger holding onto the edge and let myself plummet into ecstasy.

My body quivering inside and out must have clued Night to how close I was to another orgasm. He released my breast, slid his hand between my hip and the bed, and started rubbing circles around my clit. My last fingernail of control began to slip slowly. I wanted it to hurry and just let myself fall, but it was like my body was still waiting for something.

Night's growls turned into deep moans again as his cock throbbed deep within my ass, indicating he was also close to orgasm. He changed his pace, picking up a little speed with each hard, deep thrust.

He continued for a few more minutes before he grunted out. "Come."

That one word was what I'd waited for. My body exploded, and my hot liquid pleasure coated my insides as my orgasm pulled me into overpowering ecstasy. My mind blanked. Nothing but the complete short circuit of each nerve and body part was left. My body convulsed as each wave of bliss slammed into me in pure unadulterated pleasure. I gripped the sheets tight and clawed Night's hand around my throat. This orgasm was three times stronger than the first one.

My body's reaction must have been what Night wanted to experience before he let himself go. Because now, he was hammering into my ass, which only prolonged my orgasm again. It didn't take long before his own climax barreled into him, and he stiffened, filling my ass with jets of his hot seed. He collapsed onto my back, and we both lay there riding out the last waves of our orgasms.

I'm not sure how much time passed before I could reboot my brain and body to move again. Once I could breathe somewhat normally, I uncoordinatedly rolled to the side, making Night slide off me. Even though my body still felt liquefied, I clumsily moved into my sleeping position and passed out.

CHAPTER SIX: THE WEATHER ON EARTH

My full bladder woke me early the next morning. Not ready to open my eyes, I groaned and tried to roll off my stomach to get up, but I couldn't move. My brain, hazy with sleep, was confused as to why I couldn't move. I tried again and met the same resistance. A little panic kicked in. I cracked open one eye to find an arm and a leg flung across my back. Then flashes of the night before surfaced, and I remembered who was in bed with me. Pushing up enough to turn my head, I came nose to nose with Night. It was his arm and leg holding me down. I turned back around and gently slid out from under him, then dashed to the bathroom before I had an accident.

I returned to the side of the bed. Instead of getting back in, I stood there for a minute, just admiring all that raw masculinity lying there. Night was a fine specimen of a male. His golden skin stretched over his well-defined back that now bore a few scratches from last night, which I didn't remember doing. The eagle stretching across his shoulders just added to his allure. I wanted to crawl back into bed and wake him for round two. But instead, I returned to the bathroom so I could shower and get started for the day. Sometimes being an adult and the leader sucked, I thought as I stepped into the shower.

"Vega."

"Yes, Ms. Atlantis?"

"What time is it."

"It's eleven forty-five am."

"Thank you."

"I will activate the clock feature in your bedside table."

"My what? You know what, never mind. Thank you."

"Yes, Ms. Atlantis."

"Wait, Vega? Were you able to figure out what day of the week it is and what month it is?"

"I did find out the month. It's July. I am still working on narrowing down the specific date and day of the week. I should have it figured out in about thirty minutes."

I called for the shower, remembered to specify the temperature, then stepped into it. The hot water pelting my skin felt heavenly. I had to force myself to wash instead of just standing under the running water. I shampooed and rinsed my hair and then scrubbed my body. I was about to add conditioner to my hair when I felt large hands on my shoulders.

I looked back at Night and smiled. He kissed my lips and then worked his way down my neck to my shoulders, where there were a few faint bite marks from our last encounter. I closed my eyes, enjoying the feel of his lips on my wet skin and his hands roaming over my body. I basked in the sensations for several minutes more before I reluctantly told Night I had to finish showering so I could get my day started. He expressed not liking the idea but begrudgingly agreed, and we finished our shower.

Once dressed, we joined everyone else in the dining room. Breakfast was laid out on the table, so all I had to do was eat. Which was a relief — I wasn't sure I was up to cooking. I was exhausted, but in a good way. I sat there and ate while everyone else was chatting about things they had discovered. I was starving and not quite ready to get the day started.

I missed my soda and quiet time during my morning drive to work to get me ready for the day ahead. Here there was no soda, no drive to work, and no quiet time . . . so far. The only caffeine we had was tea. As I poured myself a glass, I noticed Cash lifting a mug to his mouth.

I turned and gaped, pointing and waggling my finger at his cup. "Hey, Cash. What's in the mug?"

Everyone stopped, looked at me, and then at him.

"Coffee?" Cash replied.

"We have coffee! Why didn't anyone tell me? Please tell me we have cream and some kind of sugar for it." I started to get up.

"Sit, Mom. I'll go make you a cup." Verruca smiled and shook her head as she headed toward the kitchen.

"Love you, baby girl!"

Everyone started laughing.

"What? I need some real caffeine. Since we have no soda, coffee will have to do. I mean, tea is great for the rest of the day, but to get started, I need real caffeine."

Night patted me on the shoulder, giving me a placating smile. I glared at him, frowning and holding back the *fuck you* that I wanted to say. He just laughed, then turned back to his food and conversation.

I was about to take a bite of food when Verruca waved a cup of coffee in front of me. I dropped my fork onto my plate and grabbed the mug. I took a tentative sip. Not only to see how hot it was but also to see what it tasted like. I closed my eyes, sighing softly because it was that good. It would be a great kickstart for my day.

We had been eating and chatting for a while when Kilian spoke up. "I think we should talk about who to wake up next."

"I agree." I took another quick drink of my coffee. "We also need to hash out some rules or laws—really, we could call them whatever—and the corresponding consequences. The info could be added to the introduction to the ship video Cash and Juniper are putting together. Plus, I think we should do this before we wake anyone else."

"Yeah, that would be a good idea because we don't want

too much input. We want to keep it simple," Ryo said.

"That's what I was thinking. I want this group right here" — I made a circular gesture, including the whole group — "to control as much as we can, especially while we are on this ship. If too many people are giving input and fighting to take control, it will be bad for all of us. Once we're on the ground, everyone can do as they please. Until then, the council will make the decisions, and I, as Iksen, will make sure things are getting done."

"Honestly, I agree. I know I haven't said much because this is all so crazy and new." Juniper glanced at everyone timidly. "But so far, I feel I can trust you guys. We do not know anything about the other people on this ship. I don't want our safety and security threatened by anyone or anything. It's scary enough up here without a power struggle going on."

Most of the group was nodding and saying, "Agreed."

"How many exactly are we going to wake?" Cash's tone held a hint of apprehension.

"Only enough to help us with running the ship. Maybe ten or so?" Verruca responded.

Cash hesitated for a moment, then slowly nodded his agreement.

"Okay. While we decide who to wake next, we can also determine who we want as the last two council members. So, are we ready to start reviewing the profiles of the other passengers?" I glanced around the table.

"Why not?" Ronan said. "It's not like it will go away or get easier."

"True. Vega, what do the sleeping volunteers do for a living." I grabbed Verruca's tablet.

"We have a doctor, a nurse, an x-ray tech, a construction foreman, two lawyers, a chef, a tattoo artist slash research biologist."

A weird combination but okay, I thought, nodding my

head in acceptance.

"A Navy pilot, a police officer, a natural healer, a banker, a bar owner, a social media star, a stockbroker, a translator, a professional surfer, a store manager, an import-exporter . . . The list goes on and on." Vega finished and suddenly materialized in front of us.

Verruca startled. "I'm not sure I'll ever get used to him doing that."

"Wow, we have a variety of professions, it seems." Juniper bounced in her seat excitedly.

"It seems that the company tried to mix it up as best they could," Night agreed.

"Yeah, but we need to be flipping strategic in who we wake. I still agree we should not wake everyone. Whoever we wake up needs to be able to help run this ship and get us to Earth. I ain't babysitting some damn fool," Jax stated.

I chuckled mentally because his Texan nature came out there at the end. Texan drawl and all.

"Then who do you think we need to wake? Let's go through the pros and cons of each person." I barely kept the amusement out of my tone, still mentally laughing at Jax. I pulled up a blank document on the tablet to make notes.

"I think we should wake all medical people. Even the natural healer." Kilian appeared business-like as he studied the list of passengers. "I think the construction person should be woken, along with the chef, the two lawyers, the pilot, and the police officer. These are people who can help us. Well, if they don't completely freak out about our situation."

"I concur with all the professions Kilian just mentioned. Besides, you never know what kind of skills people have besides their profession," Cash chimed in.

"I can agree with that. I have a lot more skills than what I did for a living." I nodded as I made notes. "Okay. So, are we all in agreement we will wake the people Kilian mentioned?"

"Yes," everyone said in unison.

"Okay, so do we want to spend the day doing their orientation, or do we think we need to do some other things also?"

"Why don't half of us start the waking and orientation? The other half can see if we can start scouting the Earth," Verruca suggested.

"I like it," I said. "Who is doing what?"

"I'll stay and help with the new people. If you don't need me," Verruca said.

Ryo raised his hand. "I can stay and help Verruca."

"We can stay to help with the new people," Juniper waved her thumb between her and Cash.

"By any chance, did y'all get that introduction video done, Juniper?" I mentally crossed my fingers.

"We did, but we just barely finished it. It's a little rough."

"That's okay, as long as we have something that gives them an idea of what they are facing. Thank you both for getting it done so quickly."

"It wasn't a problem." Cash said. "It gave us a chance to explore the ship ourselves. I know it a little better now."

"Okay, Kilian, come with me to the bridge. Jax, come with us." I looked from one to the other, and they both nodded their agreement.

"Okay, call me if you need me for anything." I gave Verruca a stern look, "Vega, please follow Verruca's orders. She is in charge of the people being woken up."

"Yes, Ms. Atlantis." He turned and followed Verruca to another set of tables.

"Thank you, Vega, and thank you guys for doing this while I take care of other things." I turned to leave.

"Wait," Ronan called. "We didn't set up any laws or rules."

Night turned towards him. "Shit, we didn't."

Kilian spoke up, "Well, I have been thinking of some extremely basic laws to live by for now. I mean, they couldn't be simpler."

"Go for it," I gestured for him to continue.

"Okay, this is what I was thinking." Kilian moved to the front of the group. "One. No stealing. The punishment will fit the crime. Depending on what was stolen will determine the penalty. Anything from extra duties to confinement. I'm not sure what a third option could be.

"Two. No physical harm up to and including death. Punishment is jail time. In the event a person kills someone, they will be permanently imprisoned. Depending on the level of brutality of the crime, we could space them, or once we land, a trial can be held to determine final punishment." He shrugged, looking around at everyone.

"Three. Everyone must contribute to our survival. If they don't, we could assign punishments like confinement to their cabins, maybe rationing their food, or whatever we think would work to inspire them to contribute.

And that's all I have. Like I said, it couldn't be simpler than those three rules."

"Sounds like the perfect start." I looked around the group, waiting for someone else to speak up. "Anyone else have any thoughts or want to add anything?"

After a few more seconds, when no one said anything, Night wrapped it up. "I think that covers the basics."

I nodded. "Okay then. Well, we can always add to them later if we need. Ronan, can you make notes of the rules and send them out to all of us."

"Yes, Iksen."

"Atlantis, I'm going to join you all on the bridge." Night walked toward us.

"Okay, come on," I motioned for him to follow us.

As Kilian, Jax, Night, and I left the dining hall, I heard Vega going through the list of people with Verruca. Then I heard Verruca give everyone else an order to make more food and drinks just as we walked down the hallway. She made me proud when she stepped up and took control of a situation. It meant I didn't have to worry about her surviving life.

I lost myself in thoughts of Verruca being so grown up on the way to the elevator. She had always been a happy kid. Inquisitive, ready to learn and explore all the time. As she grew older, she became a little anti-social, but it was only because she had begun to understand how people were. She had made me so proud when she got her cosmetology license, then turned around and got her instructor's license. Then she'd got a job at her school as an instructor, all before she was twenty-two. Then after teaching for two years she had bought her own salon. I was still smiling at the memories when Kilian's voice snapped me back to reality as we stepped onto the elevator.

"So, we should be on the Earth side of the moon now, right?"

"We should be. It has to be around eleven in the morning. We usually come around to the front side of the moon by about ten-thirty-ish." Jax looked like an excited kid. "I have been trying to track our days to get my internal clock reset. I used to have a good one, but the last few days have been all ass-backward."

"I know, mine used to be fairly good, too, but I couldn't tell you what time it was right now if I had to. I just hope my internal compass is in better shape." I stepped off the elevator onto the bridge.

"When y'all were inventorying things the other day, how much weapons, ammo, and other stuff did you find?" Jax looked over at Kilian.

"We found enough to last us a while, especially up here. Depending on what we find on the ground, we may not have enough for long periods. As for the drones, we found four small ones in cases with their batteries."

"I think all the council should learn as much as they can about all aspects of the ship. It will make it easier for us to understand our primary jobs, but also be backups for each other just in case." Night said to the group.

"I like that idea," Jax said, "Let move over to the control station and I'll show you what I learned so far."

I sat back, listening to the men talk. Not only did it seem like Night and Kilian were acting slightly competitive, but also that Kilian was giving Jax orders like he was in charge. Not that I wouldn't have asked the same of Jax, but I didn't know if it was the way he said it or the way he was doing it. It just rubbed me the wrong way for a few seconds. I knew he was a council member, but he was acting kind of weird.

"I agree," I said. "But for now, let's see what we can find out about Earth."

They all turned to look at me like they had forgotten I was there, just like any guy when *dick measuring* kicks in. I shook my head and turned toward the main screen, which had cleared, giving us a view of Earth. I stared at what used to be our home, seeing large patches of blue and green peeking through all the swirling clouds that appeared today. The land masses were still distinguishable, but the shapes appeared changed somehow. We were looking at North America, but the clouds made it hard to tell for sure what part.

"Vega, can you spare me some time?"

"Yes, Ms. Atlantis. The new people are being awakened, and that is all automated. What can I do for you?" Vega flickered into view next to the main screen.

"What part of North America are we looking at?"

"We can see all of it but the cameras are positioned to investigate North America's east coast."

"Awesome. Can we begin our trip back to Earth? But instead of investigating the east coast, can the cameras be repositioned to explore Texas first? I would like to see what it looks like."

"Yes, I will set that into motion."

"Thank you, Vega."

I continued staring out the window, observing everything I could. Visually there were some differences. It seemed crazy when thinking about all that had happened and where we were now — on a spaceship, hoping and praying we could make it back to Earth where it might be safe. I was brought back to the present when someone bumped my hip.

Kilian looked down at me. "What are you thinking about? You look very lost, confused, maybe even a little sad."

"I was just looking at the Earth and wondering what changes we are going to find."

"Yeah, I stopped trying to wrap my head around it. I'm focusing on the present."

"Hey, guys," interrupted Jax. "I am going to run down to the engine room. I had asked Vega to pull up some manuals and run more reports. He just sent a message saying they are ready."

"Sounds good to me. We will start pulling today's weather reports and get the cameras zoomed in while the ship maneuvers into place. Let us know if you need anything," I called out to Jax as he got into the elevator.

"I will. Let me know when everything is on the map, and I'll come back to study it," Jax said just before the door closed.

I returned my attention to the Earth. We had gotten a little closer, and it appeared Vega had aligned the trajectory to meet my request. I mean, not that we couldn't see all of North and South America, but it seemed we were headed a little more southward. I could now see the outline of the Texas coast clearer through the cloud breaks.

Clouds seemed to be swirling violently over the southern portion of the continent. As I watched, the clouds turned darker and swirled faster. Kilian looked at me with his eyebrows raised and a questioning expression. I shrugged because I didn't know what was going on.

"Vega, can you tell me what is going on with all the cloud activity we're seeing right now?"

"I will display the reports from the weather monitors, which will keep you informed of all current activity on the continent."

"That is perfect. Are there other Earth monitoring systems that can be turned on as well?"

"Yes, I will turn them all on now."

All the screens on the ship began to illuminate with charts and reports. I tapped on the weather report that popped up to the right of the main screen, dragging it closer so I could read it. I must have triggered something, because a computerized female voice started speaking.

"The southeast portion of what was known as Texas and Louisiana is currently experiencing severe tornados and snowstorms. This mega-storm is the result of a collision of an extreme cold front pushing snow and ice north from Mexico with a high-pressure zone moving south, fronted with strong winds and high heat index."

"Holy shit, what kind of backward weather shit is this?" Night blurted after hearing what was going on.

The door to the elevator opened, and the robot I had seen on my first night rolled onto the bridge. I was slightly taken aback because I had not seen it since that night and had never been around one this advanced. It began vacuuming with the quietest vacuum I had ever heard. We all stared at it curiously for a moment, then turned our attention to the screens to continue our reviews.

Night joined Kilian and me in front of the main screen. I was still somewhat distracted thinking about the robot when Kilian pressed slightly against my right side. I gave him a quick smile and looked back at the reports.

"What is going on down there?" Night glanced at the different reports on the screens. "Is all of the US like this? I mean, all the weather being backward and crazy?"

"I have no idea." I patted his shoulder, reassuring him that he wasn't alone in his confusion.

I looked over to find another report had popped up. I pulled it toward me, seeing a weather forecast for the next week for the southern part of the US. It called for snow the whole week. Snow in the south? Our planet had apparently been turned upside down. At least weatherwise. I slid the report over for Kilian to read and tapped on a few more pages that had appeared.

One was a report for other areas of the US. It appeared as if the weather patterns had flipped. Regions known for cooler temperatures and snow before were now hot and kind of wet. More like the South had been before the bombs. The South was now more like what the North had been.

I tapped on another report, which had a date stamp on it. I pulled it closer for a better view and saw the date showed July 2137. I checked the other reports, looking for a date stamp. It wasn't until I returned to the first weather report that I saw a date stamp in the corner. It also read July 2137.

"Vega, did you ever figure out what day of the month and day of the week it is?"

"Yes, Ms. Atlantis. I have finally worked out that it is July 15th, 2137, and the day of the week is Wednesday."

"Wait, you are telling me it's the middle of summer right now?" Kilian turned, looking at me with wide-eyed surprise.

"Yep. I have had Vega working on this for a couple days. I wanted us to have some sense of time."

"I was wondering about that myself," Night said.

"Vega, can you add the date, day, and time to every monitor on the ship? I'm sure a lot of people will want to know this. Please and thank you,"

"Of course, Ms. Atlantis."

I returned to skimming reports as the pages popped up on the screen. One displayed images from a storm that had hit the South the previous week. The pictures showed trees ripped out of the ground and snowbanks around six feet tall. The snownadoes, which is what I decided to call them, were crazy storms.

After several long minutes of reading report after report of upside down weather, I threw my hands in the air and blurted, "It would seem we are smack dab in the middle of summer and there is a huge snownado wreaking havoc on the South. Monsoons are drenching the Pacific Northwest, which is more desert nowadays than forest."

I closed my eyes and pinched the bridge of my nose in utter disbelief at what I was reading and seeing. I had no idea how to navigate this mess. Or how to find a place that was safe for us to land. Earth didn't even make sense anymore. I felt someone step closer to me, and a large warm hand took mine, gently squeezing it.

"We will figure it all out." Night's softly spoken words offered reassurance.

I squeezed his hand back and opened my eyes to look at him. He smiled at me, and I nodded as I took a deep breath.

"We've got a lot to learn more about the conditions down there before we can land on earth." Kilian nudged me with his elbow.

"I know, it's just a lot to take in at one time." I shook my head, hoping reality would set in better before I had to address the rest of our group and the new ones. "Sorry, I didn't mean to freak out there. Let's drop this info onto our map." I turned toward the table with our living map on it.

"Don't apologize for needing a minute to freak out. You have been calm, cool, and collected this whole time. You have kept everyone else grounded and have not let anyone panic.

That includes me. If you were not so calm, I don't know if I would be as settled with our situation as I am. You deserve a minute to freak out." Night stepped forward and kissed my forehead.

I smiled slightly at him, then closed my eyes. I took a second to clear my thoughts for now. When I opened them, I took another deep breath and nodded to Night.

Kilian grabbed my hand, pulling me away from Night, and half dragged me to the map table. We all stepped up on the platform, and the table lit up.

"Kilian, can you open up that folder and pull out the pics?" I looked up with a smile.

Kilian tapped the folder, then began flicking out pictures of the storms around the edge of the map. I dragged them to the areas of the country where the storms were happening and dropped them into place. We took a step back and looked at what we had created so far.

The world we knew no longer existed. Our map showed us only a fraction of the lunacy going on with Earth. The mutation of the animals, the flipped upside down weather, and the new landscape were only the tip of the iceberg. *I'm sure once we land, we will find a whole slew of things we have no idea about now. Okay, snap out of all this worrying. You can only do so much with what you know, and there is plenty of stuff to keep you busy on the ship right now. Stop running down rabbit holes of what-ifs and could-bes.* With a short sharp nod, I returned my attention to the map on the table.

"The nuclear bombs fucked up the Earth's entire weather pattern. Everything we knew before is no longer valid. We're going to have to learn everything from scratch. But with the ship's help, it should be easy," Kilian assured me as he slid an arm around my shoulders.

"Mom," I heard from my wrist.

"Yeah, what's going on?" I raised my arm, and Verruca's face appeared above my communicator.

104

"The new group of awakees is in the dining room." Verruca said. "Vega is about to start the videos. Do you want to join us to answer questions?"

"In a few. I want to set some programs to monitor the Earth before we come back."

"Okay, I'll let you know when we're going into the introduction to the ship video."

"Okay." I tapped off the communicator and turned to Night and Kilian. "What do you think we need to monitor?"

The men followed me back to the main screen, which no longer showed the reports and pictures. We all started at the Earth, hauntingly floating in the distance. They both stood close with their arms pressed against me. An image of them pushing me to the floor and fucking me flashed through my mind. I drew in a sharp breath at the thought and bit my lower lip.

"What are you thinking about?" Kilian looked down at me.

I cleared my throat, hoping no trace of the thought of being ravished by the two of them showed on my face.

"What do you mean?" It was difficult to keep my lust from coming through in my tone.

Night turned and was now staring at me. I kept my focus on the screen so they wouldn't see my lustful thoughts reflected in my eyes.

"You are smiling, but that's not a happy smile. That is a wicked smile." Night flashed a wicked smile of his own.

I glanced at him out of the corner of my eye. "I don't know what you are talking about. I was thinking about what I was going to say to the newly awakened passengers."

"Sure, you were." Kilian's smile echoed Night's.

"I was thinking somewhere along the Gulf Coast of Texas would be a good landing spot. Even though the weather has changed, it is still the area I know best. It gives us access to the Gulf for food and travel. We can find an area where a river spills into the ocean. That way, we have access to fresh water as well. I know the Nueces River comes out around what used to be Corpus Christi. So that area would be good." I secretly crossed my fingers, hoping the abrupt change of subject would distract them from the sexual tension that seemed about to explode between the three of us.

"What?" they said in confused unison.

"What are you talking about?" Kilian asked.

"Where I think we should land when we go back to Earth. I think that would be a good place."

"Okay, but maybe we should monitor more than one spot. Take some samples and see where the best spot would be." Kilian still sounded confused.

"Ignore it all you want" — Night looked me up and down — "but you won't be able to deny it forever."

I glanced at Kilian. "Agreed. I'll have the ship start monitoring." I purposely ignored Night's remark and continued looking down at the Earth to avoid eye contact. "Vega, please start monitoring the weather and atmosphere along the Texas Gulf Coast, the Oregon coast, and along the East Coast from Delaware to North Carolina. Also, I would like to be close enough to Earth to send the sample drones by the day after tomorrow."

"Yes, Ms. Atlantis. I will set all that up and have us in Earth's orbit in two days. Is there anything else you would like me to monitor?"

"Yes. Please keep monitoring the rest of the US as well. I would like to get as clear a picture as possible of the conditions. We never know what information will be needed."

"Yes, Ms. Atlantis. The weather patterns will be easy to monitor. If you wish samples of atmosphere or soil for a specific area, you will have to launch the drones, and we will have to move directly over the area for that."

"Understood, Vega, thank you."

We stood in silence for a while, just staring at the Earth or maybe nothing. I really couldn't focus on one thing. My mind was just too full, thinking about how to keep us all alive and safe, trying to figure out the best place to land when we reached Earth and what we would need once we got there. Now, on top of everything else, I was lusting after two men. It would drive a lesser person insane. *Thank God, I have always been good under pressure. Dad always told me I would need those skills at some point in my life, but I am not sure this was what he had in mind.*

Night and Kilian each took one of my hands, jerking me out of my mental rambling. I squeezed both of their hands and was about to lead them off the bridge to the dining room when Night's holo beeped.

"Night?" Jax's voice came through loud and clear. "Could you come to the engine room? I would like to talk through these reports with you and Ryo."

"Sure." Night kissed my hand. "Be there in a few."

He gave me a smile, let go of my hand, and made his way to the elevator. "Good luck with the new group of people. I'll find you when we're done." The elevator doors closed, leaving me alone with Kilian on the bridge.

Kilian let out a heavy sigh. I turned toward him to see what was wrong, but before I could form a thought or question, he slammed his mouth on mine. I stumbled back a step from the force of his kiss, and my back hit a wall. He wrapped both arms around my waist, pulling me tight to his body. I could feel every hard line of his chest, stomach, and hips pressing into me. He was holding me like he feared I would be taken away by someone or something. His tongue explored every inch of my mouth, and I returned the favor with relish.

One of my weird turn-ons has always been a hot man towering over me, and Kilian definitely towered. He was a good eight inches or so taller than me. In fact, I had to stretch on my tiptoes to return his kiss. I know it's silly, but standing six feet myself and plus-sized, it has always been hard to find a man who makes me feel like a dainty woman.

Kilian nipped my lower lip, then kissed his way down my neck until he reached my collarbone. I leaned my head to the side and sighed at the sensation of his soft lips against my sensitive skin. He apparently took my reaction as approval of what he was doing and pulled my hands up over my head, pinning them in place with one of his. His free hand slid under my shirt, and he returned his lips to mine as his fingers glided up my ribs to my breast. He slipped his hand under my bra and molded my breast in his palm until my nipple hardened. Then he pinched it and rolled it between his fingers.

My body responded quickly to his actions. I mean, it had always loved some heavy nipple play, but the heat coiling low and deep inside me happened more quickly than normal. I swore our hormones were all out of whack and on hyperdrive. He kept up his actions until a moan escaped me. That was when he pressed his whole body against mine, allowing me to feel just how turned on he was.

Damn, he was well-equipped. I sucked his lower lip and caught it between my teeth. A deep gravelly moan escaped him, and his cock throbbed between us. He released my hands, and I immediately wrapped my arms around him and explored every inch of his well-defined body I could reach. I ran my fingers along ridges and grooves, feeling the sexual tension straining each muscle I touched. He growled when I dragged my nails up his back. He feathered little kisses from my neck to the top of my shoulder, where he pulled my shirt to the side, exposing the skin underneath. Then he bit me in the crook of my neck. I grunted out a moan of pleasure and wrapped a leg around his upper thigh, pulling him closer to where I wanted him. He ground his rock-hard cock against me, creating yearning zings in my core. Oh, how I wished there was no fabric between us right now.

He worked his way back up my neck with kisses and nips, then made the return trip down to the swell of my breast. He kissed and nipped it through my shirt, but it was not enough for me. I wanted his skin against mine. I wanted to feel the electricity crackling between us. Determined to make that happen, I reached down with one hand and pulled my shirt up and over my head, tossing it to the ground. His mouth immediately found bare breast again, kissing and nipping it. I grabbed the hem of his shirt and pulled it up over his head, dropping it to the floor. Once his shirt was off, he pulled me tighter against him, rubbing his hard cock against my aching pussy. I was about to move this foreplay along to the main event when my communicator pinged.

"Mom, we're midway through the last video. By the time you get here, it will be finished."

I cleared my throat before answering, trying to be as composed as possible. "Okay, we're on our way. Call everyone and have them meet us back in the dining room."

"Okay."

Kilian growled after I closed the channel. "Well, that was the worst flipping timing ever."

"I know, right." I chuckled lightly.

I took a deep breath to steady myself. I pushed Kilian back a step and bent to pick up my shirt. Before I could put it back on, I had to adjust my boobs and bra. Once they were back where they belonged, I pulled my shirt over my head. Kilian frowned slightly as he pulled his shirt over his head. I shook my head, smoothed my hair back, and re-did my ponytail. Once I'd finished pulling myself together, I headed toward the elevator. Walking took a little bit of effort because my legs were slightly wobbly. *Damn, if that's what he does to me with just foreplay, imagine actual sex. I may not even be able to move afterward.*

Kilian followed but paused to adjust his cock. I snorted to

myself, but he must have heard, because he glared at me before continuing to walk. At least I wasn't alone in my struggle. We stepped onto the elevator, and he adjusted himself again.

"Having a few problems there, Kilian?"

"Yeah, he doesn't want to behave. Says that wasn't enough for him."

"Reeaally," I retorted in a lilting tone.

"Yes, this is not done, Atlantis. I want you, and I will have you."

"I'll think about it." I flashed him a wicked smile before stepping off the elevator.

Kilian followed me and slapped my ass. "I *will* have you."

I turned and frowned at him. "We will see."

He didn't know it, but he'd just issued a challenge that would have him chasing for a while, which was the fun part for me.

We walked into the dining room, which kept him from making another smart ass remark. We headed to the front of the tables where all the new people sat. I heard a commotion coming from the doorway and looked up to see Jax running in to join us.

Chapter Seven: Round One of Awakees

The mumbles of the new people were beginning to grow. The screen disappeared and the rest of our nine-man group began taking positions at the head of the tables.

"Everyone calm down," I let more of a southern drawl out than usual. I smiled mentally because I sounded a lot like the overly dramatic mothers from one of my favorite movies. Even Verruca looked at me with a smirk. "I'll explain things. First let me introduce everyone to you. To my right is my daughter Verruca. Next to her are Ryo, Juniper, and Cash." I pointed to each as they raised their hand in acknowledgment. "To my left are Kilian, Night, Ronan, and Jax. And last but not least, I am Atlantis, the Iksen of this group."

A tall, dark-haired woman with dark eyes raised her hand. I called on her to speak.

"Hi, I'm Savinka Azeem."

"Hi, welcome to our crazy new normal." I smiled.

"I'm a doctor, well, an oncologist. I can help with medical stuff if we need it."

"We will need your help. So far, no medical issues have arisen, but there are a lot of other medical type things to figure out, and your expertise will help. For now, how about you tell us about yourself? Just whatever you want us to know."

I stared at her as she looked around at everyone. She was a very pretty woman, medium build with deep bronzed skin. She had natural highlights in her skin, like someone had splashed honey across the high points of her face. I could tell by her slight accent she was Middle Eastern, maybe Indian, but her gestures and body language were all American. I tuned into her story as she got into where she was from.

"I currently live in Houston, Texas. My family also lived there. They volunteered for this program, but I am not sure if they are here. I play the violin and the qanun. I love music, all kinds of music. That covers most of the important things for now."

"Thank you, Savinka." I gave her another reassuring smile. "Before anyone else goes, let me just give you guys a little more perspective of what is going on here. You saw the videos. You know that the governments of the world we knew destroyed it trying to get rid of the vampires. What you may not have put together completely yet is that we have been placed on this spaceship asleep in our cryo tubs. From the time that happened to now has been just over a hundred years."

The awakees began to chatter again. I even heard a few gasps and *what the hells.*

"This ship currently is flying closer to Earth to get some current reading of the weather and atmosphere, but we learned earlier that the weather is backward. The things we knew no longer apply to the Earth from the info we have been able to gather.

"I know it's a lot, but you need to know that the people on this ship are the last two hundred and fifty humans left that we know of. If you had family that was supposed to join the program with you, we can check if they are aboard. The family and friends that were waiting for you to complete the sleep program are no longer there.

"Vega is our ship's AI." As if on cue, Vega appeared. "He will look through the rest of the manifest to see if your family members are here. I know it's a lot to digest, and I want you to take your time to grieve. Just remember we have a lot to do and to understand if we're going to get back to Earth. And I plan to do just that."

Everyone looked around at each other trying to see if they recognized anyone in the crowd. No one knew each other or were one another's family, it seemed. Verruca had gone to check on the food and Kilian asked for more people to tell us about themselves. I sat down on the tabletop behind me to listen to the new people tell us their stories.

A guy around six feet tall with lightly tanned skin, blue eyes, and brown hair stood up. He turned around and looked at everyone and I saw that he had a Navy Seal tattoo on the back of his left shoulder. He faced forward again looking at all of us for a few silent moments before speaking.

"I'm Shade Griffen. I am twenty-five years old, and I was a pilot in the Navy among other things. I signed up for the program after I got shot. My superiors suggested it since the world was in chaos. Anyway, my hometown is New Orleans. That's all I can think of right now."

Shade took his seat, and we waited for the next person. Just to make people feel a little less pressured, I turned to Kilian and started talking. The rest of our group followed suit. After a couple minutes another person stood up. She looked to be about five feet seven inches, with golden honey skin, green eyes, and tight super curly hair. I would have guessed she was mixed race. She and my daughter looked similar in their features.

"My name is Clover Drum. I am twenty-six years old and from Seattle, Washington. I was a police officer back home. I decided to join the program because I didn't have any close family left. I figured why not try something new." She shrugged sadly. "So that's me in a nutshell."

Another female stood. She seemed to be about the same height as Clover when she stood up next to her. She had light skin, long pin-straight black hair, dark almond-shaped eyes, and a thin build.

"I'm Lotus Haze from Seattle, Washington as well." She turned and glanced at Clover. "I am twenty-seven years old, and I am, was, a scientist with Phaser. I volunteered for this program. My adoptive parents had passed away, and I had no other family."

Lotus took her seat again, then a male and a female stood up. The female was very thin, like she worked hard at being that thin. Her hair was bleached blonde and her roots were beginning to show. Not that I had room to talk—my dark roots where beginning to peek through the top of my blue hair. Her eyes were a dark brown, and her lips appeared to be slightly too big. At first glance everything looked perfect, but when you really stopped to take her in, her lips were just a bit out of proportion to her face. She had a slight upward tilt to her nose which gave her a hoity toity air.

I was not much for judging people, but I was good at judging their character right from the start. I could tell she was going to be a prissy pain in the ass, and she had not even spoken yet.

The male gestured for her to go first. She sniffed with a hoity chin lift and began to speak.

"I am Lita Quinn from Dallas, Texas. I am twenty-eight years old and a lawyer. I was top of my law class at Harvard and the highest-ranking junior associate at one of the top law firms in Dallas. I would like to be part of any decisions going on and I would like to be in a position that suits my abilities." Her Southern drawl was way overdone.

It took everything I had not to roll my eyes. *She really thinks she is hot shit. She obviously has anxiety because she kept counting her fingers the entire time she gave that speech, and she keeps looking at everything like she is disgusted by it.*

"I will take that into consideration, Lita. If I find a good fit for you, I will let you know. What other skills do you have just in case we need you to fill in somewhere else?" There might not be a need for a lawyer right now.

"Being in charge is my skill. I am extremely smart, and I always know what's best." She turned sharply to retake her seat. She was a walking, moving contradiction. Here she was declaring how smart she was, yet her drawl might make some think different, but that hair flip was definitely dumb blonde. I saw her game a mile away. Those little gestures might fool the guys, but she would learn real quick not me.

Verruca leaned over and whispered in my ear, "She is going to be trouble."

I just nodded my agreement as the male who had been standing began talking.

He appeared to be slightly taller than me, maybe about six feet one inch, blond hair, green eyes, very thin build, and dark tribal tattoos running down both arms. The arrogance exuding from him was almost palpable. He fixed a smug smile on his face and began walking toward our table. He positioned himself right in front of me and faced the group.

If that wasn't a cock blocking alpha male move, then I didn't know what was.

Kilian bristled at his rudeness and interrupted his hello before he could even get it out completely. "I'm sorry, can you step to the right here?" Kilian pointed to the end of the table on the other side of us. "You are blocking our view of the group." His tone was polite but firm.

The male ignored him and turned back to the group and prepared to speak again.

I nodded to myself and hoisted myself from the table to stand right next to him, just to show him I was not about to play games with him. I felt someone try to join us but no one appeared on either side.

After a sideways glance the male began to speak again.

"I'm Ryker Devin from Dallas, Texas. I'm thirty-three years

old and a famous chef. I own the number one restaurant in Dallas, The Wild Moon. We put a high-end spin on southern classics. I'm sure if y'all are from Texas you know who I am." He paused and looked around at everyone. "If not, that's okay, I'll tell y'all about myself. I am great at a lot of things and am more than happy to share my expertise." He finished in a fake Texas drawl.

He didn't even have the correct drawl. Not only was his drawl more like someone from Georgia or Mississippi, the word *y'all* didn't flow out of his mouth right. He was not originally from Texas, that was easy to hear.

He looked over at me and smiled wide in what no doubt he thought was a charming, award-winning smile, but all it did was set my instincts on high alert. The tension grew from the council behind me. Someone's hand tried to grab mine in support, but I didn't dare break eye contact with Ryker, who was outright challenging me. My inner monologue for him was worse than the one for Lita. *They have chosen the wrong one if they think I will back down.* Finally, after many long seconds he nodded and turned to walk back to his seat. I took my seat again to wait for the next awakees to introduce themselves.

I looked over at Verruca, who was shaking her head. I widened my eyes at her and mouthed *What the hell.*

She mouthed back *I know, right.*

Now I was shaking my head in disbelief at Ryker's bullshit.

"We're going to have to watch those two," Kilian whispered to me.

I nodded once to indicate I agreed. The next person stood up, a young guy with dark hair. He wasn't but a few words in when my thoughts drifted back to Lita and Ryker. I did manage to catch his name, Rogue Nightshade, and that he had been a famous social media star. Then a set of twins stood up. They caught my attention a little more because they were hot, and from New Orleans. Ace and Vox Stokes. Ace was a banker and Vox had owned a restaurant and bar.

It wasn't until a Hispanic male, who looked about six foot two inches when he stood to introduce himself, that I truly got out of my own thoughts and started paying attention like a good leader should. If I didn't, people were going to think I was losing my mind instead of mentally talking myself off the edge of yelling at people.

"Hi, I'm Gage Delgado. I used to work in construction. Well, I owned my own business. I am from a city in South Texas called Corpus Christi. I had no other family and decided to take a chance on the Cryo program. That pretty much sums me up."

Gage sat back down, but something told me that he would be the perfect person for the role of mediator. There was something about him that seemed honest. I made a mental note to talk with everyone later about him.

I leaned over Kilian and Night to Verruca. "Can you go check the food? I don't want to leave in case anyone else gets the bright idea to challenge me."

Verruca nodded her head and quietly got up and went to the kitchen. The next person was another male, Dash Zager, from Maui. He was about six feet four inches, medium build, dark curly hair down to his shoulders, hazel eyes, and a beard. He had been a store manager for a hardware store.

"Aloha, Brah," Ryo and Ronan said to Dash.

"Aloha," he responded and waved the universal surfer hand gesture—I think it's called a *Shaka*.

The next person was another male named Garret D'Orzo. He looked to be about six feet, with dark eyes, short black hair, and a well-toned body. He said he was Italian and worked for his dad's import, export business, but his accent was totally Jersey.

Next a female stood up. She was about five foot nine inches, maybe a little taller, with long, black, straight hair to her waist, olive skin, and dark eyes. She looked Native American.

"Hi, I am Onyx Drake. I am a natural healer or medicine women." She gestured toward Night, who dipped his head to her. "I owned my own shop on the edge of our reservation in New Mexico. I had no other family besides my tribe." She made to retake her seat and then turned back toward us. "Oh, I am thirty years old."

Another male stood up. He was maybe about six foot five inches, blond hair, and brown eyes. He had a broad build. He looked like he worked out all the time or had a job doing hard labor. Then he spoke and shattered my preconceptions. His name was Knox Fuller, and he was a stockbroker. He didn't look like a stockbroker to me but what did I know about stockbrokers?

The last three people to speak were all females. They looked around at each other and the others before I had to step in to get things going again.

An amber-skinned women stood up. She looked around five foot seven inches, with thick, textured, black hair down to the middle of her back, dark eyes, and a pierced nose.

"Hello, I'm Zahirah Harber. I am half Pakistani and half white. My mom was American, and my dad was from Pakistan. I was married, but he passed away several years before the vampire issue. I have three kids. Sefa is thirteen years old, Kyril is seven years old, and Talora is five years. I worked for the courts as a translator. My biggest question is, are my kids here as well?"

"When we're done, I'll help you communicate with Vega and find out if your children are here." I reassured her. I prayed that they were among the children on the ship. I know firsthand what it's like to lose a child. Verruca reached over and grabbed my hand and squeezed. She must have seen the look on my face and knew where my thoughts had gone. I squeezed her hand back as I looked at her and smiled slightly.

The next woman stood up. She was Hispanic, around five foot eight inches, with medium brown hair to her shoulders, light brown eyes, and a very curvy build. She had an authoritative air about her. I bet she would be good at being a mediator, I thought, just as she began to speak.

"Hi, I am Camela Tack. I was the District Attorney for Muskogee, Oklahoma. I had an exceptionally large family, but so far, I do not see any of them here, except for Sybella over there. She is my ex-sister-in-law." She gave the other woman a sharp look. "I can help in any way you need me to."

Finally, we were down to our last person. Another Hispanic female around five foot eight inches rose from her seat. She had short, black hair cut into an angular bob, light brown eyes, and a curvy build. She looked very similar to the previous women.

"Well as you already know I am Sybella, Sybella Faden. I used to be a dentist in Muskogee. I was married to Camela's sister, and we have a sixteen-year-old daughter, Isadora. She was supposed to be here. Would you please check when you check for the other women's kids? And I am willing to help wherever I am needed."

After she took her seat, I stood up. "I know there are still a lot of questions. First and foremost, I'll check with Vega about everyone's children." I heard several sighs of relief. "The council and I will talk about everyone's skillsets. We will assign job duties accordingly. Most jobs are being created as we go. The more we find out about surviving on this ship, the more jobs we're needing someone to do.

" We need everyone doing what they are assigned to do to keep things running aboard the ship. It is crucial that y'all participate in our survival on this ship. Some jobs may seem unnecessary, but we have people doing them because they are needed. No contribution is too small or unnecessary. My goal is to get us back on Earth as soon as possible, but I do not have a time frame yet. The council and I will let y'all know when we do and share everything we decide."

Verruca called to me from the doorway of the kitchen. The rest of the council went to help her bring out the food. I continued to talk to the awakees as the others placed trays of food down.

"The rest of the day will be y'all's to choose a cabin on whichever floor y'all want. Please remember the three bedroom cabins are for families. Once you have chosen a cabin, y'all will find clothing and hygiene items. All the cabins are equipped for men and women. Anything that you cannot use, please bring it to the black deck, room Twelve-B. We're starting a clothes closet slash supply closet in that room.

"If y'all would like to tour the ship, please see Juniper, Cash, or Verruca for that. They know the most about the ship for now. If you feel there is a safety or security issue, please see Kilian or Ronan. Tomorrow, we will fill y'all in on what we know so far and what plan we have come up with. Our plan is constantly being revised. I mean, we have only been awake for about five days. So nothing's in set in stone yet."

Some people close to me laughed a little but most were focused on the food being set upon the table behind me.

"Okay, I'll stop talking. Come get food." I waved them forward. Everyone got up and moved toward the food.

I snuck into line behind the first five and got myself a plate. Then I went into the kitchen. It was the most privacy I could get for now, and I needed to check on the kids.

"Vega, can you tell me if the following kids are on the ship?"

"Yes, what are their names?" His form slithered into view.

"Isadora Faden, Sefa Harber, Kyril Harber, Talora Harber."

"We have Kyril and Talora aboard."

"That's all? What happened to the other kids?"

I have no children by the other two names. But I do have two young adults by the name of Isadora Faden and Sefa Harber."

"Oh my God, Vega, you gave me a heart attack. Why did you not tell me that to begin with?"

"You asked for children, not young adults."

I rolled my eyes at Vega because I was about to pass out if I had to tell those moms that their children were not here.

Vegas tone was slightly alarmed. "Ms. Atlantis?"

"Yes."

"Would you like me to call someone for your heart attack?" He had pulled up a screen in midair that showed all my vital signs.

"What? No, it was a figure of speech, Vega. I was scared because I thought the other two children were not on the ship. I didn't want to tell their moms they were gone."

"Oh, I'll add that to my database."

I finished my food and pulled myself together before I went to talk to the moms. The whole time Vega stood watching me.

"Vega, do you need something?"

"No, Ms. Atlantis, I was just observing."

"Can you stop, please?"

"Yes." And just like that, he shimmered out of view.

I was really hoping the parents would decide to leave the kids asleep until we made it to Earth, but I had a feeling they might not agree.

"Excuse me." I had to raise my voice to be heard over all the chatter and clanking of silverware. "Sybella and Zahirah, can you two come to the kitchen with me?"

They both got up in a hurry and followed me to the kitchen.

"The children are all on board."

Their faces lit up and relief washed over them. Before they could start asking to wake them I went through my reasons for not waking them yet. I let them think about it for a few minutes.

Sybella spoke first, "No, I want to wake my daughter. I need to see her and know she is okay."

Zahirah nodded her head in agreement. "Yeah me too. I get why you want to wait, but I need them."

"Okay, I completely understand, but how about we wait a few days. I want y'all to settle in and make sure y'all understand how this new life works. There are some new dangers the kids will have to look out for."

They were quiet for a few minutes thinking about what I had said.

Sybella's tone was stern, "Fine, I can wait three days, but no longer."

I looked at Zahirah.

"I can agree to three days as well."

"Good, go finish your food."

CHAPTER EIGHT: HIDDEN TALENTS

The next morning was chaotic. All the new people trying to find their way to the dining room for breakfast was funny. They kept going in the wrong directions, and Vega was redirecting them at every wrong turn. I redirected several people along the way, and by the time I reached the dining room I had a long line following me. To my surprise, the guys had already made breakfast. Juniper and Verruca had drinks, plates, and silverware out for everyone. We all lined up and began serving ourselves.

When I was done eating, I moved to the front of the group. I looked around and could see that mostly everyone was done eating.

"Please keep eating. I am just going to fill you in about the meeting we had late last night.

"First, we would like to ask Savinka and Zahirah to take the positions of the last two council members.

"Second, we would like Gage, Camila, and Lita to be mediators. If you have a problem with another person, you will speak with them, and they will help both parties resolve their issue.

"Third, Clover, Knox, and Dash, we would like for you three to be agents of our slowly growing security force. Ronan will be the Inspector and Kilian is sergeant at arms. Shade, we would like for you to train with Night and Ryo to be another pilot. Ace, for now we're going to have you working with Jax."

"Fourth, Vox, Ryker, and Garret, we would like you three

to take chef duties for now.

"Fifth, we need Lotus, Savinka, Sybella and Onyx to work together to set up a clinic. Pick whatever empty space you can find on the gold deck or black deck. We will also need your help with testing samples we will be taking from Earth's surface. We have two labs that the four of you can use. Get with Juniper if you need anything.

"Those were the topics we felt could not wait to be ironed out. I hope everyone is agreeable to their new assignments. After you're done with breakfast, everyone will report to their leaders and begin learning their new positions. Gage, Camela, and Lita, if you can meet me on the bridge in thirty minutes, that would be great. "

I walked back to where I had been sitting, picked up my plate, and went into the kitchen. I refilled my coffee, then decided to grab a couple of biscuits to take with me. I had just gathered everything to make my way to the bridge when Verruca walked in.

She gave me a hug. "So, what do you need me to do?"

"Can you help Ryker, Vox and Garrett get settled in here? Then after that can you help Juniper take Savinka , Lotus, and Onyx to the labs? Oh, also can you and Juniper get Twelve-B open and ready to collect the extra supplies." I tapped my chin, thinking. "I think that's it for now."

"Okay. I'll get everyone started, then monitor their progress throughout the day," Verruca assured me with a pat on the shoulder. "Oh, when we were passing out jobs you forgot Rogue. You know, that young guy that was a social media star. I think he should help in the kitchen until we know what else he can do."

"Sounds good to me. If I forgot anyone else just find them somewhere to help."

"Got it." She waved two fingers in the air as she walked out.

I grabbed my stuff and made my way to the bridge. I stepped off the elevator, and the bridge lit up for me. I walked to the main display, tapped the large file folder. It flipped open and several pages streamed out into a line on the screen. They were new reports of the weather.

There had been two more of those crazy snownadoes across the panhandle of Texas and back to the border of Louisiana. The two storms dumped five feet of snow on the affected areas. The atmosphere was stable for now, no storms pending.

The next report showed that oxygen was at seventeen percent, nitrogen at seventy percent, and all the other gases were right about normal. It was a bit thin but breathable. The second page of the report showed only small amounts of radiation in the air but nothing harmful.

I heard a noise behind me and turned to see Kilian and Night entering the bridge.

"What new info do we have this morning?" Kilian pointed to the screen.

"New reports of the weather and atmosphere from yesterday and overnight." I pulled the pages back up for them to read.

While they caught up, I went to our map table. I tapped the screen and began adding the current information. After dropping everything in place, I reviewed it. Heavy rain in the north flooded the affected area. Then snownadoes in the south dumped more than five foot of snow. It was a remarkable sight. I couldn't even imagine what it would be like to live in. A thought came to me as I studied the map. Were Earth's cardinal directions still in the same direction? If they were off, that could account for this crazy weather.

"Vega, can you tell me which direction is north and south?"

"Yes, I will put it on the main screen."

"Actually, could you indicate it on the map we're already creating?"

"Yes, Ms. Atlantis."

The directions flickered into focus on our map. North was semi-north. It was showing more northeast than directly north. So not exactly reversed but definitely out of whack.

"This slight shift in polarity could account for this chaos."

"This is a total cluster fuck." Night shook his head side to side in utter disbelief. "Nuclear bombs did all this? How many damn bombs did they set off at one time? Did anyone know that this would happen? How are we supposed to survive on this planet?" He dragged his hands down his face in complete frustration.

I put my hand on his shoulder and squeezed. Kilian hadn't spoken yet and I was wondering what was going on in his mind, because mine was racing through a million possibilities. Then the logical side of my brain kicked in.

"All we can do is take it day by day and moment by moment. If we overthink things, we will drive ourselves crazy. Let us stick to the plan and get started doing drone searches and collecting samples.

"I think we should check out three different areas of the US, starting with a location from each of the three areas we had Vega begin monitoring. We can choose new ones if one of those doesn't work."

"That sounds like a good plan for the next couple weeks. Where do we start for today?" Kilian finally looked at me and Night.

"Vega, where are we closest to right now?" Night turned his face toward the ceiling, eyes closed, and hands behind his head.

"We are closer to Texas right now, since that is where Ms. Atlantis had wanted me to monitor first."

"Then let us start there. Vega, please bring us as close as

we can to the Earth. We're going to launch a drone today and see what happens," Night instructed Vega.

"Yes, Mr. Night. I will let you know when we are in place."

"Thank you, Vega," I said. "Now can you also let Gage, Camila, and Lita know I'm ready for them? Oh, and can we just stay orbiting the Earth instead of going back and forth from the Moon to Earth?"

"Yes, I will keep us orbiting the Earth until otherwise instructed."

"Vega, thank you for everything."

Vega did as I asked, and I moved to the seating area in the back left corner of the bridge. I sat down scrolling through my notes on the tablet. After pages of notes, I found the one with the laws slash rules. I wasn't sure what to call them, but we needed them. The guys chose a chair on each side of me, and they began reading something on their tablets. We had been sitting there reading for about ten minutes when the door to the bridge slid open.

"Welcome, guys. Come sit." I motioned toward the empty seats.

Gage, Camila and Lita each claimed a chair on the far end of the sitting area directly across from myself and the guys. They looked around the bridge, taking in the strange surroundings. I gave them a minute so they could look at everything.

"The reason I wanted to meet with you three is to give you the rules slash laws we developed. They are simple—we didn't want anything complicated or hard to follow."

Gage looked around at everyone nervously. "I have never been involved in politics or law making. I only followed the laws made by others. Why would you want me to be part of this?"

"Well, because you seem like an honest person. I think you would listen to all sides of a story and make a fair decision about the punishment. Camila and Lita know laws and how a justice system should work. Between the three of you, the council feels y'all will be good at handling issues that arise and make a fair judgment on outcomes."

"Is there something we can write on? I would like to write these laws down," Lita's tone was skeptical.

I raised my index finger gesturing for them to hold on a moment. I went to the cabinet and pulled out three tablets and three holos. I returned, passed them out to each person, and explained what they were. "If you have any trouble with working either of them, Vega can help."

None of them answered, but I could almost see the wheels in Lita's mind spinning extremely fast. I was surprised smoke wasn't coming out of her ears.

"We have decided on three rules. All y'all must do is listen to the parties involved and decide on the outcome. We need people we can trust to do this and be fair. Of course, if y'all need anything, the council or I will be right here to help."

Again silence, but Lita's face told me she was planning something—what, I wasn't sure. A *whatever, bitch* snort escaped me that wasn't supposed to be aloud. I had to cover it with a cough. Slightly peeved with my private thoughts escaping, I continued.

"Y'all don't have to do this. I can find something else for y'all to do. I just thought the three of you would be the best fit."

We sat there for a couple of minutes letting everyone think about what I was asking. I knew I was asking them to jump in headfirst, and they had barely had time to digest where we were. I didn't want to push them, but we had to get these things decided and move forward. I took a deep breath and interrupted the silence.

"Okay, these are the laws. Like I said, they're simple and to the point.

"One. No stealing. The consequences will fit the crime. Depending on what was stolen, you will determine the punishment—anything from extra duties to confinement, and I'm not sure what a third option could be.

"Two. No physical harm up to and including death. Punishment is confinement for a set time frame. The mediation team and council will decide that time frame. In case a person kills someone, they will be permanently confined to their quarters until an investigation can be completed. Then a trial will be held for final judgement, which would be confinement for a specific time or permanent confinement. Depending on how heinous the crime is, we reserve the right to space the offender.

"Three. Everyone must contribute to our survival. If an awakee refuses to contribute, consequences will include rationing of their food, confinement, or a creative solution that would motivate that individual to pull their weight.

"So that is what we have. Do y'all have any input?"

"I know this might sound harsh," Night added. "But we need everyone to contribute to the functionality of this ship and our survival. If they don't, there will have to be consequences. We can't have a few carrying the weight of the many. " His eyes held a hint of sadness in them as he spoke. It would seem he didn't like having to have such harsh consequences.

Kilian gave them all a stern look, like a commander giving orders to their troops. "All grievances need to be brought to y'all, the mediators. We must help solve conflict so it doesn't evolve into chaos. "

Camila nodded, looking around at each of us. "Those laws and punishments are fair. The use of extra work shifts, like cleaning duties, or some type of community service, can be used as consequences. For repeat issues or severe issues, confinement to living quarters is a good start. I'll see if I can find a few other options and add them."

Gage looked a little confused as he gazed around at us then he said, "This sounds good to me."

I looked over at Lita, who rolled her eyes as she was typing notes. She hadn't said much or added anything helpful to our discussion.

"I would like to leave spacing for the very last option, so I will always be open to any other ideas y'all have. The council, myself, and y'all will sit down and discuss any alternatives available before we chose floating." I looked around at everyone and saw them nodding their heads in agreement.

"We should always be prepared for anything," Night added. "People can do cruel and unthinkable things to each other when scared and panicked. We must have a system in place to handle these issues when they arise. We hope these rules are sufficient for now."

Kilian patted my shoulder- "Well, hopefully they are and we don't have to use the punishments."

I smiled back at him. I let everyone sit in silence for a few minutes to think about our new laws. I kept running through them all trying to think if I was forgetting anything that needed to be in writing.

Night looked between Camila, Gage, and Lita. "Do you guys think you can write this all up and be ready to present it to everyone tonight at dinner?"

Camila's tone was cautious, "Can you just clarify what you want each of us to do?"

Lita scoffed, and I looked at her out of the corner of my eye. She was looking down at her tablet.

"Simple—listen to each person involved in the disagreement. Discus the issue between the three of you and make a fair judgment on an outcome. Y'all will decide if one party or the other was right, wrong, or something in the middle. Y'all will give the parties involved a ruling and the parties will abide by it. If they don't, then further action may be needed.

In that case either y'all will take more action or come to the council for help."

"Okay, that clarifies it better for me." Camila nodded as she typed on her tablet.

Lita didn't say anything or ask questions but merely continued to look down and scroll through something on her tablet.

Ignoring her attitude, we left them to it and went to the black deck to look at drones. Vega had informed us that we were an hour out from being in place. Just before I stepped into the elevator, I asked Vega to call the rest of the council to cargo bay B1.

We walked on to the top deck of cargo bay B1, and all the lights flickered to life. On the lower level sat large cargo crates held to the floor by huge retaining nets. In the center of the room sat a large sleek black and chrome drone. It was shaped like a giant almond with one small engine exhaust port in the rear.

"Like most things on this ship, the drone is a prototype." Vega shimmered into view in front of it. "It is the first of its kind and a bit of a hybrid machine. The inventor combined the knowledge of single occupant space craft and the knowledge of drones to create what you see in front of you. But I must warn you, it has never been tested in space. Only in an antigravity chamber."

I didn't have words for the information Vega had just laid on us, so I continued to study the drone.

"The cockpit has almost a three-hundred-and-sixty-degree aluminum silica glass pane. Well, actually three of them, to withstand the pressure. On top, four black arms extend with shiny silver engines at the end of each arm. These engines pivot, allowing the drone to maneuver in different directions. This model only allows for two passengers." Vega finished just as he returned to the front of the drone.

When I was done admiring that beautiful piece of work, I noticed the guys were standing in the control room. It was located up on the catwalk in a narrow room between cargo bays B1 and B2. It had large windows that looked over each bay. Below the control room was a long wall that had two doors. One was a normal size door, but the second was a large sliding door.

"Vega, what do those two doors lead to?" I pointed to the wall.

"That is the launch room for the drones. All drones are launched from there to make sure the rest of the bays are safe from depressurizing."

"Good to know."

This ship had things I couldn't even imagine a ship would need. It left me in awe every time I found something new.

I walked over to the first stack of crates, but before I could open them, I had to get the cargo net unlatched. I used all my weight to pull on the net, giving the end with the hook enough slack to unlatch it from the ring in the floor. The first attempt almost worked. I took a deep breath and let all my weight pull against the net again. This time I got the hook out of the ring.

Flicking the laches open on case one, I found two mini versions of the large black drone. The only difference was these had propellers on the ends of each arm. I put the lid back on and pulled crate one to the floor. I flicked the latches on crate two and inside were large cylindrical metal devices. I picked one up, turning it in my hands looking to see what it was. On the opposite end I found several lines of short metal prongs. After pondering what they were for a few seconds, it hit me that they were batteries of some kind.

After I placed it back in the crate and dropped the lid down, I moved to the second stack of crates. Walking around it I saw that these cargo nets had ratchet straps. I lifted the latch to one of the ratchet sections and pushed the side button to release the strap. I repeated the action on the second strap and was able to flip the net off the crates. Lifting the lid on the first crate, I saw two more mini versions of the large drone in blue. We had enough for scouting.

I pulled out a blue drone and then got a black one out. I turned each one on. I heard the guys mumble something.

"What's going on up there?" I called to them.

"The screen changed, and it startled us. That's all," Night yelled as he leaned out of the control room door.

I sat the drones down and climbed back up the ladder. I walked into the control room pushing Kilian over so I could see the screen.

"Mom, what's going on?"

I looked up to see the rest of the council walking through the door. They all squeezed in to look at the screen.

"Oh, this is easy." Cash stepped up to the screen and began tapping.

He pulled up a screen that looked like a flight simulator. He tapped it again, and it divided into four identical looking screens. He began tapping an icon—I couldn't see what it was—in the corner of each simulator. Live feeds for drones came up. The two that were on showed close-ups of the bay floor.

"Okay, how do you know how to do this, Cash?" I looked at him with a questioning expression.

"I used to play a lot of video games. There was one that was a flight simulator where I had to fly drones around on missions."

I looked at Cash, pondering what other secrets he was hiding.

He continued working with each drone and after a few minutes longer he had the two of them up in the air flying around the cargo bay. Cash then began manipulating all their accessories. He had one picking up objects — one had a trowel-looking thing trying to scoop air. I was amazed at what people could learn from video games. Next, he began making a flicking motion in each of our directions.

"What did you just do?" Verruca looked down at her wrist.

"Check your tablets and your holos."

We all looked down at our tablets, then I looked at my communicator and saw that the feeds were indeed on each device.

Chapter Nine: The Unknown Nature of Space

"Ms. Atlantis, we will be in place in fifteen minutes," Vega announced.

"Thank you, Vega." I then turned to the group. "Okay, can we be ready in fifteen minutes to send our first two drones to the surface?"

They all looked at me with blank stares. Then Cash blinked and turned to the main control screen.

"Yes, I think I can. The batteries are fully charged. Let me get the other two out and fly them around a little bit. I'll message y'all in a few with an update. "

"Cool, I am going to head back to the bridge. I would like to watch everything from there." I pushed my way through the group heading for the door.

I looked back to see Verruca, Ryo, and Jax carrying the two drones into the flight room. Smiling, I exited the bay and headed for the bridge. Just before the elevator door closed, two hands stopped it. Night and Kilian stepped through the reopening door. Of course, I sighed inwardly — my two shadows were there. I leaned against the back wall. Night picked right and Kilian chose left and they leaned against the back wall on each side of me. No one said anything, but they both pressed against me slightly.

Leaving the elevator, I went to the main screen and pulled up the live feeds for the drones. The guys each went to a different control panel.

Once I had the feeds pulled up and knew that they were working correctly, I went to the map table. I pulled the reports from earlier and began adding the new info. In the middle northern states of Montana or maybe North Dakota, there was a huge thunderstorm system that had rolled in overnight and was still pounding the area with rain. The system had dumped about seven feet of rain across the affected area. There had also been a wind slash sandstorm that wreaked havoc on the Oregon and Washington coast.

Kilian walked up next to me ,placing a hand on my back as I leaned over the table. He began rubbing soothing circles on the small of my back. I closed my eyes for a few seconds and let his touch do its job.

"The weather was violent last night. There is a thunderstorm system like I have never seen before still dumping rain up north. A wind slash sandstorm attacked Oregon and Washington overnight. Then of course the snownadoes that keep rolling through the top half of Texas." I looked over my shoulder at Kilian, but before he could say anything, Vega spoke.

" Ms. Atlantis, you are cleared to launch the first drones."

I tapped a button on my communicator, which opened a channel to the hangar.

"Cash, we're clear to launch the drones. Are you ready?"

"We are ready. The rest of the council is already on their way to the bridge."

Pleased with his progress and abilities I left the map table and returned to the main screen. Night and Kilian joined me, one on each side. Seconds later the door to the bridge opened and the rest of the group entered. On the screen a counter appeared. It began counting down from ten. When it hit five, another camera view came up on the screen. It was of the launch area for the drones. When the counter turned from one to zero the drones shot out of the door and the door snapped closed behind them.

I watched the drones descend to the Earth like four little rockets. Midway through the atmosphere, they began to look like two balls of flames, then they broke through into white fluffiness.

I heard a loud exhale behind me. I turned to look at the council and saw relief written across each face. While I was looking at everyone else, Night and Kilian each slipped a hand into mine, squeezing. Everyone had been afraid this wouldn't work. I turned back to watch the drones drop farther through the clouds.

After what seemed like forever but was really only about ten minutes, the drones began to reach the tops of trees. We could see land, and drone two was giving us a shot of what looked like a beach with water. Out of the corner of my eye I saw Verruca lift her wrist closer to her face.

"Cash, could you use the drones to collect samples? We need samples of the soil, vegetation, and the water." Verruca dropped her wrist and returned to watching the feed.

"Of course." His voice sounded as clear as if he was in the room. "I can use the drones' attachments to collect all the samples."

I could tell he was pleased with himself for knowing how to work these drones. I was just grateful he did, because learning how would have slowed us down more.

Verruca inserted herself between me and Kilian. He reluctantly released my hand, and she took it. We stood in total silence, watching the drones collecting samples. She leaned her head on my shoulder and I leaned mine on top of hers.

"Mom, how are you holding up?"

"I'm here. You know me. I try to take it one step at a time. Tackle each issue as it arises." I lowered my voice. "So, you and Ryo? I saw y'all looking at each other."

"We've been talking. Other than that, I don't know yet. It's not like you haven't been playing."

"Me?" My tone was innocent. "I have no idea what you're talking about."

She lifted her head and looked at me. Then she leaned over and looked at my left hand where Night still had it gripped in his. Then she looked me in the face again with one eyebrow raised questioningly.

"I have no idea what you're talking about," I shrugged and turned back to the screen.

"Um, okay, sure no idea. That's why I had to squeeze myself between you and Kilian who was holding your right hand in a death grip and didn't even want to turn it over to me, your daughter."

We both chuckled, and I wrapped my arm around her. I let go of Night's hand and led Verruca to the captain's chair. We watched the drones some more while everyone else did different things. Night, Ryo, and Jax were at one panel looking over something. Kilian, Ronan, and Savinka were standing over another panel studying something different. Then Juniper and Zahirah were sitting in the back watching something on their tablets.

I turned my attention back to the feeds on the screen. The feed showed mostly flat land, but occasionally there were things that looked like large rocks. Some looked like strange-shaped hills. Neither of us could tell what they were.

"Cash, can you back out the cameras? We need a wider view of what they are flying around."

"Give me a second. Let me figure it out."

After a couple seconds of the camera turning and zooming in and out quickly, he found the right position for us to get a better view. Now we could see it was a large pile of concrete. The pile was about a foot from an exceptionally large misshapen hill.

He brought the drone up and flew around the hill. It was

covered in grass with a couple small trees on it.

"Wait, go back. It looks like there was a hole not too far from that second tree."

Cash backed up the drone.

"Freeze, right there. See that dark spot? See if you can maneuver the drone into it."

"I will, hold on. Let me get the other drone through scooping up some dirt."

I studied the hole and its surroundings. The edges of the opening appeared natural, but as I examined it I could see smooth edges of something grey. I followed the edge I could make out and they formed a large rectangle. I still wasn't sure what we were looking at or if my mind was just trying to make it make sense. I moved my attention back to the opening, but beyond it was nothing but darkness. I leaned over to Verruca who was also studying the image.

"What does this look like to you?"

"I'm not sure, but it does look familiar. I just can't put my finger on it." Verruca continued looking at the screen, puzzled.

The drone began to move into the darkness. Cash used the attachments that looked like pincers on a crab and pulled the grass away from the hole. He then slowly moved the drone past the opening. All we could see was black. Before I could ask, he'd found a light on the drone.

He moved in further. There was a large blob in the corner. He maneuvered closer, and the blob turned into a dented-up fridge.

"Is that a refrigerator?" Juniper stepped closer to the screen.

"Yeah, I think it is," Verruca stood up to examine the video better.

Cash moved the drone around the space, and we could see a TV missing its screen, half hanging on the wall. There was damaged furniture scattered all around the room, the pieces ravaged by time and the elements. As the drone maneuvered around the space, there was something still wrong with what we were seeing. Trying to put my finger on it I stared hard at the screen. It clicked when the drone passed the damaged TV again, everything was on an angle, leaning toward the right.

"The building must have fallen over to the right." I turned my head lightly.

Several people turned their head to the right as the drone approached another wall.

"It must have, for everything to be on that angle," Verruca said as she straightened back up.

"Damn," Juniper exhaled softly.

We refocused on the drone. It was heading toward a wall with different sized squares on it. As the drone drew closer, we could see the squares held family photos. The drone focused on each photo. The pictures were damaged from the edges toward the center barely leaving the faces of each special moment frozen in time. Suddenly I felt someone's hand on my face. I looked toward it, finding Verruca wiping a tear from my cheek. I smiled sadly at her and looked back at the screen.

"This was someone's home. It's crazy that all these things have survived, yet they haven't. They had been living their lives, then in a blink it was all gone." I took Verruca's hand.

A red light started flashing on the corner of the screen. Cash began backing the drone out of the opening.

"What is that?"

"It's the battery light. It's telling me that it is time to bring them back. I am setting the return launch now."

We watched as the drones gathered, pulling in all their attachments and blades, then shot into the air. At that exact moment alarms sounded throughout the ship. They were loud trumpeting sounds that held the note for three counts, dying out on the fourth. The sound repeated over and over just like a hazmat horn. I jumped to my feet, calling to Vega.

"What is going on, Vega?"

He flickered into view right in front of me and began speaking quickly. "We have a coronal cloud coming our way fast, Ms. Atlantis. You need to get everyone to a secured location."

"What do you mean? I don't know what kind of protection we have. You are supposed to know those things," My tone was harsh as I looked at him expectantly. All eyes were on me for how to handle this, so I just started blurting out instructions.

"Verruca, Savinka and Zahirah, go gather the rest of the people and take them to a communal area to wait for more instructions. Jax, Night, Ryo, go to the engineering room and start monitoring the engines and ship-wide systems. Juniper and Ronan, go help Cash get those drones back on this ship and secured. Kilian, you stay with me to figure out where to put everyone."

Everyone scattered like ants to follow my instructions. I paced the floor for a minute and then yelled at Vega.

"Pull up the blueprints for the ship now." The blueprint popped up. I paused with one hand on my forehead and one on my hip. I was trying to calm myself so that I could think rationally. "Vega, what is a coronal cloud?"

"It is a cloud of high radiation-charged particles that the sun ejects after a large powerful solar flare. A cloud can contain a billion tons of these radiated particles. Some clouds move fast, some move slowly. Unfortunately, this one is moving fast. It will hit us in forty-five minutes."

"Son of a motherless goat," I shouted, and Kilian tried to touch me. I backed away. I didn't have time to be coddled by him.

I turned to the blueprints. Scanning the layout I scrutinized all the mechanical and electrical rooms. None of them were big enough to hold everyone, and I didn't want us split up. "Vega, why isn't the ship made to withstand these clouds?"

"It is to a point, but this is a strong one and the amount of radiation coming our way could breach our protections. So the alarm sounded for you all to find cover."

"Okay, so where on this ship has the most protection?"

Vega was silent and had a faraway look on his transparent face.

I knew that meant he was processing something, so I shook my head and returned to the layout. Kilian was studying it with me and then turned to one of the control panels. Not seeing any other options I turned to Kilian and he turned to me with an excited look.

"The engine room has the best protection on the ship. It has lead re-enforced walls to help keep the radiation from escaping that area in case of any kind of leak from the nuclear core."

"Okay, we have maybe twenty minutes to get everyone into the engine room and secure the doors." I lifted my wrist and clicked the speaker icon on my black holo. "Listen up, everyone. We have a coronal cloud heading our way and fast. Please get yourselves to the engine room. This room has extra fortifications due to the engine core and is the safest place for us."

Changing channels I called out to Cash.

"Are the drones back?"

"Almost."

"Okay, get them in and secured as fast as you can. Then y'all hall ass to the engine room."

"We will."

"Kilian, get to the engine room."

"Not without you. In fact, you go now, and I'll stay and do whatever you were going to do."

"NO! Do what I told you to do this one time, damn it. I'll

be there in just a few minutes once I know the drones are back and the cargo bay doors are secured."

"Then I'll stay with you."

"Look." I spun on him quickly. "I know you feel like you must protect me or something, but I am a big girl. I know how to take care of myself. Now go to the damn engine room. I'll be there shortly." I pointed toward the elevator.

Pissed and cursing, Kilian got on the elevator. I gave Vega orders and he disappeared with a pop. Once I was receiving all the reports of the coronal cloud on my holo, I headed for the cargo bays. When I got to B1, Ronan and Juniper were crating the drones. Cash was on the deck above banging on the control panels.

"What is going on, Cash?"

"The hangar door is not sealing completely. I don't know if it is closed enough to keep the radiation out."

"Okay, let me look at it."

I ran over to the side door of the launch area and slipped into the launch bay.

Cash began yelling. "Iksen, you can't go in there. If that door re-opens it will suck you into space. At the very least you could suffocate from lack of oxygen."

"Then don't let the door open while I'm in there!"

Running up to the door I began searching for an issue, but I didn't see anything blocking it. Yet I could tell it wasn't closed completely which meant it wasn't sealed correctly. I went back to the cargo bay.

"Ronan, Juniper, y'all get out of here. We need to open the door again. Then we will be right behind y'all."

I went back up to the control room. I watched as Ronan clipped the last cargo net in place. Then they both joined us in the control booth. I stared at them for a second but before I could say anything Ronan put his hand up.

"We will all go together. Let's just get this door shut

correctly."

Cash reopened the door and then closed it. Still, it didn't shut right.

"Do it again."

Cash opened it again and closed it. I got a ten-minute warning on my holo.

"All of you go now to the engine room."

"No, we're not leaving you," Ronan protested.

"I didn't ask what you wanted. I am telling you to go. NOW!"

They all looked at me, horrified. I pointed toward the door. Cash and Juniper left. Ronan tried to argue with me again.

"I am not leaving without you. Even if that means I must pick you up and carry you."

"Just go, Ronan. I am going to try and get this door closed and then I'll be there."

Just as I finished my sentence, Night came in.

"What the hell are you doing?"

"I am trying to get this door to close. Why are you not in the engine room helping watch everyone?"

"Because I looked around and you were not there. So I came to look for you, and Vega told me where you were. We have like seven minutes before that cloud hits us."

"I know," I angrily slammed my hand on the button as I opened and closed the door again.

"Ronan, will you help me?" Night looked at him with a slight nod of his head.

Without another word Night walked up to me, picked me up, and threw me over his shoulder caveman style.

"What the hell are you doing? That door is not sealed correctly."

I saw Ronan open it and close it one more time. It closed better than before but the light still did not turn green. Night was already in the hallway, and I saw Ronan come out and seal the hallway door behind him. They began to run to the opposite side of the black deck to the engine room.

"*Chingoa!* Put me down. I can run on my own."

Night set me down, then he and Ronan grabbed my hands. We ran to the engine room, making it through the door with only seconds to spare. As the door was closing the countdown on my holo hit zero.

"I can't believe you, Mom!" Verruca grabbed my arms and shook me. Night, Kilian, and Ronan stood behind her, all of them with their arms crossed and giving me a death stare as she scolded me.

"I would have been here in time. I was trying to get that damn door closed correctly. I don't know if it's closed good enough to keep the radiation out."

"That doesn't mean you sacrifice yourself to get it done," Verruca yelled at me again.

"Okay, enough. I'm here and I'm fine." I hugged her. She squeezed me tight, while Night and Kilian just stared at me, still pissed off. I just rolled my eyes at them.

We took a seat on the floor. It was easily ten or fifteen minutes before Verruca stopped holding onto me in some way and the guys stopped glaring at me. We all sat on the floor waiting for the cloud to pass. I felt helpless sitting there not doing anything. I was not really the sit-and-wait type. I turned my attention to my black holo and began reading through the info Vega was sending.

It showed that the radiation from the first section of the cloud was extremely high. It was all the way to the ten Gy level on the gauge. I continued to watch the gauge, and after a few minutes slowly went down to eight. Verruca put her hand over my holo, pressing my hand down to my lap. She then laid her head on my shoulder and closed her eyes. I leaned my head on hers and closed my eyes as well.

My holo vibrated jerking me awake. I looked down, and the new readings were showing. Now that most of the cloud had passed us, we were in the three Gy range. At least three sounded better than ten, because I wasn't sure at all what was an acceptable amount of radiation. I switched over to the ship's level, and the inside was around the same as the outside currently. According to the report it had never reached above a level three inside. Thank goodness, because who knew if that would have damaged the embryos, or seeds, or us.

I removed my arm from around Verruca and began typing a message to Vega.

After the cloud passes, if the radiation is still high in the ship, can we purge it by venting the spaceship?

It is not high enough for that. I will turn on the scrubber and purge the water between the inner and outer hulls, then refill the space.

I have no idea what you are talking about, but okay. Let me know when it's safe to leave this room.

I will, Ms. Atlantis.

I returned to waiting with everyone else and hoped it wouldn't be much longer. Leaning my head back, I closed my eyes for a minute to think.

"Mom, wake up." Verruca shook my shoulder. "Vega announced that it's safe to come out."

"Okay, Verruca, stop shaking me now."

I stretched and began to get up when Night and Kilian both grabbed a hand, pulling me up.

"Everyone, listen up. If you want to take time off this afternoon, that is okay. I know this was scary and you may need to decompress from it. If you have any questions or concerns, please let me know, or any other member of the council. Also, I need the council to hang out for a minute. We need to discuss some things. Vox, Ryker, and Rogue, can you three still get dinner made? I mean, take some time and relax but we will still need dinner for everyone."

"It's not a problem," Vox winked. "I am used to taking crazy weather in stride. I'm from New Orleans, after all."

We both chuckled, and I thanked them and turned to the council.

"First off, is everyone okay?"

I looked around at all of them, and they were nodding. I still waited for a few minutes to see if anyone wanted to talk.

"Does anyone have any concerns about what happened?" I paused, "Anything anyone wants to go over?"

Jax raised his hand. "I am going to stay in the engine room and run diagnostics. If Night and Ryo will join me, that would be great."

"Yeah, I'll help," Night answered.

"Me too," Ryo echoed.

"If Ronan will help me, I want to go back and try to get that hangar door closed correctly and see what needs to be done to make it continue to work correctly." Cash looked over at Ronan. Ronan nodded in agreement.

"Okay, I am going to go to the bridge and look over the reports and make sure we're all safe. Verruca, Juniper, and Zahirah, can y'all just walk the halls to make sure that everyone is okay? Just be available if people start to freak out. Savinka, can you be available if people feel sick? I'm not sure what we have as far as meds, but use whatever you can."

"I'll see what I can find in the labs. Maybe there's something I can make a medicine out of if I have to," Savinka answered.

"Absolutely, that's a great idea."

"Okay, I'll see everyone at dinner. Call me if you need me."

CHAPTER TEN: THE GRAVITY OF OUR SITUATION

I reached the bridge, but before I could start, I plopped down on the couch and breathed deeply and slowly. I closed my eyes and continued to breathe. My mind was whirling so fast I couldn't land on one single thought. I was getting a headache from it. I don't know how long I sat there, but finally I shook my head and got up.

"Vega, show me the reports. Was there any damage? I want to see it all." The main screen lit up and reports started appearing on the screen. I tapped on one, but the light of the screen just hurt my eyes.

"Vega, can you just read the reports to me? My head is hurting, and I can't stand here looking at this screen." I took a seat in the captain's chair.

"The first report just tells you about the cloud and how much radiation it hit us with at each stage as it passed. Which you know because you were monitoring it as it happened. The next report is a ship damage report. There is no real damage to the outside of the ship. I ran diagnostics on the systems and did not find anything. The bay door is the only issue we must correct."

"Perfect. Two things. One, can you put the drone feeds on the main screen here? Two, can you help them with getting that door working correctly?"

"Yes, to both."

"Thank you."

The video feeds popped onto the screen. I reluctantly stood back up and went to the screen. I tapped on the first feed and let it play through some. It was mostly just video of the land and the samples the drone took. Feeds from two and three where the same as one's. It had to be drone four's that I was looking for. I tapped it and let it play, pausing a few times to study the land formations. When I got to the apartment, footage I stopped it just before the drone got to the pictures.

For us, it felt like everything happened yesterday or last week. I couldn't imagine the pain, craziness, and the absolute absurdity of living through it. Tears rolled down my face. I closed my eyes taking time to mourn the loss of the world, of people, of what we knew to be life. After a minute, I broke out into full sobs. I didn't know if it was all because of the loss on Earth or partly from what had just happened, but I gave myself a few minutes to cry.

I was wiping my face and trying to blink back the rest of the tears when I felt a hand on my shoulder and jumped. I looked over my shoulder to see Kilian standing there. He pulled me into his arms and just stood there silently holding me. We let our closeness console each other where words would have failed.

"You okay? " Kilian broke our hold to look at me.

"Yeah, maybe, I don't know. I don't know if it was what we just had to deal with or if it was because the reality of what happened on Earth just hit me or a combination of both. But I'll be fine now. Just needed a minute to freak out or panic or whatever you want to call it." I waved my hand dismissively and stepped back.

"You have the right to have some feelings about what is going on. Hell, we all do."

"I don't have time to freak out at every little thing. I must keep everyone moving forward or we will have mass chaos on our hands, and no one will get back to Earth."

"You don't have to do it all by yourself. I'm here, the council is here. We all want the same thing. It's not all on you."

"Whatever, you don't get it. I'm fine. My moment of weakness is over, and I don't need you to rescue me or take care of me. I'm a big girl. I can do it on my own. Been doing it since I was about seven."

"You are so damn frustrating," Kilian yelled and stormed off the bridge. He turned in the door of the elevator and stared at me for a minute before speaking. "I don't think any of us have taken the time to truly process what has happened down there or to the people that were left behind. Have you ever thought that we're all having issues with this?"

We just stood there staring at each other as the elevator doors closed.

"Ms. Atlantis, Vox wanted me to let you know that dinner is ready."

"Okay, Vega, thank you."

Not wanting to deal with what Kilian had said, I stood staring at the main screen. Remembering I needed to mark where we took samples today, I turned to the table and tapped on the toolbox icon. The menu dropped down allowing me to search for something resembling a flag. I found country flags at the very bottom. Those would work. I tapped the US flag. It showed up on the screen. I dragged it to the coast of Texas. After I marked where we had taken samples today, I gathered myself to go to the dining room. I was about to walk out from behind the map table when the elevator door opened. Kilian came marching toward me. He grabbed me by the arms, pulling me into him and planted a kiss on me.

He walked me backward into the screen, then pinned me against it with his body and deepened the kiss. I lifted a hand to the nape of his neck. I ran my fingers up into his hair and then grabbed onto it taking control of the kiss. I flipped our positions and now had him pinned against the screen with my body. I tip toed to kiss him along his jaw slowly moving down to his neck. His pulse kicked up a notch, and I smiled. I kissed along his pulse until I reached the crook of his neck. Then I bit him.

I pushed away, walking off the bridge. Kilian caught up by the time the elevator door opened. We both stepped into the lift. I was still smirking from teasing him as I leaned against the back wall giving him a smoldering stare. He grinned wickedly, and as soon as the door closed, he picked me up, wrapping my legs around his waist and shoving me against the wall. He kept one arm tightly around my waist and used his free hand to slide up under my shirt. He cupped my left boob, giving it a squeeze while he kissed me hard.

Not liking that he had all the control, I again grabbed a handful of hair, pulling his head back and to the side exposing the other side of his neck to me. I then licked from his collar bone to his ear, maneuvering his head to accommodate my licking. A shudder rippled across his body, and I chuckled. I kissed his neck, nibbled on his ear lobe, and when I felt the elevator begin to slow, I bit the soft skin along his pulse point. This caused him to lose his grip on me, which allowed me to place my feet on the floor. I shoved him back and straightened my clothes just before the door opened.

He was rubbing his neck when I stepped out into the hall-way. I shot him a shit-eating grin and walked to the dining room. When I walked in, people were scattered around the tables. Little groups had begun to form. It was nice to see everyone finding their people. This would make things easier for them to survive. I spotted Verruca at a table close to the kitchen.

"Hey, baby girl."

"Hey, Mom."

I hugged her before sitting down. I hadn't gotten food yet. I just wanted to sit for a minute and talk to Verruca. Do something a little normal. We used to talk every day, and it was usually at dinnertime.

"Hey, I was going over the videos from the drones. I realized that we only have one person who really understands how to run tests on our samples from today. I decided we should wake a few more people. I already looked at the list and found a couple. I want to wake them first thing in the morning."

"Okay, I'll get with Vega in the morning."

"Great, now I need food."

"Wait, you said one person, but we have two."

"We do?"

"Yeah, Savinka and Lotus."

"Oh shit, I forgot about Lotus. Well, I think we still need the help."

"Okay."

I turned, heading to the kitchen, but before I could take a full step, Night stood before me with a plate of food. I thanked him and sat back down. I dug in like I hadn't eaten in forever. The food was so good, but I barely made it through a third of what was on my plate. *He must think I eat like two grown men.* I went to the kitchen to get something to cover my plate. Once that was done, Verruca and I went back to our cabins together.

Stepping off the elevator, Verruca slipped her arm into mine and laid her head on my shoulder. We talked about everything that needed to be done tomorrow as we walked. When we reached our doors, we hugged and went into our cabins. It was such a strange thing for her to be in her own place — we had always lived together. Frowning slightly at the thought, I placed my plate in the fridge and went right to the shower. After my hot shower I just climbed into my bed. No clothes, no anything. I just needed to sleep.

The next morning, I woke to the sound of a blaring alarm and Vega's voice. I sat up quickly from my bed looking around trying to remember what was happening.

"Ms. Atlantis, can you hear me?"

"Yes! Vega, I can hear you. What do you want? And why do you keep waking me like this?"

"Ms. Verruca asked if I could let you know that the new people were awake. They are in the dining room."

"Okay, a text would have been a lot better. I didn't need you here yelling my name and the alarm going off."

"You would not answer me. I needed something to help wake you."

"Well, next time leave the damn alarm out of it."

I got up and put my clothes on. I had never liked the sound of an alarm clock. I headed to the bathroom, still glaring at Vega, to finish up my morning routine. Once I was put together, I headed for the dining room. I was waiting for the lift when Kilian stepped up behind me. We both stepped into the elevator and then he spoke.

"I came by last night, but you didn't answer."

"Yeah, I fell asleep really early."

"Maybe I can come by tonight."

"We will see. It really depends on what happens today." I smiled and stepped off the lift.

I walked through the door of the dining room and scanned for Verruca. She had the two new females sitting with her. I walked over to introduce myself.

Morning , I'm Atlantis. I am the leader, or Iksen, of the group. Do you have any questions about what you saw?"

"Are my husband and son on this ship?"

"Yes, I checked already, and if you would like we can wake them tomorrow, or if you choose, we can wait."

"Yes, tomorrow."

"I'll set that up. Can y'all tell me about yourselves?"

"Well, I'm Vashanti Tate. Most people call me Shanti. I am twenty-eight years old, and I worked as a nurse and a lab tech in Austin, Texas. I have a husband and a son. My husband was an x-ray tech. We saw that things were getting a little crazy and decided to volunteer for this project."

Vashanti had naturally curly hair, amber eyes, and a deep, warm, cinnamon complexion. The other girl, who seemed to be a little freaked out by everything, had purple over her naturally dark hair. She had a lot of tattoos, a pierced nose, and blue eyes.

"I'm Sphynx, and I'm twenty-six. I worked as a research Biologist by day and a tattoo artist by night. I am from Dallas via the English Midlands. I had a mum and sister, but my sister refused to join the project with me because our mum had been ill. I knew when I woke up that my mum might be gone, but now they're both gone," she finished in her Midlands-mixed-American accent, but she barely got the last part out before tears streamed down her face.

Vashanti reached over and placed a hand on her shoulder.

"Well, guys, I know this isn't what any of us expected when we woke up. I still don't know how I feel. What I do know is that we're here, I am doing my best to get us back to Earth, and that we have more than we can ask for in this situation.

"After you eat, we will have Juniper show y'all around and let you choose a cabin. Y'all will find clothes and hygiene products in each cabin. Anything you can't use, please get with Verruca about. She will collect it to take to our supply room. Vashanti, you can pick from the family units. Then tomorrow we will show y'all where the labs are located. We need y'all's expertise in running tests on samples we collected yesterday from Earth."

They both looked at me and nodded in agreement. I shook both of their hands before I went to find my mediator team.

On my way I checked my holo, it was almost mid-day and there was still so much to get done. I spotted Gage and Camila sitting at a table together but didn't see Lita. I looked around for her and found her sitting with Ryker talking. I went to the table where Gage and Camila were sitting. I took a seat and then called Lita on her black holo. When she saw my face, she rolled her eyes and declined the call. I stood up and turned in her direction.

"I was calling because I wanted you to join us. Please come over here," I yelled over everyone.

She looked at Ryker with fury in her eyes. He touched her hand and motioned in my direction with his head. She stood up and came over to the table. Once she made it to the table, the people who were watching went back to their food.

"Now that we are all together I wanted to see if y'all were ready to present the rules to everyone?"

"Yes, I wanted to add a few things, but Camila wouldn't let me. She stuck to the extremely simple laws you had approved," Lita said in an irritated drawl.

"Good, I would like for you guys to present them to the group tonight."

"We can read them to the group now if you like," Camila offered.

"Yes, go for it. I'm going to go get a plate of food while y'all read them."

"Iksen, I changed the name to the *Three Edicts*. I hope that's okay."

"I like that. It's perfect."

I got up from the table heading for the kitchen. Right before I walked through the door, I heard Camila call for everyone's attention. When I got into the kitchen, Rogue and Vox where still moving about.

"Hey, can I get y'all to go out and listen to Camila explain the new laws to the group?"

"No problem," Rogue and Vox said almost in unison. Then they headed out to the dining room.

I busied myself making a plate of food. Once I had everything I needed, I turned and saw Ryker leaning against the door facing me. *Chingoa!* I hadn't noticed him standing in the doorway, but I'd be damned if I let him see that he'd surprised me.

"Can you also go and listen to the laws? I want everyone to know them."

Ryker didn't say anything, just stood there eyeing me. Then he made a sucking noise with his teeth like he was disgusted by me and walked out the door.

Okay, whatever. Hope he didn't think he was the first to look at me like that.

I took my plate and went back out, taking a seat next to Verruca. Camila was finishing up reading out the laws to the group. A couple of people had questions. Ryker had scoffed at every law read by Camila. Another thing I noticed was that he watched Lita with a hungry stare.

Camila finished answering everyone's questions. Gage then introduced himself and explained what the mediators' role was on the ship.

I had just stood up ready to address the group when Lita stepped forward and began speaking.

Who does this little girl think she is, cutting me off like that? I stood there quietly and eyed her up and down as I kept a slight smile on my face.

"Hi, everybody. I would like you to know that I am here for you all. If you need assistance or to talk, I am here to help you," she said in her overdone Texas drawl.

I stepped out into the aisle to address the group as I made my way to where the mediators were standing.

"Afternoon, everyone. I just wanted to follow up on what the mediator team just went over. I want y'all to know the three edicts go into effect immediately. If you have any other questions about them, you can reach out to any of us. If you feel like something should be added to the edicts, please let the mediator team know. Other than that, have a wonderful day, y'all."

I went back to the table and picked up my plate. Verruca stood up with hers and we walked to the kitchen.

"That chick is unbelievable. I mean, what does she think she is going to gain by acting like that with you in public?" Verruca practically growled out under her breath.

"Who knows, I'm not worried. She's just a little girl acting out because she isn't getting her way." I waved my had dismissively. "I'm heading to the bridge. You want to join me?"

"No, I have some other things to check on." We hugged and then I went to the bridge wanting to check on the weather. The reports had not been up when I'd first entered the bridge. I took a seat with the intention to check messages I received earlier. Instead I got lost just staring at the Earth. I wasn't really thinking about anything, just staring. It was quiet in the room and the view was mesmerizing. I sat like that until my attention was caught by pages appearing on the screen. I blinked a few times to refocus myself and stood up with a sigh.

No new storms on the horizon, just the ones from last night playing themselves out. Another report showed the results of the final checks run on the ship from yesterday. The ship was holding up well after yesterday's coronal cloud ambush. The guys had got the hangar door working properly. There was a damaged seal in the door-facing, which was the reason it hadn't closed.

I decided to wait another day before we tried to send the drones back to Earth. I wanted everyone to have enough time to recover from yesterday. Well, maybe *I* needed another day to recover.

"Vega, we're going to take another day before we explore

our next site. Until then, I want you to turn your focus to making sure that there is nothing else coming our way."

"I can do that, Ms. Atlantis."

"Also send a ship-wide text to let everyone know that we are taking tomorrow off from exploring."

"Done. Is there anything else?"

"No, that will be all. Wait, let Verruca know that I'll be in my cabin. Give her access to my cabin. That's it, I think. Thank you for all your help."

"You're welcome."

I went back to the dining room and gathered stuff to make lunch and dinner for tonight. Once in my cabin, I didn't plan on leaving if I could help it. I planned on watching movies and doing nothing.

Chapter Eleven: Getting Back on Track

I sat up quickly, startled by a loud banging. I gazed all around trying to figure out what to do first. Blinking several times to clear my eyes I looked at the nightstand to see what hour it was. A glowing *2.15 am* floated in the air over a small black box.

Flinging the blanket off myself, I stumbled to my feet and walked to the door of my cabin.

"Who the hell is it?"

"Kilian."

"Oh."

I opened the door, scowling at him for waking me up at this hour.

"What do you want? It is way too early to function right now." I waved a hand dismissively at him and turned to walk back to my room.

He grabbed my forearm and spun me back into him.

"I told you I wanted to come by tonight. But you disappeared. That's why I am here knocking on your door."

I made a disgruntled humph and waved him in. He hadn't taken but two steps in the door before he pressed our bodies together. My hands rested against his chest. He splayed a hand in the middle of my back as he tightened his hold on me.

"What do you want, Kilian? It is late. I'm tired and I don't want to talk about anything to do with the ship right now." I stared into his eyes.

159

"I didn't come here to talk." His tone was gravelly and lust-filled.

His free hand slid up my back to the nape of my neck and grabbed a fistful of my hair. He pulled my head backward and a soft groan escaped me. I approved of his dominant move but resented it at the same time, because he was always trying to take control of me. He kissed and nipped my neck maneuvering from right to left, controlling my head with the handful of my hair. Payback for me doing him the same way, I assumed. He pulled my mouth to his. This action forced me to tiptoe to reach. He wouldn't even bend his head to meet me.

Okay, this was the second dominant move he'd pulled, and that didn't work for me. I retreated from the kiss and bit down on his lower lip hard enough to draw blood. He growled and jerked back. I grabbed a fist full of hair and pulled his mouth down to mine. I kissed him hard and demandingly.

A growl combined with a moan escaped Kilian, and he shoved me against the wall. Before he could press into me, I flipped our positions. I slammed my mouth onto his, forcing my tongue inside. Seconds after the kiss, he slid his hands down my hips to the globes of my ass and lifted me up, which for most men was not easy. I'm not exactly petite. Unsure whether he had the strength to hold me up for long, I wrapped my legs around his waist. To show me he approved, he pressed his thick hard cock against me. My inner walls clinched with the anticipation.

He shoved off the wall and carried me to my room. He dropped me onto the bed unceremoniously. I landed with a *humph!* Before I could chastise him he began pulling my pants off me. Once they were off, I stood up quickly in front of him. Grabbing his shoulders I pushed him to his knees. I lifted a leg and rested it on the edge of the bed. Then I moved his face into place. He didn't waste any time sliding his tongue through my folds and finding my clit. I moaned from the sparks that shot out to every nerve ending in my body. He was talented with that tongue.

He licked and nipped my clit, sending pure pleasure to ignite the build of my orgasm. My head fell back when he slid his tongue into my core adding new sensations to the pool of liquid fire that ignited deep in my center. As good as it felt, oral sex never completely got me to my orgasm, so I pulled his mouth free. I then stepped over him onto the bed. He rose up from the floor, and I pointed to his pants. He stripped them from his body without protest. I then pointed to the bed, indicating for him to lie down. He didn't. Instead, he tried to grab my feet and pull me down.

Glowering at him I moved up the bed. I was not about to make this easy for him. He needed to work for it. Once I was out of his reach, I snapped my fingers and pointed to the bed again. He stood up, crossed his arms and just stared at me. I shrugged my shoulders, pulled my shirt over my head, removed my bra, and began to step off the bed. I could go to the shower and take care of myself. He made a grab for me, but I moved to the other side out of his reach.

"Lie down, damn it," Kilian growled at me.

"You lie down and I will give you what you want. Otherwise, you can leave, and I'll go to the shower."

He stared at me for a few seconds and then did what I asked. He lay down on the bed. I slowly stepped forward until I was standing over him, one foot on each side of his hips. We just stared at each other for a few long seconds. Then I lowered myself down to where I was straddling him. Before I could get positioned correctly to take him in, he grabbed my hands and flipped me over onto my back. He smoothly pulled both my hands over my head and held them with one of his.

He lowered himself enough that the tip of his cock was barely touching me. He then used his free hand to reach down and pull my right leg up, allowing him to slide into me — which he did slowly while he held my gaze the entire time, letting me see his eyes that were completely filled with need. It was a turn-on, knowing he wanted me that much. He continued to move in and out of me slowly, making sure I felt every inch of his dick filling me.

He let go of my hands and sat back on his knees. He lifted my other leg and wrapped them both around his hips. This gave me the perfect opportunity to switch our positions so I could be in control again. It was a bit of a struggle, but I got him over and me on top. Before he could fight me, I slid down on his dick. I began moving my hips back and forth and he forgot about trying to fight me. While I was basking in his lust, he moved his hands to my hips. He gripped them tight like he was about to change our positions again. I raised my body up. He growled in frustration.

"Tsk, tsk." I wagged my index finger from side to side. "Bad boys don't get rewarded."

A low disapproving grunt came out of Kilian and with all his strength he flipped us. Now he was on top of me staring at me with a smirk on his lips. With a quick head dip he latched onto my left nipple with his teeth. I sucked in a sharp breath of pleasure. I grabbed the back of his head as he began to roll my nipple between his teeth. He flicked it with his tongue several times and then sucked the whole thing into his mouth. My body arched toward him. I wanted more of the pleasure he was currently spreading throughout my body.

He managed to free his head from my grip, moved to my right breast and repeated all the same torturous pleasures. I writhed under him wanting more.

"I love your breasts. I have imagined sucking on these nipples since I first saw you," Kilian said through his teeth as he still gripped my nipple between them.

A deep moan was all the answer I could give him now

because my brain could not form words. Then he elicited several panting moans as he swirled his tongue around my nipple roughly. I ran my hands over his shoulders and down the top half of his back. On my return I dug my nails in deep. His muscles tensed and he grunted. He retaliated by swiftly lifting my left leg and slamming home. I dug my nails in deeper and grunted out a long moan of pleasure. He bit my nipple a little harder, growling, and tightening his grip on my body. Kilian then started moving his hips in a circular motion. He released my nipple and raised his head. He was moaning low and deep in his throat as he continued the circular motion.

This motion might have just become my new favorite move. Every nerve ending was sparking in all directions, and I didn't want him to stop.

"Don't stop," I commanded in a husky voice.

"I'm the one in control here, I don't take orders," he said in a deep, low tone that made his chest rattle. The vibrations sent tiny shocks of pleasure through my nipples.

I moaned softly from the pleasure and dragged my nails down his forearms leaving red trails in their wake. He looked at me for a second before he changed his movements. Instead of circular now it was hard and deep like I hoped for. It felt amazing as his thick head pressed through the last ring of nerves before his crown was nestled against my cervix, but I still needed better friction. I tried to move to encourage him to give me what I wanted, but the pig-headed ass ignored me and continued his pace. With each deep thrust he sent electricity shooting through my nerves and my body was beginning to quiver with the intensifying build of my orgasm.

I remembered a move I used to use to get out of holds in judo, and with a growl of frustration I rolled us so that I was on top. Now that I had control again, I slammed myself down onto his cock. His long, thick shaft filled me completely. Yet that hunger was still riding me, so I picked up my speed. The faster I rode the less he tried to reverse our position. Soon his hands dropped to my hips and his eyes rolled back in pleasure.

"Damn woman, you know how to work that cock better than anyone before you," he rasped out between gravelly groans.

"That's why you need to stop fighting me for control and just let me lead."

He was helping guide my hips as I moved atop him. Then Kilian slid his left hand from my hip to my clit. He made light circles around it and immediately my orgasm began to build faster deep inside of me. I allowed the sensations spreading through my body to fill my mind. All I wanted to do was chase that pleasure building in me until my orgasm engulfed me. The faster I went the faster the circles on my clit got. We were now in a battle. My inner walls quivered as our battle of wills continued. His cock throbbed which made a spike of pleasure shoot through me and I bore down on him wanting that pleasure to expand throughout my body. With his free hand he reached up and pinched and twisted my right nipple. The surge of pleasure must have been what I needed because my orgasm exploded in me. My movement stilled and my mind plummeted into a nirvana of pure pleasure as wave after wave overtook my body. My whole body clenched and reverberated in pleasure. My reaction must have been what Kilian was waiting for because he stiffened beneath me and grunted out a long raspy moan as his climax hit him full force.

We stayed in place, letting our orgasms wash over us until we had ridden out every wave of pleasure. I collapsed onto the bed next to him.

"You know where the door is." I barely whispered. I meant to wave a hand in the direction of the door, but my body could not move after all that.

I barely turned to my side facing away from him. My limbs

were heavy with exhaustion and contentment. He ignored me and pulled me into his arms. I rolled my eyes, but I was too tired to fight about it.

The next morning, I woke up to a large hand on my ass. For a second I was alarmed, but then the escapades of last night came rushing in. I rolled over and looked at him. He was sprawled on his back, taking up most of the bed. I slid out from under his hand heading for the bathroom but just before I stepped through the door I turned to look at his overbearing possessive ass lying there. *Damn alpha males thinking they own everything they touch or look at.* Shaking my head, I turned and went to the shower. I stood under the hot water letting it soothe my still heavy limbs. I don't know why, but there was nothing better than a hot shower to get your day started. Reluctantly, I began my daily ritual.

Clean and feeling like I might be able to face the world, well, at least our world, I stepped out. I grabbed a towel from the rack. I went to the sink to brush my teeth and hair. Finishing up my poor excuse for a beauty routine, I hung the towels on the rack and walked back into the room.

He was still sleeping. I shook him.

"Wake up, handsome. It's time for you to go to your room."

I turned toward the closet and asked it to open.

He scooted up against the headboard rubbing his eyes. "Why would I do that? The view here is much better than mine."

"Because you have your own cabin and this one is mine."

"Well, this one could be *ours*."

I looked over my shoulder at him. He was smiling a shit-eating grin. I narrowed my eyes at him, but he was for real.

"Yeah, that doesn't work for me. One night of sex does not a relationship make."

"What?"

"Go to your room and take a shower. Get ready for today, and let me do the same."

"Okay, I am going. But I will be back."

"Sure, I'll let you know when that is." I shoved him, wearing solely his pants, toward the door.

He stepped out into the hallway and turned to face me. The door shut quickly, and I returned to my room to get dressed. I had barely put on a shirt when I heard knocking at my door. I walked into the front room irritated and loudly asked, "Who is it?"

"It's me. Why?"

"Oh, come in."

The door slid open, and Verruca stood there smiling wide. "Why so irritated at this hour?"

"Oh, it's nothing."

"Yeah, that means a guy was here and didn't want to leave."

I looked back at her scowling playfully.

"Uh-huh, I know you and I know what irritates you early in the morning. One, no soda. Two, a guy who has overstayed his welcome. Since we haven't had soda since we woke up, it must be number two."

"Yeah, yeah. Whatever. Why are you up at this hour? You been out playing yourself? That looks like yesterday's clothes. Doing the walk of shame this morning are you?"

"First off, all our clothes look the same, so you wouldn't know yesterdays from today's. Second, I'm grown. I can stay out all night playing if I want."

I narrowed one eye at her in a disapproving look. "Smart ass." We both started laughing.

"I was with someone. Nothing too serious, at least so far. I was with Ryo, and when he left this morning, I saw Kilian leaving. I just wanted to get the scoop. But this attitude told me he overstayed his welcome."

"Well, he shouldn't have stayed all night. And he damn sure shouldn't have suggested he move in. He was acting like a typical alpha male, thinking because we had sex, he owned me. If anyone had a claim, it would have been Night. He beat him to the punch a week ago."

"Really now, which one was better?"

"I am not discussing that with you."

Verruca busted out laughing. When, she caught her breath she said, "Come on, let's go get breakfast."

"Nope, I brought food back with me. I am staying in today. We can pick up exploring and everything tomorrow."

"Okay, what if I join you?"

"I'm okay with that."

I went to the kitchen to get out the food to make for breakfast and Verruca went to find our first movie. Once I had our breakfast ready, I joined her on the couch. We rarely moved the rest of the day. In between movies we talked about things we used to do. It felt so nice to just do things we used to do regularly. After our last movie we just sat there talking for who knew how long until Verruca decided it was time for her to go to her cabin. After a quick good night hug, she left. I went to my room and fell over into my bed.

"Mom! Wake up!"

"What do you want? Why do all of you insist on waking me up so early and so loudly?"

"Well, if you would stop sleeping like you're dead. We wouldn't have to yell at you or sound the alarm full blast," Verruca retorted with humor in her tone.

"Whatever, go to the front room while I get dressed."

After a quick shower and fresh clothes, I walked out to the living room.

"Okay, I guess I am ready to get this day started."

"Aren't we scheduled to check out another location

today?"

"Yes, we are, but I need food and caffeine before all of that."

We left my cabin and headed for the dining room. When we exited the elevator, I ran smack dab into Night.

"Sorry, I wasn't paying attention."

"It's okay. I was just heading to the bridge to check our systems. What are you doing?"

"We're fixin' to get breakfast and then to see what needs to be tackled first today."

He stared at me for a long second.

"Come on, I am starving. I need food." Verruca grabbed my arm and dragged me toward the dining room.

"Why are you pulling me down the hallway?"

"I didn't want to stand there watching you two ogle each other."

I shook my head at her as we entered the dining hall. About half the awakees were up and eating. We got our plates and sat down. After a few bites in silence, Verruca began with our agenda for the day. She had the schedules lined out for all of us.

"Send everyone their assignments. Make sure they know I need regular updates. Since I'm going to be supervising the exploration of the new location today. I would like you to personally take Shanti and Sphynx to the labs.

"First, we need them to get familiar with what capabilities the labs have. Ask Savinka and Vashanti to join y'all so they can help them. They will need to read through all the info on the computers. My biggest concern is they understand that the embryo labs are to be kept quiet. We need to get started on growing an animal, but I want it kept between them and the council. Well, us too."

"Okay, but why don't you want anyone to know we can grow animals in an external womb?"

"For one, if it doesn't work, we will need to research what happened so we can make changes to the wombs or fix whatever mistake we made. But some people aboard might have a moral issue with it. I'm not debating morals with anyone if this process mean food or no food. Besides, even if Lita and Ryker have no real issues with it, they will use it to cause issues. That I'm sure of."

"Got it."

Once we were done going through everything, I took my plate to the kitchen. On my way back through the dining room I saw Kilian standing at Lita and Ryker's table. There were several other people sitting at the table, just staring at him. When I got close, I could hear his tone was reprimanding. I stepped closer listening to what he was saying.

"It doesn't matter if you agree with Atlantis's decisions or those of the council. We are the ones in charge. So, if I hear y'all spreading rumors about Atlantis again, there will be consequences."

I grabbed Kilian by the arm and started pulling him away. I heard Lita retort a smart ass comment about needing a big strong man to stand up for me. I ignored it because she was trying to goad me. Kilian, on the other hand, was about to get it.

"How dare you stand there and speak for me?"

"I was putting a stop to her causing dissention in the ranks."

"First off, this is not the military. Second off, I don't need you standing up for me. I am more than capable of doing it for myself. Now she is going to think she can challenge me at every turn. She is that kind of person, and you also just solidified her and Ryker's relationship. He already thinks he should be the alpha male in charge. Now he will join in with anything Lita suggests to remove us from leadership."

"I didn't think about it like that. I was just trying to stop them from causing chaos."

"You being an overbearing alpha male may have just set them off. I must be the one that cuts them off at each turn, or Lita will keep at her shit."

"I was just trying to help."

I waved him off and made my way to the bridge. On the elevator ride up I sent a message to all the council members letting them know about Lita and Ryker. Then I asked if we should have a meeting in the early afternoon to discuss this new issue. Most agreed and I put it on everyone's agenda for today.

The rest of my trip to the bridge I spent stewing over Kilian's interference. I walked on to the bridge to see Night leaning over a control panel.

"Vega, on the left side of the screen can you pull up a live view of Earth this morning? On the right put up the new reports."

"Yes, Ms. Atlantis." Vega flashed into view and began doing what I asked.

Night turned to look at me I smiled and patted him on the shoulder as I passed. The Earth's live feed came up, and I stared at it. I just wanted to find a place for us to land. Somewhere we could all start over. The only problem was we did not know this new, dangerously broken world.

I kept running different scenarios in my head. If we chose the site in Texas we'd sampled yesterday, we would have to deal with wintry weather and snow right now. That didn't include what animals were around that location. If we chose today's location in Oregon, we were looking at hot summers, extraordinarily little plant life, and most of the rivers had turned to streams. A chime sounded and drew my attention back to reality. I began opening reports and reviewing the data.

Last night seemed to have been slightly calm over Texas

with no more snownadoes. But the temperatures had held out in the low twenties. I pulled up a second page and saw that South Texas temps hovered in the upper forties. I made a mental note that somewhere around old Corpus Christi might be a viable alternative. I became lost in my thoughts and planning what to say to the others.

The area we are going to explore today had a massive thunderstorm that set fire to a section of what used to be a dense forest. After the bombs it was nothing more than a patch of shrubs and dying trees. After last night it was ashes and a few fires. Our location is closer to the ocean, so I'm hoping that the fires will not have affected it much.

"Mom, stop rubbing your earlobe. We will get you some earrings soon."

Night jerked his head up and looked at me. Then he looked around at everyone else.

"What?" I said in surprise. I had not heard the door open. Then I realized I was rubbing my earlobe and dropped my hand.

"What did you want to talk to all of us about, Iksen?" Jax walked onto the bridge looking energized.

The rest of the council filed onto the bridge one after the other. Once they were all seated, I spoke.

"The first thing I wanted to fill you in on is what happened with Lita and Ryker this morning."

Kilian stood up and took over. "I was walking past their table this morning and overheard her telling the other awakees that Atlantis didn't know how to get us back to Earth. She went on about how Atlantis was old, uneducated, and just trying to keep the power to make sure herself and her daughter here were safe. Ryker joined in saying he had overheard Atlantis say she didn't care about the rest of the people on the ship, just herself ad Verruca. "

Jax shrugged. "Who cares what they say? We know better."

Still giving Kilian a death glare, I explained. "It's

important, because if she can cause dissension, then it will make it harder to keep everyone focused on our goal."

"I stopped them from talking shit and reminded them that we"—Kilian moved his hand in a circular motion—"are in charge of this ship. And that Atlantis has done nothing but put everyone else first."

"Oh god, you didn't," Verruca put a hand over her eyes.

"What did he do wrong?" Savinka asked.

"He made her look like she can't fight her own battles." Verruca stood up and came to my side. "Lita and Ryker are the type of people that will use that to try and convince others that my mom can't stand up for herself. They will challenge her and push others to do the same."

"You really think they will do that?" Zahirah looked at me and Verruca.

"I do. So going forward, please tell me if you hear them saying anything and I'll address it. This way I can keep them in check." I looked around at everyone and they all nodded.

Verruca stepped forward. "I have something I want to talk about quickly." She paused, and I waved her on. "Now that we have two more people that can work in the labs, I thought we should start with growing an animal. Savinka, if you could assign everyone duties in the lab, maybe three of you to run samples, then one of you can research thoroughly how to grow an embryo. Then let's put one of the smaller animals in and see how we do."

Savinka looked around at all of us. "Do y'all mind if I recruit Vashanti's husband to help with some of the smaller jobs? Or maybe he could work with the plants. Other than that I'll get everyone started."

"Not at all, get him started wherever you need him. He can even bring their son to the plant lab—only the plant lab, though." I paused, thinking whether there was anything else we needed to address when a thought hit me. "Savinka, he might be perfect to really take charge of seeing sick awakees, since you will be running the labs."

"You're right, he would be a good fit for that. And if anything serious comes up, he can get with me." Savinka nodded her head in agreement.

"Okay, I think that's everything for now. Who's ready to get the drones launched?"

Cash jumped off the couch, flexed his hands, and cracked his neck. "I am."

Ronan, Juniper, and Jax laughed and followed him out of the room to go and prep the drones.

"Where are we researching today?" Zahirah looked at the main screen, searching the feed of the earth.

I answered her while I pulled up the video feeds from the drones. "Today we're exploring a section of Oregon where Lincoln city was located. Like last time, we're going to take samples and look around as much as we can via the drones.

"The day after tomorrow we're going to explore a spot in North Carolina."

We all busied ourselves while we waited to hear from Cash. Vega sent the weather reports for last night and I began reviewing them.

Chapter Twelve: Settling into Our New Lives

Cash called over everyone's holos that he was ready. When I looked up, only Verruca, Kilian, and Night where still on the bridge, each working at different stations. I flicked the reports in the direction of the map table and began placing the current info quickly into place while the countdown began. Zero sounded and I looked up just as the drones shot out. While they descended, I leaned over the table studying the land formations from yesterday's scans. There didn't seem to be many around the area we were exploring today except the giant rocks on the coastline. The mountains looked to be several feet lower than they used to be, or maybe it was just because they were bare now.

"Mom," Verruca blurted out in annoyance. "Stop drumming on the table. It's annoying."

"Look, you know I do that. Get over it."

The guys chuckled at us bickering. I returned to what I was doing.

"The drones made it through the clouds." Night called out to us.

I went to the main screen to get my first look at Oregon. The drones were still too far up to discern anything, so Verruca and I made our way to the captains' chairs. The guys came and sat on the platform in front of us. Our gazes were glued to the screen as the drones got closer. Cash had two drones flying around giving us an overall view. I was in shock from what I was seeing. A once lush forest-covered land now looked like a desert wasteland.

"Wow, it looks nothing like it used to. Remember when we lived there, the forest was so thick and green. The mountains used to be covered in snow. It was beautiful. Now it's a desert." Verruca stood up and stepped closer to the screen to stare at the images.

It was crazy to see Oregon looking like this. I just watched in disbelief as the drones collected samples and flew around the area.

"I'm not sure I like this choice of site. There are no natural protections, since the forest is gone. I think it would be too unprotected. Another thing is it doesn't look like the soil can grow anything. At least the Texas site had grass, trees, and shrubs." Verruca pointed to the feed.

"I don't know what it is about this location, but it gives me the creeps. There is something not right." A shudder ran across my body.

"I think I might agree. It has a strange feeling, and we aren't even on the surface," Night echoed.

As I watched the drones move around, I began to wonder what the samples from two days ago had to tell us. The drones had done all their work and were rising into the air to get ready for the return trip when one caught a strange movement within the bare, branchless tree trunks. I jumped up and walked toward the screen.

"Wait, what was that. Vega, run that video back."

"What? What did you see?" Verruca asked, looking at me like I was crazy.

Vega ran the video back a couple of minutes. I watched until I saw the movement.

"Freeze! What is that?" Kilian appeared next to me.

I pointed toward a strange shape. "It looks like a giant Gila monster weaving between the dead black trees."

It was easily the size of a Saint Bernard with a black and tan body. I asked Vega to play the video in half speed. We could now see that it was half slithering and half waddling on its stocky legs.

"Oh my god. That is the biggest lizard I have ever seen." Verruca squeezed my arm.

"I know, and they're poisonous. This can't be our site. I don't want to have to deal with that on a regular basis."

"Yeah, me neither." Verruca shuddered on my other side.

"Vega, drop this picture onto the map, please."

"Yes, Ms. Atlantis."

"Okay, I need a break. That was more than I needed to know about our new planet." I turned back toward the chairs. Night was still sitting on the platform.

I plopped into the chair and just sat there for a minute. What the hell were we going to do if we had to deal with animals like that at every site?

"Mom, do you want me to bring you food back? I'm going to go eat and hope I forget about what we just saw."

"Yeah, something to drink for sure, and then whatever looks good."

"I'm going to go check in with Cash," Night said as he walked toward the door.

"Me too." Kilian followed Night to the elevator.

I waved bye without a glance toward them. I had closed my eyes and leaned back into my chair. I needed to relax after that scare. After I felt like I had a handle on what awaited us on Earth, I got up.

I went to the main viewing window to stare out at the Earth. I marveled at the secrets she was holding in this new world. *How can we survive with monsters like that now walking on it? My Earth plan is going to have to include more survival skills and hunting lessons than anything else.* The longer I stared, the more I felt like I might be up against an opponent I couldn't beat. I jumped and looked over my shoulder.

"Night, I wasn't expecting you to come back."

"We have not been able to have alone time in over a week."

"I know, but there has just been a lot going on."

"Yeah, and other people have been keeping you busy."

I turned to look at him, to read his expression. I saw it in his dark questioning eyes. He knew about Kilian.

"Yeah, I slept with Kilian."

"So, what about us? I thought you liked me."

"I do. I like him too. I am grown. I know who I do and don't want to sleep with. None of us have made any commitments to each other. Until that time comes, I will continue to see him. If I don't hurt him first because of his damn alpha male bull-shit."

Before Night could answer, Verruca barged in talking.

"I got you a big glass of tea." She froze and looked at us, surprised. "Oh, I didn't know y'all were trying to have alone time."

"Smart ass. No, he was asking me some questions."

"Oh, do you normally cuddle with people who ask you questions?"

"Yes, I do if they are really hot."

"I'm going to go check in with, umm, Cash." Night hurried from the bridge.

We both started laughing. "Why do you always have to embarrass the guys I'm seeing?"

"Because it's so fun to see them blush and want to hide. You know you always date these big, manly men. It is so funny to see them get all shy around your child."

"Smart ass!"

"I learned from the best."

I stuck my tongue out at her. "Why don't we take our food to my cabin? We can put a movie or music on."

"Yeah that sounds good."

I took my tea and plate from her and we headed out.

We had just stepped off the lift when Verruca paused.

"Shit, I forgot that I was supposed to meet up with Ryo, Jax, and Sphynx. We were all going to hang out.

"Okay, baby. Well, go meet up with them. I am still going to my cabin for some quiet time."

"Okay, I'm so sorry. I totally forgot until right now."

Verruca leaned over and hugged me and then headed back to the elevator.

"Love you, have fun." I waved at her as I continued to my cabin.

"Love you too."

I sat on my couch, turned on a movie and stuffed my face in peace and quiet.

I woke up needing to pee and checked the time as I passed the nightstand. Six am shone at me in red block numbers. It was a little early, but since I had fallen asleep early I had some energy. I decided to go see what was going on around the ship. I showered, dressed, and headed out. I wasn't sure where I wanted to go first, so I got on the lift, closed my eyes, and picked a deck. The gold deck it was. I went to the embryo lab and saw Vashanti working.

"What are you working on?"

"Oh, shoot! You scared me."

"Sorry, I didn't mean to," I patted her on the shoulder as she caught her breath. Once she dropped her hand from her chest, I spoke again, "So what you working on?"

"I was running the samples. Savinka asked me if I could start them while she went to grab some food with Ronan."

"How's that going?"

"First, I had to figure out all this equipment. I mean I understand the basics, but these are more advanced than the ones I'm used to."

"I think most of this equipment on this ship is more

advanced than what any of us are used to."

"I know, right. All the voice commands had me stumped at first."

"I had the same issues at first. But I can't wait to see the results from the samples."

"Yeah, me too. I can't stop thinking about how we're going to survive."

"I know. It's been on my mind as well. Sorry, I forgot to ask how your son and husband are doing with all of this?"

"They are okay now. My son thinks it's some wild adventure. You know kids, they take it all in their stride. My husband, I think, is still a little freaked out, but he jumped at helping with the clinic."

"Fortunately, kids are resilient. I'm sure your husband will settle in soon. I think we all will as we get more into the groove of life here."

"I'm sure you're right. I guess I have had a lot of stuff to keep me busy and just moving forward."

"I think it's a mom thing. We always move forward through all tough times trying to keep the kids settled and happy."

"You may have something there. The last thing I want is for my son to be scared."

"I do have one more question . . ."

"Shoot."

"Did Savinka tell you about the animal embryos and the artificial wombs?"

"She did. She also told me that you wanted to start growing some of the embryos to see if it would work. But you don't want me to tell anyone?"

"Yes, I don't want anyone to freak out or have some moral issue with it. Whether we like it or not, we will have to grow the animals to have food and to re-populate these animals."

"I understand your thinking. I am sure someone on the

ship might have a problem with it, but I don't. I have always hoped that science would get artificial womb technology up and running to help all the women out there that have trouble carrying a baby to full term."

"I had always hoped they would find something to help with that problem as well. Now you get to spearhead that technology right here in our own high-tech lab."

"It's exciting."

"It is. And I know we will have to tell people at some point, but until that time comes just keep it hush-hush for now."

"I will. I totally understand the situation. I don't want to give anyone a reason to cause trouble either."

"Thanks for understanding." I waved her to follow me. "I think we should try a rabbit for now. It's small and easy to take care of once it is born, and gestation only takes three weeks. I'll have Vega keep the birthing lab locked unless it's me, you, Sphynx, Savinka, Lotus or Verruca. The rest of the council knows but they will trust I am handling things."

We walked out of the embryo lab over to the birthing lab.

"Okay, I am good with that. No one else needs to be in here anyway."

"Vega, can you set the birthing lab doors to restricted access? Authorized access granted to me, Verruca, Sphynx, Lotus, Savinka, and Vashanti only."

"Yes, Ms. Atlantis."

"Thanks for understanding. Please send me the reports from the samples as soon as the results come back. If you or your family needs anything, please let me know or any of the council."

"I will, thanks for the offer."

"And now, I'll leave you to it."

"Yes, Iksen. Thank you for checking in on me."

I left the lab and continued walking. When I got to the end of the corridor, I heard noises coming from a large room on the left. I opened the door and found Ronan putting something together.

"What are you doing? I thought you and Savinka where getting breakfast together?"

"We did, after we did a little workout. She went to go shower and change. I found some items in one of the large containers in cargo bay B4 that I can turn into workout equipment. I wanted to use this frame for us to do pull ups on and create other workout equipment, but it is being stubborn and doesn't want to go together."

"Did you look for the instructions on how to put it together?" I could barely keep myself from laughing at him.

"Does it look like it came with instructions?"

"You never know until you look."

Rolling his eyes and fighting a smile he went on about his ideas. "I figured once we assigned the agents for the ship we could work out in here. But anyone could work out."

"That reminds me, did you ever figure out a schedule for our workouts? I need to be in better shape."

"Yeah, I'm still good with first thing in the morning. You used to do judo and aikido, right?"

"Yeah, years ago. It's been a while since I have done any of it. Marching band, judo, aikido, track, or basketball. But I became cute and fluffy." I grabbed my love handles, chuckling.

"Yeah, well I can fix that," Ronan said with a snort of laughter.

"Thank you, how about starting for real tomorrow? I know I said that already, but things got in the way."

"I'm good with that. I like to get my day started with a workout."

"Well, what if we try mornings for now and then make adjustments when we need to?"

"Sounds like a plan to me." Ronan walked me to the door. "See you in the morning, Iksen."

"Good, see you then."

I left the — um — gym? Well, it was *the gym* going forward. I made my way toward the cafeteria. I ran into groups of people moving around doing different things on my way, I even almost tripped over the kids playing tag as they headed to the dining room.

I got my food, a glass of tea, and a cup of coffee.

"Thank you, guys. I appreciate all the cooking y'all have done. Ryker, I would like you to do an inventory of drinks and snacks. I think it would be good to let people take some things to their cabins, if they want. Vox, offer leftovers, to anyone who wants them. I don't want anyone to feel like they can't have food in their cabins."

"Yes, Iksen," Ryker answered drawing out the N and then punctuating it hard.

"Thank you, Iksen," Rogue said with a big smile like he was trying to defuse the tension.

Vox cut Ryker off before he could speak again. "I'll inform everyone throughout the day, Iksen."

"Again, thank y'all. I really do appreciate everything y'all do."

I had barely stepped out the door when I ran into Night.

"Where are you going?"

"I'm fixin' to go take a seat right there and eat."

"Okay, I'll be back to join you?"

Sitting his plate on the table, Night sat in front of me. "Can we finish our conversation from yesterday?"

"Sure." I chuckled.

"I want to spend some time with you again. But it seems like you are trying to avoid that."

"No I'm not, I have been busy, in case you can't tell."

"Well, you're sleeping, aren't you?"

"Yes, but if you were there I wouldn't be."

Night smirked wickedly at that comment and his eyes filled with lust and need. It was so strong I wanted to say *to hell with breakfast* and take him to my cabin right now, but I knew other things had to be done first. "I'll make a deal with you. Meet me here for dinner, and I'll let you know if I'm up for a visitor tonight."

His grin widened and he agreed. The rest of our breakfast talk was filled with what was going on for the day and new systems he had learned. He had found a communications hub in one of the maintenance tunnels. He spent some time yesterday running diagnostics from there just learning how the communications of the ship truly worked.

"I'm glad you got the time to work with that hub. You never know when you may need to go fix something from there."

"I know, that's why I did it."

"I'm heading out to go check my agenda for the day. But I'll be here at dinner time so you better not be late." I wagged my finger at him playfully scolding him. Then I leaned over and kissed his forehead before I headed for the exit.

I was studying weather reports from last night when Verruca came in. I looked at her, puzzled because she had a slight smile.

"I'm guessing last night went well?"

"Maybe."

"Umm, you are not a morning person. You would rather kill someone for waking you up before noon, let alone have a slight smile on your face."

"Fine, we had a good time last night. Now can we get to our agendas for the day? Because I am not discussing my date night with you."

"Oh, so it went extra well. Okay, I see how it is."

Verruca rolled her eyes and flicked our agendas for the day

onto the main screen. I hip bumped her when she stepped close to me and she did it back. After a quick laugh we went through what we needed to do. Since the girls in the labs had just got to running samples, Verruca and I decided it might be wise to wait until tomorrow to check another possible landing site.

It wasn't smart to just keep piling on the workload with the other project they were working on.

"What's next?"

"Either you or I need to check in with the mediators. I was thinking since the kids were awake, we might want to start some kind of school or something to keep them occupied," Verruca suggested as she checked down her list.

"I'm good with that. Talk with Juniper about starting something. Let her know she can find someone else to help if she needs it. Okay, what else?"

"Not everyone else has let me know what they are doing for the day."

"They should all know what they want or need to do today. I don't think I need to assign anything."

"No, I don't think you do either. They also all know to get with you if there is something you need to know."

"I agree. Well then, I am going to drop this new info on to the map table and begin looking at our next possible sites."

"I'm going to go check in with everyone and talk with Juniper," Verruca informed me as she stood. "Love ya."

"Love ya too."

Verruca head off and I began my tasks for the day. I called for Vega.

"Yes Ms. Atlantis?"

"I would like to go over the options for our next site."

"Yes, what areas where you thinking?"

"We have to be close to fresh water for sure, but I would like to be close to the ocean as well. That way we have more options for food and travel."

"Let me pull up the map on the main screen and we can go over the options."

"Perfect."

Vega and I began looking over our choices. We pulled all the info he had for the east coast and we scoured it to look for the best ones. He set the ship to maneuver us more in line with the east coast. He looked at new pictures, compared them to old ones and finally narrowed it down to two options. I was stretching from sitting for so long when I remembered I was supposed to meet Night.

"*Chingoa!* what time is it?"

"It is six forty five."

"Shit, I was supposed to meet Night forty five minutes ago."

"Go. I will leave any new info on the main screen for you to review tomorrow."

"Thank you Vega. You're a life saver."

I quickly got on to the lift and hurried to the dining hall. Walking as fast as I could, I entered the dining hall and saw Night standing by the front table talking with the rest of the council.

"And who was late?" Night wagged his finger at me.

"I know, I know. I got lost in what I was doing and didn't realize how late it was. I'm sorry."

"You will have to make it up to me."

I crossed my arms and rolled my eyes.

"I know just how you're going to make it up to me. You're going to let me cook for you. In your cabin tonight. Let's go." Night grabbed my arm and started dragging me from the dining hall.

"Wait, Give me thirty minutes. Let me run and get cleaned up." I gave him a pleading look.

"Okay, thirty minutes and then I'll be there."

"Okay."

Once I reached my cabin, I snatched some clothes from the front room area and threw them toward the bedroom. I grabbed a couple dirty glasses and placed them in the sink. The I turned, giving the area a once over to make sure it looked decent. On the way to the shower I picked up the clothes and put them in the closet for now.

"Vega, play some rock, alternative, grunge, anything that falls into those categories."

One of my favorite songs came over the speakers. I sang the intro as I climbed into the shower.

I stepped under the hot water falling from the ceiling and groaned at the feeling. It never failed. A hot shower always relaxed me. I was trying to hurry, but when I heard the knock, I still needed to scrub my body.

"Vega, can you let Night in and tell him I'll be out in a few minutes?"

"Yes, Ms. Atlantis."

I grabbed the puff from its hook and poured body wash on it. I scrubbed myself as quickly as possible. I could hear bits and pieces of Vega talking to Night, but I stood in the shower a few more seconds relishing the feeling of the hot water. With a long sigh I ordered the water to turn off. I wrapped myself in a towel and then did the same with my hair. I continued drying myself as I went to the closet to pull out fresh clothes. I really had to make time to go to the clothes closet slash supply closet and get a couple more pieces of clothing. Three outfits made it hard to stay fresh all the time.

I ran back to the bathroom, brushed my hair, and pulled the front back into a rubber band. I walked out to the living room and found Night setting the table. Where he found a candle, I will never know. I slowly approached the table in awe. That's when I saw it was not a real candle, but a hologram projected from a small black square.

"How did you get this ready that quickly?"

"Well, while you were taking your thirty minutes, I asked Vega for some help. I have seen you running around doing all these things making sure everyone and everything is working the way it should and I thought it might be nice to pamper you a little."

"Well, this is a good start."

He pulled my chair out and gestured for me to sit down. I was starving now that I smelled the food. Once I was seated, he took his seat. We ate in silence at first. To my surprise it was not awkward, and we both seemed to relax into it.

"I was able to talk Rogue into making us some brownies. He will bring them in just a few."

"Yum, I haven't had a sweet since we woke up. I didn't know if we even had anything sweet."

"He found the ingredients and mixed it up after bugging Ryker to tell him how. Ryker didn't want to tell him because I was asking for it."

"No, it was probably because you were bringing them to me. You know he has a problem with me. So does Lita for that matter."

"Well, Rogue wanted to make enough for everyone, so Ryker finally gave in."

"That was nice of him. He's a sweet kid. He had a big head from his social media fame, but he is settling in, finding his groove."

"Yeah, he is." He took a sip of tea. "Why do you think Ryker has something against you?"

"The way he acts when I speak. He looks at me blankly or with disgust. I see him and Lita together, so I figured it was coming from her. She acts like she is too good to listen to me when I speak, and did you see her when we were addressing the group? She stepped in front of me and began speaking over me."

"I did see that, but you handled it well. You didn't let your anger get the best of you. That's all you can do when in front of the whole group."

"Yeah, she was trying to make a show of power. But I am not too worried about her. I must focus on what we're doing every day."

"Well, don't worry. We all have your back. Everyone can see you have been doing everything possible to make sure we are all safe and get back to Earth."

"Yeah, but with me being so firm, trying to keep everyone busy, and not wanting to wake the rest of the people, I am sure that I have rubbed some people the wrong way,"

"Don't be so hard on yourself. You have been doing good to keep us together as well as you have. This many people to keep organized is not easy."

"I am used to a classroom full of crazy kids or a store full of adults acting like crazy kids. I have a little experience corralling people."

Night took our plates and rinsed them at the sink. He then brought two spoons to the table. "Well, you have done an excellent job so far. Don't let them get to you."

"I know, but I might have to give her a verbal smackdown, so she understands I'm not the one to play with."

A knock on the door interrupted us. Night got up and went to the door. It was Rogue with the brownies. Night brought the pan to the table. He sat back down and picked up his spoon holding it out toward me. Confused as to what he wanted, I slowly held my spoon up.

"Cheers," He clinked his spoon against mine.

We both dug into the brownies and brought our first bite to our mouths.

"Umm, damn." I closed my eyes. "This is so good. I'm not sure I have had any as good as these."

"Or has it just been so long that anything sweet would taste like heaven?"

"You could be right," I mumbled around another bite.

We talked some more while we ate. Night told me about missing his little ranch and how much he loved drumming at the pow-wows. I told him about playing the drums from junior high through college. After stuffing ourselves so full we couldn't wiggle, Night ushered me off to the couch. I asked the video system to play a movie. Night cleared the table

I had let my eyes close for only the briefest of moments when I felt Night take my hands.

"Come on, let's go to bed."

Night led me to my room and pulled back the blankets. Once I was lying down, he pulled the blanket over me and then walked to the other side. He climbed into bed and snuggled up to me. I relaxed into his arms and drifted off.

CHAPTER THIRTEEN: SABOTAGE

I'm not sure what time it was when I woke up with Night between my thighs. The sparks that were shooting through my body were exquisite. I sank my fingers into his hair, holding him in place tight. He half-purred, half-growled in approval of my handhold. The vibrations flooded my core, making my climax begin to pool readying itself for release. He continued to rev my body until I was too close to my orgasm exploding through me. Not wanting it to be over so quickly I pulled his head up.

He looked at me and I sat up, rolled him over, and slid down his body until my mouth was level with his cock. I licked around his crown with a quick swirl of my tongue. He groaned while his eyes fell shut. Pleased with his reaction, I sucked his cock into my mouth hard and fast. His hands flew to my head holding it in place as he arched into my mouth. His crown was in the back of my throat begging to be allowed access. I relaxed my throat and he pushed in further. He groaned from the sensation. That groan spurred me on, I wanted to hear more of his pleasure. I began to swallow which caused my throat to constrict around his cock.

His breathing became short and breathy. His grip tightened in my hair, and I knew I had him on the edge. I swallowed two more times and his cock throbbed hard. He roughly pulled my mouth free from his cock. I caught my breath while watching Night lying there with his eyes closed tight and a low growl radiating from him.

I gently removed his hands from my hair and placed them

190

on the bed. As he continued to gain his composure, I decided to climb on top. I gripped his cock and placed it at my opening. I slowly sank down onto him. My head fell back from the pleasure of him filling me. I slowly began making circles with my hips as I ground on his cock. This was always one of my favorite moves when on top. Well, if the guy was big enough to reach all the right spots. Luckily, Night was big enough. My climax was beginning to pool again and I sped up my movements.

Night groaned deep as he grabbed my hips, helping me move. "You're so hot and tight."

I answered him with a moan.

"I could drown in the feeling of you. I want to stay right here in this moment, in this feeling, and never leave."

I leaned my head down to look him in the eyes. In that moment, the lust that peered out at me spurred my orgasm to build quickly. The raw honesty I also saw in his gaze almost broke my heart. He held my gaze as he slipped his thumb over my clit, then manipulated it fast and rough. My inner walls clinched tight around his cock and made my mind return to the task at hand.

A strong need to prolong this moment rushed through me. I changed my movements and slowed them. I slid up and down, dragging out the sensations of our bodies moving together. Night growled low and deep, making electricity shoot through me, lighting every nerve with hunger for him. I was enjoying the feel of Night beneath me and the control I had over his pleasure as I rode him.

"You're killing me, Atlantis."

"Good."

He answered with a growl and gripped my ass, stilling my body above him. Night smiled wickedly and began thrusting into me hard and fast. I gripped his wrist tight and leaned my head back moaning. My inner walls instantly began to flutter.

I gasped and moved my hands to my breast, pinching my nipples. He groaned and moved a thumb to my clit again. In seconds I fell over the edge as my orgasm flooded my body in the mind-numbing bliss I loved. Before I could even begin my come down Night's own orgasm hit him, and he groaned out my name.

Neither of us moved, we just relished the mind-blowing sensations still spreading throughout our bodies. I felt like I was floating into the stratosphere. Several strong aftershocks racked us both as we enjoyed the high. Night's hand still gripped my hips tight and I still had my hands on his chest bracing myself. My head hung between my arms with my eyes closed, panting and letting the last of my pleasure dissipate. Once I felt like my limbs were no longer wobbly like Jell-O, I opened my eyes so I could move from atop of Night when I realized we were actually floating.

"What the hell is going on?"

Night opened his eyes and looked around. He grabbed my thighs in surprise.

"I don't know what is going on. Why are we floating in the air?"

"Vega, what happened to our gravity?"

"It would appear that there is some kind of issue with the gravity generator."

"Okay, so how do we fix it?"

"I'll get back to you on that. I need to go through its manual."

"Okay, can you wake Jax and Ryo? They have been learning about the systems together," Now I had to figure out how to move with no gravity.

I used Night's body to push off from so I could find my clothes and put them on. Night used the momentum to try and reach his side of the bed, where his clothes were.

Frustrated with trying to get my clothes on, I blurted.

"Getting dressed in a swimming pool would be easier. Grrr."

Night chuckled and reached out his hand for mine. I took it and he held me still so I could get my pants on. Then he dragged me along as we left my cabin and began floating our way to the elevator intending to go to engineering. As I passed Verruca's door, I saw Ryo come out, which I expected, then I saw Jax come out. That I hadn't expected. Before the door slid closed, I saw Verruca and Sphynx. I made a mental note to ask about all this later.

Ryo and Jax wouldn't look at me the whole elevator ride to the gold deck. Which in all reality was funny. We were on an elevator, floating at the top of it, and they were trying to avoid looking at me. I really wanted to mess with them but I decided against it, since I needed them focused on our issue.

Night was still holding my hand and used it to pull me toward him. When my body reached his, he wrapped an arm around my waist, holding me still. I wrapped an arm around his neck to help hold me to him. He then whispered in my ear, "Tonight was amazing. I was floating in pleasure before I realized we were actually floating."

I smirked and agreed with him by nodding my head. Before we could reminisce any more about our fun-filled early morning, the elevator stopped. I let my arm drop from his neck and we pushed our way out of the elevator behind the other two.

We all floated our way to engineering. Once in, the guys began to look for the generator. I did the smart thing.

"Vega, where is the gravity generator located?"

"It is the medium-sized cylindrical machine on the front right side. It is next to the vertical cylinders that filter the ship's water."

We all turned toward the front of the room, and on the floor was a horizontal, cylindrical machine. The guys floated over and began examining the machine.

"Look right here. It looks like someone was banging on the generator." Ryo waved everyone over to look.

The guys continued their inspection when Jax cursed.

"Fuck. Look, someone cut this cord. It's not all the way through, but enough to damages the wires."

"No doubt it caused the generator to fail," Ryo said and took the cord from Jax's hand.

Night looked at the cut while Ryo held it. Jax took out a tool that looked like needle-nose pliers and reached out his hand for the cord. Ryo placed the cord in Jax's outstretched hand. Jax began cutting back the rubber coating to better expose the damaged wires. Once the rubber was out of the way, they could see only two of the wires that made up the power supply cord had been damaged. Night and Jax went to work repairing them. Ryo grabbed some tool from a work bench across the room.

"Vega, can you make sure all power to the gravity generator is off?"

"Yes, Mr. Ryo."

Ryo opened the damaged end of the generator to inspect it for internal damage.

"I think I can Three D print some connectors for these wires," Jax informed us as he continued to look at the cable. He ran his hand along the cable on the floor and followed it up the wall as far as he could reach.

"Are there any other cuts?" I looked at Jax hopefully.

"There is one small nick over here by the wall." Jax pointed down to indicate where the nick was located. "Other than that, I didn't feel anything."

"This looks deliberate. But who would do something like this?" Night was still examining the cut in the cable. "The edges are smooth. Something sharp made this in either one hard hit or one smooth slice."

"That coating is thick. I don't know how they would have

done it that easily." I was examining the cut with Night.

"If they had enough upper body strength, they could have got it done in one strike," Ryo said as he stood back up. "I don't see any damage inside the machine, but we really won't know until we can get it back on."

"Vega, if this machine cannot be fixed how do we restore gravity?"

"There is a work around, but it is difficult to enact, Ms. Atlantis."

"What kind of difficult?"

"It will require some re-wiring to happen."

"Really, do we have any electricians on board?"

"No, Ms. Atlantis. But if it comes to that I have step by step instructions."

I shook my head. "Okay, thank you Vega. Oh, one more thing, please send out a ship-wide message letting everyone know that we're safe and the issue is being corrected."

"Yes, Ms. Atlantis."

"We got this, Iksen. Go check on everyone make sure the awakees know things are okay," Jax said as he patted my shoulder.

"Yeah, that's a good idea. Maybe I'll go start breakfast. I'm sure most people will be waking up from this." Night kissed me. "I'll find you when we're done."

I nodded and headed for the dining hall.

I used the pipes to the plants to pull my way to the elevator. If it wasn't for the pipes, I wasn't sure how I would have made it down the hall. There were very few things to use as leverage to pull or push myself forward. I stopped at the door to the lift. As I paused to try and figure out what was the best option for pushing the button, before I made a decision the door swooshed open. I floated in, then realized I needed to push a button. Luckily the interior of the lift had a decorative grate, made of different sized circles, over the lighted walls. I used it to pull myself down enough to push the correct button.

The elevator descended to the deck below. After exiting, I pulled myself along with the pipes again. Once I was in the dining hall I pushed off the wall to propel myself toward the door to the kitchen. I reached the other side slightly off from the door but my aim wasn't too bad.

I pulled out food from the freezer for breakfast. I laid the packages on the table but they began to slowly float up. Not wanting them to float too far away, I quickly turned to the stove and turned it on. The fire began to float.

"*Chingoa!* What the hell. Why is the fire floating away? Vega, help!"

"What is it, Ms. Atlantis?" Vega answered with just as much alarm in his tone as I had in mine and popped into view.

"I turned on the stove and now the flame is floating. There are four balls of flame floating. How do I extinguish them?" The pitch of my voice rose. A flame was floating in my direction, and I had to move out of the way.

"You can capture them in a container with a lid. This way the flames are deprived of the oxygen. Or there are fire blankets in the bottom of that cabinet on the left." Vega pointed to it.

I decided to try the container idea first. I looked around the kitchen and found a large metal bowl. I slowly gathered the flames in the bowl, then slowly turned the bowl upside down and placed it on the metal table. I had to grab a potholder to help hold it down, because it was getting hot. After a few long seconds I lifted the bowl a little and the flames were out. I quickly gathered the other three flames into the bowl and then turned it upside down on the table.

I took a deep breath. "Son of a motherless goat." I exhaled. "Vega," my tone was very frustrated, "How do I cook food with no gravity?"

"You will have to use the microwave."

"Will that work?"

"Yes."

"Awesome, next time please tell me important things like *don't light a fire in zero gravity.*"

"Yes, Ms. Atlantis. I must go now. I have multiple people calling for me. They are frightened."

"Can you direct them all to the kitchen?"

"Yes, Ms. Atlantis." And he dissolved like sand falling through an hourglass.

Changing my plans for breakfast, I decided to look for things I could just warm up in the microwave. I rummaged through the storage containers. In a large metal box I found fresh baked loaves of bread. In another I found some freshly made biscuits. That was going to have to work for now. I warmed them in the microwave and placed them back in the metal boxes to keep them warm. I snatched myself a piece of bread before I closed the box, and then spread butter over it. There was nothing better than warm bread with butter, except maybe some honey butter. I looked up and shook my head as a metal box of bread floated by.

I decided to try and make some sliced potatoes in the oven. I found two large metal clips. I cut the potatoes up the best I could and placed them between two shallow metal pans. I clipped them closed and put them into the oven.

I sliced some ham and cheese. These were a little easier, since I could stick them to the plate and then cover it with a lid. I decided to take a chance with some jelly. I stuck a butter knife in it and waited a minute. The knife stayed, so I took what I had out to a table. Verruca was hovering over our table. I waved her over to watch the food so I could return to the kitchen.

This was defiantly a trial in survival. I was not sure I was liking this pilot episode of extreme cooking. I wanted to get drinks, but liquid would float right out of a glass. I looked around to see if we had anything I could improvise into glasses with lids. I squatted to look at some tall containers that had lids. There were a little big but they might work.

"What the hell are you doing in my kitchen?" I heard a deep gravelly voice behind me. I jumped and stood up quickly, turning to see Ryker staring at me with his arms crossed. I guessed that his previously smooth, polished voice was an act.

"I am making food, since people are starting to wake up."

"You put me in charge of the kitchen, and I don't like other people messing in my stuff."

"Well, first, this is everyone's stuff. Second, I did not put you in charge. If anyone is in charge in here it's Vox. Third, I will make food for everyone when I feel like it."

Just as he was about to retort, Rogue floated in.

"Morning, Iksen."

"Morning, Rogue."

Ryker rolled his eyes and walked over to the oven.

"Those should be done if not close to it. I was trying to see if something would cook in the oven or burn. The clips were my solution to try and keep things from floating all around or burning "

He pulled the clips off and lifted the top pan.

"Be careful, things might float away." I was too late. The top pan was off and several pieces of potato floated upward.

I didn't say anything. I just tried to pour some tea into one of the containers with a lid. Unfortunately it didn't work — the liquid just kept floating up and not going into the container. With that option failing, I decided to just wait for a drink. If I continued, we were going to have a mess to clean up when the gravity returned. Leaving the guys to figure the rest of things out, I headed back to the table.

Verruca was already sitting at the first table with Sphynx. Well, they were trying to sit. No gravity was making it extremely hard. Sphynx had tucked her legs into the bars of her seat.

"Here, me duck." She reached her hand out to Verruca. "Sit and tuck your feet into the bars under your seat."

Verruca was doing just that while Sphynx helped hold her in place. Chuckling, I floated to the opposite side of the table.

"Hey, baby girl." I sat on the seat and attempted to tuck my feet under the bar. It took me a minute, but I found the right position to hold me in place and not hurt my feet."

"Now can you tell me what happened, because it was interesting to wake up floating around my room. But I don't want to do this for long term."

"The gravity generator stopped working. The guys are down on the gold deck's electrical room working on it right now."

"How exactly did that happen?"

"I am not exactly sure, but I'll be looking into it."

I got up from the table and let myself float over to the center table where Lita sat. A large group of people had gathered around her, and she was already talking to them. Her gestures indicated she was on her soap box.

"Morning, Lita. How are things? I see you are helping the group understand everything is okay."

She looked at me with narrowed eyes and then plastered a fake smile on.

"Morning, guys, I just want you to know I am going to address the issue as soon as more people get here."

"Yes, Iksen. We're all glad you have everything under control. We know you have our best interests at heart," Lita said in a sickly sweet, sing-song voice on top of her already sickly sweet Texas twang.

I smiled and nodded before I pushed off the table and floated back to my table. When I saw a few more of the awakees enter the dining hall I decided to go ahead and address the issue.

I pushed off my table toward the doorway to the kitchen. I was going to try and use the doorway to position myself so everyone could see me and hold myself upright. I pressed my toes against the side of the door facing and held on to the top. It wasn't the most graceful pose, but it would work.

"Morning, everyone. I just wanted to let y'all know that Night, Jax, and Ryo are working on the gravity generator. The generator had a few issues last night. The repairs seem simple enough and they guys are working hard to correct the issue. Hopefully, it won't be much longer, and we can walk instead of float."

"Can you tell us what happened? Is it something wrong with the ship, or did someone make a mistake?" Clover asked shyly, while Knox, Dash, and Lotus looked on.

"It looked like the power cable got damaged somehow." While I was talking, Kilian had floated over to me.

"May I?" Kilian gestured toward the group.

"Go ahead."

He turned toward the group and did his best to float in a good direction to address them. "I was just down in engineering. Jax almost has the fix for the wire printed. It won't be much longer. I know it's a little awkward trying to sit and eat. Just hang in there. They are working as quick as they can."

We let the group go back to trying to eat. Kilian pulled me into him so he could talk to me without anyone hearing him.

"Can we go to the bridge? I would like for us to talk to Vega without everyone hearing."

"Sure."

I waved to Verruca as Kilian and I floated our way out of the dining room. The ride in the elevator was just as strange as the last two rides. Riding in an elevator while floating was definitely one of the strangest things I have ever done. My thoughts scattered about all the strange things I might still have to do once we get to land, when the elevator door opened.

We floated out onto the bridge, and I saw that new reports were waiting for me on the main view screen.

"Vega, do you know what happened to the gravity generator?" Kilian spoke to the empty room.

"No, I am not sure how it stopped working, Mr. Kilian."

"Do you have a way of looking anything up?"

Before Vega could answer him, I had sent Vega a command to not tell him about the video surveillance.

"No, Mr. Kilian, not currently but I am checking several different reports to see if I can find a cause."

"Aggh," Kilian growled.

"Look, I will continue to work with Vega." I faced Kilian and ran my hands down his arms to calm him. "Maybe we can find out who did this. Why don't you go talk to Ronan about getting the security team up and going? Y'all set up a schedule for the people already assigned. Then see if y'all need to recruit more, even if that means waking a couple people."

At that moment, the gravity decided to make an appearance. We both slammed into the floor.

"Son of a motherless goat, that hurt." I lay on the floor groaning for a few seconds. I opened my eyes to get up, and Kilian stood over me reaching out his hand. I took it and he pulled me to my feet.

"You, okay?" He pulled me into a hug.

"I'm fine," I mumbled into his shoulder. "Go get Ronan and get started. I am going to work on things from here. I think we might have to take a day off from exploring the Earth."

"Okay, I'll check in later and let you know who we have chosen."

He kissed me hungrily before he turned and walked off the bridge. *Chingoa*, that was good. I fanned my face as I walked back to the main view screen.

"Vega," I said shakily. I cleared my throat and tried again.

"Vega." The words came out clearly this time. "I want to see the video of the electrical room on the gold deck."

Vega slithered into view. "I was going to suggest that you view the video when Mr. Ryan asked about what options we had for finding out who caused the damage. But then you cut me off."

"I don't want anyone but Verruca and myself to know we have video surveillance of the inside of this ship."

"Yes, Ms. Atlantis."

"Thank you. Now put the video on the main screen. And please put this room into private mode and do not let anyone into this room until I tell you it's okay."

"Yes, Ms. Atlantis."

Vega did as I asked and disappeared. I pushed *play*. I watched intently expecting to see someone, but there was nothing so far. Deciding to work backward I went to the time when we had begun floating. I skipped to that time and then ran the video backward. The video had only gone back a couple minutes when I saw movement. I slowed the video to watch what was happening.

Nothing happened. I tapped on the sidebar to access the list of cameras. Luckily, whoever named the cameras did so with names that made sense. I pulled up the camera that was outside of the electrical room. I ran the two feeds next to each other.

I saw a shadow but not the person. Then seconds later there were sparks in the electrical room. I rolled the feed backward for a few seconds to make sure that the sparks came from the area of the cut. They did, and that confirmed the cut caused the issue. Now I needed to go back more and see who caused the cut.

I rolled the video back around ten minutes from the spark

when I found two people exiting the electrical room in a bit of a hurry. I let it roll back to where the people entered it. There was not much light in the room, so I enlarged the video so I could see more details.

I could see the person well enough to observe them using a small ax to hit the machine over and over. Then another person came in and snatched the ax from the first person's hand. The new person walked over and took one swing at the area where the cable was located. Sparks shot into the air as the two people jumped back.

I could not make out who they were, because while in the room their bodies blended into the shadows too well. Their faces were covered with towels with just a narrow hole cut out for their eyes. After they looked at their handiwork for a few seconds, the second person pulled the first quickly out the door. I paused the video there.

The two subjects were close enough to the camera that I could make out some of the details their disguises were meant to distort. The subject closest to the camera was a male. He had stuffed something into his shirt trying to make him look like he had a gut. I continued to inspect the male and I saw just the tip of a tattoo peeking out from under his collar.

I moved the video forward one frame and inspected the second person. This person had also stuffed something under their shirt to make them look larger all over. Not being able to tell much, I moved it forward one more frame. The second person turned and looked in the direction of the camera. I was able to see they were female by the eyes. I looked at the towel wrapped around her head like she had just got out of the shower, and I saw a strand of bleached blonde hair sticking out from the side of her towel wrap.

Something told me this was Lita and Ryker. I couldn't prove it, but my intuition had never led me astray before.

CHAPTER FOURTEEN: FINDING OUR GROOVE

Furious with what I had seen, I tapped my communicator and selected Kilian's name.

"Kilian, what's your progress on getting our security force together?"

"We are talking with everyone right now," Kilian answered.

"I want it done ASAP. I want people on patrol tonight. I want all of the black deck and all electrical rooms locked down from everyone other than council members."

"Okay, why the hurry?"

"I just don't want any other issues. We are already losing a day of exploring."

"Okay, I'll let you know as soon as we have it set up."

"Thank you."

I paced back and forth thinking about how to handle this little girl who thought she was so smart. *I don't want to divide the awakees, since she already has people following her or so it appears. But I cannot have her causing chaos.*

"Vega, please store that file in a location only I can access."

"I will store it in a folder named AR and assign biometrics of your fingerprint to open it."

"Thank you."

"Will there be anything else?"

"No . . . Well, yes. I need you to safeguard yourself against hacking or breaches in your security. None of us know much about each other, let alone our extra-curricular activities. I don't want you to be vulnerable."

"Yes, Ms. Atlantis. I will start running security protocols immediately."

"Thank you. I think that is it for now."

I sat down on the couch and worked on getting my temper under control. I really wanted to walk out there and call Lita on her bullshit, but I didn't want to give her the chance to play the victim since I had no real proof. I stood up, stretched, and went to the table. I dropped the new info on the map and looked it over. The same weather issues continued to crop up in the same areas. After several week of monitoring, we were beginning to get a good picture of the weather on earth now.

After seeing the giant Gila monster, we hadn't seen any animals shapes on the scans or in the pictures that Vega had been taking each day. I was sure each location had their animal issues, but I wished we could get some on camera so we knew what we were up against. I continued studying the map because we probably needed to choose two more locations just in case this next one didn't work out.

"Mom."

"*Chingoa!* You scared me." I clutched my chest breathing hard.

"Oh, stop being dramatic, woman," Verruca said with a sarcastic tone and a big smile.

I stuck my tongue out at her and she copied me. Both of us chuckled. She joined me at the map table. She studied as I turned to the main screen tapping a few buttons to bring into view the section of Earth we were currently over. It was the middle of an ocean. The blue water of the Pacific was beautiful. I was admiring my view when the door slid open. Night, Ryo, and Jax came in. Night walked over and kissed me while Ryo and Jax did the same to Verruca.

"I have evidently missed something here."

Verruca rolled her eyes, cocking her hip out, placing a hand on it, and wagging her finger at me. "You have no room to talk, first off, but yes, Ryo, Jax, Sphynx, and I are seeing each other. It's not like there's a lot to do and we all get along great. I want to date Ryo and Sphynx. And Sphynx wants to date me and Jax. So we all decided to hang out and see where things go. I'll let you know when there is more to know." She continued to stare at me, challenging me to say something.

So of course I took that challenge. "Well, first off, I made you, so I will ask all the questions I want. Second off, I was just asking. I know who you are and as I have said many times before I don't give a shit if you like guys, girls, or both. I just expect to know what's going on, that you're happy, and that you're safe."

We were still staring at each other when Kilian walked in. He had made it almost to me when he stopped dead in his tracks. He looked at me puzzled and then looked at Verruca. Next he looked at the guys. They all shook their heads and raised their hands, palms out in a surrendering gesture.

"What did I miss?"

"Nothing."

"Mom being a hypocrite," Verruca answered.

"About what?"

"She was about to give me a hard time about seeing three people at the same time."

"As I said, I don't care," I said.

"Why don't we go get lunch?" Night said, trying to defuse the tension.

Then Verruca and I began to laugh.

"I have to stand up for myself with my mom and let her know I will do what I want when I want."

"I just like to rile her up. She falls for it a lot."

Night walked over to me and took me by the hand. He led me to the door, and the rest followed. Verruca joined me on my free side with Ryo and Jax on her far side. Kilian walked behind us. Verruca linked her arm in mine as she laid her head on my shoulder. I leaned my head onto hers as we all rode the elevator. Jax and Ryo exited quickly, and Verruca followed. Night, Kilian, and I exited together. We continued down the hallway quietly. Kilian was eyeing us up and down. I nudged Night, silently encouraging him to go ahead. I stayed back to walk with Kilian. He looked like he wanted to ask me something.

We were about to enter the dining room, and he still hadn't said anything, so I asked.

"Did you need to say something? Because you keep acting like you're going to speak and then don't."

He continued to look at me. I just shook my head and waved him off. I walked into the dining room, got my food, and took a seat next to Verruca. Eventually, the table filled with members of the council. They wanted to talk about what had happened and what we needed to do about it. Kilian had beaten Night to my empty side even though Night had entered before us. Now Night had to sit across from me. He reached his leg across under the table and rested his calf against mine.

"So, what are we going to do to make sure nothing happens to any more of our equipment?" Juniper looked around at everyone.

I gestured for Kilian to speak. It took him a minute to swallow his food and clear his throat.

"Ronan and I have been working together today to create a schedule for the few agents we have. They will start their first shift tonight. We also looked over who's asleep in case we need more agents."

Ronan spoke up. "In the morning we would like to wake up Asp Mabin. He was a paramedic previously but I think he would be a great fit. We just wanted to make sure that would be okay with everyone."

"Yes, I'm good with y'all waking Asp. But if he has family on board, try to convince him to let them sleep a little while longer. I'm not sure this is the best time to increase our numbers until we know who damaged the generator."

"I can agree with that." Ronan said.

Zahirah looked toward me. "Do we know who, if anyone, did this? Is it fixed, or do we have to worry about anything else going wrong?"

I nodded my head towards Ronan-"He is investigating the issue, but I am also looking at a couple people."

Zahirah nodded-"Good I would hate for anything major to get damaged and delay us from returning to Earth."

"Exactly!" I exclaimed.

We turned back to the group to see what everyone was talking about. They were deep in conversations about who they thought had damaged the generator. I listened for a little while then I remembered I wanted to discuss something with them.

"Hey guys, I want to discuss something." They all turned toward me. "Earlier while I was on the bridge I was looking at the map and all the things we have discovered about Earth. The more I reviewed, the more I thought about the fact that we need to have at least two back up spots to research. I have a feeling that we're putting too much faith in the North Virginia spot."

"Okay, so where else do you want to look?" Ronan asked.

"I was thinking around Corpus Christi, Texas. It's farther down the Texas coast. I figured it was far enough away from the snownadoes that it would be safe. The other spot I'm not sure yet, but we can work on figuring that out."

"I think it's smart to have some back up spots just in case tomorrow doesn't work out," Juniper agreed.

"Yeah, we can definitely look and have a plan ready for just in case," Ryo chimed in.

"Good. I'm glad we all agree on that. Now, this next idea is a little more crazy. But hear me out before everyone says no. I think that whichever site we decide on, we should send a couple people down to investigate it in person. It's all good and well for the reports and samples to tell us it is livable, but it's another to know firsthand."

"Absolutely not," Kilian blurted out. "I can already see it in your eyes—you want to be one of the ones to go down."

"I wasn't thinking about it, but if I did you would not get a say so. Anyway." I rolled my eyes and turned to the rest of the group, "What do the rest of y'all think?"

"I would like to volunteer to go to the surface." Cash raised his hand.

"Okay, I'll keep you in mind. It's still a few weeks away, probably."

"I think I want to be one of the ones to go down also," Night said.

"Okay." I nodded to Night. "Everyone just think about it. We will need to all agree before we send anyone."

The group answered, with several saying *Yes, Iksen* and some nods. After everyone had agreed to think about it, we returned to eating and chatting.

Kilian leaned in and whispered in my ear. "I don't want you to go to the ground. I don't want you hurt."

"I'm a big girl, I can handle myself. I don't need a big bad man to protect me."

"I am asking you—no, begging you—to not go to the planet. I could forbid it, but I am asking you not to go."

I stood slowly and looked down at Kilian. For a few seconds I thought about just walking away, but then I thought, to hell with it.

"Let me tell you something. No one will tell me what I can and cannot do. You don't own me. If I remember correctly, around nineteen-twenty, women won rights, and around eighteen-sixty-five, slavery ended. Which means you have no claims over me, and just because you stuck your dick in me doesn't mean you get to tell me what to do. I am grown and will make my own decisions without permission from any man." My tone was sharp and dangerous.

"You don't think anything of us sleeping together? You don't think that gives me the right to care what happens to you?" Kilian yelled back.

"A woman can have sex with someone just to have sex with someone. It doesn't mean that they are madly in love with that person. Again, I am grown. If I want to fuck you or any other person on this ship, I will. That still doesn't give you or anyone else the right to try and control me. You don't see Night trying to tell me what to do. He just goes with me to do it."

"What the hell does he have to do with it?"

"Well, we have slept together twice. Yet he is not telling me what I can and cannot do," I walked away.

The entire dining room was watching what was going on. I didn't really care if they were watching right now. I was so tired of him trying to make decisions for me. I truly didn't understand him. He was fine when I was issuing orders to everyone, but the moment I tried doing things, he acted like an alpha male asshole.

I was halfway down the damn hall before I realized it. I paused my ranting and took a breath. Then I giggled, then I giggled again, and soon I was in full blown laughter. I was so furious that it was funny. Or maybe I just wanted it to be funny so I didn't cry. I just needed to go to my cabin and forget about his stupidity for the rest of the night.

I stepped through the door of my cabin and took a deep breath. *Maybe I should just stay in for the rest of the day. Everyone knows what to do. We don't have anything planned.* I walked into the kitchen to get some water. Out of habit I opened the fridge, but there was nothing in it. By the time I finished my glass of water, I decided to stay in for the rest of the day. I tapped Rogue's name on my holo.

"Yes, Iksen."

"Rogue, would you do me a huge favor? Later, as it gets close to dinner, would you bring me some food to my cabin? I'm going to take the afternoon off."

"Yes, of course. Anything specific?"

"No, whatever you have ready or just whatever you can put together for me."

"Okay, I'll get something good together for you."

"Thank you, you are the best."

"You're welcome, Iksen."

I flopped on the couch and put on another of my favorite chick flicks. I worked hard for the first ten minutes or so to get lost in the movie and clear my mind. But once I did, I relaxed and was sucked in.

I jumped at the sound of a knock on my door. Quietly I made my way to the door.

"Who is it?"

"It's me, open the door," Verruca said with a hint of amusement.

"Open. You know you have access to my cabin. You can let yourself in."

Verruca walked into the room still smirking at me. "So, why did you choose that venue for that fight?"

"I didn't, he did. I ignored his first comment, but he had the balls to tell me he would refuse to let me do it. And so I let him know that he was not going to bully me into anything just because we slept together. He's a great guy, but this old-fashioned idea of the woman must obey the guy is for the birds. You know I am not that person and that is why I am not married." I stopped my ranting and plopped down on the couch.

"Oh, I know how you are. I also know you like it when a man gets possessive over you. You like that he doesn't want you to get hurt," said Verruca, still smirking at me.

"You are having too much fun with this." I shook my head at her. "You might be right, but just because I like the idea of a guy not wanting me hurt doesn't mean I want one to physically keep me from doing something that I want to do.

"I want a guy to care about me and I want to care about them. I just want us to support each other, to be partners, and for it not to be one-sided one way or the other. When a relationship is one-sided in either direction, it doesn't work."

"Yeah, yeah, I have heard it all before. You talk all of this, but you have never found it. So, have you ever thought it might be an excuse to not truly believe in someone? To not truly trust them?"

"Look, I know I have trust issues. I know I always say show me, don't tell me. But trying to keep me from doing things is not the way to show me he cares. I am truly capable of going to the surface and looking around without getting hurt."

"I know you are. But guys want to keep their women safe, so you need to learn how to deal with him better than having a fight with him in front of everyone."

Before I could say anything there was a knock at the door. "Who is it?"

"It's Rogue."

"Open," I instructed the door. Rogue stood there with a big smile on his face holding a box. "What is all this?"

"I brought snacks and something for dinner."

"Thank you, Rogue, I appreciate it."

"I know, Iksen, so you're welcome. "

"You are a sweetheart. " I patted his shoulder.

Rogue gave Verruca a quick wave and headed off. I turned

back toward the kitchen smiling. I placed the box on the counter and began unpacking it.

"I think you have an admirer. He was flirting with you."

"He is barely legal."

"You don't know. You might like being a cougar."

I looked at Verruca flatly. "I am not into the whole cougar thing. I want my men to be old enough to understand my jokes and my music."

Verruca busted out laughing. "Well, what does that say about me? I understand your music and most of your jokes."

"I raised you right, so you don't count."

We both laughed, I poured us both some tea. Rogue really did know how to keep me happy. With tea in hand we went back to the couch and continued bullshitting

We eventually started watching the movie again between our talking. By the time it was over I was snacky. I went back to the kitchen to see what kind of snack there was. I pulled up a dish with some brown paper covering it and peeled back the edge of the paper to find brownies.

"I got something." I waggled my eyebrows at her. "Rogue brought us something special." I walked toward her with the dish behind my back. When I reached her, I pulled the plate from behind me.

"Brownies? Where did he get those?"

"He forced Ryker to show him how to make them. Night had got him to make some the other night for us. Night said that Rogue had been cleaning and organizing the kitchen when he found the chocolate, flour, and other baking supplies."

"He will become every woman's best friend now that he knows how to make brownies. I can't believe we had this stuff, and you didn't find it."

"Yeah, well I wasn't looking for that kind of stuff when I was in the kitchen."

We took two spoons and went to the couch. I put on another movie and we went back to talking.

A loud knock jerked me out of my sleep. I looked round the room. Verruca was on the other end of the couch dead asleep. The knock came louder the second time.

"Who is it?"

"It's Ryo."

"Open."

"How can I help you?"

"I was looking for Verruca. I was wondering if you had seen her?"

I stepped back from the door and gestured wide with my hand to indicate the direction of the couch, where she was still asleep.

"Ahh. Is it okay for me to wake her? We were all supposed to hang out and have dinner together."

"Yeah, go ahead."

Halfway to the couch he stopped, turned back, and looked at me like he wanted to say something.

"What?"

"Are you really okay with what is going on with all of us?"

"Why?"

"Well, it's hard to wrap your mind around for most people. Hell, it's not always easy for me sometimes. So I was wondering if you were okay with it." Ryo watched me as I thought about my answer, but before I could say something, he spoke again. "I want to know because I don't want anyone close to us to cause problems. I don't want anyone to be injecting their ideas or thoughts in the background behind our backs."

"Ryo, I like you and I like Jax. I don't know Sphynx well, but she seems like a good person. But I love Verruca. She is my daughter, and it has always been her and I. Now I don't care who she chooses to sleep with or be in a relationship with unless it is not right for her. If she is happy and safe, I'll have no problem with y'all's arrangement. If she ever becomes unhappy or is hurt because one of you did something stupid, I will rain down fire on that person. And to hell with what anyone thinks about it or me being Iksen. Do we understand each other?"

"Yes, Iksen. Or can I call you Mom yet?" Ryo said with a shit-eating grin.

"Don't push your luck. Let's wait and see what happens."

He laughed and woke up Verruca. "Wake up, my little *wahine o ka po.*"

She jumped and looked around like she was lost.

"What did you call her?"

"My little spirit lover. It's hard to really translate it to English correctly, but for me I use it because we have a great connection. More than just physical. We connect on many levels."

I nodded my head in understanding. I could see he really cared for Verruca.

Then he got her to her feet, and they left. Just before the door closed, Ryo winked at me.

I smiled and turned to the kitchen. I was pouring a glass of tea when I heard the whoosh of the door closing. I shut the fridge door, but before I could turn, large arms snaked around my waist and a low, smoky, gravelly voice spoke softly.

"Hey, I was wondering what happened to you. Are you okay after all that stuff in the dining room?"

I leaned back into Night, enjoying the feeling of him being close. "Oh, yeah, I'm fine. I meant everything I said to him. You don't act like him. You let me do my thing, and if you're worried you just go with me. He keeps trying to control me. That doesn't fly with me."

"I decided when we became a thing it was easier to work with you, not against you," Night finished as we sat down on the couch.

"Honestly, I wasn't looking for relationships. I just want to get us back to Earth. But y'all came along, and neither of you were bad looking, so I decided why not have some distractions from this crazy new world?"

"What do you want from either of us? Are we just something to distract you, or do you like us? I mean, it's been nice, but if you are not looking for something real, I am not going to waste my time." Night looked at me sternly but hopefully.

"Look, I don't know what I want. We are stuck on a spaceship a hundred years past the last time we knew anything. The only thing I know is I want us to get back to Earth and create a safe place for myself and Verruca. It's the only reason I accepted the role of Iksen. For now, I would like to take things as they go. Which mean you and Kilian will have to get along. I cannot have you two fighting over me while I am trying to lead these people. We already have two trying to cause problems."

"What do you mean we have two causing problems? What did you find?"

"No one knows anything about what kind of security we have on this ship. I'm not going to tell you what I found or how I found it, and Vega is under strict orders. So don't think you will get it from him. Let just say we need to keep an eye on Lita and Ryker."

"I wouldn't tell anyone what our security is. You can trust me. I will keep it to myself."

"I know you would, but I don't want you to have to lie. I also don't want you to just be on edge about things. I need you to be my relaxation. My escape. Just know we have more security than anyone knows."

Without another word he pulled me into his lap and dropped the whole subject. I loved that he knew what I needed and when I needed it. I told the TV to play another movie. We spent the rest of the night together.

CHAPTER FIFTEEN: CAN'T CATCH A BREAK

I woke to banging on my door. Stumbling to the door, I yelled, "Who is it?"

"Kilian."

"Open." The door slid back. "What do you want at this hour? I don't have time to fight again. I need food, coffee, and I have a workout date with Ronan before we get started for the day."

"I just wanted to talk about the things that were said yesterday."

Before he could continue, Night walked out from the bedroom.

Kilian just stood there looking dumbfounded.

"Morning," Night said and walked over to kiss my forehead before pouring himself a glass of tea.

"What is he doing here? Why didn't you tell me you were seeing him too?"

I took a deep breath and looked at him. "First off, I am grown, and I can have anyone I want in my cabin. Second, I did, but I don't have to explain myself to you. Third, I like both of you, and if you want to continue to be with me, you are going to have to learn you cannot control me. You are also going to have to learn to get along with Night, because I am not giving him up and I don't want to give you up. So, deal?"

"Are you okay with this?" Kilian asked Night.

"I am not sure yet, but I know I can't force her into

anything, and when you try, she does the exact opposite. I want to be with her if she will have me, and I am willing to deal with you to do that."

Kilian just stood there for several long minutes without saying a word.

I had things to do, so I decided that I was going to leave them to work it out. I went to my room and got dressed.

"I have a workout to get to. You two play nice." I kissed both of them bye and headed off for my workout.

I got to the workout room and Ronan was waiting for me.

"Go easy on me. It has been many years since I did any major workouts. I damn sure haven't taken any falls in many years."

He laughed and waved me over to some open space on the far side of the room. He started me off with an aikido kata. We ran through it several times, which had my calves burning. Then we moved into some running in place to really get the blood flowing. Once I was out of breath and thought I was dying, he moved me into some stretching and groundwork. By the time we were done, I had been worked hard, but it felt good.

I was on my way back to my cabin for a shower when I saw Lita talking to someone in the common area. I paused and watched. The man turned to the side, and I saw it was Kilian. Lita appeared to be laying it on thick when she reached over and placed her hand on Kilian's forearm.

That bitch, she really thinks she can undermine me. I strolled over to Kilian, stepping directly in front of her, kissed Kilian, and then continued to my cabin. I heard Kilian tell her that he had to go but that it was nice talking to her.

I had just walked into the cabin when Kilian stepped in behind me.

"So did you and Night play nice while I was working out?"

"Ha, ha, we really didn't talk much. He left shortly after

you did. I then went to clean up. I was coming back from breakfast when I ran into Lita. She was consoling me for you being so mean to me."

"Oh, I bet she was."

"What's that supposed to mean?"

I looked at him flatly.

"What?"

I rolled my eyes. "I have been keeping my eye on her. I don't trust her. I think she is angling to try and take over as leader, along with her lackey Ryker."

"Really? I don't see those two together. She is too hot for him. Besides, she is well-educated, and he is just a cook."

"First, he is a chef. He went to school to become one. Second, he had a well-known restaurant at one time in Dallas. Besides, she doesn't need him to have brains to lead him around by his dick. That is where those hot looks come in." I waggled my eyebrows at him.

"I guess. I don't know how that would work. It wouldn't work on me."

Trying hard not to laugh in his face. "Really, you don't think a women can lead you around by your dick?"

"No. I have more will power than that."

"Well, you're not a follower, and he is." I was still stifling a laugh. "He needs someone stronger than him to follow, and it doesn't hurt that she is hot. I also bet she keeps promising him more—if you get my drift—if he just helps her become leader."

I left him sitting on the chair in the kitchen and headed for the bathroom. I turned on the hot water, stripped off my clothes, then stepped under the water. I had just finished soaping my body when I felt hands slink around my waist. I turned in his arms and wrapped mine around his neck. His eyes were molten sapphires of desire as he took in my body. I stretched up placing my lips on his. I slid my hands over his wet, slick shoulder, feeling his muscles bunch and flex as he moved. He took the scrubby from me and began to wash my body. He turned me making sure to get every inch. He took his time when soaping my breasts, even giving my nipples a few pinches. He smiled wide at the soft, panting moans he elicited from me. He slid a soapy hand down, but instead of delving in finding my clit, he just teased me. Coming close to touching it but never actually doing it. Believe it or not it was fucking hot. The anticipation was driving me wild. I was ready to take what I wanted when he stopped.

He reached to place the scrubby on the shelf. My hand shot out and took it from him. It was my turn to torture him. I ran it across his chest and when he didn't stop me I continued. I made sure to get every inch of his body leaving the best for last. I raised myself from cleaning his legs, letting my chest graze his cock, stomach, and chest as I came to my full height. I placed the scrubby on the shelf then returned my soapy hands to his cock. I grabbed his shaft, twisting and sliding a hand up and down. With the other hand I rolled his balls. He sucked in a sharp breath and slammed a hand on to each wall bracing himself. His eyes closed and a low steady groan emanated from him. I continued my assault on his cock as I watched every expression on his face. It was shortly after the groans turned into grunts that his cock began to throb in my hand.

He grabbed my hands, stilling them and then slowly pulled them away from him. Once my hands were nowhere near his cock. He closed his eyes and took several deep breaths. I smiled at the power I was exerting over him in this moment. Eyes still closed he pushed us under the water to rinse the soap off our bodies. Not wanting to give up the power I dropped to my knees and sucked his cock down hard.

"Fuck," he snarled and wrapped his hands in my hair.

I slid back and rolled my tongue around his broad head

making him groan. Slowly making my way back down his shaft I messaged the underside with my tongue until my lips reached the base. He tightened his grip and pushed my head down on his cock forcing me to open my throat to him. When his crown pushed into my throat he let out a long groan. Kilian released his grip slightly then pushed my head down again.

I swallowed several times, making him roughly pull my mouth from him. Jerking me to my feet, he slid his hands down to my ass and picked me up.

He made low gravelly moans of pleasure as he backed me against the wall. He hungrily moved his mouth down my neck until he reached the crook of it. He bit down hard and I arched into him as a shot of pleasure ran throughout me. He chuckled softly as he lifted me, so he could slide me down onto his cock. My head fell back as I let out a long, deep moan. Kilian groaned with me as his head dropped to my shoulder and he continued until he was completely sheathed.

After a few seconds, he slid out slowly and back in hard. He repeated the move over and over. The slowness of him pulling out was the sweatiest of tortures, but the hard thrust was exactly what I wanted.

"I need more," I rasped.

"You will get what I give you." He growled.

I rocked my hips showing him what I needed. Yet he just held me in place and kept doing what he was doing. I groaned, letting him know I was displeased with that answer, but he just kept on. I felt his cock throb inside me just before he slid out of me and dropped me to my feet. I was about to protest when he spun me around, placing my hands on the glass door. He pulled my ass out and dropped to his knees.

I gasped as his tongue slid through my folds finding my clit. He flicked it, sucked it, and nibbled on it. Heat spread through me as it caused that delicious liquid fire to pool deep in my center. My head fell between my arms as I panted out deep moans. He slid his tongue back circling my entrance before he plunged it into me. At the same time he sank two fingers into my ass. A gasping moan escaped me as his fingers and tongue moved in and out. He pulled his tongue back, circled my clit again and then spread it back inside me. I was groaning and panting in pleasure as he made his way back to my clit. He was alternating between sucking and nibbling when my leg began to quiver from the overwhelming sensations spreading throughout me.

Just when I though he was going to push me over the edge he stopped. He stood up and pushed his cock into my ass. I sucked in a raspy breath and my arms collapsed, leaving me pressed against the glass door. My nipples hardened at the touch of coolness from the glass.

Kilian leaned over and grunted. "Who's in control now?"

Smart ass, I thought. Opening my mouth to retort something, I was cut off by him placing a finger on my clit. All thoughts melted away. Once he knew I was lost in the sensations he removed his finger and began fucking me hard. My moans tuned to screams as he sank into my ass over and over. He had pushed me to the edge. I was holding on by a fingernail when he stopped. Now I really was going to say something but he spun me around and hoisted me up, slamming home.

Kilian grunted when my inner walls clamped down on his cock. I growled from the zaps of pleasure that shot through me, yet my orgasm still eluded me. I writhed against him trying to speed things up. I reached up and grabbed the top of the glass door for leverage. Then I picked up the pace, finally getting the friction I needed. Kilian grunted several times. He then took over and he was slamming his body into mine. The warm pool was now fire spreading throughout my body, pushing me closer to falling over the edge into ecstasy.

Soft whimpers escaped me as I tried to push myself over that threshold. Kilian knew I was chasing my orgasm which he drank in for several long minutes before he slid a hand down to my clit.

"Yes, baby, give me what I want. Come for me," Kilian growled in demand.

He made only a few circles, and I exploded.

"Yes, come all over my dick." He continued to make circles giving me no reprieve from the pleasure spreading through me. "Give me all of it. I want every last drop of your pleasure."

Not being able to take any more, I stilled his hand and dropped my head to his shoulder. The sensation felt like I had fallen off a cliff into an ocean of pure ecstasy. But the high didn't last long enough. I was already coming down when I opened my eyes to look at Kilian. But movement caught my attention. Night was standing in the doorway watching.

Kilian was still moving in and out of me as I watched Night over my shoulder. After a few more minutes Night pulled his shirt over his head. He kicked off his boots and dropped his pants. Kilian jumped at the click of the shower door opening.

"What are you doing?"

"Joining," Night said in a low husky tone.

Neither said another word. Kilian let me go and I slid down the wall to my feet. Night grabbed me by the nape and pulled me into a hard punishing kiss. Kilian growled, the sound a mix of arousal and jealousy, which caused that fire in my core to reignite. Kilian stepped toward me running his hands up my backbone to my shoulders. He gripped the top of my shoulders and forced me to bend forward.

"Open your mouth," Kilian demanded.

I ignored his demands, which earned me a slap to the left ass cheek. He issued the command again and again I ignored him. To my astonishment Night made the next move and pinched my nose, making me gasp to catch my breath. As soon as my mouth opened, Night slid his cock in. Kilian slid his hard, thick cock into my hot swollen center. I moaned around Night's cock, and he tightened his hands in my hair. I don't know if it was my moans or the sight of my mouth on Night's cock but Kilian fucked me hard. The sensations of his thrusts was making my inner walls quiver and my second orgasm begin to build.

Night was guiding my mouth up and down on his cock. I decided he was not moaning enough, so I sucked him down hard. The head of his dick was pushing at the back of my throat. I began swallowing causing my throat to constrict around the head of his cock.

Night let out a low gravelly, "Oh my god."

I continued my actions for several minutes when I felt his cock throb. Night quickly pulled my mouth off his cock with a pop. Kilian stood me up and spun me around. Night gripped my hips tightly, pulling me backward onto his cock. Kilian then pushed my head down, pressing my lips to the tip of his dick. I ran my tongue around the head before sucking him down hard. I slowly slid my mouth back to where my lips barely touched the tip. Then I sucked him down again.

"Son of a bitch," Kilian growled out and gripped my head tight.

I repeated this sequence several more times, causing Kilian to curse loudly. Night moved in and out of me at a steady pace causing tiny zings of delight to shoot throughout my body. He stepped to the right, causing the head of his cock to slide against my left inner walls. The new friction flooded my body with delicious new sensations, causing my inner walls to quiver. I let out a long moan as the building blaze of my orgasm intensified.

Kilian's cock throbbed in my mouth. I knew he was close, so I teased him some more by making a wave motion with my tongue. He grunted and forced his cock all the way into my mouth causing me to gag on it. He let me catch my breath, then forced his cock back down my throat again. He did this several times before he pulled my mouth to his. He kissed me hard as he growled his pleasure into my mouth.

While I was distracted by Kilian, Night pulled out of me and pressed the head of his cock to my ass. He pushed in slightly, which caused me to jerk and bite down on Kilian's lower lip. He pushed in a little more. I dug my nails into Kilian's chest from the sting of pleasure and pain.

Night pushed in completely and a deep loud moan raced out of me from the pleasure. He pulled out slowly then pushed back in. He continued his pace while Kilian kissed me hungrily. Kilian's hands slid down my shoulders to find my nipples. He rolled my nipples between his fingers hard, sending sharp sparks of pleasure shooting to my clit. The flames of my orgasm flared to full burn. Feeling my body quiver in rapture Night knew I wouldn't last much longer, He lifted me up. Kilian stepped forward catching my legs in the bend of my knees.

Kilian pushed into me, and I screamed out in pleasure. I had never been so full in my life. I was panting from the overwhelming sensations sparking each nerve in my body into overdrive, engulfing my mind and body. The guys found a perfect rhythm that was pushing me further to the edge. I had an arm wrapped around each of their necks, but my head was bowed between them as deep moans escaped me. They fucked me hard in this position until I felt each of their cocks jerk and spasm in me.

I knew they were close, and I was about to slide my own hand down to my clit when Night beat me to it. He made slow circles around it at first then he pinched it. I screamed.

"Night."

My orgasm slammed into me, setting every inch of my

body alight with the purest gratification I had ever felt. Fireworks burst behind my eyelids and left me quaking in their arms. My mind still in a dark haze, I slightly registered that they both went stiff under me. With one last hard thrust they growled out their release as their orgasms hit them hard. Night stumbled back into the wall and Kilian braced himself with one arm as they continued to spill themselves into me.

Kilian's head fell to my chest and Night's to my shoulder. They held me there for a few more minutes regaining their composure before they pulled out and slid me to my feet. My legs were weak and wobbly, so I leaned back into Night as Kilian pressed into us. I was positive being pressed between them was the only reason I was still in an upright position.

I had almost fallen asleep between them when Kilian pulled me forward under the water. Night stepped forward and proceeded to wash me as I clung to Kilian for support. Once I was clean Night scooped me into his arms. Kilian turned off the water, grabbed a towel, and dried us off. Then Night picked me back up and took me to the bed. He laid me down, and they both crawled in with me.

Chapter Sixteen: Squashing Drama

I wasn't sure what time it was when I heard Vega calling me. "Ms. Atlantis, you need to hear this."

I slid out of bed, grabbed a towel from the floor wrapped it around me, and went to the living room. "What do I need to hear, Vega?"

"Lita. She is in the dining room trying to gather enough people to listen to her talk about how you can't lead them."

"Show me."

Vega pulled up a live feed from the dining room where Lita was standing on the bench seat of the front table talking about my fight with Kilian. She looked smug standing up there running her mouth.

"My fellow survivors, please join me in a discussion about our leadership. I don't believe that Atlantis has our best interest at heart. She is too worried about who she is sleeping with instead of the fact that our ship is falling apart around us. She is taking too long to decide where to land us, and by the time she decides we may not be able to land this ship." Lita's tone was innocent and caring.

Several people were looking around at each other with questioning looks on their faces. When Lita saw the looks and heard the whispers, she began speaking again. I continued to listen to her as I went to get dressed, and then I completely planned to interrupt her little speech.

"This ship has more issues than she can keep fixed. She doesn't know that the ship's AI has not told her about the engine issues. I have a friend that knows computers well and has looked throughout the systems, and he has found issues all throughout our ship. If I was in control, I would put us on the ground immediately so that way we're not stuck in this tin can of a ship."

I walked in the door of the dining room clapping just as she finished talking. I walked up and stepped up on the bench with her, still clapping. Then I turned to the people who had gathered.

"Bravo, she gave a great speech. Don't y'all think? She is convincing. I can see why she was a good lawyer. But despite her being convincing she is also a liar. Not one piece of that info is true."

"What do you mean it's not true? I would never lie to my fellow survivors."

"Except the information that Ryker — I am assuming that is your friend" — I used air quotes — "found on the system is all fake. I knew someone had been trying to hack into the system, so I had Vega set up false info so that I could catch them. Well done on playing yourself."

"Well, what about the gravity generator going out?" Lita said in a rush, trying to deflect the focus off her lies.

"Oh, well, should I tell them or you?"

"Tell them what? I had nothing to do with that."

"Oh, I am pretty sure that you and Ryker did something to the generator to cause it to stop."

"We had nothing to do with that. I was asleep and I don't know what Ryker was doing," Lita said in a hoity, whiney voice. She sounded like a petulant child.

"I think it's time for you to go do the jobs you have been assigned and stop trying to cause unrest and discord between everyone."

She stared at me side eyed, and then turned with a huff and stomped out of the dining room.

"Now, for everyone else, I am sorry that I had a personal

argument in front of y'all, but I had to say what I did when I did for him to understand me. I'll try hard from now on not to let my temper get the best of me. Have a good rest of your day and see y'all around the ship."

I turned toward the kitchen to get food. I walked into the kitchen to find Rogue by himself.

"Hi, Iksen. What can I get you?"

"Hello, Rogue. I was wondering if you could help me get out enough supplies to make dinner in my cabin tonight. Also, a sandwich for now would be good."

"Sure, let me make your sandwich first. We have some left-over chicken from last night. I can make some chicken salad."

"That sounds good. Thank you. You're really catching on to this whole cooking thing."

"Thank you, Iksen. Vox has been a great teacher, and Ryker as well."

"Well, I'm glad you're enjoying it."

While Rogue worked on the chicken salad, I went to the freezer to see what kind of meat I wanted to make for tonight. We had all kinds of meat in here, almost anything you could think of. I was surprised that it had survived so long. I guessed their experimental preservation system worked.

I looked through the supplies I was torn between blackened salmon and chicken fried steak. With the salmon I could add some squash, and with the steak I could do mashed potatoes and gravy. I leaned out the freezer door.

"Rogue, do we have oil? Like enough that I could fry something in?"

"Yeah, we have several large bottles in the cabinet. But we also have a five-gallon drum that I found in that back storage room over there," he said and turned to point toward the alcove with the brooms.

"What, there is a storage room back there?"

"Yeah." He waved his hand for me to follow him. "Come

on. I'll show you."

I followed him to the alcove. He then pushed on the side, and a door swung open. I followed him in, and in the room was extra dry ingredients for cooking. There were bags of flour, cornmeal, oats, rice, beans, and sugar. On the shelves were jars of chocolate powder, powdered sugar, and several jars of powdered fruit flavors. There were also large jars of different nuts. I picked up a jar of almonds to examine them. It had a strange seal around the jar.

"They all have that seal. I guess it is what has helped them survive all this time."

I turned the jar in my hand. It had a large white plastic band that wrapped around where the lid met the body of the jar. In the front was a square with a small red button. I pushed it, and there was a hiss and a pop. The white band loosened and when I pulled it up there was membrane that came loose with it.

"Once the white band is positioned, you push the red button, and the membrane is sucked tight around the lid of the jar. And they are reusable," Rogue said excitedly as he showed me how it worked.

I smiled at him, nodding my head to let him know I was following. When he was done, I walked over to some large five-gallon drums in the far corner. One said *canola oil*. One was empty, I assumed so that old oil could go into it. The third said *olive oil*.

"Whoever set this kitchen up was trying to make sure we had everything we needed to cook."

"I know, it is crazy how well stocked it is. I'm just glad it is, so we're not really missing out on anything. I am not sure how long I could have gone without chocolate." He laughed.

"Me either." I smiled and patted him on the shoulder.

I walked out to the main kitchen, and Rogue walked back to the table. I looked around trying to decide what I needed for dinner tonight. I saw a few of those mesh bag things and pulled them off the shelf. I then began collecting the pots and pans I would need to cook and placed them in one bag. I then decided to go with chicken fried steak, so I gathered all the necessary supplies for that plus the potatoes. That took up the other two bags I had pulled down. By that time Rogue had finished the chicken salad and had made us sandwiches, I had everything ready to go back to my cabin.

We had just sat down to eat when Verruca came in.

"Mom, we need to talk."

"Okay, what's the problem?"

"No, we need to talk alone."

"I'll leave, and you can have the kitchen." Rogue picked up his plate and went out to the dining room.

Verruca watched him as he left the kitchen and then turned back to me looking a little urgent.

"Lita's little stunt this morning has caused a few issues. There are several of the newer awakees that are saying that you don't care about them. That you are only trying to save yourself and me. They think someone like Lita who was a lawyer should be in charge. They are saying this to anyone who will listen to try and get them to agree that Lita should be in charge."

"Okay, well I know how to stop it. We are going to have to call an emergency council meeting. Then we're going to have to show everyone what the Earth is like right now and why I am looking for the right spot."

"You want to tell them about the Earth now? I thought you were going to wait until we had more. Until we knew where we were going to choose to land."

"I was, but now we need people to know exactly what we're seeing, because if not, Lita will gain traction, and then we will have a coup on our hands."

"I still don't like it. I don't want people to be freaked out over any of this. It will add additional stress to an already stressful situation."

"I know, but if everyone knows the truth then she doesn't have a leg to stand on. Vega, can you let the council know we're going to meet in an hour on the bridge?"

"Yes, Ms. Atlantis."

"You cannot say anything to Sphynx. She is not part of the council, and she will hear everything with the rest. But since you are here, can you help me carry this to my cabin? I am going to make dinner tonight for Night and Kilian. I am making them play nice together, so I thought the least I could do is make them dinner."

Verruca laughed and shook her head as she picked up one of the mesh bags. I grabbed the other two, and we headed off for my cabin.

Once we'd put the food in my cabin, we made our way to the bridge. We talked about this new life we'd found ourselves in.

"So how is it going with your little foursome? Quartet?"

"Our group is good. We are figuring out the dynamics. You know . . . what everyone's roles are, how we fit all four of us into everyday life. There's been a few bumps, but we're figuring it all out."

"Are you happy with the arrangement?"

"Yeah, at least for now. Really, it's all so new I am just trying to enjoy the difference instead of worrying about things. I mean, why create issues if there aren't any?"

"You're right. That just makes everyone miserable. I just want you to be happy and protect yourself but your heart too. If anything makes you feel like you're not important or less than them, you better stand up for yourself and tell them."

"Seriously, when have I never stood up for myself?"

"I know, but it's different when you care about someone. You don't want to hurt them, so you keep hoping things will just magically change. But they never do until either it's too late or someone says something."

"What about you will Kilian and Night?"

"Oh, I'm more likely to be the bully in that situation. They won't run over me no matter how much I care for them."

She laughed. "You're probably right."

"Like I said, I just want you to be safe and happy."

"You, too. Besides if this isn't the world to try new things in, I don't know what world would be."

"Smart ass."

We both started laughing. We were still laughing and teasing each other when we stepped onto the bridge. To my surprise, when we walked in, we saw several council members already there. Night, Kilian, Cash, Jax, Ryo and Ronan were all sitting and talking. Verruca made a beeline to Ryo and I sat in the chair between Night and Kilian. I listened as everyone continued talking. After about another ten minutes the rest of the members began straggling in. Juniper and Onyx came in chatting away, but as soon as Juniper saw Cash, she diverted herself to him for a quick hello. Savinka and Zahirah made their way in. Savinka went to stand with Ronan. They both waved Zahirah over to join them. Now that everyone was present, I stood up.

"Hello, everyone. We have some things to discuss. I'm sure most of you guys have heard about Lita's little stunt in the dining room this morning. I put a stop to it at that moment, but there have been some mutterings from some of the newer awakees that she should be in charge."

"That's bullshit," Jax exclaimed.

"I agree, you have done nothing but put us first," Juniper said.

"I know, but the reality is that she could cause a lot of problems with the few that are showing her support. All it takes is for the few who don't agree to cause chaos, and we could be in serious trouble in space."

"Miss Atlantis, we have incoming asteroids," Vega interrupted me.

"Explain." My tone went from calm to panicked.

Vega appeared in front of us. "I had no warnings of asteroids coming in our direction. I monitor all activity as far out as my sensors will allow. Then a data stream came in from the satellite. It showed an asteroid storm heading our way."

"Can we avoid them by changing our trajectory?"

"I have set the ship to evasive maneuvers, but I'm not sure if that will allow us to miss it completely. The asteroids seem to be made of some kind of metallic alloy. The satellite did not pass on much info about them."

"So, what does that mean?"

"Depending on their size, they could do severe damage to the ship."

"What do we need to do to prepare for this storm?"

"Get everyone to one common area. Keep them away from outside walls or windows. I will turn the ship with the exhaust ports facing the incoming storm. Then I will do my best to avoid what I can, but the ship does not move fast."

"Yes, I know. What else do we need to do to prepare?"

"Secure everything that we don't want damaged."

"Okay."

"*Chingoa!*" I took a deep breath. "Okay, Jax, Kilian, Savinka, and Zahirah, y'all find two more guys and take the embryo containers out of the lab and move them to an upper deck that has power to plug them back in. Then find something to secure the lids."

"I am not sure that they can be moved. I believe they are hard wired to their power supplies," Savinka said.

"Okay, y'all go see what can be done. We cannot lose all those embryos. Also find a way to secure the seed cabinet ,even if that means screwing one of the metal lab tables over the drawers."

"We understand and we will do everything we can," Jax assured me. Kilian gave me a kiss, and they all left the bridge. "Ronan, Cash, and Juniper, go to the cargo bays. Take whoever you can find to help and move all our drones, weapons, and anything else to a safe place."

They all got up and headed out. I looked at the rest of the group trying to decide what would be best for them to do. "Vega, can you make a ship-wide announcement that all people aboard need to meet in the dining room?"

"Yes, Ms. Atlantis."

"Onyx, can you go see which common area would be the best for everyone to ride out the storm in? Once you find it, send everyone a message."

"Yes, Iksen," Onyx answered with a nod of her head.

"Night and Ryo, can y'all work from the bridge?"

"Yes," they answered.

"Vega, give them manual control access. If you feel like you need to take over, do it. Get us out of the storm as safely as you can."

Verruca and I headed for the dining room to meet the group. The elevator ride and the walk were quiet and tense. I was running through what to say in my mind so that I wouldn't make everyone panic. As we walked in, the group turned to stare at us. The stares followed us until we made it to the front tables. When I reached the front, I looked over the group, and of course there was no Lita or Ryker. I leaned over and whispered to Verruca that I didn't see them.

She began typing on her holo texting Vega to look for them.

"I need everyone to listen to what I am about to say and not to panic. We are well underway to try and protect us and the ship from as much damage as possible." Low mumbles broke out in the crowd. "An asteroid storm is coming our way. Vega has been monitoring as far out as he can, but somehow this storm didn't show up on his sensors until now. We now have about forty-five minutes before the storm is upon us. Vega is maneuvering us out of the way as quickly as possible, but the reality is we don't move as fast as we would like. Believe me, I have teams working to secure everything we can. Right now, I need everyone in this room to stay here until Onyx contacts us with a place to ride out the storm."

The crowd was looking at each other and mumbling. I let them talk as we waited for Onyx to contact me. I told Verruca to stay and watch the group and I stepped into the doorway of the kitchen. I lifted my communicator to my mouth and called for Vega.

"Vega, I need you to be ready to seal off any decks that have hull damage or any kind of air leak. Next, I need all our cameras to be recording every inch of this ship."

"I can seal any deck that needs it. The cameras have always been running since people have been awake."

"Thank you."

CHAPTER SEVENTEEN: SPACE IS OUT TO GET US

L ita and Ryker not being here meant they could be up to something. That knowledge put me on higher alert than the asteroid storm. I looked over the group making sure no one was beginning to panic before I returned to my black holo.

"Vega, do we have equipment to fix hull breaches if necessary?"

"We do have some supplies to patch hull breeches, but we only have four AGSs."

"AGSs?"

"Anti-Gravity Suits or AGSs."

"Gotcha. Okay, so we will be able to fix some of the damage. That is good."

I could hear the group getting a little louder. "Just keep me informed of all news of the ship, even the smallest details. Just send it to my communicator."

"Yes, Ms. Atlantis."

I returned to the group just in time to see Onyx walking in. She came straight to me.

"It looks like the best place to ride out this storm is the blue deck common area. When we get there we will need to move all the furniture into one of the empty cabins."

"Let's go, everyone, and get ready to ride out this storm."

Everyone slowly nodded and began moving toward the exit. I instructed Onyx to lead the group to the blue deck and get them started. I wanted to check a few things before I got there. I held Verruca back with me. Lifting my communicator to my mouth, again I called to Vega.

"Vega, can you tell me where Lita and Ryker are?"

"Not at the moment but I will scan the ship to find them."

"Thank you. Can you announce that the blue deck common area is where we will ride out the storm? One last thing. Can you up grade Verruca's security clearance to the same as mine?"

"Yes. Ms. Verruca, how would you like to access the system?"

"What do you mean?"

"Would you like fingerprint scan, retinal scan, password, or any combination of?"

"Oh, I guess a retinal scan for high security items and a password for mundane items."

"Agreed, please look at your communicator. I will scan your eyes and then please speak your password."

Verruca did as she was instructed and then quietly spoke, "Lyra."

It took a few seconds then Vega confirmed that everything was set up.

She checked a few things to make sure it was working and then we headed for the blue deck.

We rode the elevator in silence except for my tapping toes. I was pissed that Lita and Ryker were nowhere to be found so far, and anxious about this storm. Verruca took my hand squeezing it reassuringly. I smiled at her, squeezing her hand back.

When we arrived, all the furniture had been moved and everyone was sitting on the floor just talking. Verruca and I sat down with Onyx and Juniper. Verruca picked up with their conversation while I just watched and listened to everyone. I wanted to make sure everyone was okay. As I studied the group, I saw that everyone was more scattered than was probably safe.

I came to my knees. "Guys, let move against the walls and huddle up. Let's use each other to hold on to and keep from being tossed around too much."

Everyone began moving around grouping up against the walls, then the chatter broke when Vega announced how far away the storm was.

I looked at my communicator to see the countdown that Vega had started. We had roughly fifteen minutes until the asteroid storm hit us. I was starting to worry about where the rest of the council was. I waited a few minutes longer before I really got nervous. The countdown now said we had seven minutes. I called each group and told them to come on regardless of what they had gotten done.

I sighed in relief when they began making their way in. They joined us at the front of the group. Kilian took a seat on my right and began to fill me in on what tasks they had been able to complete and I was relieved they were able to finish everything. They had tied the large drone down the best they could and moved all the crates out of that bay so they wouldn't damage it. They had moved the small drones to one of the empty cabins.

My communicator began to vibrate. Our time had run out. I rose to my knees.

"Listen, the storm should be hitting us any minute." I was interrupted by a large shudder that spread across the ship. "Okay, I guess it's here. Hold on to each other. It should pass quickly."

I sat back leaning into Kilian. I looked over to Verruca, Sphynx, and Jax huddled together.

"Mom, where are Night and Ryo?"

"They are on the bridge. They are our pilots. I had them stay on the bridge just in case we need them to get us out of the middle of this storm."

I looked over the room. People were huddling together, holding on to each other with a little more fear in their eyes than a few minutes ago. As bad as this current situation was, it was nice to see that people had found something as normal as human connection in our current crazy world.

Another shudder rocked the ship. Then we all began grasping for something — anything that would hold us steady. The ship swayed to the right and then to the left. It repeated its movements several times over what seemed like forever but really was only a few minutes. We had all relaxed slightly, hoping the worst was over when the ship swayed to the right again and kept going. We did a complete roll, and everyone fell to the ceiling and then back to the floor. Banged up and head pounding I lay for a minute sprawled out like a starfish. I opened my eyes slowly to see Kilian looking over at me. He was also dripping blood on me from a small cut on his forehead. I sat up slowly with his help, ignoring my head pain.

I looked for Verruca first. She was okay, but Sphynx was knocked out. I looked at Kilian gingerly touching his head wound. We were leveled out, but before I could get to my feet, Vega spoke.

"We are out of the storm with min—" His words broke off at the sound of an alarm.

"Vega, speak to me," I commanded.

"We have two breeches on the black deck. One is a small hole in the wall of the drone bay. The other is larger. It will be dangerous to fix."

"And what is the third alarm?"

"It is alerting me that the oxygen levels on that deck are very low."

I felt my communicator vibrate just before he finished his sentence. I looked down to see a message from Vega. I opened it.

The third alarm is informing me that there is an oxygen scrubber that has gone down on the blue deck. I will seal the black deck until we can get someone to fix the hull breeches. This will keep the oxygen levels steady until the scrubber is fixed.

I typed a message and sent it to Vega.

Understood. Please have the video from the workroom of the blue deck waiting for me on the bridge. Do not let anyone else onto the bridge after the guys leave until I give you the go ahead. Don't say anything to Night or Ryo. I will let the council know when I know more.

"Vega, please silence the alarms." The sound cut out mid wail. "Anyone here know how to weld?"

Slowly, a hand raised into the air. The hand belonged to Clover. "My dad and brothers are welders. I used to weld with them in high school."

"Perfect, you will go with the guys to fix hull breeches."

"Yes, Iksen," Clover said and nodded her head.

I looked around. There were several people knocked out, several more with bleeding wounds, and everyone had bruises.

"Okay, Jax, go with Clover and get the repairs started. Call Night and Ryo if y'all need help. Savinka, we need to do some wound checks. Juniper, Onyx, and Shanti, get whatever y'all need to doctor the injured people. Ronan, take the rest of the security team and check for damage throughout the ship. Everyone else go check on your cabins. Make sure the sensors didn't miss any damage. Let me know if you need anything."

Everyone began to clear from our stronghold, spreading out in all directions. I grabbed Verruca by the hand.

"Leave Sphynx in the hands of the medical people and come with me. We need to do some things." I dragged her by the hand to the elevator. Every time she tried to ask what was going on I shook my head. The lift door opened, and I dragged her in and pushed the button for the bridge.

"What is going on? My girlfriend is hurt." Verruca said, irritated with me for dragging her from Sphynx's side.

"Lita and Ryker never showed up. Then during all those alarms, Vega sent me a text telling me that the blue deck oxygen scrubber is not working."

"Wait, what does that mean?"

"He said things will be fine as long as the black deck stays sealed until the breeches are fixed."

"So, you think Lita and Ryker did something to it?"

"I do. They damaged the gravity generator."

We walked on to the bridge to find Night and Ryo still there. They were standing over a control panel scrolling through screens.

"What's the damage?" I called out as we approached them.

"We are pretty banged up. But I'm only seeing the two holes on the black deck. Then we had another alarm saying there is an oxygen scrubber not working on the blue deck," Ryo answered.

"So not really anything different from what Vega informed me of. Could I get you guys to go look at that scrubber and see what needs to be done to fix it?"

"Yeah, no problem." Night then looked up at me for the first time. His eyes went wide and he moved to me quickly reaching for the bruise on my forehead just above my temple.

I winced at the thought of him touching it and grabbed his hand. "I'm good. I'll go get checked as soon as I know the ship is safe."

"Yes you will, even if I have to throw you over my shoulder and carry you to get checked out."

I nodded my head and kissed him. "Ryo, hun. Sphynx was knocked out. Savinka, Vashanti, and Onyx are taking care of her and will message us when she awakes."

"Oh my god. Are you okay? Is Jax okay?" Ryo asked, as he turned her head side to side and then slid his hands down her arms and ribs. almost like he was patting her down before he hand cuffed her.

"I'm fine and Jax is fine. We are a little shaken up, but that's it. Tomorrow might be a different story."

Ryo kissed Verruca, then left the bridge with Night.

Once the guys had left, I had Vega set privacy mode again. Then I immediately launched into what I knew.

"Vega didn't have much info on that faulty oxygen scrubber, so I had him pull the video from the blue deck electrical room. We are going to review it right now."

I clicked *play* on the video of the electrical room. I started it an hour before the storm and ran it until the storm was over. All we found was the spark of wiring shorting out. So, I went back another hour, then another, and then another before I found someone entering the workroom. This time the person only covered their head with a towel. It wasn't enough to disguise his build from me. It was Ryker. No doubt Lita put him up to it. I pulled up the other video from when the gravity generator went out.

"So, they are trying to sabotage the ship," said Verruca.

"Kind of. They haven't really broken anything important or that couldn't be fixed. Lita has chosen things that had a good chance of scaring people but are not important enough to put us at risk. She wants hysteria so that she can swoop in and save the day, but I beat her to it the last time. I'll beat her to it again this time. That is why they tried to hack the system."

"So, they are a bigger problem than you have let on about. Why?"

"I wanted to wait until I was sure, but then she gave them away the other day in that speech. I knew someone had tried to hack into Vega but wasn't sure who. After her speech and now this, it's time to share my theories with the council. As for as the rest of the awakees, I am going to just share the info about Earth."

"It's risky, but I think you're right. If we have nothing to hide, then she will not have any leverage."

"They are not going to have leverage anyway, because I am having them arrested."

"Wait, you were serious about all that?"

"Yes, because of people like them. If we're going to hold everyone together, then we must show them we're serious about the laws we set into place. Once we hit the ground, I don't care what everyone does. I'm willing to give anyone who wants to set out on their own some supplies to do so, but until then they must be controlled. Otherwise, we may never get to the ground or anywhere else."

Verruca sighed heavily and stared out the main window. After a few seconds she turned back to me. "Okay, you might be right. I'll follow your lead, but if you start to get tyrannical, I will overthrow you."

We both laughed. Then we got to work collecting reports from everyone.

Chapter Eighteen: Recovering from Another Road Bump

It took about thirty minutes to begin hearing back from everyone. Ronan and his team had found a crack on the green deck. He'd already informed Clover, and it was up next for repairs. After speaking with several groups of awakees, we learned they'd only found wrecked cabins. Things flung everywhere, broken furniture, and hydroponics fluid drenching the walls and floor. At least the ship structural damage was minimal, though.

"Onyx, can you give me an update on everyone?"

"Yes, we have treated everyone. Three required stiches but Vashanti's husband was able to take care of that. We still have one person out, but we're monitoring him. As for us, Shanti and I are banged up. Juniper has a bump on her head and Savinka has a hurt hand. Nothing that can't heal easy."

"Good, I'm glad that everyone is doing better. The rest of the ship is also banged up. The awakees found nothing but tossed cabins. Ronan's team found a small crack on green deck. Clover is working to get all the breaches sealed. That's all I know for now. Please let me know if you need anything or if the anyone's conditions change."

"I will. But you and Verruca need to come get checked out."

"We will. I need to check on one more thing and then we will come get checked out. And thank y'all for all the help today."

"You're welcome."

I closed my conversation with Onyx and opened a line to Ronan. "Ronan?"

"Yes, Iksen."

"I need you and your team to find Lita and Ryker. I have not seen them, and they have not emerged after all this chaos. If they are awake, I want them arrested, and if they are knocked out somewhere, get Savinka to check them out and then arrest them."

"Why? What has happened.?"

"I'll tell y'all as soon as all the repairs are done."

"Okay, I'll grab Ace and Dash and we will start searching."

"Thank you."

Verruca grabbed my hand before I could do anything else and dragged me to the elevator. We walked on to the blue deck to see Onyx leaning over Knox. Savinka was sitting against the wall with an ice pack on her hand, and Juniper was next to her with an ice pack on her head. When they saw us, Savinka waved us over and I kneeled in front of her. She ran her hands across my body checking for bumps, cuts, and any other injuries. When her hand ran just above my right temple, I winced. She gently touched the sore spot but she didn't find anything other than a goose egg. She made me sit back so she could check my legs. Savinka grabbed my right knee and I jerked my knee out of her grip.

"Son of a motherless goat! That hurt."

I pulled up my pant leg, and my knees were already turning purple. Savinka turned to a med kit sitting between her and Juniper. She turned back with a needle in hand.

"Stop right there. I do not do pain killers."

"Why? It's a small dose," Savinka looked at me totally confused.

"No, I have severe reactions to all pain killers. Like throw up, pass out, and go into convulsions type reactions."

Savinka stared at me for a minute and then lowered the needle. "I have never heard of that before. Most people can't wait to get the pain meds, but okay, we have ibuprofen," She reached back into the bag and pulled out a white medicine bottle.

I took the bottle from her and shook out three pills. Vashanti handed me some water and Savinka moved to examining Verruca.

"What did you do for any surgeries that you needed ?" Savinka continued to examine Verruca as she questioned me.

"Well, I have only ever had one surgery in my life. It was an emergency c-section to deliver my son. It took the anesthesiologist an hour of calling colleagues for advice before she found something that would work, and I still had some reactions."

"Where is your son?"

"Unfortunately, the emergency c-section was to deliver him because I lost him."

"Oh, I am so sorry," Savinka and Vashanti said at the same time.

"It was a long time ago. Well, I guess a very long time ago now."

"Ouch, that flipping hurt," Verruca winced from Savinka's touch.

Savinka pulled up Verruca's shirt, and there was a large bruise starting to form on the back of her right rib cage. She reached back into the bag and pulled out an ace bandage. She wrapped Verruca's ribs and handed her the ibuprofen.

"Savinka, thank you for everything you have done today. In fact, thank all of you, but I need to have a meeting with the council. Then we're all taking the rest of the day off."

"Okay, let us move Knox to the clinic, then we will meet you on the bridge," Juniper said.

"That works for me. We will see y'all up there."

Verruca and I headed back to the bridge. On the way I called the other council members. The bridge door slid open, and I headed to the couch to lie down and wait for everyone. Verruca did the same on the other. That was the last thing I remembered until Kilian woke me up.

"Come on, sleepy head. Sit up. We are all here for your meeting."

"Yeah, yeah, I'm getting up." I smacked his hands away.

I stood up and stretched. While I was stretching, Night came in, kissed me on the cheek and then plopped down next to Kilian. I walked over to the main view screen and pulled up the two videos.

"If y'all would please turn your attention to the main screen, I have two videos that I need to show y'all."

The group got up and came to stand with me. I tapped *play* on the video of the gravity generator being damaged. They watched in silence. When it was done, I played the next one. When that one was done, I turned to them.

"What did y'all see in these videos?"

Kilian gave me a disgruntled look. "Wait, you're just now telling us that we have surveillance cameras on this ship?"

"We do. Almost every inch is covered."

He stared at me a with the same look for a second. "Why were we not informed about them?"

"I didn't think it was relevant until now."

"I thought we were running things together. This is something we should have all known about."

"Now you do. I wasn't really hiding it from y'all. I was hiding it from the rest of the awakees. But why is it a surprise that we have CCTV?"

Kilian scoffed, "I honestly didn't think about it, but the fact that you knew and didn't say anything feels like you don't trust us."

"That's not it at all and you know it."

Juniper interjected, "We know you were not hiding it from us."

I nodded. "Thank you."

Zahirah spoke up. "Who are the first two?"

"I believe that they are Lita and Ryker. I think they used towels or extra clothes to make themselves look bigger. But Lita's hair was not completely tucked under the towel-wrap thing on her head. The guy moves like Ryker. Since they are so close, it's only logical it's them."

Cash gestured to the video- "It is definitely Ryker in the second video. He obviously doesn't know we have cameras everywhere."

"Well, not for lack of trying, but I did instruct Vega to keep our camera coverage to himself."- I turned toward the group- "Ryker tried to hack Vega to gain control of the ship, but I already had Vega set up security protocols for just such a thing."

Kilian's tone was still irritated when he spoke, "Wait, you're telling me they have tried to hack our ship and we're just now hearing about it?"

"I was waiting to have solid proof they were causing problems, but after these two attempts to damage the ship, I have it. Then with her little speech the other day, she was able to rile up some of the awakees. I wanted to make sure I had evidence before I accused anyone of anything. You forget I used to do investigations for a living." My tone was indignant at his unspoken allegation.

Ryo interjected, trying to break the tension. "You were right to wait. You were right to want more evidence of what they were up to."

"Thank you," I patted Ryo on the forearm. "Wait, where is Ronan?"

Ryo looked around the bridge, "I don't know."

I tapped my communicator. "Ronan, where are you?"

"Sorry," he replied at once. "We found Lita and Ryker knocked out in an electrical room on silver deck. Lita is still knocked out and Savinka is checking her right now. Ryker woke up shortly after we found them. I have him locked in his cabin with Dash standing guard."

"Okay, keep us updated. I'll catch you up when you're done."

"Copy," Ronan answered.

"So, my next thing to discuss is I want to tell the rest of the awakees what is happening on Earth. But I'm not sure if we should tell them everything we have discovered about Lita and Ryker's escapades."

The group was quiet for a little bit before Juniper spoke.

"I think we should tell them about all of it. One, they have the right to know. Two, we do not need anyone else thinking they can do what Lita and Ryker have done. Any more damage to the ship could keep us from landing."

Cash leaned forward in his seat, "I agree."

Then one by one everyone agreed. We decided to tell them at dinner after we had checked on all the repairs of the ship and the people who were hurt. Everyone headed out. Verruca and I went to check on Knox and Lita.

When we walked into the clinic, Knox was awake.

"Hey, hun, how are you feeling now?"

Knox smiled slightly, "I'm okay, I guess. My head hurts like a son of a bitch and I am still a little dizzy when I move too much, but other than that nothing broken."

"That's good."

Savinka said pointedly, "Yeah he has a concussion. I have ordered him to stay right there and rest."

I patted him on the shoulder. "Rest — get Vega to play you a movie on your communicator or play some music for you."

He smiled and turned to his side, tapping his communicator.

I turned and walked to Lita's bed. She was still knocked out. I looked her up and down and noticed she had rope around one hand restraining her to the bed. As much as I was pissed at her for all her bullshit. I still wanted her to be okay. I turned to Savinka to get an update on her. "So, how is our resident troublemaker?"

"Her vitals are steady, but she has a huge knot on the back of her head. She banged it against something hard."

"I'm not sure what they were doing, but hopefully she will be okay."

"I am sure it's just a concussion, like Knox. She should be waking up soon. I can call you as soon as she is awake."

"Yes, please let me know, and call Ronan. He will need to come help escort her to her cabin. She is being placed under arrest."

"Wait, what? What did she do?" Savinka asked with wide eyes and her hand over her chest. "Is that what y'all talked about in the meeting?"

"Yeah, I'll tell everyone what is going on at dinner tonight. I want to make sure everyone hears what I have to say."

"Okay, I'll be there ready for whatever is next."

"Thank you."

"You're welcome, Iksen." Savinka squeezed my shoulder.

Verruca and I left. Then she turned and looked at me.

"Mom, has anyone checked the birthing lab? I want to go down to the labs. I want to see how things held up and to see if Sphynx is down there."

"Okay, let's go down."

We went to the birthing lab first. As we approached the cabinet, the lights flickered on. Now we could see that each artificial womb had one side exposed through what looked like glass—observers could monitor the growth of the embryo. In the middle row were two baby rabbits growing in their artificial wombs.

"Oh my god! They are so cute," Verruca said softly.

"They are. I so glad they made it through the damn storm."

Baby rabbit one twitched a back foot.

"Aww," we both cooed at the sweetness. We stood watching for a few minutes. Watching this new life growing right before our eyes reminded me of what we were trying to save and why I was dealing with all this bullshit.

"Wait, I thought that it had died," Verruca said.

"The first rabbit did. The second one was getting weak, and Savinka, Vashanti , Sphynx, and Lotus scoured the computers to find something. Finally, they found some notes from the original trials. It had the recipe for a nutritional liquid that can be injected into the wombs. They followed the instructions, and it worked."

"Thank God there was notes on this in a random file. Now these two are doing great, it seems," Verruca cooed.

"Yes, I was relieved too," Shanti said,

"Actually, baby rabbit one, in the womb, is technically baby three and a boy. He will be ready by mid next week to be born," Sphynx said excitedly.

"Holy shit, that's awesome. I want to be here for that."

"Okay, he will need to be bottle fed for a while so maybe you can help with both. I am hoping to get the baby goats into the wombs next week, and I was thinking about trying a calf as well."

"Oh, please do the calf. You know I have always wanted a cow."

"I know, but you've got to remember they are also going to be our food. I don't want you to become attached, because eventually we will have to kill some of them."

"I know, but the first one can be mine." Verruca pouted and gave me puppy eyes.

I hmphed and shook my head.

Verruca smiled smugly because she knew she would get

her way. We left the lab and stepped into the embryo lab. Sphynx and Lotus had the first baby bunny out feeding him. Verruca walked to Sphynx quickly and hugged her tight.

"'Ey, ducky, I'm fine. Just a little goose egg on the head, but Doctor Savinka said I looked good."

"Babe, I was still worried. I know Savinka wouldn't let you out of her sight until you were fine, but I was still worried." Verruca kissed her.

I walked up to them and hugged Sphynx. "I'm glad you're okay, honey.

"Thank you, Iksen."

I checked on the baby bunny, which we had not even named yet. "Lotus, how is he?"

"He is okay. His little box is very cushioned, so I think that helped with the rough ride."

"Good, I think we should call him Hopper."

The girls laughed. Then they nodded in agreement.

"That's cute and is a great name for a bunny," Lotus said.

I was still wired from our excitement today.

"Verruca, do you want to work out a little?"

"No, not right now. I really want to check on everyone and see how our cabin is doing."

"Okay, give everyone a hug for me, and I'll see y'all at dinner."

"You don't need to do anything but go home. Your knees are banged up, and I'll be surprised if you can walk tomorrow."

"I'm too wired right now to just go to my cabin and sit."

"Iksen, that's just the adrenaline talking. You need to rest," Sphynx said tentatively.

"Okay, I'll go try to rest."

Verruca hugged me and then gave me a stern look before she let go of me. I waved bye to everyone on my way out.

I walked into my cabin to find Kilian and Night

straightening things up. I smiled at them in relief. I had not been looking forward to cleaning up a mess. I walked up to Night and kissed him and then I moved to Kilian. I left them cleaning, and I went to the shower. I stripped, walked into the shower, and let the hot water run down me. After a few seconds the left side of my head began to sting. I reached up to feel my head.

"Ouch!"

The water hitting my goose egg hurt. I gently touched it trying to get a better idea of how big it actually was. It hurt too bad, so I just leaned my head back. Slowly but surely, my body begin to relax under the hot water. I finished my shower, surprised the guys didn't join me, and went to the room to get dressed. I looked at my small selection of clothes and sighed. We needed some more options, I thought to myself and chuckled.

I pulled out clean clothes that looked just like the dirty ones I'd just taken off. After getting dressed, I lay across the bed. I stretched across it feeling my body move easier after that hot shower. I was lying there thinking about how to express the information I needed to tell everyone.

The next thing I knew, Night was leaning over me telling me to wake up. I opened my eyes and blinked slowly as I tried to look around. Kilian was standing at the end of the bed.

"What, wait." I shook my head and blinked again. "What is going on?"

They both laughed and Kilian spoke. "It's dinner time. You were going to tell the rest of the awakees what is going on down on Earth and what Lita and Ryker have done."

"Oh, yeah. Damn, I can't believe I fell asleep again and that hard."

I got up and stumbled. My knees were killing me. Night reached out and steadied me. I took a minute, then I took another step toward the bathroom, and that was when the room tilted sideways. Night picked me up this time and sat me on the bed.

"Kilian, stay here with her, and I'll go talk to the group."

"No, Night, I'm good. I'll go tell the group."

"No you will not. You are going to sit right here and let me take care of you," Kilian commanded me.

"I'm sorry but I agree. You need to stay here. I can talk to the group on your behalf." Night gave me a stern look.

I ignored both of them, got out of bed, pulled my hair back into a messy bun, and walked out of my room.

CHAPTER NINETEEN: PUTTING AN END TO STUPIDITY

I stood, with Night and Kilian on each side of me, at the front of the tables waiting for everyone to enter and get their food. Night had been bugging me for several minutes about eating something myself, but I just couldn't think about food at that moment. Not only was I quiet due to the dizziness from hitting my head, but I was also a little nervous about telling the awakees about everything. As I was waiting, I noticed one small group watching me as intently as I was watching everyone else. They must be the few that wanted to follow Lita. They were about to find out what kind of person she was.

Finally, everyone had made it into the dining room. I cleared my throat and began.

"I am standing up here tonight so that I can give you the run down on Earth. I had been waiting to do this because I didn't want anyone to freak out, because it sounds scary. But I am not just going to tell you. I am going to show you. Vega, pull up the map."

He did as I instructed, and the map I had been plotting everything on hung in the air above the tables. The crowd all looked upward at it. Some pointed, others raised their eyebrows in surprise, and the small group huddled together rolled their eyes. Ignoring them, I continued.

"This is the map I have been using to plot what we have learned. Let's start with Texas. As you can see, I have dropped several tornado-looking shapes at the border of Louisiana. That is because there have been snow tornados happening almost every night." I paused to let them study the area. After a few minutes a hand slowly raised into the air.

"Yes, Lotus."

"The weather is that messed up down there?"

"Yes, from what we can tell the weather has flip-flopped. The north, which used to be the cold, snowy part of the US, is now the dry, hot region, and the south is the cold, snowy region."

The crowd immediately started to chatter, and I let them for several seconds before I went on.

"Crazy weather is not the only thing we have found. Over the years Vega has been able to capture pictures, so I have had him pull up the last six months of pictures. In those pictures we saw animals that are extremely different from what we knew."

"Like what?" several voices asked.

"Well one picture caught a black panther-like cat, which we have been calling a razor cat. The reason for that is that the appear to have something white sticking out of their skin along their tails. We believe it might be pieces of their spine. What we can tell is that they have leathery skin and neon-green eyes." I pointed out each feature on the picture.

As I looked around, there were a lot of wide eyes studying the creature in the picture. I made a swiping motion with my hand and the next picture came up.

"This is what we have been calling a venom dog. We're not sure if it is venomous, but if TV taught us anything, it's that neon-green means toxic. So logic dictates that green drool hanging out of its mouth is toxic."

Garrett's tone was worried, "You are telling us that these things are everywhere?"

"No, they are in certain areas, according to where these pictures where taken. At the already explored Texas site, we have only seen what looks like a polar bear with patches of translucent skin . We haven't caught pictures of many other animals in the area as of now. The second Texas spot we're looking at is a little farther down on the coast just out of reach of those snownadoes."

"This is crazy!" several voices said.

"What are we going to do?" a few others said.

"Okay, settle. We are looking at another site on the east coast either tomorrow or the next day, depending on how we all feel after today's surprise meteor shower. The new location is in a now warmer part of the US. We will take soil and water samples for testing, along with air samples, but I can tell you the air is a little thin in general on Earth. That means we will all have to adjust to this."

Shade raised his hand- "Why haven't we just landed and taken our chances with whatever is out there? I am tired of being on this ship."

"Well, I didn't want to put us in any more danger than I had to. I wanted to know as much as I could before we made a choice on where to land. I have a responsibility to all of you to keep you as safe as I can."

The whole group rolled their eyes and Shade scoffed. I couldn't believe Dash was in that group. I might have to re-think him as an agent. I ignored their doubtfulness and continued.

"Besides crazy weather and weird animals, we still don't know if there are actual people left down there. We have been sending drones down to collect the samples for us to test. But other than the animals, we have not seen any people. For that matter, we haven't even seen the animals except a large lizard at our last spot. We have had to rely on the pictures that Vega already possessed to tell us most of what we know."

With a venomous tone Shade blurted, "So, what are you going to do about it, Iksen?"

"We want to decide on which landing spot is the best

option. I am hoping for somewhere with the best advantages possible, like fresh water and an ocean. The council and I have also discussed sending a scouting team down, but we're still discussing the particulars of that."

Verruca stood up. "I know there are a lot of questions and any of the council members can answer them for y'all, but we have one more thing to discuss that is very important."

When she said that last part, she looked over at the group of Lita's lackeys.

I took a deep breath and cleared the map. Then a file folder icon dropped on the screen. I tapped it and the two video clips appeared. I tapped the first clip and let it play. Once it finished, I tapped the next one.

I didn't say anything after the second one played. I let everyone sit there for a minute to realize what they had watched. I glanced at Lita's group quickly while the second video was playing. They all looked a little surprised but not Dash. Maybe he didn't buy into Lita's bullshit as much as I first thought. I made a mental note to try and talk to him. The rest of the group all had varying expressions on their faces. Garrett seemed to be the one that was not convinced.

"I wanted to show y'all this because I know Lita has been trying to recruit people that might help her become Iksen. Everyone knows that she was a lawyer. Just like we know how capable she must be to have achieved all the things she did before all this happened.

"But those accolades can be applied to many of us on this ship. Being the leader is about more than your education, or prior jobs. There are so many aspects that you have to try and look at all the time. That is why there is a council to help me with that but also to temper me. I hope everyone knows I am trying to do my best for the whole."

Ryo stood and addressed the group. "Atlantis didn't just appoint herself as Iksen. The ship nominated her and we all agreed."

Zahirah stood up. "She discusses everything with us. She has rarely made a decision without letting us know about it. And they have all been for the welfare of everyone on this ship. We have the right person leading us."

"There is a lot I have been doing without bothering everyone. Not that I think you guys couldn't handle it, but because I wanted to let as many of you as I could just try to create a new normal. Believe it or not, it has helped me to see everyone finding lovers, creating a routine of life, and making this ship a community. We will need all of that once we land, to survive. Thank you, I appreciate that. I will say I took on the job because I felt it was what I could do best. I'm not good at doing nothing."

"That's for sure." Kilian said, only loud enough for me to hear.

Ignoring him I went on. "I do want y'all to know that I was not purposely hiding anything from y'all. I just wanted everyone to try and create a new normal without worrying about everything else going on. I thought it would help everyone feel safe."

"Please believe us when we say she was not making these decisions on her own. We all" —Savinka motioned to the whole council— "have put our opinions in on every decision."

"But I'll go with what the majority wants." I added quickly.

The council stood up and looked around the room, then Onyx spoke, "I believe that you have been doing everything you can to keep us safe and on track to get back to Earth. I want you as my leader."

Speaking in unison, Juniper and Cash added, "I agree!"

Jax said, "I know most of you have not really got a chance to see all of what we have been doing in the background, but I assure you it has all been in the interest of keeping everyone on this ship alive and getting us back to Earth. Atlantis might run a tight ship, but she has been working harder than all of us to get us back to Earth." He looked at me. "You will always be my Iksen."

The rest of the council agreed with him. Kilian and Night both took my hands and squeezed them.

I continued. "Hold on, hold on. I'm not the only one that has been working hard. Ryo, Night, Jax, and Kilian have been working diligently to learn how the nuclear core works. How it powers the engines of the ship and the electrical systems. Juniper has jumped in anywhere she has been needed. Cash jumps in where needed and runs all our drone missions.

"Ronan has put in overtime for selecting and training the security team, especially since Kilian has been more focused on the nuclear core. Savinka, Vashanti, Lotus, Onyx and Sphynx have set up the sick bay, already have plants growing, and have been testing samples from the first two sites we visited. Then Vox, Rogue, Garrett, and even Ryker have planned three meals a day for all thirty of us that are awake. Not to mention all the special requests that they have managed to pull off.

"So by no means have I been doing all this by myself. None of this would be happening as smoothly as it has been without each person's dedication. We must hold on a little longer. When we land we can make different decisions about how to run things." I turned to look at the council. "Thank you for everything you have done and will do. Thank you Vox, Garrett, and Rogue for feeding us all. And thank you to all of you who have done what has been asked of you."

I looked out over the crowd and didn't see any hostility, really. I smiled at the crowd and breathed deeply. Hopefully, this would make everyone stick together long enough to land. Then I didn't care what everyone did. That will be up to them, I thought to myself as I continued to smile at them.

Everyone returned to their food, and I finally felt like I

could eat. Night went to get me food as I sat down next to Verruca and leaned my head on her shoulder. My knees were hurting so badly. I rubbed them while waiting for Night to return.

We sat eating and talking about anything except what I had just shown the whole ship. It was such a relaxing night as we all told stories from before. I think it really brought the group together. Ryo was talking about how his family would get together and play cards at least twice a month. Then Ronan jumped in with his side of the story and they had the whole table laughing. I leaned back into Kilian, listening as Night held my hand. We all listened and laughed. Verruca even made me tell stories of when she was young.

"It was nothing fancy. My friends would come over on weekends and we would barbecue, drink, and tell stories from high school or college. Verruca knew that meant she would get to see the other kids her age, but also everyone spoiled her. I always believed being spoiled was her favorite part. Most of them would bring something special for the kids."

"Tell them about your escapades when you were in high school and college," Verruca said smirking.

"We didn't do anything more than other kids growing up in a small town did. We would race my Mustang down our main street. We would toilet paper our friends' houses and our band director's. From high school through college, we went to Mexico for spring break. And so what if we went to a few strip clubs down there? Got really drunk a few times, it was Mexico. You know what happens in Mexico stays in Mexico." I shrugged my shoulders. "It was just what we did back then."

The younger ones couldn't believe I had once been the wild child. The older ones laughed.

Kilian said with a mischievous smirk, "I remember toilet

papering a friend's house."

Teasingly Ronan said, "So, in other words you were the troublemaker."

"No, I was a perfect angel." I grinned wickedly, waggling my eyebrows.

"I don't believe that for a second," Jax said with a hardy laugh. "I know a fellow troublemaker when I see one."

That made us all laugh. Then I settled back into Kilian, and Jax picked up with a story.

"One night, when I was still a prospect, Luke, who was my sponsor — you know, everyone, that prospects have to have a sponsor who vouches for you — he took me drinking. Of course, I was young and a dumb ass. I had been talking shit about how much I could drink. So, Luke and a couple other brothers taught me a lesson. They got me so drunk I passed out. They got some makeup and a dress from the server. They put the dress on me and did my makeup and then put me on my Harley in front of the bar. They taped my hand on the handlebars and tied my hips to my seat, so I stayed sitting upright for the most part. Then they took pictures of me, but the icing on the cake was they left me out there all night. I was so mad, but it was my own fault."

'I'm sorry, bro," Ryo said and patted him on the shoulder.

"Aww, you're my big strong man, aren't you, chuck," Sphynx said and kissed his forearm that was around her shoulders.

Cash picked up with a story. I was listening, or at least I thought I was until Kilian nudged me.

"Hey, you are dozing off. Are you ready for bed?"

"I am not dozing off. I am listening."

"Yeah, so those soft snores I heard weren't you?" Night smiled slyly at me.

Night pulled and Kilian pushed until I was standing up. Then they both led me to our cabin. *Wait.* I paused mentally for a second to think about it. *I think I like the idea of it being our cabin.* Not that I would tell the guys that, but still it was nice.

We walked into the cabin. I headed for bed, and the guys were in the kitchen getting drinks. I flopped in the center of the bed. It had been an awfully long day, and I was glad it was over. The soreness of being slammed from the floor to the ceiling and back again was starting to really settle in. I got comfortable in the middle of the bed. A few minutes later the guys joined me. Night lay down in front of me and Kilian behind me. I snuggled into Night with my head on his chest. Kilian snuggled into me and placed his head on my back with his left leg entwined with my right since I was lying on my stomach. He also threw his left arm over my hip since Night's hand was on the upper part of my shoulders close to his face.

They had been getting a little more comfortable touching each other when we were snuggled like this. It was nice they were relaxing into this relationship. As we lay there, my mind began to drift to other things we could be doing, but when I tried to move, I was pinned in place. Both guys were dead asleep. I smiled, adjusted myself between them, and drifted to sleep.

I woke early the next morning with Night's knee driving into my kidney, which in turn was pushing against my bladder. I wiggled my way from between them and ran for the bathroom. *Chingoa!* I almost peed on myself. My bladder just wasn't what it used to be after carrying two kids.

Once I was done, I decided to get my day started. There was a lot to do today. We had to research the third landing spot, and I had to talk with Lita and Ryker. I needed to call them out on their bullshit. I stepped up to the sink to brush my teeth. When I was about done, I felt a hand run up my back. I opened my eyes to see Kilian standing behind me. I smiled but before I could say good morning, he had pulled down my pants and slapped my ass. Not that I didn't enjoy it, but I needed to get started for the day.

I was about to voice just that, but before I could, my thoughts were cut off by a thick hard cock sliding into me.

I gasped from the warm tingles that shot to my clit and spread throughout my body. He growled as my inner walls gripped him tightly. His fingers dug into my hips, his eyes closed, and he moaned in pleasure as the crown of his cock pressed against my cervix.

"I love the way your body grips me." His tone was deep and full of lust.

His deep tone stoked the embers of lust building in me. "Harder," I moaned breathily.

Gripping my hips, he rocked into me. Now a moan escaped me as warm pleasure spread out engulfing me in need. I pressed back to encourage him to fuck me faster, but he was not taking the hint.

I physically pushed him back a step and then I had the room to take over. I moved myself on his cock finding the pace I needed. Nails dug into my skin as I went faster and slid a hand between my thighs finding my clit. I made small circles around it and then I felt that familiar build starting deep in my core. Kilian finally got the hint and began moving at the pace I had already set. I allowed him because I really wanted this orgasm to keep building.

I was moaning softly when he picked up the pace and began slamming into me. His thick cock pounding into me amped up the build of my orgasm. I was inches away from floating into an oblivion of pleasure.

Kilian then ran his hand up my back,-wrapped it into my hair and jerked my head back. A breathy moan escaped from the pleasure pain of his move. My ass automatically arched, and he pushed deeper. I growled out my pleasure. This dominating move was super-hot and pushed me to dangling on the edge of oblivion. I wanted to give in, but I couldn't. I pushed back on Kilian and made more space between me and the counter. Then I turned to face him with his hand still wrapped in my hair. He changed his grip to cupping the nape of my neck, and that was when I swept his feet out from under him. He hit the floor hard and grunted in pain, but before he could do anything else, I was on top of him.

I positioned myself over his cock and then slid down on it fast. His hips arched into me, he returned his hands to my hips, and his eyes rolled back. That only encouraged me to ride him harder. I leaned backward and placed my hands on his thighs, which angled his cock where it was rubbing against my g-spot. Short breathy moans were elicited from me at this new sensation, and I rode harder. This caused my whole body to ignite with the need to fall over that edge. My orgasm built more and more, but I still wasn't quite there yet. Getting impatient, I leaned forward and grinded on his cock moving my hips in circles. That was what my body wanted. His cock was hitting every sensitive spot of my inner walls, but I was still missing something.

Kilian was groaning in pleasure while guiding my hips. Then without any prompting he slid his hand to my clit and made a circle. Just one circle, and my orgasm exploded through me, and that oblivion of pleasure I was chasing engulfed me. My inner walls quaked around his cock while my body quivered on top of him. At some point he had interlocked our fingers, and we were holding hands. He used this leverage to hold me up as I rode out my orgasm.

Shortly before I completely came down, he began to slide in and out of me quickly. This drew out my pleasure and made me moan in short pants. Each thrust caused a new sensation to spread through my body. While I was enjoying each sensation, Kilian's orgasm slammed into him. He growled out, "Fuck" deep and low in his chest. His cock throbbed in me as jet after jet of his come filled me. I flopped on top of him as we enjoyed the aftermath of our morning sexcapades. We lay there until we could move again.

When my limbs stopped being wobbly I stood up and got into the shower, since starting my day had already been delayed. Kilian stepped in behind me. He showered quickly and left me to enjoy my very hot shower alone. Well at least I thought I was going to be alone, but now two hands squeezed my shoulders. I knew it was Night from how he touched me. He massaged my shoulders for a few minutes, which almost put me to sleep. Night moved closer, kissing me on my wet shoulder as his arms snaked around my waist. His lips moved their way up my shoulder to my neck as one hand moved down to my clit and the other moved up to my left breast. My clit was super sensitive. My body twitched from his touch, and I moaned softly.

Night groaned while his kisses turned into nips and bites along the column of my neck. This change of tactic made me shiver. I felt his lips pull into a smile against my skin. Then he applied a little more pressure and speed which sent intoxicating jolts of bliss to every nerve ending. Releasing a gasping moan my body reignited with need. Night's erection was growing quickly between us and I rubbed my ass against it. Now he was the one that inhaled sharply. I smiled wickedly to myself, enjoying his deepening breathing.

Abruptly his hand left my breast and slid up my back. He wrapped his hand in my hair and spun me around, pushing me to my knees. It was the most dominant move he had ever used. He placed my closed mouth on the tip of his dick. I glared up at him defiantly from my knees and that is when an oh so sexy and wicked smile crossed his lips. He leaned over, kissed me hard and then collared my throat. He stood back to his full height then squeezed my throat slightly. I gasped, partly in shock at how dominant he was being, and partly because it was hot as fuck. But he shoved his cock in as soon as my lips parted. I glared at him, and he glared smugly back. He used his grip to move my head in the directions he wanted. He forcibly pushed all the way in until I choked on it and then repeated the action several times. On the last time he held my head in place, so I closed my lips around his shaft and began to swallow. A loud, long, gravelly moan rumbled up from the pit of his being. Now I was the smug one. His cock throbbed, then throbbed again, and he roughly pulled my mouth from his cock.

"You are going to be the death of me," he growled as he pulled me to my feet.

Night shoved me against the wall. He leaned in and kissed me hungrily. He pulled back, breaking the kiss and dropped to his knees. Slinging my right leg over his shoulder he dived in, tongue exploring until he found my clit. I dug my nails into his shoulders while my head fell back against the shower wall. I was breathing hard in between deep moans while I writhed against his mouth. I didn't know if he was that skilled or if I was that sensitive from my previous exploits. But his tongue was sending pure, hot pleasure spreading out from my clit to the tips of my toes.

My orgasm built fast and hard. I went from stepping on the bottom of the ledge to dangling off it by one finger. My body was quivering with the need for release, but just when I thought I was going to fall he stopped. I spluttered and whimpered my disapproval, but before I could make coherent words, he had spun me and bent me over. He slid into me hard and fast. He never relented in his fervor and slid a hand down to my clit to continue the knee-buckling assault on it.

I was whimpering and shivering from the overwhelming pleasure that was coursing through my entire body. He had me again hanging on by a thread when he stopped. I was about to lose my mind when I felt the crown of his cock press against my ass. Pressing in slowly, we moaned in unison. I was filled by him and needing release.

"Fuck me hard, now," I growled out.

He did what he was asked. I ran a hand down to my clit and it only took three circles to toss me off the cliff headfirst into ecstasy. My whole body tensed up, my legs quivered, and waves of galvanizing rapture washed over me again and again as he continued to fuck me hard. As long as he was moving, my orgasm was dragged out. Each stroke of friction causing new mind-blowing sensations to overwhelm each nerve again and again. Even his hand on my skin caused fire to burn there. Night continued his assault on my body for a few more strokes before his orgasm blasted through him. My name spilled from his lips in a loud primal growl that echoed throughout the shower. He thrust deep one last time and then collapsed against my back, shaking and breathing hard.

I relaxed, letting the top half of my body sag against the wall. While I was deciding if my legs were trustworthy enough to continue standing, I felt Night's lips pressed against my skin several times before he pulled out of me slowly and stood up. He then reached over and pulled me upright, but my knees tried to buckle. Night caught me by the waist and held me up. Thank God I had already washed my hair before Night had made his way into my shower. Now we worked together to wash my body. Once we had both got clean and stepped out, I was steadier. He snatched a towel from the rack and wrapped it around me, kind of, then led me to the bed, where he laid me down.

"No, I have a lot to do today," I protested.

"Kilian and I have it. Rest, and let that bump on your head go down. Yesterday was a rough, demanding day. Let us help you," Night demanded.

"Well, by that logic we should all take a break. That would include you and Kilian," I retorted.

"I'm okay. I just have some bruises on my legs and arms. Kilian has a couple bruised ribs but has some pain meds to help. You, on the other hand, have refused to take anything and started running the moment the storm passed."

"I did take some ibuprofen. That's as strong as I can take. I am allergic to everything else. Since we don't have more than heart monitors aboard, I can't take a chance of taking pain meds because it might kill me."

"Wait, what? Why is this the first I am hearing of this? What if you had been seriously hurt yesterday? What if Savinka had given you something while you were knocked out?"

"Verruca knows. She would have said something."

"That is all the more reason that you should stay in bed and rest. I am not going to argue with you about it. I let you be strong all the rest of the times, but today you will listen to me and stay in bed."

"Fine." I rolled, over sprawling out on the bed. I had intended to get up after I heard them leave the cabin but the longer I lay there, the less I wanted to get out of bed. Sitting up against the headboard, I put a movie on.

CHAPTER TWENTY: TALKING TO THE PRISONERS

"Mom, wake up. Mooom, wake up," Verruca said in a whiney kid's voice.

I rolled over, eyes still shut, and shoved her. "I don't want to wake up."

"Get up, it's dinner time. You need to eat something. I brought food."

Verruca got up and went to the kitchen. I rolled out of bed, grabbed my rubber band from the nightstand, and pulled my hair back on the way to the kitchen. I plopped down in a chair at the small table.

"Why did you wake me?"

"Night said to come check on you. He told me he wouldn't let you get out of bed this morning and do any work."

I scoffed. "That's not exactly what happened, but okay."

"What happened? Oh, by the way, make sure your men know things about you. I didn't need Night bitching at me at that hour of the morning about you not being able to take pain killers."

I chuckled. "Sorry he was bitching at me, too, about why I didn't take a pain shot for my head. I told him why, then he flipped out about what if I had been seriously hurt yesterday and they gave me something without knowing. I told him you would have said something."

"If I was awake, yeah, but what if I wasn't? He is right. You should have told at least Savinka."

"You know me, I didn't even think about it until something happened where I might need some pain killers. But Savinka knows now."

"I know, but this is a new world. No one but me knows you here, and I can't always be there to inform people. I had to tell my little group about my allergies."

"Yeah, I know. I'll make sure Night and Kilian know. Speaking of your little quartet, how are things going?

"They are good. We have found a rhythm for now. We have set some ground rules along with some *living in one cabin* rules."

"How's the living in one cabin going? I know you hate to share your space."

"That part has been the hardest for me. You know I love alone time in a quiet space. They have all learned to read me, but I am working on telling them when I need that alone time."

"That's good. I'm glad things are settling in."

"What about you? You are no better than me when it comes to your space and things."

I frowned playfully at her. "Well, falling asleep has been hard. I am used to falling asleep in a king-sized bed all to myself. Now I must make room for two more people. Although last night was easier. I am still trying to break Kilian of his domineering attitude, though."

"I'm surprised you are still putting up with it. Usually after the first time a man tries to control you, you get rid of him."

"Yeah, normally I would, but I don't know . . . there is something about him. It's just I don't want to give up on him yet. We only have problems when he lets that macho attitude out. I'm sure most previous girls allowed him to act like that because they thought it was manly. But I'm showing him not all women like that. Besides, it's a new world, so I'm trying to be a newer me." I laughed. Then went to the fridge and got us some waters.

"Well, I guess we are all trying something new. Hopefully, we can create a new world where everyone is equal."

I leaned over, kissing her on the top of her head. "It would be nice." I got the food she had brought, and we sat eating and talking about our possible new world. We had about finished our food when Kilian walked in and paused briefly.

"Hey, girls, what are y'all doing?" he asked just before he leaned down to hug me.

"Not much. Just sitting here talking about life." It was crazy to think about *life* since we really didn't know what that meant anymore.

"Oh, so some deep meaningful conversations going on," Kilian said with amusement.

"Yeah, it was super deep. We were talking about our relationships," Verruca said with a chuckle.

"Verruca." Kilian's tone had a harsh edge to it. "Could you give us some alone time? I need to talk to your mom," he said, a bit demandingly. That attitude set me on edge, and I didn't like it one bit. "Well, she and I were not done talking. So until then we are going to sit here."

"I just wanted to talk to you about some things and I didn't want to do it in front of her."

"Okay, that's fine but you don't just get to tell us we're done talking."

"All I did was ask if she could leave so you and I could talk."

"No, you demanded. I am not sure where you switched from the polite man who walked into this cabin to the snotty one who just spoke to my daughter with all that attitude, but that rudeness will not cut it with me. Now, I am sorry if you didn't like us talking about you or whatever flipped your switch, but you will not act like that with me or my daughter."

"Well, I don't talk about personal stuff in front of family

and friends. That should be kept personal, between me and you."

"Verruca and I talk about everything, there are very few things we keep from each other, so I'll talk to her about whatever I choose to. This macho bullshit doesn't work with me. I have done everything, including telling you that you will never control me, but you don't seem to get it. I like you. I have seen the sweet side of you, but this is not working. I'm sure previously plenty of little girls thought this was cool and manly. But those girls were only looking for someone to take care of them, not be their partner.

"No grown man should have to take care of a grown woman and no grown woman should have to take care of a grown man. So if you're looking for someone who needs you to take care of them, then you have chosen the wrong one. Because I don't need you. I wanted you, and there is a huge difference."

When I quit talking, I noticed Verruca was standing behind me with her arms crossed, glaring at Kilian.

"All women want a man to take care of them, and the ones that say otherwise are lying to themselves," he retorted.

"Really, because there is not a damn thing that you can do for me that I can't do for myself."

"Well, there's one thing you can't do for yourself," he said with a smart ass tone.

"Oh no, I can even do that for myself. Used to be I could go to the store and buy one in any color or size I wanted, but I am sure I can find something on this ship that will suffice. So as of this moment we're done. Get your shit and go back to your cabin."

"You will want me back soon enough."

"Don't count on it. I rarely make the same mistake twice."

"You don't deserve to be in charge," he said in an ugly tone as he walked out the door.

Just as he walked out Night walked in. "What is going on? I could hear you yelling down the hall."

"Kilian with his macho man bullshit. He thinks he can tell me what to do and what to say and I am not going to have it."

"Mom, calm down. He is not used to strong women. He doesn't understand our relationship, because you know most women would give up their kids for a man. Especially their grown children. Also everyone is trying to adjust to a new, crazy, and uncertain world. Maybe he feels like he has no control."

"I get all that, but he is going about it all the wrong way, especially with me."

"Look, I know you care about him, so give him time to realize he has made a mistake," Night said.

"I don't know. He would have to really make a change and apologize his ass off. Besides, you don't act like that," I said, pointing at Night.

"It's different for me. I grew up differently. I had tons of strong women around me. In our tribe women are equal in mostly everything, but we're also taught family is everything. So I understand you and your daughter are close. In fact, I love that."

"Well, I am glad you understand. I would hate to have to throw you out too," I said with a wicked grin just before I kissed him on the nose.

"What if we all do dinner here tonight? I'll go to the kitchen and get food, and Verruca and her . . ." Night paused, looking for the right word.

"Quartet," I said.

"Partners," Verruca said.

"Okay, partners can come over to eat. We can make it a late dinner. Since y'all just had a snack."

"Sounds good. I want to go talk to Lita and Ryker anyway."

"Yeah, that should be fun. I'll let everyone know," Verruca said. She hugged me and left waving bye to Night as she walked out.

"I am going to go talk to them now. Hopefully Kilian can do his job without issue. I would hate to have to relieve him of his duties, too, after all of this."

"Hey, don't worry, and I'll talk with him tomorrow."

"No, just leave it, unless he wants to talk to you. You don't need to play referee."

I walked over to him and kissed him for real this time and then left to go see the prisoners. I was running through the possibilities of what I might have to do with Lita and Ryker if I could not get them to stay in their cabins peacefully.

I stepped off the elevator on the green deck. I was only a few steps down the hallway when Knox and Clover came into view guarding Lita and Ryker's doors.

"Hello, guys, how are y'all?"

"I am good. A little sore today, but good," Knox answered.

"Same here," Clover said.

"Clover, thank you for welding the holes. Without your skills we would have a lot of problems right now."

"You're welcome. Repairing them made sure we all survived. Me included."

"Well, thank you again." I reached out my hand to her. She took it. "Okay, how have they been?"

"Ryker has threatened us a lot. Lita has tried to seduce me, and when that didn't work, she tried to push past me," Knox said.

Clover chuckled. "Well, Ryker tried to hit on me, but to his disappointment I didn't bite. Which made him mad and led him to try to manhandle me. I put him on his ass and he yelled like a little bitch. By the time Ronan and Knox came in I had him rolled over and was sitting on him."

"I expect everyone to stand up for themselves in those

situations. But I do not want it to be the way we handle every situation. Unfortunately, for you guys, you're held to a higher standard. Just like the council. As much as I would like to hit certain people, I can't. We have to create the world we want to live in, and I hope your vision is close to mine. Which is everyone being equal and treated fair all the time. Do y'all understand?"

"Yes, Iksen," they answered together.

"What are you telling them now?" Ronan said with amusement. "I wouldn't listen to her if I was you all."

"Whatever, I'll show you who's boss. Let's go to the gym," I replied.

Ronan laughed even harder. "I am not going to make that mistake again."

Clover looked at us quizzically.

Ronan smiled. "She has a mean choke hold. Once she gets you locked into it, you cannot get out of it. I will not make the mistake of letting that happen again."

"I told you I used to do judo, and that I was damn good at it. Not my fault you thought I was old and out of shape. I am, but I still have some skills." A mischievous smile spread across my face.

"Okay, enough busting my balls. Let's get the prisoners questioned, and then we have a decision to make," Ronan said as he waved me toward Ryker's door.

"Vega, open the door please."

"Yes, Ms. Atlantis."

The door slid back with a barely audible swish. Ryker was sitting on his couch looking pissed. I looked around the cabin. Its color scheme was dark brown and beige. The wall behind the couch was like Verruca's. It was made of squares at different depths, and the wall was painted dark brown. Around the living room were different shades of green as accents. I looked back at him, and he was glaring daggers at me. Well, he could be pissed off all he wanted. He shouldn't have allowed himself to be led around by his dick and he wouldn't be paying the consequences now.

"What is y'all's plan? Why have y'all decided to undermine everything we have been working to accomplish?"

Ryker simply stared at me.

I watched him as he sat turning over things in his mind. I looked him over, observing his demeanor. I had met guys like him before, the ones that pretended to be a follower while all along they were getting other people to do their dirty work so they could accomplish their goals. That also explained why he was letting Lita lead this little plan to take over leadership of this ship.

I stood a few more minutes learning as I watched him. He was basically a coward hiding behind a skirt to get what he wanted. I was not a fan of that, either, and Lita wanted to be in charge of something so bad she was naïve enough to do what he was guiding her to do.

"Okay, well, the longer you're quiet the longer you stay confined. I'll move over to Lita, and I am sure she is more than happy to spill her guts."

I waved Ronan and Clover to follow me, and we went next door to Lita's cabin. Vega opened the door for us, and Lita was nowhere to be found as we walked in.

"Lita?" No answer, so I called again. Still no answer. I walked to the bedroom. I didn't see her on the bed, so I stepped into the room to walk to the bathroom and that's when she tried to jump me. To her surprise she missed as I simply stepped forward and she fell to her knees.

"Ambush, really? Even you should be smart enough to know you are not skilled enough to pull this off." I waved my hand to indicate her on the floor.

She stood up glaring at me. I stared back for a few seconds and then gestured for her to lead the way to the front room area. She turned with a humph and slowly walked to the living room. She glowered at Ronan and Clover. Then she stood in the kitchen leaning against the counter.

"What do you have to say for yourself? Why are you trying to sabotage this ship and us trying to get back to the ground?"

"I have no idea what you're blathering on about," Lita said innocently in her heavy Texas twang.

"You have no idea how the gravity generator was damaged or how the oxygen scrubber on the blue deck got damaged?"

"I have no idea. Besides, I am under no legal obligation to tell y'all a thing."

"That's where you're wrong. You seem to be under the impression that there are laws here other than myself and the council. You forget the laws and government that used to be there no longer exist. I can make any law I choose when I choose."

She remained standing and didn't speak, but I could see she was processing this information. Then I saw that eye twitch that told me she just truly understood my meaning. Now the realization that she didn't really know me like she thought she did dawned on her as fear and then stubbornness crossed her features.

"Ah, so it has finally sunk in. I'll ask again, why are you trying to sabotage this ship and us getting back to the ground?"

"I still don't know what you're talking about, but why should you get to be the leader when you are old and uneducated? I am the most educated and accomplished person on this ship. I am a lawyer. I should be in charge."

"So, you truly believe that you are smarter than everyone else on this ship?"

"I know I am. I was head of my class in pre-law, and I was head of my class in law school. I was valedictorian of my graduating class."

"Well, let's test your theory. What do you know about a nuclear engine core?"

"That its nuclear and it's an engine," Lita said with an eye roll.

It took everything I had not to bust out laughing. I knew she had to be older than she was acting, because she was a lawyer. She had to be in her late twenties, but she was acting like a two-year-old.

"Yes, but what does it do for our ship?"

"It makes it fly," she said in a hoity tone, but I could see in her eyes she wasn't really sure that was correct.

"It does make the ship fly, but a regular engine could do that. A nuclear engine makes us fly longer, smoother, and helps power the majority of the flight systems on this ship."

"So, what does that prove?"

"Well, what about this? How long does it take a rabbit to fully gestate?"

"What?"

"Well, you're smarter than me. So how long?"

"I don't know. What does that have to do with being in charge on this ship?"

"It has to do a lot with being a leader on this ship. If you were smarter than me, you would know this. Just for your info, though, I too attended college. I was a music education major at first, then an art education major, and then an early childhood development major. Now I didn't get to finish my degree, but I was on the dean's list every term in my last go around. When I started my career as a loss prevention manager, I became very good at what I did and moved to the top very quickly.

"Kilian was a weapons specialist for the US Navy and then ran a weapons development department for one of the top weapons companies in the world. Night has a degree in aviation mechanics. Ronan has run a successful business for many years. Verruca has a cosmetology license and had begun to travel all over doing trainings for some of the top companies. Not to mention we have a doctor, nurses, x-ray tech, lab scientist and so on, on this ship. I did not just appoint myself leader. The ship kind of chose me when he woke me first, but then the council agreed with Vega's choice and appointed me as the leader.

"And I'll be damned if I let anyone screw up our chances to get back to Earth. Since you want to stand here and pretend that you're smart and dumb all at the same time, I will leave you confined to your room until we land on Earth. Ryker will suffer the same fate. Oh, and just FYI, you should pick your minions better, because that one is all about himself. He is more than happy to let you take all the punishment."

She just stared at me trying hard not to say anything else, but I could see it was killing her. I'd given her all the chances she was getting from me to own up to her shit. I turned and walked out the door. As the door slid closed Lita screamed.

"You're just a stupid, fat, old, bitch!"

I burst out laughing. I laughed so hard I was crying and couldn't stop to catch my breath. Ronan was just staring back and forth between me and the door. Clover had a hand on my shoulder but was stifling a laugh.

"It's . . . okay . . . you can . . . laugh," I said between my own laughs and gasps of air.

Clover started laughing, hard. Her laughing made me laugh even harder. Knox and Ronan looked at us confused. After several more minutes of laughing, Clover and I caught our breath enough to explain why it was so funny to the guys. Fanning my face with one hand as I wiped tears away with the other, I gave Ronan instructions.

"Ronan, these two are to stay confided to their cabins with guards around the clock. If need be, choose a few more people to induct as agents, or we can wake someone. I don't want any one person having to stand guard all the time. That means shifts will have to be established."

"Yes, Iksen. I will look and see who we have that I feel will be good at the job."

"Okay, just let me know who so I know what they are doing. Or if we need to wake someone."

"I will."

"Thank you, Clover and Knox. I know it's not easy to stand here when I am sure you would like to be doing other things. I appreciate your dedication to us getting back to the ground."

"You're welcome, Iksen," Clover said, still smiling and wiping her face.

Knox inclined his head in a quick nod. I smiled at them both. Then Ronan and I walked away. When we got to the elevators, Ronan assured me he would find two more agents and let me know imminently. We stepped in together, but I went back to the blue deck heading for my cabin. Ronan proceeded to the black deck.

CHAPTER TWENTY-ONE: THE FIRST FAMILY DINNER

The closer I got to the cabin, the more I realized I was a little nervous about all of us being in the same room. Was I really going to like their dynamic, or was I going to get mad at how Verruca was being treated in the quartet?

I paused at my door and took a deep breath. "Open."

I walked in to find everyone already there. Night, Verruca, and Sphynx were in the kitchen area, cooking and laughing together. Jax was pouring glasses of iced tea, but I was not sure what Ryo was pouring. The boys were throwing in comments. No one had noticed me yet until I stepped up to the table.

"Hey, Mom," Verruca said through a laugh.

"Hey," Night said and walked over to kiss me.

"Hello, Iksen," Jax and Ryo said.

"'Ey up, Iksen," Sphynx added in her Midlands accent. Which seemed a little heavier today.

"No, no, we don't have to be so formal here. Y'all can just call me Atlantis in these situations."

"Or Mom," Ryo said, then smiled mischievously.

"Maybe if y'all stay around long enough." I looked at him pointedly but amused.

The guys laughed uneasily, which made me smirk. They went back to getting the table set, and I walked over to see what Night and the girls were cooking—spaghetti. I looked over at the other two pots and saw a red sauce in one and the other was an Alfredo sauce.

"I see Verruca told you she doesn't eat red sauces," I said to Night and chuckled.

"Yeah, when she saw it, she made a disgusted face. So I went back to the kitchen and found some stuff to make a creamy sauce. I just hope it turns out right. We didn't have quite the right ingredients." Night stirred the sauces.

I saw an additional pan on the stove covered with some wax paper, or at least it looked like wax paper. I lifted it and it was garlic bread.

"Where did we get garlic bread?"

Before anyone could answer a beeping noise sounded and I looked around at everyone questioningly. Verruca snapped her fingers.

"That would be the reminder to go get the potatoes. Let me run get them." She headed out the door.

I turned and looked at Night in an enquiring manner.

He smiled at me and patted my arm. "Rogue was making bread today, and I got him to make an additional loaf for us to turn into garlic bread. He was also keeping an eye on some potatoes that Verruca was roasting for dinner. That's what she left to go get." He waved the sauce spoon toward the door.

"Oh, poor Rogue. I need to do something nice for him. He is always doing nice things for everyone."

"Did you let Ryker and Lita go?" Ryo asked as he placed some silverware on the table.

"No, and I don't see them getting out of their cabins anytime soon."

"Really, so he admitted to damaging things?" Jax asked in surprise.

"No, he didn't, but his smug ass said way more with his gestures and facial expressions than he realizes. Lita almost let her ego get the best of her, but she caught herself before she admitted to any of it outright. She really thinks she is so much smarter than the rest of us, and she did say that out-right."

"Blimey, she didn't!" Sphynx said in shock.

"Yep, she really said that. She thinks I am too old and not smart enough to lead us. But that just shows how young and naïve she is."

The door slid open, and Verruca came in holding the pan of potatoes. She walked over to the stove and set them down. As she walked by, the smell was delicious.

"Well, everything is ready now. How do we want to do this? Does everyone want to make their own plate, or do we want one person to serve?" Night asked, looking around at all of us.

"I think everyone can make their own plates." I said decisively.

Everyone agreed, and I gestured to Night to make his plate first. He did, then headed for the table. I tried to let everyone else go first, but Verruca and Sphynx weren't having it, so I made my plate and joined Night at the makeshift dining table. Ryo and Jax had pulled two additional tables and chairs from neighboring empty cabins to make enough table space and seating for everyone.

Our first few bites were in silence. Me, personally, I was just enjoying the food. It was so good. Who knew Night could cook so well? I picked up my glass of what I assumed was water and took a big drink. I choked on the liquid because it burned. I swallowed quickly so I could take a deep breath.

"Damn, that was strong. I could have used a warning," I said fanning my face with one hand.

Jax and Ryo snorted out chuckles before speaking.

"I am so sorry," Ryo said. "I forgot to tell you. The other night when Ronan and I were doing a late-night patrol we found this being made in one of the electrical rooms on the green deck."

"We have someone onboard making moonshine. From the taste of it, they are using potatoes so it's a moonshine-vodka-combo thing," Jax said after taking a taste of his.

"Do we know who it is?" I asked between a couple small coughs.

"No, not yet, but Ronan said he had an idea and was going to question them about it."

"I mean, I am not mad about it. But it doesn't need to be in an electrical room where the additional heat could cause problems. Did y'all at least take down the still?"

"Ronan took most of it apart and then went back for the main part which had this in it." He lifted his glass indicating the clear liquid. "It was hot so he couldn't carry it. He had to wait until it cooled."

"I guess their loss is our gain for tonight."

Everyone picked up their glasses. "Cheers, salud," we all said in unison and raised our glasses above our heads at the same time. Then we chugged our moonshine quickly. We all dropped our glasses back on the table with our faces twisted. I grunted in relief as I cleared my throat. Everyone else echoed my sentiments in the form of grunts and whoops. We all reached for our tea and took a big drink.

"I think that is going to take some getting used to. That shit is strong, *chingoa!*"

"Bloody hell! Sorry my British came out. But that was rough. I thought I had drunk some strong drinks before, but wow. Can you pass me the pitcher of iced tea? I need some more to wash that down," Sphynx said to Jax.

He reached over to the counter behind him, picking up the pitcher of iced tea and passing it to her.

Sphynx took hold of the pitcher. "Thanks, me duck."

"Me duck?" I asked. "You said that to Verruca one time."

Sphynx smiled wistfully. "Oh. It's a term of endearment from back home. I always liked it, so I still use it."

"I think I like it too."

Night patted his chest and coughed hard to clear his throat, "I thought the old men on the reservation made some strong alcohol, but I think this one might beat theirs."

Once we had settled from our moonshine, we began eating and talking.

"So Sphynx, how did you get from the English Midlands to Dallas?"

"Well I grew up in the Midlands until I was eleven. Then my dad moved us to London because of his job. Just about the time I settled in, he got promoted and moved us to Dallas. Well actually, my Mum and I stayed in London until I finished the current term in school, then we joined him in the summer."

"Was your family still in Dallas when you volunteered?"

Verruca broke in , "Mom, stop being nosy."

"It's okay, I don't mind." Sphynx patted her arm. "Well, my parents moved back to the Midlands after my dad retired. But Mum passed away shortly after I finished grad school."

"I'm sorry. That must have been hard on everyone."

"Thank you, it was, but I went home to visit Dad as much as I could, and we talked all the time. I think talking regularly helped both of us. But having my sister in town also helped him. Now I'm not sure what happened to them. I tried to talk him into joining the program, but he wouldn't."

"The not knowing has to be hard. I'm sorry you are having to deal with that now."

"Thank you. Having these three with me has made dealing with all this much easier, but we all have our days." She smiled at Verruca, Jax and Ryo.

"Yes, we do." I nodded in agreement.

Sphynx started a conversation with Verruca and I went to get a little more bread and pasta. When I returned to the table I decided it was Jax's turn to be interrogated.

"Okay, Jax it's your turn. Spill your guts. Are you a native Texan, or a transplant?"

"Texan, born and raised. My story is pretty simple. Y'all know most of it. I lived in Austin my whole life. My family was typical. Dad was a teacher at a local high school. He taught PE and shop. Mom was a kindergarten teacher."

"What happened to them?"

Jax shrugged casually, "They went out on a Friday night for one of their date nights. It began raining at some point that night, and when they were on their way home, a car hit them head on. The other driver had been drinking and he lost control of his car when he hit a large puddle."

"Damn, that had to be hard to deal with at that age." I smiled softly at him.

Jax's smile was tight but he went on, "It was, but what made it harder is that the only family left was my mom's mom, and she was in a nursing home. I had to go into foster care. I bounced around until I aged out. I had no idea what I wanted to do, but one of my case workers gave me a bunch of pamphlets on different schooling I could take. I decided on mechanics because my dad and I had always worked on an old mustang he had in the driveway."

"Bettering yourself is always a good way to set yourself in a direction and see what happens."

Jax nodded in agreement, "It was. I did really great in school. I got a good job at a big mechanics garage. They worked on everything, but they specialized in motorcycles. I loved the bikes and quickly became one of their top mechanics and that's when I found out that the people who owned the shop were actually a Motorcycle Club. I became a prospect shortly after that and then at the end of that year I was a fully-fledged member. It was actually just what I had been looking for, somewhere to belong."

Verruca and Sphynx hugged his arms. Verruca softly told

him he now belonged with them.

I felt bad for them not having anyone from their past life here with them, but they were making new lives for themselves. Not that any of us had much of a choice, but it was better than all of us dwelling in the past.

After we finished dinner, we all moved to the couch and chairs in the living room area and continued talking for several more hours. We even took our chances and had two more shots of moonshine. Verruca told Night some stories about me that I tried to keep her from telling, so of course I paid her back by telling stories of her. I made sure they all knew she used to have a whole Chinese-alien language that she and her cat, Kitty No, would talk to each other in. I also told them about the Chingoa Meow song she wrote for Kitty No that had all of us laughing at her creativeness.

"Oh, let me tell you about the first party I went to as a prospect," Jax said animatedly. "There was several of us prospecting that year, and the MC threw us a welcome party. Of course I thought I was hot shit and could out-drink everyone because I always had out-drunk my high school friends.

"So, my sponsor and the vice president kept just handing me drink after drink by ten or ten thirty I was gone, passed out in one of the guest rooms at the club house. They swear that I was the one who had stripped all my clothes off, but who knows. The VP started drawing on me with a sharpie and my sponsor had a couple of the girls doing weird shit to me. Then my sponsor tied me to the bed and I almost pissed myself trying to get up. It was a wild night."

"And after all that they still got you again when they duct taped you to your bike?"

"Well let's just say it took me a while to learn my lesson around those guys."

"It would seem. I hope you did and then got some of them back."

"I did."

We all laughed at the wicked grin on Jax's face when he answered me. "How about you, Ryo? Did you get into any trouble growing up?"

"Maybe. I tried not to be too much trouble because my sisters and brother were raising me and my younger sister. But I do remember one time before our parents passed. Ronan and I had been picking at our sisters for days for being annoying girls. We had even tied their hair together around one of the bed posts. They were so mad at us because they had to cut some of their hair off because we had caused huge knots in it.

"So in retaliation they took our surfboards, the brand-new ones we had worked our ass of for all summer, rubbed honey all over them and laid them on top of ant beds. The ant beds were also in the sun. By the time we found the boards in the back yard they not only were covered in ants that bit you all over, the honey had hardened in several places. It took us forever to get those boards clean and usable again, not to mention all the ant bites we had. Poor Ronan even had an allergic reaction to the bites and had to go to the hospital. Of course, we were all in trouble for it."

"Okay, since Mom interrogated my people, it's my turn to interrogate you." Verruca pointed at Night. "Tell us about you."

"Like what?" Night's tone was slightly worried.

"Anything, something we don't know. Something funny from when you were young. Whatever, I just want to know a little more."

Night pondered for a minute, "Okay, let me see. I guess I was about thirteen, my cousin was twelve, we were at a Puberty Rite Ceremony for one of the young girls in our tribe. The ceremony is to celebrate a young girl moving from childhood into the next stage of life. But for us boys we didn't care, we were young and bored. So we went looking for something to do. As much as my mom and aunt tried to make us stay with them and behave, they just couldn't. We had been roaming through the ceremonial area for a while when we came across what we thought was a few joints and a bottle of tequila. We took a joint and the bottle.

"Then we went off and found a spot behind the main building to smoke and drink. What we didn't know was the joint wasn't weed, but jimsonweed. We use it in ceremonies to help us have visions, it's a hallucinogenic. Not only were we drunk, but we were seeing all kinds of things. To this day I cannot stand snakes, I was hallucinating that a giant snake was trying to eat me. I ran all over screaming for help. My cousin thought he was a bear, he was roaring at everyone. It took us hours to come down. When we did we were so sick we threw up everywhere and we couldn't get out of bed the next day. My mom and aunt had to stay up all night with us, but once we were okay and no permanent damage had been done, we were in so much trouble with them. I think I was grounded for like a month and had so many chores to do that I didn't have time to do anything else."

I laughed hard, because I remembered doing something close to that. "I think that was the point. She didn't want you to have time to get into more trouble."

"I see now why you like my mom. One troublemaker knows another when they see one."

"I never did anything wrong my whole life," I said in mock innocence.

"Whatever, wild child," Verruca retorted and the rest just said, "Uh huh, sure."

I just shook my head at them in disbelief. Night slung an arm over my shoulders and pulled me into him kissing the top of my head. I settled into him, smiling, as everyone continued to talk.

It was nice to get to know Verruca's quartet more on a

personal level. They all seemed to be good people. I was looking around at everyone as they were talking, and I noticed that Sphynx had fallen asleep on Jax's shoulder. I pointed to her, and Verruca turned to see what I was pointing at. Verruca smiled and then pouted slightly as she looked at Sphynx.

"Let's get her home. It is already late, and a few of us" — Verruca turned and looked at me pointedly — "have to get up early and get this last site sampled."

Jax jiggled his shoulder up and down to wake Sphynx.

She jumped and flung a hand to her chest, looking around in confusion. "Eh, you little bugger," Sphynx said and slapped Jax on the arm.

I chuckled. It was funny how she bounced back and forth between her British words and her American words. It reminded me of myself with Tex-Mex.

They gathered themselves and some food to take with them. Then we all said our goodbyes, and they left. Before the door closed completely, Verruca stepped back in for another hug.

"You will tell me what you thought in the morning," she whispered demandingly in my ear.

"You know I will," I whispered back.

We both laughed and then she headed back out the door to join the rest of them.

I turned and walked into Night's waiting arms and we made our way to the bedroom. We both got undressed and climbed under the covers.

"I think that went well tonight. I mean, it was the first night that felt like something we would have done before." I pulled the pillow under my head.

"Yeah, it was almost normal. In fact, it was really nice and relaxing. I can't believe I'm about to say this, but the only thing missing was Kilian."

I rolled over to look at him to see if he was joking. But he didn't look like he was joking.

"Really, why?"

"Well, I know you like him. That you like having him around. I was getting used to him being around. So, it felt a little weird, like we were a bit lopsided."

"Okay." I snorted. "That was not what I was expecting, but I guess I can invite him to dinner tomorrow and we can all talk."

"I think that would be good."

Then Night rolled over and pulled me under him, planting a deep kiss on my lips. I wrapped my arms around his neck and my left leg over his butt. With that he slowly slid into me. I moaned softly as he pushed the last few inches in until he could go no further. He stayed in place not moving as he deepened the kiss. I wrapped the other leg around his butt giving him better access and encouraging him to move by digging my heels into his ass. At first, he didn't take my hint. I nudged a little harder with my heels. He laughed softly against my lips.

"Okay, I get the hint."

He began moving in and out of me slowly, making sure I felt every inch. I moaned as small rivers of fire washed through every nerve ending. The embers roared into full flames as he changed his tactics. He pulled out slowly then slammed home. Out slowly, slam home. He repeated this over and over. Panting moans escaped me as I begged for him to pick up his speed. He moaned as he thrust into me hard again. Then he stopped and pulled out, lifted me up, and turned me around onto my hands and knees.

He pushed my head down and dragged his nails down my back until he reached my hip. He gripped them tight, and my core tingled with anticipation. He slid the crown of his cock between my wet lips rubbing my clit. Flares of flaming desire spread out all over my body repeatedly with each pass of his crown on my clit. Just when I thought I could not take any more, he slammed home eliciting a gasp and a deep moan from me. I slid my hand down to my clit. It didn't take long before the liquid heat begin to pool in my core as my orgasm built.

Night moaned as he slid into me, and my inner walls clamped down tight. He slid his hand down my back until he reached the nape of my neck. He wrapped his hand into my hair then pulled my head back as he pushed completely into me. He rotated his hips, hitting every spot that pushed me to the edge of my orgasm. I was so close now I was whimpering and quivering.

He stopped his circular motions and went back to fucking me hard. It was just what I needed to push me toward oblivion. I begged him for more and he obliged. He let go of my hair and gripped my hips as he picked up his speed. Each thrust was deep, hard, and fast.

I gripped the sheets tight as I fell over the edge into bliss and screamed out. "Night!"

Right after my orgasm slammed into me, Night's slammed into him. His cock jerked and throbbed as my inner walls clinched around his cock milking every last drop of come from it.

We didn't move as wave after wave of our orgasms racked our bodies. My legs and arms felt weak as I came down. Instead of trying to get up I just collapsed onto the bed and wiggled my way up onto my pillow. Night laughed and flopped down on the side of me. He sighed deeply, turned into me, and flung his arm over me. I rolled over on to my stomach and passed out.

CHAPTER TWENTY-TWO: MEN ARE
MORE DRAMATIC THAN WOMEN

I groaned as I rolled over to break the blaring alarm. It was too early for all that noise. I slapped the little black square off the nightstand and rolled on to my back, stretching across the bed, procrastinating on getting out of it. I gave myself five more minutes to lie there before I forced myself out of the bed and into the shower.

Once I was showered and dressed, I headed for breakfast in the dining room and left Night to sleep. I figured it was the least I could do after he let me sleep almost all day yesterday.

I walked in, and most of the awakees were already enjoying their breakfast. I entered the kitchen, and Rogue, poor thing, was working hard at making sure everyone received food.

"Morning, Iksen," Rogue said with a big smile.

"Morning, Rogue. Where are Vox and Garrett?"

"I'm trying to let Vox have a morning off, but as you can see, my skills are limited. Vega has been a huge help. He has been walking me through things. But I don't know where Garrett is."

"Good, I am glad you have had some help. I know this got sprung on y'all. Talk with Vox and Garrett and y'all decide if another person is needed. If so I will find someone. "

"No problem. Here you go, hope you like it," he said and handed me a plate with three breakfast tacos on it.

"Thank you."

I took my plate and found a seat. I was halfway through my second taco when Kilian sat down across from me. I looked over at him with a skeptical look. He didn't say anything until he had finished his first taco.

"Are we going to talk about what happened or are you going to continue to act like this?" Kilian said condescendingly and continued eating, not looking at me.

I sat there trying to hold my temper. I took a few more bites, gathering my thoughts and trying to keep my cool. Finally I took a deep breath and raised my eyes to meet his. I raised one eyebrow and pursed my lips together as I looked at him indignantly. I held this look for a few seconds to see if he was going to change his question. When he didn't, I finally spoke.

"Excuse me? I am not sure I heard you right."

"No, you heard me right."

Oh, the bastard. I so wanted to go off on him, but I had more important things to do. I got up, taking my last taco with me and left.

Just before I walked through the door he yelled, "You're just going to run away. What happened to the big tough girl from the other day?"

I paused in the door, warring with myself over whether I should respond or walk away because it wasn't worth it. But my logical side didn't win this one.

I turned, set my plate down on the closest table, and began a slow walk back toward him. He stood up and walked toward me.

"Let me tell you something. I don't care who you think you are, but you will not talk to me like that, at all. It's not just because I'm Iksen, but because I am a woman who will not put up with it. You think because we had something you can treat me however and talk to me however, but you can't. If that means I have to physically kick your ass I will, but you will not behave this way with me."

"I wouldn't have to act like this with you if you would just do what you're supposed to. I know you're Iksen, that doesn't mean you can't be a woman too."

"Honey, I am all woman, something you should know well. What I don't get is your obsession with me acting like some helpless woman. Have you never been around a woman who is strong and capable of doing things for herself?"

"I have been around a few, but none like you. You refuse to let me be a man at all. You won't let me do anything for you. You won't let me protect you, take care of you, hell you won't even let me be in control in the bedroom."

"If I thought you wouldn't let that little bit of control go to your head. If you wouldn't think that gave you the right to try and control every aspect of what I am doing, I might let you have some control in bed. But I know if I give you even that tiny bit of control, you would try to control all aspects. If you want to be Iksen that bad when we land, we can vote for a new Iksen and you can run against me."

"I don't want to be Iksen." Confusion flashed across his face. "You are excellent at being Iksen. You turn each situation and look at it from every angle making sure every possible issue can be handled. Not many people do that."

"Then what the hell is the problem?" I threw my hand in the air.

"I just want to take care of you on the flip side of things. You spend all day taking care of everyone else. Including me and Night. I just want to take care of you."

I heard swoons come from the crowd watching our little showdown. It took everything in me not to roll my eyes at those women.

"Well, that is not how it comes off. It comes off as controlling. I am not nor have I ever been looking for someone to take care of me. At least not in that way. Even when I am tired or sick, I get up and handle my shit. I have never had anyone else to do it for me nor would I have let anyone else do it for me. Not that I couldn't have used help sometimes. but because it wasn't anyone else's responsibility, it was mine. If you can't handle being in a relationship where we all take care of each other and it's not one sided then we need to call it quits right now."

Just as I finished speaking, I felt an arm brush mine, and a hand slid into mine. Night had walked up at some point. Night was staring at Kilian with a calm look, but his body was slightly behind me, indicating where he stood on the matter.

"Are you still okay with this?" Kilian looked at Night.

"I was the one who suggested she speak with you today and try to work things out," Night said in a firm tone. "But I am not okay if this is how it's going to be all the time. You have to learn to stop trying to control her. You can plainly see it doesn't work."

"I just—" Kilian tried to speak, but Night cut him off with a raised hand.

"I heard what you said, but after the first time, you should have got the picture. At the very least, you should have just told her what you were trying to do, so she understood you better. You have to stop goading her into a fight. I will not put up with it anymore."

"Why does she always have to rise to everything?" Kilian replied in a childlike tone.

Ignoring that last little childish dig, I spoke to him again. "You now have both our answers. We miss you but neither of us will put up with this behavior. Think about it for the rest of the day, then come to the cabin for dinner with your answer ready." I kissed Night, then Kilian before I headed for the bridge.

When I got to the bridge, Ronan and Verruca were already there looking over reports and communicating with Cash, who was getting the drones ready for launch today. We had lost four days already. We needed to explore this possible landing site and gather the needed samples. I felt good about today. Today was our day to get this done.

"Morning, guys."

"Morning," they mumbled back at the same time.

"Ronan, I think we may need to wake up some people. You need some for agents, and we may need two more people to help in the kitchen. Rogue, Garrett, and Vox are doing their best, but they need some down time too. "

"We can do that. I only need two more people for agents. I think we have two who are awake that will work," Ronan answered as he continued to look at the map table.

"I was thinking we probably need like five more people. One, we need the extra help guarding Lita and Ryker, but I think we need to have some extras already trained for when we land. We don't really know what is down there."

Ronan was quiet for a minute. "Okay, I can see that. It would be nice to have enough to rotate on Earth while we're building."

"Exactly, since we're in as much of a controlled environment as we're going to get here on the ship. It is probably the best place to train some more agents. You can get them physically ready, and then once we land, Kilian can finish the weapons training with actual firing classes."

"Okay, do you want to go through the list now and pick out who we want?"

"Yeah, if you're done helping Cash."

"Hold on. I have a question." Verruca came to join me on the couch. "When are we going to wake the rest of the people in general?"

"I thought we were going to wait until we landed?" I looked between the both of them.

"Yeah, at the time I thought that was the best idea, but I'm not sure now. I am looking at these landing sights. There is a lot of unknown elements. I don't think we should have newly awakened people in this unknown environment. What if some of them panic and run off? They will be killed or lost and die of hunger."

"Yeah, I could see how that might be a possibility. But what if having them all awake causes even more chaos than what Lita and Ryker have caused?" Ronan said.

"That's true," Verruca conceded.

"I have thought about this over and over. I have had the same concerns. I have thought about how pissed they will be that we didn't wake them up while we were still in space. I mean, when you stop and think about it, it's cool. We are in space, but I would rather them be pissed at me then put everyone in danger."

"Okay, it was just a thought. I was trying to think of things we could knock off the list before we landed. We will have our hands full with building, farming, and taking care of what animals we have managed to grow."

That actually reminded me that Verruca and I needed to go check on the progress of the animals growing. I made a reminder on my communicator.

"If that is settled, let's look at this list of people we still have asleep," Ronan said and flicked the list of people from his tablet into the air so we could all see it.

We scrolled through the list looking at their brief profiles, but after a while they all started to blur together.

"I think we should just pick. They have all started to merge into one. I think Echo Vallencourt is a good choice. Echo was a paramedic, so that would help in emergencies."

"I like her for an agent," Ronan agreed.

"Who else do we have that might be good options?" I asked.

"I think Asp Mabin and Crux Rubio might be good choices.

Asp was also a paramedic and Crux had been a bartender, but he is six feet five inches. Just his size alone would intimidate people," Verruca said with a smile and a shoulder shrug.

"Asp for sure. Crux . . ." Ronan paused for a minute as he looked up his profile. "Okay, he looks like he could handle it. Anyone who had to go through the foster system can handle anything thrown at them."

"So that's three down. I think this other guy Sage Fox would be good. He is another mechanic, but he could help in the kitchen and train as a backup mechanic if needed," I suggested, to round out our choices.

"He looks like he can handle himself. I think everyone we chose will work out," Ronan said.

"Good, that is figured out. Ronan, can I trust you to wake them and get them fed, show them the videos, and get them up to speed on everything else?"

"Actually, I need to go down and meet with Cash, Night, and Kilian," he said.

"Oh, yeah. Damn, I forgot. I need Verruca with me. Who else could do this?"

"Sphynx could do it. She has been wanting to do more," Verruca offered.

"Do you think she can handle all of them? You know the awakees are a bit confused when they wake up. Some have been a little aggressive at first."

"She can handle it. I'll see if Jax and Ryo can go with her."

"Okay, message them all and then we've got to go take care of some other things."

I waited for Verruca to tell everyone their assignments while I looked at the latest weather reports. I was just reading through the info on the Texas Louisiana border when Verruca said she was ready.

"Hold on, let me finish reading this." After a few minutes, I continued.

"Son of a motherless goat, did you see that report from the Texas Louisiana border? That was a crazy storm last night. Not only did two snownadoes spawn from the system, but it also dumped hail the size of softballs and about three inches of rain. The wind gusts were up to fifty miles per hour. I'm glad we decided to look farther down the coast for another spot." We stepped onto the elevator.

"I saw it. I was thinking the same thing."

"In fact let me get Vega started with gathering info on that area. Vega?" I looked up. A faint wave of shimmer appeared in front of us. It looked like heat rising from the black top in August. As it continued, Vega's form became more visible. It seemed today he wanted green eyes. Normally he had blue.

"Yes, Ms. Atlantis," his deep smokey voice said as his form solidified into view.

"In one of our last meeting we decided to look for a landing spot around Corpus Christi, Texas. Can you begin pulling any info you may have on that location? Also, we're going to need you to take pictures and scans of the area."

"Yes, I can do all those things. What type of area are you looking for?"

"The same as our last spots. As close to fresh and salt water as we can get. Calmer weather if that's possible."

"Yes, Ms. Atlantis, I will get started as soon as we are done with today's exploration."

"Thank you, Vega."

I finished just in time to step off the elevator onto the black deck. Vega popped out of sight. He was becoming more dramatic with his entrances and exits. I dropped my thoughts of Vega as Verruca and I walked into the labs. We walked in to see Savinka and Vashanti holding the baby bunny.

"Aww," I said with a big smile and reached my hands out for him.

"No, I want to hold him first," Verruca said and stepped in

front of me.

I let her hold him first. He was too cute. He only had fur around his ears, nose, and tail. He looked like an old Kung fu master. But miniature.

I reached over and rubbed his little ears. "How have the guys over there been doing?"

Vashanti walked up to my side. "They have been doing good. We added a lamb instead of a goat. He needs more of the additional nutrition and sooner than the others. He needed it within days of being in the womb."

"Well, as long as they stay healthy and grow. I mean, I know as a scientist you want to know why. I would like to know too, but for now let's just focus on keeping them alive. Then once we have a few born, we can look into the why."

"Okay, but do you mind if I store their afterbirths to study when I can?"

"Absolutely. We will need to know everything we can if we plan to rebuild healthy, non-mutated animals."

Vashanti smiled wide. I squeezed her forearm and went to take my turn holding the baby bunny. I gently took him form Verruca's hands. He was so tiny, mostly pink with just peach fuzz for fur. His eyes were not open yet, but his nose was working. It was twitching away.

"How are y'all feeding him?"

"We have been using a syringe to feed him right now, but we're going to have to figure out a makeshift bottle as they get bigger and for the others," said Savinka.

"We have been trying out some different things. I think we're close to having one for the large animals. Still working on one for the smaller ones."

"Well, hopefully we will be on Earth by the time the lamb gets here." I handed the bunny back to Vashanti. "We've got to go and see how the drone prep is coming along. Send me updates on how the bunny is doing, and I'll try to be back soon to see him for myself."

"We will," they said in canon.

Verruca and I headed over to the cargo bay to check in with Cash. We needed to get this place checked out today and check our second site in Texas. I just really wanted to get us on the ground. I was tired of being on this ship. I mean, it was beautiful up here, but we could only go between four decks. I would love to be able to go outside and see some land.

CHAPTER TWENTY-THREE: LAST MINUTE DECISION

We walked into the cargo bay, and I shoved my mental bitching down so I could get back to the task at hand. Today we were exploring our third location, North Carolina, between the Roanoke River and Tar River. Right at the top of Albemarle Sound. It was a great choice of sites. It had all the necessary attributes for us to survive.

"Hey guys, how's it looking?"

"They're ready. I'm waiting for the batteries to charge and top off the fuel for the thrusters," Cash answered.

"Wait, these things have fuel?" Verruca looked at the drones curiously.

I looked at him questionably also, because I didn't know they had fuel. "What kind of fuel?"

"It's a hydrogen fuel mix. It is in these tiny canisters that you can fill and re-insert. It just helps the drones push through the atmosphere on the way down and back through on the way up."

"Oh, I just didn't know they had fuel. I thought it was all batteries. How much longer before we can launch?"

"It should be about another five minutes and we will be ready." Cash smiled wide. He really liked doing all of this. I could see it in his eyes.

"Good, let's get this done. I would like to have a quick council meeting and just go over a few things. You know, make sure everyone is on the same page."

"Okay, we will meet you up on the bridge once the drones have launched," Night assured me.

I nodded in acknowledgment. Then Verruca and I headed for the bridge. On our way out, Juniper came bouncing through the door.

"Hi, guys. How are y'all doing?" Juniper asked as we traded places in the doorway.

I turned back to face her. "I'm good, just trying to get caught up from our little asteroid storm the other day."

"I'm good too, just trying to help Mom get us back on track," Verruca chimed in.

"You look like you're in a good mood."

"Yeah, just trying to stay positive. You know how that can go."

"Yes, I do. We will catch up more at the meeting. I just need to go prepare for our exploration today."

We all waved bye to each other. Verruca and I headed for the elevator, my mind turning over what Juniper said about *just trying to stay positive*. Which made me think we should do something to boost morale. I stopped dead in my tracks when another thought took over my mind. It was one of those things that happens when someone says something that triggers a completely different thought. One that has nothing to do with what triggered it.

"I think this is the site for me and someone else to go to Earth? Right now, in the large drone," I blurted out, looking at Verruca excitedly.

"What is wrong with you?" she shouted.

"It just hit me. I want to know for myself what it is like down there, so I know I am making the right choice to take us back to the ground."

I turned and walked back into the cargo bay. Once I was in the middle of the room where everyone could see me, I spoke.

"I'm going to Earth."

"Wait, what, when?" Cash blurted out from the top level.

"Right now. I want to personally know what it's like down there. I want to know if we are making the right decision to go back."

"Absolutely not," Verruca and Night said together.

"I didn't ask for permission. I'm telling y'all and asking for a partner."

Everyone erupted into chaos, all of them talking at the same time as they climbed down from the upper level. Some saying I couldn't go, others just cursing about how crazy it was. Finally all four stood in front of me.

"Look," I said and raised a hand to silence them. "I already know what y'all want to say, but I don't care. I want to go down. I would like it if Night joined me, but Jax or Ryo will do."

They broke out in choruses of *No* and *You can't go.*

I raised my hand to silence them again. "I'm going. The only question is who is going with me."

"Mom, you cannot go. What if you get hurt? You cannot take pain meds if you get hurt. What if the drone can't come back?"

I pulled her into a hug and kissed the top of her head.

"What if you die? I can't do this without you," she said, the shaky, muffled words from her face buried in my shirt-covered shoulder.

"I'll be fine, baby girl. I always am," I whispered and squeezed her tight.

She pulled out of the hug and stared at me with tears threatening to spill down her face.

"I'll be fine," I said imploringly.

I heard Night sigh hard and heavy. "Fine, I'll go with you. Only because I can plainly see you will not back down. Even though there are plenty of us who could go instead."

Rolling my eyes at him I turned to Cash. "Do you know

where the AGSs are?"

"Yes, they are in the other hangar's storage cabinet," he said as he waved us to follow him.

Night and I accompanied him to the other hangar. The suits were black with blue stripes around the shoulder areas, the wrists, and one on each side of the zipper that ran up the center of the suit. The suits were made from what felt like a hybrid between rubber and latex. We put them on, and they fitted snugly to our bodies but were extremely flexible. They also changed temperature according to your body's needs, because mine was cooling down. There was a helmet that went with the suits, and when it was locked into place, the suit was airtight. There was a square device about the size of a lunchbox that two tubes from the suit attached to. The little box created the AGS's oxygen supply. It was a mini air scrubber. It took in the air around you, scrubbed it, and turned it into oxygen. Once we were suited up and everything secured, we walked back to the other cargo bay.

"A few things about the suits. They are made for short term use. Like taking the drone down and back or needing to go out of the ship for a repair. The little air scrubber cannot work for extended periods," Cash dictated as he double checked the suits.

"Understood," I yelled through the helmet.

Cash moved to face me and pushed a button on the collar of my suit, and a radio clicked on. I smiled at him.

"If there is any indication that there is a problem on the way down, I will return the drone to the ship immediately." Cash stared at me.

I looked over at Night, who was locking his helmet in place. He looked up at me. "That was for you not me. I wouldn't even be going if it wasn't for you."

"Me!"

"Yes, you. Ms. Recklessness." Cash shook me by my

shoulders.

"Okay, I get it. You will bring me back if there are any issues."

Juniper and Verruca had opened the large steel sliding door that led to the drone launch area. Cash and Night began maneuvering the human-sized drone into the launch area. Verruca stood there glowering at me. I walked over to her and hugged her again. After they got the drone in place, Night reached over and placed a hand on her shoulder.

"I'll do my best to keep her safe."

Verruca pulled out of my hold and nodded at Night. Me, on the other hand, she returned to glowering at.

Ignoring her death stare, Night and I made our way to the drone. We climbed into the drone and began securing everything for our flight. Once that was done, I waved at everyone still standing in the doorway. Night began flipping switches and pushing buttons. They slid the large metal door closed and locked it, ensuring the seal engaged to keep the other hangar safe when the launch doors opened.

The radio systems connected with a screech that made us all wince.

"Do you understand how it all works, Night?" Cash's voice came over the radio.

"Yes, I have flown plenty of times, and these controls are very similar to a helicopter."

"Okay, at any time if there is an issue I can take over. Now, let's check camera feeds." He clicked a few buttons. "Camera feeds are working well. I also have all your gauges and systems pulled up on the main screen so I can monitor everything."

"Okay, sounds good," I answered him.

"I got this. I am a good pilot." Night continued to flip switches and check gauges.

I reached over and squeezed his forearm to let him know I

had faith in his abilities.

"Okay, countdown has started." Cash came over the radio again.

I turned in my seat to look at the flight deck. Knowing I couldn't look at Verruca anymore I turned back to face the launch doors and whatever lay beyond them. My nerves tingled with anticipation, and not the good kind. Night looked over at me, and my emotions must have been written on my face, because he took my hand and intertwined our fingers. I looked over at him and smiled slightly.

"Holding your hand is not for you. It's for me. I need reassurance." The left corner of his lips turned up.

The countdown hit zero and the launch doors snapped open. We were sucked out, and the doors snapped closed behind us. Night began pushing buttons. Then he leaned back in his seat relaxed as could be.

"Is that all you need to do?" I was a little horrified at his lack of action.

"Yes, I set the auto landing sequence. The drone does the rest." He squeezed my hand.

"Okay, if you're sure."

I looked around at space—outer space. I was flying through outer space. *How crazy is this? How crazy is all of it?* Amazed at what I was seeing, I tried to take it all in as we smoothly descended to Earth. Well, it was smooth until we began to enter the thermosphere. Our smooth ride became bumpy as we were jostled around. I began grabbing for the *oh shit* handle when the flames began slithering up the windshield and all around the outside of the drone, but we didn't have any handles inside. Night took my hand to help calm me. Then as we entered the next layer, the mesosphere, it got downright rough. The jostling became jerking from side to side.

I gripped Night's hand tighter. I was expecting it to get

unbearably hot inside the cockpit, but to my surprise it didn't. Even though everything seemed to be going well, I still had Night's hand in a fierce grip. Then out of nowhere everything stopped, and blaring bright light hit us in the face. I snapped my eyes shut from the overbearing sharp light. We were entering the troposphere. As we descended, little by little I cracked my eyes open trying to see what was happening. All I could currently see was white fluffiness. We evidently were passing through the cloud banks.

I continued to open my eyes sliver by sliver, but it was a hard fight. The light of the sun was unforgiving to our poor eyes. We had been in artificial light for so long now that our eyes couldn't handle real light. I said to hell with it and opened my eyes. They immediately watered and made everything blurry. I blinked several times before they cleared enough to see we were getting closer to land, but I still had to partially shield my eyes with one hand to see anything. Night began pushing buttons and flipping switches as we got closer to land. Just as we touched down, a loud screeching echoed in our helmets and the drone. I tried to slap my hands to my ears, but the helmet was in the way.

"What was that?"

"Mom!" Verruca's voice came blaring at us from all directions.

"Stop yelling." I winced from the noise.

"Then answer me when I'm talking to you, and I wouldn't have to yell at you."

"Smart ass."

Verruca's laughter came over the radio loud and clear. I had not realized we had lost radio contact once we left the ship, but it seemed to be working fine now. Then I jerked back, startled by the four drones hovering in front of us. I waved at everyone.

"See, we're okay."

"Yeah, things are good. Everything is working." Night waved at them too.

I heard a large collective sigh come through the radio. I guessed they all had been holding their breath.

"Your video feed is coming through clearly. The small drones are working great as well. All your other equipment is working, and all vital signs are reading strong," Cash assured us.

Night and I looked at each other and nodded our heads.

With a big smile on his face Night unlocked the doors to the drone. We stepped out and placed our feet on the Earth for the first time in a hundred and five years. I reached up and took off my helmet. I clipped my helmet to the back side of the small air scrubber where it had a built in hanging spot. I then turned back, took a deep breath, turned my face up to the sun, and raised my hands over my head. I was taking in this moment of being back home. I let my arms fall on top of my head and I looked around at my surroundings. It kind of felt like discovering a new world. It made me wonder if that was how the first guys to land on the moon felt. I looked over at Night and could see he was less moved by being back on Earth. He was already walking back and forth looking at a map projected from his holo.

Our drone was sitting in a small clearing. It was longer and more narrow than wide. The tree line of the forest was maybe three feet from us. When I walked to the front of the drone, I could see that the other side sloped slightly, about another three feet away. I was guessing but I bet that slope led to the rushing water sound I was hearing. Looking directly ahead in the same direction the drone was facing, I could see remnants of structures. What those structures were, I could not tell from here. Then I turned to look directly behind the drone, but all I could see in that direction was trees.

"I say we head toward those structures and see what we

find." Night reached out his hand for me.

I took it, and we walked down the slope. We looked over to see that the small drop led to another piece of more steeply sloping land. This land led to a sidewalk that ran next to a gently moving river. The river was moving in the direction of the overgrown structures, and we followed it. We walked along the sidewalk with its almost completely rusted railings until we hit a dense wall of foliage. In this section the vines had grown out over the railing of the sidewalk and created a thick wall. Night began pulling on the vines. After pulling several large handfuls loose Night still had not cleared a path. I began to help him pull on the vines. I was pulling hard, but they were not budging. I grabbed a handful with both hands and used all my weight to pull. Nothing was happening at first. Then I heard a crack, then a snap, and then I was on my ass because all the vines I was pulling on came down.

"Son of a motherless goat, that flipping hurt."

I could hear Verruca laughing over the radio. Trying to stifle his own laughter Night reached out both his hands and pulled me to my feet.

"You okay, Iksen?" Cash called out.

"She looks okay," Night answered as he helped me dust dirt from my pants.

"I'm fine. Just didn't expect to end up on my ass."

"Come on now. The vines are cleared, and I can see a sort of path through them." Night took my hand.

Dragging me, he led us into the foliage. Once I was inside the greenery, I could see that something or someone had made a path of sorts through the tangled mess. After ducking to miss another thick vine, we ran into another large wall of vegetation.

Night examined the foliage. Then he grabbed a handful in both hands and yanked each hand in the opposite direction, like he was opening a set of stage curtains. The vegetation gave way, making a big enough gap we could slide through.

"Cash, are you getting all of this?"

"Yes, Iksen. Both feeds are coming through clearly."

"Good."

Night and I stepped out of the greenery into a remarkably preserved town. The buildings were in desperate need of repair, but there was no vegetation growing all over them. The grass was very tall in some sections, and some of the shrubs were now almost as tall as some of the trees. There was no trash on the ground, and most of the windows were still intact. There even appeared to still be items in the buildings. You could tell by looking that the visible damage was due to aging, not people purposely damaging them.

The first building to my left was a convenience store. The next one looked like it was a restaurant, by the number of tables and chairs scattered on the inside. Attached to it looked like a boutique of some kind. The clothing mannequins were still in the windows. The clothes, on the other hand, looked like just strings and strips of fabric hanging on the mannequins now. We continued down the sidewalk next to the water.

We had not walked far when the sidewalk opened onto a large round grassy hill. Night dragged me up the hill. I was not prepared for a hill. I had to stop and catch my breath at the top. I looked over at Night. He wasn't even breathing hard. Shaking my head, I stood upright and looked around.

"You guys seeing this? It looks like some kind of town center. The building to the left looks like a courthouse or city hall. It also looks like the river opens into a bay farther down from here."

"We see it. But what's that large dark object at the far end of the bay?" Verruca came through the radio.

"I don't know. Let me get closer."

I began making my way down to the side of the river,

trying to remember not to lean on the railing because I might fall in. Night kept pace with me, focusing on our surroundings looking for any signs of danger. The shape was coming into view better, but my brain couldn't make out what it was yet. The farther down the sidewalk I got, the more I could see that the shape was triangular-ish. It looked like dark, burnt or rusted metal, but I still couldn't tell. I walked a little farther, and then it hit me. "It's the bow of a ship. It looks like the stern sank, leaving the bow sticking almost straight up in the air."

"Wow," I heard several voices say.

"Yeah, it looks crazy."

"Let's go back and explore some of those buildings." Night pulled on my arm.

Chapter Twenty-Four: Exploring What Was Left

We began making our way back down the sidewalk to the town center. When we got there, Night headed toward the second building to my right.

"Hold on." I pulled on Night's hand, "Cash, can you set the small drones to collecting samples while we explore?"

"Yes, Iksen."

I caught up to Night at the second building. He was trying to look through the dirty glass of a downstairs window.

"What do you see?"

"I can't really see anything."

I walked up on the porch. Some of the boards bowed under my weight, and I had to step carefully up to the large wood and glass door. I pushed on the door, but it didn't move. I shoved it with all my weight, and it slid back barely enough for us to slide through. Slipping through the opening into a poorly lit entry way, I could see a large wooden staircase dead center. To one side there was an entryway table that was half standing. On each side of the entryway were large square doorways. I chose to walk through the right one. There was barely any light coming through the window at the far end. I could make out several rows of chairs on each side of an aisle.

At the end of the aisle was a dark, odd-shaped blob. I couldn't tell what it used to be. I slowly moved up the aisle toward it.

Night grabbed me after a few steps and pulled me back.

"Let me go first."

Rolling my eyes at him, I gestured for him to go ahead of me. We made it about halfway up the aisle, and I realized what it used to be. It was what was left of a baby grand piano.

"That sucks, I bet it was beautiful at one time. I would love to play an instrument again." My tone was wistful.

"I bet it was," said Verruca.

"Why does it sound like you two are about to cry?" Ryo sounded worried.

"It's always sad to lose a musical instrument. It's almost as sad as losing a pet," answered Cash.

"Exactly," I said.

Shaking his head, Night led me to the room that was on the left of the entryway. This room had floor-to-ceiling mirrors. Along the mirrors were remnants of wooden bars running the entire length of the room. On the wall that was on the same side as the doorway were also floor-to-ceiling mirrors. On this side of the room there were three-wheeled bases scattered. I recognized what this room once was. Night was still looking around at everything.

"This was a ballet studio once upon a time," I told him. "Those three-wheeled bases over there were for mobile ballet bars."

"How do you know that?"

"I spent some time in dance studios when I was young."

Looking around, I could see the beautiful space it used to be. At the front of the room were large windows. There were also windows above the mirrors and skylights in the ceiling. It once was filled with tons of natural light. I could imagine all the little girls dancing in their little ballet outfits. Now the windows were dirty, the room was dark, and the mirrors were tarnished.

"This must have been a music and dance school at one time. Now it's just sad. It holds no more beauty in it."

"Let's go over to that main building," Night suggested.

We exited the building and then froze at the sound of a plopping, splashing sound coming from the water. I turned around and ran back to the railings and looked over. The railing groaned a little as I leaned against it looking down at the river. I didn't see what had made the noise, but I heard the snapping noise just before the railing gave way. Night barely caught me by the collar of my suit and pulled me back.

"You are going to give me a heart attack before we get back."

I shrugged my shoulders and turned back to head for the other building. "It must have been an animal or a fish."

"It was almost you plopping into the river," said Verruca sarcastically.

"Whatever."

We reached the official-looking building, and Night began peering through windows. Again, the windows were so dirty he couldn't see anything, so he shoved the door open. We walked into a wide, long, rectangular room. Against the wall with the door were chairs. Between the chairs and the long wood counter were the last pieces of line dividers. All in all, it looked like a waiting area of any official building.

We made our way through the trash on the floor to the wooden counter. This building looked like it had been trashed on purpose. I hopped up on the counter and swung my legs over to the other side. I could see now that everything on this side had been trashed as well. I slid off the counter until my feet touched the floor and I heard crunching under my feet. I lifted my right foot and looked down, then lifted my left and that was when I saw some glass. I carefully picked my way through the mess on the floor to the back side of the dilapidated desk and saw the rusted beat-to-hell remains of computers, printers, and other office supplies on the ground.

"What are you doing?" Night's voice was a hushed growl.

"Relax, I'm just looking around."

I continued to the left, picking my way through. Night hopped up on the counter, swung his legs over, and joined me. He followed me as I made my way through the mess into the hallway. The floor was clear of trash, but the first office was a mess like the front area. The florescent light was hanging from the ceiling, rusted and damaged. The desk was nothing but a pile of wood. There was another pile of wood in the corner that might have been shelves or a chair. I couldn't tell, so I moved to the next office.

Night was in the next one looking around at what was left standing. In this office was a very rusted filing cabinet.

We continued down the hall looking through the doors, and each office was in as bad shape as the first two. We made it to the end of the hallway. Directly at the end was a mostly glass emergency exit. and to the right was another hallway. I looked out the emergency exit to see what was outside of the door, and a quick movement to the right caught my eye. I turned my attention in that direction but didn't see anything. I looked back down the hallway, but Night was in an office. Also, the windows of the hallway were too high up for it to have been a reflection.

"Cash, where are the drones?"

"Right now, there are two a few yards behind the building you are in. One is collecting dirt, and the other is pulling leaves. The other two are collecting water. One from the bay, the other from the river."

"Okay, I thought I saw someone move at the back of the adjacent building. But then I thought it might be the drones. The movement was right at the edge of that really overgrown area at the back of that building."

"Which building? There is one on each side of you."

"The one on the left side when facing the building I am in."

Night came out of the office holding something in his hand.

319

He held it out to me, and it was a snow globe.

"Out of all the things to survive, a snow globe?"

We both laughed as I turned it in my hand. The scene on the inside was a volcano erupting. The lava was running down into a forest, and as I turned it, the lava still sparkled like it was flowing. I turned it upside down to swirl the snow, or maybe it was supposed to be ash.

"Hey, that looks like home," Ryo said, amused.

"I'll bring it back for you."

Ryo just laughed.

"You said you saw movement?" Night asked, looking out the emergency exit.

"Yeah, out toward the end of that building." I pointed out the door in the direction I had seen the movement.

"Guys, something just happened to one of the drones in the back of your building. Something knocked it out of the air, and it is still knocking it around."

We pushed open the emergency exit, and to our surprise the alarm sounded. It sounded like it was drowning in deep water, but it worked. We quickly but quietly made our way to the back corner of the building.

"The camera is showing flashes of the ground and what looks like a paw. So something has it," Cash whispered.

Night gestured for me to hold back, and he looked around the corner of the building. He tiptoed to get a better look. After a few more seconds he turned back to me.

"I can't make out what kind, but I can tell it's an animal. This bush is too tall for me to see much more. I am going to make my way around so I can get a good look."

He inched his way around the bush, with me following and saw that it was a venom dog pup. He was bouncing at the drone and pawing it. He thought he'd found a new toy and he was super cute playing with it.

"How do you want to get the drone back from him?"

"I was thinking of scaring him with a gun shot."

"Wait, where did you hide a gun?"

"In my boot." Night leaned down and pulled a hellcat out of his boot. "See? It fits perfectly."

Shaking my head in disbelief, I gestured for him to take the shot. We stepped out from behind the bush, and he aimed the gun at the ground behind the dog.

"Please don't hit him," I whispered.

"I won't," he whispered back.

Night shot. The pup jumped and yelped. He began sniffing the ground where the bullet hit the dirt. He sniffed hard in one spot and then sneezed all over. Then he sneezed again and again. When he was done, he ran back into the trees. I waited for Night to retrieve the drone.

"He was so cute," Verruca said.

"He was adorable." I was making my way toward Night. "He was just a baby playing with a new toy."

"If we chose this location, we would have to deal with venom dogs," said Night.

"I'm sure there is more than venom dogs that we would have to worry about," said Ronan.

"True, but that applies to all the locations," I said. "But Night, let's go explore the forest area. I don't want to go far. I just want an idea of what it looks like."

I began walking toward the trees. Night let out a loud put-out sigh and followed me. We cleared the first group of trees and entered a lush green forest. There was a very small clearing about two feet away canopied by the lush foliage of pine trees and whatever this viny plant was. The ground was covered in a thick spongy layer of lanky moss and was a rich emerald green.

"It's beautiful." I wasn't talking to anyone in particular.

"It is. I didn't expect this. I wasn't sure any forest had survived after seeing Oregon," Night sounded far away as he looked around.

"I say we go in different directions." Holding up my hand to stop him from speaking. "Not far. Just a little way so we get a better picture of what things look like."

"No more than six feet apart." Night looked at me sternly.

"Okay," I held up my hands in surrender.

I turned to the left and Night went to the right. After only a few feet I had to crawl over a log or walk a long way around. It appeared this log was actually a small tree that had fallen. I climbed over and stretched my legs toward the ground.

"Shit, son of a motherless goat." I slipped on some moss and fell a little farther than I thought I would.

"What happened?" Night called out to me.

"Nothing, the drop was a little farther than I thought," I yelled back as I rubbed my knees and elbow.

"You sure you're okay?"

"I'm fine. I just hit my knees and my elbow."

"She's fine, believe me. If she was hurt, you would know. Her body becomes extra dramatic. Too much pain and she vomits her guts up and passes out," Verruca chimed in over the radio.

Rolling my eyes at my smartass of a daughter I picked myself up and continued my exploration. As I walked and looked at things, my mind jumped to doing something for the whole ship to lift morale. Again another random though brought on by things not related to it.

"Okay, I know this has nothing to do with what I'm doing or what we're talking about. But Verruca, what if we do something for everyone to lift their morale. Maybe a movie night or game night. What do you think?"

"Yeah, that actually sounds fun."

"Oh, yeah, that would be fun," Juniper agreed.

"Maybe Jax could use the three-D printer in the engine room to print some . . ."

I trailed off because I came across a mini pond. It had a very narrow stream that fed it. But it looked like it was right out of someone's fairytale drawings.

"Wow, that's really pretty," Verruca said.

"I know it looks like someone painted a fairy bath right onto the forest floor."

The stream ran over a tiny outcropping of rocks, which turned the end of the stream into a tiny waterfall. All around the rocks by the waterfall were different types of mushrooms growing at all different heights. The taller ones even glowed. All along the edges of the pond was the soft spongy lanky moss. Then at the very back side were several flat rocks that would be perfect for small animals to sun on. Behind the flat rocks was a curtain of what looked like tiny blood root flowers. The tiny white flowers intertwined with each other, creating a curtain of white.

Verruca continued our conversation as I moved on from the little fairy pond. "The movie or game night I think would help a lot with uplifting everyone's spirits. When do you want to do this night?"

"I was thinking tonight if we could get everything together. Someone has to ask Vox and Rogue to make some kind of snacks. I don't know what they can come up with, but they have surprised us many times already."

"I'll message them and see what they can come up with" Verruca clicked off, sounding distracted.

"I didn't finish my thought earlier, but maybe Jax could print some dice, maybe some cards, or dominos. I'm not sure what the three-D printer can do, but whatever he could make would be better than nothing."

"I can do that. I'll go right now and set it to printing whatever I can find in the programs. Maybe that will take my mind off you being down there for a minute." Jax's frustrated voice came over the radio clearly.

"Okay, honey. Even though I'm doing just fine down here." I was touched that Jax was worried for me.

"Vox just answered me back. He said they could pull something together for tonight and still get dinner done."

"Perfect."

"Hey, I found some remnants of a building and what looks like a watch tower." Night cut into the conversation.

"Okay, I'll head your way." I turned and began walking in the direction Night was. "Verruca, can you and Juniper get with everyone and assign them tasks to get ready for tonight? And find a place to hold this movie night. Maybe one of the —"

The air was knocked out of me, and I hit the ground like a ton of bricks.

"*Chingoa!*" I gasped after getting my breath back.

"Mom!"

"Atlantis!" Night yelled at the same time as Verruca.

I opened my eyes quickly to see a set of blue ones looking back at me. I blinked a few times to make sure I was seeing clearly. The eyes and face looked human, but what I could see of the body was oddly shaped. Or maybe he had something on to obscure his body. His shoulders seemed to be covered in some kind of material. He turned his head side to side as he studied my face. Looking closer, I realized his skin was a golden brown with freckles across his nose.

"Hi, I'm Atlantis."

He jerked back.

"It's okay. I won't hurt you. But if you could let me sit up that would be great. You're a little heavy sitting on me like this."

He didn't get off me, but he scooted down my body enough that I could pull myself to a somewhat sitting position. I propped my back against a tree stump. Well, I thought it was a tree stump. I wasn't sure, but it worked. He was straddling my legs around my knees and watching every move I made.

"Thank you, what is your name?"

He startled and looked over my shoulder. I heard Night coming but hoped no one acted rashly.

"He won't hurt you. He just wants to make sure I am okay. I'm going to stand up now, okay?"

I used my hand and heels to push myself up onto the stump behind me and then came to my feet on the side of the stump so I was not right on top of this boy. He stayed crouched and looked up at me, still turning his head side to side. Night came into view pointing the gun at him. I held my hand out to Night to stop him from moving any farther. I could now see that the boy was in his early teens and was wearing some kind of camouflage. The camouflage was good. He blended right in with the foliage.

"Night, lower the gun. He's not going to hurt us. He is just curious, like us."

"Are you sure?" Night only slightly lowered the gun.

"This is Night." I gestured toward him. "He is my friend. He was just scared. But he won't hurt you."

The teen's attention switched to the other side of me. I turned to see what he was looking at, but it was too late. Something barreled into me and Night. Night was trying to protect me from hitting the ground too hard, but it didn't work. I hit my head hard on something and the world spun. Then I saw spots, then my vison went fuzzy, and then black.

CHAPTER TWENTY-FIVE: HOUSTON, WE HAVE A PROBLEM

I awoke sitting in the passenger seat of the drone with Night slapping my cheek. He was calling my name frantically as well as the whole group shouting my name over the radio.

"I'm awake. Stop yelling." I slapped Night's hands out of my face.

"Oh, thank god," Night exclaimed in relief.

"Mom!" Verruca yelled. "That is exactly why you didn't need to be down there. What would I do without you?" She almost choked on the last words.

It made me feel bad, but I was okay. "Baby girl, I am fine. I just have a headache."

"That's all!" Verruca said affronted. "That's all. Like you just stubbed your toe. You were flipping attacked."

"I'm fine," I said sternly but gently. "We are coming back right now."

"She seems to be fine. She is moving okay, and no slurred speech, but have Savinka waiting for us when we get back," Night instructed Verruca.

"I am fine. I just need some ibuprofen for the headache."

"You need to be checked out," everyone yelled at the same time.

"Stop yelling at me. It hurts." I grabbed each side of my head.

"Night, what happened? Who or what attacked her?" Jax asked.

"It appeared to be a humanoid creature. I'm not sure, but I think it was protecting the boy. Once it hit Atlantis, I really didn't give a shit what it was, I just got her out of there."

"Damn," Jax said.

Night started the launch sequence. When the countdown hit zero, we shot into the air along with the three small drones.

"Did you get the damaged drone?" I turned toward Night.

"Yeah." He pointed behind my seat. I watched Night as he flipped switches and pushed buttons. I could see the fear and stress etched into his face as he concentrated on making sure the drone was working correctly. When he was done, he sat back in his seat. I turned in my seat and leaned my head onto his shoulder and slid my arm under his, linking them. He reached up and caressed my cheek. Then let his hand rest on my arm that was linked with his. We rode the rest of the way in silence.

When we were about three feet from the ship, Night took over controls to manually maneuver us into the hangar. I think he just wanted something to do, because the drone could automatically fly us into the ship. He lined us up, but the door didn't open. We looked at each other, confused.

"Ms. Atlantis, I cannot open the door." Vega's face appeared on the control screen of the drone.

I sat up straight in my seat. "Why can't you?"

"Someone is trying to hack the basic functions of the ship."

"Ronan, where are Ryker and Lita?"

"I'm on my way to find out," Ronan answered, his voice was pitchy. He sounded like he was running.

"Cash, is there an override in the hangar?" Night called out.

While they worked that angle I went back to speaking with Vega.

"Vega, what is going on?"

"It's Ryker. He escaped his cabin somehow and is in a

maintenance corridor of the ship. He found a diagnostic station and is trying to use it to hack into the system. That is why he has affected the basic functions first. That station mainly has access to them, not the rest of the ship."

Vega sent me the video feed, and it popped into the air from my holo.

"He thinks he is so slick. He thinks that he can use that station to create a back door into the main system. I need you to block all his access."

"I am, but every time I deploy my own attack programs, he tries to invade another program file. I am renaming files, sending the attack programs, and trying to write code faster than him to get in front of his codes to block him. Right now, he is trying to use the communication system to backdoor his way in."

"How can we stop him?"

"I am, but he is leaving code everywhere that is still trying to break through the fire walls of each program."

"Well how in the hell do we stop that?"

"I can try purging the system and running a high security scrubber attack program, but it will take at least ten minutes and will cause a lot of the systems to shut down before they reboot."

"Do it. We have to stop him from getting any kind of control."

"Yes, Ms. Atlantis."

There was a loud static sound and then dead silence. Night looked at me, fear creasing every line of his face.

"What?"

"We have fifteen minutes before the auto pilot sends us back to Earth. We don't have the fuel or the battery power for that."

"Okay, set a timer on your holo."

We sat there waiting for something to happen. I looked at

my holo. It had been like a minute and a half since everything went silent, but it felt like a lifetime.

"Vega, are you back yet?"

Nothing. I went to my black holo. I tapped the screen and then tapped the ship-wide speaker icon.

"Vega?"

"Verruca?"

"Jax?"

"Anyone?"

"They can't hear us yet." Night pushed my hand down from my face.

We sat back in our seats. I closed my eyes.

"Fuck! Vega needs to hurry up."

"Yeah, because we only have eight minutes."

"*Chingoa!* Vega, are you back yet?" I yelled.

Now we were on pins and needles. He had to get this door open. A soft alarm sounded, and a female voice spoke.

"Launch sequence will begin in five minutes."

"Come on, Vega, we're running out of time!"

I began drumming my finger on my knee as we sat waiting for something to happen. My finger tapping quickly moved to my whole leg bouncing up and down. I have never been a patient person, but now that we were down to two minutes, I was about to burst out of my skin.

"Night, what are we going to do? We don't have enough power in the drone to get back to Earth and definitely not enough to come back."

"I know. But Vega will pull through for us."

"But what if he doesn't? We will be stuck with not enough oxygen in any situation. Our suits are not really made for long-term space exposure."

Night placed one hand on each side of my face. He then pulled my face to his and rested our foreheads together.

"Breathe, we will figure it out. Vega is having to send

329

attack programs back at Ryker to keep him from breaching any firewalls and gaining total access to the system. Then he has to run a system purge to clear anything that might be hanging around."

"Twelve, eleven, ten," the soft female voice said.

"Is there anything we can rig to keep us up here for a little longer? To help us make it until we can get back on the ship."

"We don't have to." Night jumped into action and began flipping switches

The drone jerked into motion, and we shot into the hangar right after it opened. We landed a little rough, but as soon as the hangar doors snapped close, I jumped out of the drone. I pulled my helmet off and took a deep breath to try and calm down. The side door to the hangar slammed open, and Verruca ran to me. I moved toward the front of the drone, and Night had stepped up next to me as Verruca slammed into me hugging me fiercely. She hit me so hard that Night had to catch us before we fell over.

I kissed her head and squeezed her tight. She started crying, then ducked her face into my neck and pulled me in even tighter. I held her like that for a few minutes. Then she grabbed Night, pulling him into the hug. Night wrapped his arms around us both and just held us there. Ryo and Jax stepped up to us and placed a hand on Verruca's shoulders. It still took a second, but then she pulled back from the hug slightly. She looked me over with tears still falling down her face.

"Don't ever do that to me again. No more going to Earth until we all go. I can't handle you being in danger. I couldn't survive without you," Verruca chastised me.

"I know, baby girl, but we are here, and we're fine."

"Promise me you will not go down again!"

"I promise."

She let me go and stepped back. Ryo and Jax wrapped her

in their arms, but then Jax released Verruca into Ryo's arm's and reached over pulling me to him. He kissed my cheek.

"I'm glad you're safe, Mom."

I snickered because he knew he didn't have permission to call me mom yet. I shook my head as Ryo pulled me over and kissed my other cheek. Jax bro-hugged Night as much as he could and then Ryo did the same. Squeezing out from between them, I began to walk to the door of the hangar when the rest of the council members rushed through and began hugging us, each one telling us how relieved they were that we were back. After accepting everyone's hugs, I had made it through the group and came face to face with Kilian.

I stood staring at him. Night stepped up next to me, placing a hand in the small of my back. Kilian stared at me for a few more seconds. Then in two long strides he ate up the space between us and wrapped his arms around me. He lifted me off the ground, holding me for at least a minute, maybe longer. Then he sat me on my feet but didn't let me go. He reached over and grabbed Night's shoulder. We stood like that for a while before Kilian let me go. Once he did, Verruca squeezed her way between us linking mine and her arms together. We all left the hangar in a large, huddled group.

"Guys, thank you for being worried about us and for fighting to get us back on the ship. But I am going to my cabin to relax. I'll see everyone at dinner. Verruca and Juniper, thank you for getting everything ready for tonight. Can someone let Vashanti , Savinka, and Sphynx know we have new samples?"

"Yes, Iksen. I'll message them," Cash said.

"I'll let Savinka know you're in your cabin," Juniper said to me. "That way she can check you out. You still need your head looked at."

"Okay, thank you."

Everyone headed off to do their thing while Night, myself,

Verruca, Ryo, and Jax got on the elevator. Night leaned against the wall, and I leaned against Night. Verruca leaned against me. Ryo held her hand and Jax stood on the other side of Ryo. We rode in silence and then we walked to our cabins in silence.

"Shouldn't we wait until tomorrow to do the movie slash game night?" Jax said frustrated.

"Why would we wait?" I looked at him confused.

"Because you should rest. I mean you were just in a dangerous situation."

"I am fine. Yes, I was a little scared about what we would do if the drone sent us back, but we were not hurt in anyway."

"Yes, but it was still stressful and draining," Ryo contributed.

"No more so than most days up here. I'm fine, I want to do something fun like movies and a game, because honestly, it would be the best way to relax. To let what happened today wash away."

"Guys, she's right. Having some fun tonight will be the best way to let the lunacy from today fade away. Besides, once she sets her mind to something, she won't back down. With or without us, she will still have the game night," Verruca explained to the group. Then she hugged me again.

I hugged her back. "I love you, baby girl. I'll see you in a while."

Jax and Ryo led her to their cabin. Night dragged me into ours and straight to the shower. Without a word, he stripped my clothes from my body, then walked me into the shower.

"Shower on."

Hot water fell from the ceiling, pelting my body and running down in hot rivulets. I turned my face up to the water as Night stood outside the shower and stripped his own clothes. He climbed into the shower. He ran his hands all over me like he was checking it, making sure I was whole. He pressed me against the wall kissing me hard and deep. It was an assurance we were still alive. That we were whole and here together. We kissed for a while before he pulled back. Still not speaking, he began to clean me. He washed my hair and then my body. I tried to return the favor, but he would not let me. I just stood leaning against the wall watching him, and it was a glorious site. I watched as his muscles bunched and stretched with each move. I reached out and pinched his ass when he bent over to wash his legs. He smacked my hand. When he stood back up to rinse the soap from his body I watched the soapy water as it ran across each plane of his chest and abdomen. One particular sud caught my attention when it began to run the length of the V that led to my favorite part of his body. His wet soapy body was the best thing I had seen all day.

He noticed I was watching him intently, and when I finally met his gaze his eyes were dark with I'm not sure what . . . maybe fear? I held his gaze as he finished up his shower. I think I scared him today when that person attacked me, or was it us getting ambushed and me passing out? Something was haunting him, but I didn't want to push. He would tell me when he was ready. Once he finished his shower, we got out and he wrapped us both in towels, pushing me toward the bedroom. We found our clothes and got dressed. I was sitting on the bed when I heard a loud knocking on the door. Night went to the door, and I followed, stopping at the end of the hallway.

"Open."

I saw Night's posture turn rigid, then he took a step back to reveal who was at the door. Kilian stood there looking between us, looking for permission to come in. I waved him in and made my way to the couch.

"Atlantis, can we really talk about things? Without an audience for once." He looked at Night, who retreated into the kitchen.

I slowly met his eyes and then I sighed. "I suppose we can."

I sat back on the couch and gestured for him to have a seat. He took a seat on the table in front of me. He stared at his hand for a few seconds before he looked up at me and spoke.

"Atlantis, I am not used to a woman being as strong as you are. I have not met one that eventually didn't want me to take control and do everything for them. Most women I have dated or that are in my family, no matter how strong, they have eventually wanted a man to take care of them."

"Well, I am not one of those women. I have never needed a man to take care of me nor have I ever wanted a man to take care of me. If I am going to be in a relationship, I want it to be fifty-fifty. I have never needed a man for anything. I wanted the ones that I let into my life. And to me there is a differ-ence — a significant difference."

"I really wasn't trying to control you. I just thought if I kept pushing you would eventually want me to take care of every-thing for you. Like all the rest of the women I have been around. I never thought that you may like being that strong."

"Well, I am not one of those whiney little bitches that can't save themselves. I have been saving myself for a long time and yes, it gets tiring at times. But at least I know I can handle anything and won't ever let my life be torn apart by someone. Not only did my dad not always do what he was supposed to do, not one of the men I have ever had a relationship with did what they were supposed to. I have seen my friends' whole lives get turned upside down by their husbands walking out on them. They were so dependent on their man, they didn't even have their own money, no work skills, and were thrown out of their houses with nowhere to go."

I sat there quietly waiting for him to say something.

He just looked at me for a few moments, then cleared his throat and spoke. "I'll say it again. I wasn't really trying to control you, not like that. I just wanted to take over the hard stuff and do it for you. I wanted to take care of you, but it is obvious I didn't know how to help you. Or to take care of you in the way you needed."

"That's an understatement," I said as I rolled my eyes and then took a deep breath. "Look, I do like that you're strong, willing to take care of me, and an alpha personality. But you have to learn the difference between taking care of someone and smothering or controlling them.

"You have to realize that I am just as dominant as you are, and if that is a problem for you than we need to go our separate ways."

Night had been standing in the kitchen the whole time just watching Kilian. His expression hadn't changed, nor had he moved a muscle during this conversation.

Kilian sat there just watching me. I didn't know if he thought I would change my mind if he stared at me silently long enough or what. Sadly, that would not work on me. After a few more seconds I got up to go to the kitchen. He placed a hand on my hip to stop me from moving. Then he slowly wrapped his arms around my hips and placed his head on my stomach. I threaded my fingers through his hair and held his head.

I was not sure what he was trying to say with this hug, but we stayed like this for several long minutes. Vega broke the silence. Kilian cleared his throat and released me from his grip. I reached out for his hand to pull him up, but once he was on his feet he continued walking until he was out the door.

Chapter Twenty-Six: Loss of Control

"Yes, Vega?" I answered in a slightly clipped and annoyed tone.

"Ronan, for you," Vega said.

"Did you find Ryker?"

"Yes, finally. He ran, he hid, and then he decided to try and fight us. That was his downfall. We have put him back in his cabin and I am placing two guards outside. They will be here at all times."

"Perfect. I swear if he and Lita would just give us some more time, we would be on the ground, and I could send them on their way."

"I know, but they are secured for now. Well, neither of them are talking, really. Ryker will not say anything. Lita just keeps complaining about how unfair it is that she is locked up when she is needed on this ship. What she is needed for I can't figure out."

"She is just trying to make you feel sorry for her. She thinks if she can play the damsel in distress, she can win you over to her side. I have watched her try this with all the males on the ship. She tries flirting first. If that doesn't work, she tries the damsel in distress act. She gives women a bad name." My disgust was a little too evident in my tone.

"Well, I am not going to say anything to that. I don't need all the women in my life mad at me."

"No, I wouldn't if I was you. I'm on my way to talk to

them." I headed out the door with Night in tow. "I never understood why women thought they could flirt their way into everything. All that has just never worked for me. I get laughed at or eye rolls when I try to act like that. So, I gave up on that crap a long time ago and just became strong."

"No offense, but I could never see you trying those tricks to get what you want," Ronan said over my holo with amusement.

"Evidently no one else can either." I snorted.

My tagalong and I exited the lift and made our way to Lita and Ryker's rooms.

Ronan nodded at us then turned and opened Ryker's room.

Ryker stood up. He was pissed to see me, but I didn't give a damn.

"What the hell did you think you were doing?" I asked as I walked up to him. "Did you really think by getting me killed, you and Lita could take over this ship?"

"Fuck Lita and her stupid plans. And fuck you!" he spat out, and opened his mouth to say more, but I punched him in the face first.

The room broke into chaos. Ryker lunged for me. I swept his legs out from under him, using his momentum against him and slammed him on the floor. Before I could do anything else Night grabbed me. Ronan grabbed Ryker and pinned him to the floor.

"You better be glad he's holding me down. I would beat your ass if he wasn't," Ryker yelled as he struggled against Ronan.

"Bitch, I'd like to see you try. I'm not the female that will cower to you or try to lead you around by your dick. I'm the one who will whip your ass and make you like it," I yelled back.

"Get her out of here," Ronan yelled at Night.

Night began to pull on me to make me move toward the

door, but I was not going.

"You almost killed me and Night. And you think I am supposed to just take your shit talk. I should float y'all's asses for this shit."

I was cut off abruptly by Night picking me up and slinging me over his shoulder, then stalking out of the cabin. Once we were outside, he set me on my feet and pinned me against the wall with his body until Ronan was able to exit the room. Clover and Dash looked startled and confused by all the commotion.

"What the hell where you thinking, Atlantis?" Ronan said, exasperated.

"I wasn't!" I yelled back at him. "I was fine until he said *Fuck you*, then my anger got the best of me. I am so tired of those two trying to sabotage us, just because they want to be in control. They don't care about any of us or about getting back to the ground. Neither of them are smart enough to think past their own selfishness."

They all stood there shocked at what I had done, but I didn't care. He'd got what he deserved. Night and I had almost died. Well, he'd put us in a situation that could have led to our deaths.

"Night, please get off me. The door is shut, and I am not going to go back in there."

Slowly Night released the pressure of his body pinning mine until I was free from him.

"See, and y'all think I always have my shit together. Even I lose my composure sometimes."

"That wasn't losing your composure. That was losing your shit. All over someone else," Night chastised me.

I just rolled my eyes at him and looked at Ronan.

"Leave three guards at all times no matter what. No one enters either cabin by themselves. Vega, I want a live stream coming to my communicator at all times. If there is any issue whatsoever, I want to know about it regardless of the time of day."

"The night shift will be Echo, Sage, and Crux."

"That works, but should we even be keeping them hostage, or should we put them on trial? I mean we set up a kind of justice system, but we haven't really used it yet. They have only dealt with maybe three small issues."

"I think being this close to landing we should just keep them confined. The justice system will be useful on land more than here. We only have, what, two more weeks at most, and we will be on the ground." Ronan slouched against the wall.

"Maybe you're right. I like the idea of having them under control. But I think I would like them not being on this ship better. But you're right, it's only about two more weeks. Then we can hold a trial or send them packing."

"I think you need to calm down before you make any decision on people's lives. I know what happened freaked you out, it did all of us. But you cannot make a rash decision about people's lives. It's not fair, no matter how big a piece of shit they are," Night said.

"I have to go. I need to go check in with Verruca. I'll see y'all at dinner."

I waved at them and headed for the elevator. I stepped inside and sagged against the wall. I had not planned on hitting Ryker. It just happened. All of a sudden, I burst into tears right there. I slid to the floor, willing myself to not let the tears overrun me. The magnitude of the situation finally hit me. I let myself cry a few minutes longer. Then I sucked it all up, tucked it into a neat little box inside me, and exited the elevator when it came to a stop.

I followed the long hallway to the engine room to meet up with Verruca and Jax. I wanted to see if he'd been able to make dice or cards with the 3D printer. When I walked in, Verruca was busy scrolling through a list of movies that Vega had archived. She wanted to choose two titles and give the crowd the choice between them.

Jax was leaning over the large square printer watching it intently. I walked up to one side of him, and Verruca joined us on the other side. She slid her arms around his waist. He startled slightly but then ran his hands along her arms and leaned back into her. She could handle his weight, she was only about two inches shorter than him. He looked back at her and smiled then pulled her to the front of him and kissed her. I cleared my throat so he wouldn't think he could go on with that kiss into other things. He looked at me and smiled sheepishly.

"Sorry."

"I just wanted you to know not to continue with that kiss."

He ducked his head and looked back to the printer. I watched as Verruca slid her hand into his and then she turned and gave me an admonishing look. I just shrugged. He needed to know I was not going to stand there and watch him make out with my daughter.

"Where you able to get anything to print? Cards or dice maybe?"

"I was able to get a pair of dice to print so far. I am printing another pair right now. What all do you want me to print?"

I leaned in to look at what the printer was doing. Jax would not meet my eyes, so I continued with instructions.

"If you can, we need at least six dice to play one of our favorite games. And if you could print a deck of cards, that would be awesome. A chess game would work or any game you could find in the system to print, even if it doesn't get finished tonight. There is nothing to help keep people entertained aboard besides movies, music, and each other."

Verruca gave me a *really, Mom* look when I said the last part. I rolled my eyes as I chuckled slightly and waited for Jax to answer.

"Okay, I'll try to get the dice and cards ready by the time the party starts, and then I'll work on some other things when I can."

"Thanks, Jax. I am going to go check in with Vox and Rogue then get dinner. See you guys in a few minutes."

"Yes, Iksen," Jax said sheepishly and turned back to the printer.

"Bye, Mom," Verruca said in an exaggerated tone.

I smiled and waved as I left the engine room.

I walked into the dining room. Several people were already there eating. I walked into the kitchen to check in with Rogue, Garrett and Vox.

"Hello, guys. How's it going in here?" I asked and settled myself against a large metal table.

"We are good, busy but good," Vox answered as Rogue nodded his head in agreement. Garret barely looked up at me.

"What did y'all come up with for snacks?"

"Well, Rogue has done most of the snacks. He has been working on that all day while we handled dinner," Vox said, smiling at Rogue.

"I was able to make a cake, some more brownies, some sugar cookies, and some chocolate sugar cookies. I have taste tested everything and it all tastes good," Rogue said assuredly.

"I am sure they taste fine. Thank you for all the hard work. All of you. Y'all always make sure that the food is on time, and everyone is fed. And I know that is no small feat."

"I love it. And it keeps me busy," Vox explained.

"I just enjoy doing something new and something that is important," Rogue said.

I took a plate of food that Vox handed to me and thanked them one last time before I went to sit down. I was only a few bites in when council members began trickling in a few at a time. Eventually they had all made it to the table.

We all talked and joked while we ate. No one talked about either of the incidents that happened earlier. I think they just wanted to enjoy the fact that everyone was here and alive. They didn't want to dwell on something that turned out good in the end.

Once we finished dinner, Verruca, Jax, and I went to set up the games.

When we got to the communal area, there were chairs from the empty cabins spread around the area. There were also extra pillows brought from the empty cabins. Jax pulled out from his left pocket six dice and from his right a set of playing cards. That must have been why he was so late to dinner. He had waited for them to print.

The dice were a light gray plastic type of material and the cards were a very thin version of the same plastic material. They were not flexible, but we would have to learn how to shuffle without bending the cards.

Two separate tables had been set up for games. Each had a tablet on it to keep score on. I took the table closest to me and began setting up a scoreboard on the tablet. Jax laid the cards on the other table and pulled up a blank page on the tablet. As I practiced rolling the dice with Verruca, Jax began to find a way to shuffle the cards. He finally found the easiest way just in time. People were beginning to show up. Rogue and Vox were among the first to make their way in. I looked around and there were no tables for the food.

"Jax, Verruca help me find some tables in these empty cabins for the food."

We three scurried off to find tables. I told Rogue to hold on as I passed him. The first few cabins we looked in had already been scavenged, so we had to make our way to the middle cabins. Finally, we found three of the small dining tables and brought them back to the communal area. We lined them up along the back wall of the room. Rogue and Vox placed what food they had on them and went back for more. While they were doing that, I had Vega get the movie selections ready.

Several people sat down at the table with Jax. He showed them the cards, and everyone was handling them and getting a feel for them. Some people had sat down at the table with Verruca, and they were all messing with the dice. I waited a little longer to see who all was going to make it here before I spoke to the crowd.

"Hello, everyone. I am glad you came to our movie and game night. We were able to come up with one deck of playing cards for now and some dice to play a game called Farkle. Verruca chose a couple movies and you guys can pick which one y'all want to watch. Rogue, Garrett, and Vox made some desserts and snacks which are on the tables to the left. Have fun and glad to see you guys."

I turned things over to Verruca, and I went to the Farkle table. About five other people were sitting at the table including Night and Kilian. Verruca's chair was waiting for her while she got the movie list lined out and started. Once Verruca was back, I explained the rules of the game and we started our first round. We were about halfway in when Verruca mentioned to me that it would be a lot more fun with something to drink. I laughed and agreed but we were all out of the moonshine that had been confiscated.

She called Ryo over to the table and pulled him down to whisper in his ear. He nodded his head and left. I was going to watch what he was doing but my attention got pulled back into the game.

Verruca had kicked our ass in the first game and Night didn't look so happy about it. Who knew he had that competitive streak in him? Verruca was teasing him while we started a new game. Kilian got to go first this time, which put him on the board and in the lead. He was now teasing Verruca.

"Oh, don't count your chickens before they hatch,"

Verruca taunted.

"Just wait, I'm winning this round." I smiled at them all.

Chapter Twenty-Seven: Enjoying the Moment

I had forgotten that Ryo had left, and when he came back, I shook my head at what he had in his hands. He had a box of bottles — bottles of moonshine.

"Where did you get all of that?"

"I can't tell you."

"I thought I told y'all to shut it down until we got to Earth."

"Actually, I think you told us to have him move it out of the electrical closet," Verruca said. "So we did. It's set up in the last spare room on the black deck."

"Smart asses."

They both laughed, and Ryo set two bottles on the table and then put the others on the tables with the food. He came back and picked up his turn on the next round. We played a half a shot for every Farkle we made.

The night was turning into a great night. Half of the people were watching movies and talking. When the first movie was over, they asked Vega to put some dance music on. Those of us playing games were having a blast. I had downed about two full shots by the time I won the game. Verruca had the next highest score and the guys, well, they lost miserably.

I'm not sure if they were just having that much bad luck or needed an excuse to drink more. They started another game with some fresh players. After I explained the rules, Verruca dragged me to dance. We danced several songs before the guys joined us. Night slid behind me wrapping his arms around my waist and pulling me into him. Then a few minutes later Kilian joined us. Night whispered and asked if it was okay. I nodded slightly and Kilian took his place in front of me. I looked over and Verruca and Sphynx were between their two guys dancing and laughing. Onyx and Lotus were wrapped in each other's arms swaying to the music, as well as Savinka, Zahirah, and Ronan next to Verruca's group. It made me happy to see all of them happy for the moment. The next two weeks were going to be crazy busy just getting everything finalized, checking out the other side of the Earth, and then of course landing.

Kilian was watching me. He reached down and lifted my face to his. "What are you thinking about? I see that mind working overtime when you are supposed to be relaxing."

"I know, I was just happy that everyone was having fun."

"And?"

"And about how much we have to do in the next two weeks."

"Just forget about it for right now and relax. It will all get done."

I was about to say something when one of my favorite songs came on. Verruca turned and looked at me as if to say, *how could you?* She hated this song. I just gave her an innocent shrug of my shoulders and mouthed, *Who me? I would never.* We both laughed and returned to dancing. I actually had sent Vega a message asking him to search our database for it, but she didn't need to know that. I relaxed into the song and let it guide my body along with Night's and Kilian's.

The song didn't last long enough for me, but then another good song came on. It was one of those country songs that had the additional words. I froze when everyone started singing and looked around. Then I burst out laughing. I didn't think most people would know this song and all the extra sayings that went with it, but they did. We all swayed to the song and sang at the top of our lungs. It was also a great song to end the night on. It was already close to one o'clock in the morning. I told everyone goodbye. Then Kilian, Night, and I left.

Night and I walked down toward our cabin. When Kilian headed toward his, Night stopped me and asked if he was joining us.

"He can if he can remember what we talked about."

Night looked between the two of us and then Kilian nodded. I reached my hand out to him and he took it. We entered the cabin and went to our room. I began stripping out of my clothes. Once they were off, I went to the bathroom to clean my face and do some nighttime routine stuff. I pulled a towel from the rack and wrapped it around myself. They guys entered right after me but they got into the shower. I was surprised they got in together but who was I to complain.

I brushed my hair back and pulled it into a haphazard bun. It had grown out quite a bit since we had been awake, I thought as I inspected my roots in the mirror. Movement and a slightly raised voice coming from the shower caught my attention and I stared at the guys for a few moments. Their conversation seemed to have died down and they were now just showering. Before I decided to join them I went back to examining myself. My dark roots had begun to show a few weeks back but now some of the blue was fading, so more blonde was showing through. It sucked not having hair dye to do touch ups, but even when we got back to Earth, we wouldn't have hair dye.

I was getting my face ready to use the new soap with ground up almond shell in it.

One day Rogue and I had been talking about needing something to scrub our faces with and we had searched the kitchen for something. Almond shells were the only thing we'd found. It had taken some doing, but we'd got the shells down fine enough to use as an exfoliant. We'd mixed it into a little bit of hand soap and it worked. We'd made enough to share with everyone.

Just before I poured the soap into my hand, I heard the water turn off. I glanced over my shoulder to see them drying off. I returned my attention back to the task at hand and shook my little bottle of soap then twisted off the cap. That's when Night stepped up and took the soap from my hand. He set it back onto the counter. Kilian picked up the lid and placed it back on the bottle. Night then jerked my towel from me.

"Look at me," Night growled out.

So, I did. My inner walls were beginning to flutter in anticipation.

"I want you to watch as we fuck you. I want you to watch us take you, dominate you, and make you beg for more," Night said in a low wicked tone.

Kilian watched wide eyed as if he was waiting for me to object. But this was the only time I would relinquish control to them. Night knew this, and he knew how to handle me. Maybe he could teach Kilian if he paid attention.

Night leaned over me and placed his lips to my ear. "I want you to feel my anger, my fear, and my need to keep you safe. I want to know in the most basic way that you are here and alive, so I am going to make sure you feel every inch of me and Kilian." Night placed his hands on my hips and turned me so that he was behind me. That look he had in his eyes earlier in the night was now replaced with raging lust and need. He slid those hands up my back to my shoulders. He pushed me down, making me lean over the counter. He rubbed his hands all over my smooth back causing different sensations by dragging his nails or using pressure. I moaned softly as one hand slowly slid up to the nape of my neck. He wrapped his hand in my hair and sharply jerked my head up meeting my gaze in the mirror. Then he slammed home eliciting a deep loud moan from me.

"Mmmmm, you feel so good. So, tight and hot. Was this what you needed to take your mind off everything?" Night rumbled in a dark lust-filled tone.

"Yes," I whispered barely audible.

"Tell me what you want. I want to hear you loud and clear asking for what you want," Night demanded.

"I want you inside me. I want both of you inside me," I said in a whimper of need.

Night began sliding in and out of me picking up his pace with each thrust. He settled into a hard, fast pace that caused my body to tighten and tingle with each stroke.

I could see Kilian in the mirror stroking himself as he watched Night dominate me. But every time my gaze slid to his, Night slapped my ass.

"Keep your eyes focused on mine," he commanded me and tugged on my hair to punctuate his command.

I growled at him, which earned me another slap on the ass. I narrowed my eyes at him letting him know he was reaching the end of his dominance allowance. He smirked, which let me know he knew he was approaching dangerous ground. He angled himself so he was causing more friction on the left side. Hot liquid fire began to flood my body making each nerve ending crackle with pleasure. Night stopped after one last deep thrust. He pulled out and moved over. Kilian took his place and slid home hard and fast. I moaned loudly and dropped my head down almost to the counter. Kilian groaned and dug his nails into my hips. I kept my head down as Kilian slid out and then slammed home again. He did this several times but on the third thrust Night spoke.

"Lift your head and watch him."

I did what I was told and lifted my head so I could watch Kilian. This eye contact spurred him on. He pulled my hips away from the counter and began driving into me hard. Night stepped up to me and ran his hand down my stomach until he found my clit. He began making fast, light circles around it. They were teasing circles, just enough to intensify those strands of electricity surging through my body, but not quite enough to make me fall into the darkness of pleasure. I reared my head back and thrust my hips forward trying to get more friction on my clit. When I did that, he stopped.

"I didn't tell you to move," said Night. "You are supposed to be watching him fuck you."

I gave Night a warning look, and he grinned wickedly. Then he slapped my hip and pointed toward the mirror. I glared at him one last time before I looked back at Kilian. Once Night was satisfied I was following orders, he slid his hand back down to my clit. He began his pleasure inducing, body jerking, moan eliciting assault on my clit.

Kilian closed his eyes and half groaned, half growled as my inner walls began to flutter again. After he gained some semblance of composure, he picked up his speed. He slid his hand up my back and into my hair, grabbing a handful. He then pulled my head back, making my body arch.

"I have missed this body. The way it grips me and hungrily sucks me back in," he breathily groaned.

"You hear that? He missed you, but you were being stubborn. Now he gets to pay you back for that stubbornness," Night growled in my ear as he watched Kilian fuck me harder.

Not putting up with bullshit and being stubborn were two different things. So now I was just going to make them work for it even harder. It was going to be as much torture for me as for them, but I stopped all sounds. I clinched my jaw shut and stared defiantly at them both.

Night must have seen that as a challenge, because he picked up his speed. Kilian pressed me down onto the counter and pulled me onto my tiptoes. The change in angle made his hard, thick crown hit my g-spot roughly with each stroke.

That liquid electricity was amplified, and my inner walls rippled with anticipation of release. I ground my teeth trying to not make a sound, but Kilian slid two fingers in my ass. Knowing that he was cheating he added another finger which then left me moaning and writhing. After only seconds, my moaning turned into outright begging to come.

"Please, let me come."

"I will let you know when you can come," Night said.

He had me tiptoeing on the edge. I was balanced so precariously that it would only take one good rotation of Kilian's hips for me to swan dive into that beckoning oblivion of pleasure.

"Please, Night, let me come," I half moaned, half growled.

He ignored me and continued. I watched them both. Kilian had turned to look at Night. They stared at each other for a few seconds. Then Kilian removed his fingers from my ass, pulled me off the counter, never breaking stride or leaving my body, and replaced Night's fingers on my clit with his. Night then pulled my head down to his cock.

"Open your mouth."

I thought about refusing but I wanted to come too badly. I opened my mouth but only enough that just the very tip of his crown could feel the wetness and warmth. He growled and pushed against my mouth. I didn't comply with his demands. He pushed harder against my mouth, and I opened just a little more. He grunted in frustration, so Kilian helped him out. Kilian rubbed my clit a little harder, and I gasped at the shot of pleasure that made my insides tighten. It distracted me enough for Night to slide his cock into my mouth. When his crown hit the back of my throat he moaned. As a tortuous payback, I began to clinch and unclench my throat. His hands tightened in my hair, and he took over by sliding his cock in and out of my mouth fast.

After a few minutes, Kilian picked up his speed sliding in

and out of me at almost the same speed as Night. I was moaning and panting, needing to take that swan dive and the guys still kept me tiptoeing on the ledge. I relaxed into every sensation letting myself get lost in it all, when suddenly Kilian paused for a split second before he began to rotate his hips, the tip of his dick hitting every sensitive spot, and I furiously dove off that ledge into ecstasy.

My inner walls clamped down around Kilian's dick and my legs quivered. I dug my nails into Night's thighs just to help keep me standing. I came so hard I saw spots and before I could even register all the sensations spreading throughout my body Night exploded in my mouth with a loud, long moan. Kilian released hot jets of come inside of me as he growled out my name. No one moved for several long seconds before my legs tried to give out on me. Night caught me and steadied me. Kilian picked me up and carried me to the bed. He laid me in the middle of the bed and they each took their sides.

Night was on the front side of the bed lying on his back, and I placed my head on his chest. Kilian was on the back side of the bed. He slid up to me, flinging his arm and leg over my back, and placed his head between my shoulder blades. We settled back into our places like it had been this way the whole time. We all drifted to sleep.

I wasn't sure what time it was when the guys woke me. Kilian slid into my ass. Night had my left leg thrown over his hip which allowed him to slide into my hot tingling core. This time it was slow and sensually.

This continued throughout the rest of the night, each time a little something different. Each time cementing their place with me and with each other in the most basic and primal way they knew how.

Chapter Twenty-Eight: Hangovers Are the Worst

The next morning, I didn't crawl out of bed until eleven. I was exhausted and had a hangover. I had not had one this bad since right after my daughter was born. I squinted one eye open enough to see the screen to my black holo. I typed a message to Verruca and asked her to go get me some ibuprofen, then with more effort than I thought I could muster I slid out from between the guys. I stumbled my way to the bathroom. I called out to the shower and then climbed into the hot water. I slid down the wall and sat for a while. My legs were a little wobbly, but I wasn't sure if it was from all the sex last night or from the hangover.

I was not sure exactly how long I had sat there, but I was pretty sure I would run out of hot water soon, so I hoisted myself to a standing position. Once I was sure my legs were going to hold me, I began washing myself. After getting clean I stepped out and up to the sink. I leaned into it heavily, hoping it would help keep me upright. I brushed my teeth and pulled my hair up. By the time I was done with all of this I was moving better and made my way to the bedroom to get dressed. As I walked in, I looked at the two men still in bed and grunted. They looked so peaceful and happy. I, on the other hand, looked as bad as I felt.

Once I was dressed, I called Verruca to find out where my pills were. She tried to laugh at me but then grabbed the side of her head. Evidently, she was in no better shape than me.

She whispered that she was just down the hall with them. I opened the door, and she was just steps away, shaking a little white bottle at me. She came in and we both took some ibuprofen. Then I left some on the counter for the guys. She ran next door to leave some for her people and then we entered the elevator.

"I swear, the older I get, the harder it is to recover from one night out. Well, not that we were really out, but you get the concept," I said to Verruca.

"Well, I'm not that old, and I am still tired myself." She grinned.

I elbowed her in the ribs, and she elbowed me back. Then we both winced and groaned from the shot of pain that caused our heads to pound. We exited the elevator cautiously and continued in the same manner to the kitchen. Vox and Rogue only looked slightly better than us, but at least they were making food.

"I'm so sorry, we just got started. It will be a few more minutes before the main dishes are ready," Vox said to us.

"That's fine. Is there tea or coffee made? And can we have some warm bread? Or whatever you have that would be easy to eat and that will help absorb the last of that damn moonshine." I rubbed my stomach to help soothe the queasiness.

"I got you, Iksen. Go sit, and I'll bring it out to y'all." Rogue grabbed some bread and placed it in the oven.

"I can wait. Y'all don't seem to be doing any better than us right now," I said to him.

"I'm okay, just really tired. I stayed up way too long, but I didn't drink much. Dash drank way more than me."

"Oh, well be glad you didn't."

Verruca and I took a seat at the first table. We just sat there. We didn't want to talk, because it made our heads hurt. Shortly Rogue brought some warm bread with butter, a pitcher of tea, and a cup of coffee. He poured each of us a glass of tea, then slid the coffee in front of me and sliced the bread. I thanked him. Then we buttered some bread and ate. We had both eaten two large pieces by the time Vox brought us plates of scrambled eggs and country potatoes. The bread had made me feel a little better, enough that I wanted the food in front of me. It seemed it had done the same for Verruca, because she took a big bite of potatoes.

We had finished our food by the time the rest of our group joined us. Then slowly but surely the others began waking and entered the dining room to get food. I talked with everyone for a bit and reminded them we needed to have a meeting. Then Verruca and I went to the bridge to check reports and just take time to become completely functioning people for the day.

We were talking about last night and how much fun it seemed everyone had when our conversation was interrupted as council members began to enter the bridge. Ronan, Savinka, and Zahirah came in holding hands. Next Ryo and Jax walked in talking animatedly about something. They both plopped down next to Verruca. Night and Kilian came in one right after the other. Night claimed the chair next to me and Kilian sat on the couch next to him. I think we were only waiting for Cash and Juniper now.

We all fell into conversations as we waited for them. Verruca was filling the guys in on what we'd seen, and I was telling Night and Kilian. We had been talking for a while when Cash and Juniper finally walked in.

"Sorry," Juniper and Cash said while taking their seats.

"It's okay, I know y'all were doing things. But let's get started. Here are the things I wanted to go over. One, we need to check one more site in Texas, because so far, the water and soil have had the best results. The only reason I don't like the site that we originally chose is because it is too close to those crazy storms. Who wants to have to deal with a snownado nightly?

"Two, I want to check on the rest of the world before we land. We have seen what the other side of the world looks like from space, but I think we should really research it like we have with the US. It would give us a better overview of conditions on earth. Three, I know a few of us have talked about this, but I want everyone's opinions on do we wake the rest of the people aboard, or do we wait until we're on the ground? Four, do we want to hold a trial for Lita and Ryker now, or when we land?"

Everyone sat quiet for a few minutes thinking about what I was asking.

"Let's take about five minutes to discuss with each other and then I'll ask for thoughts again."

I waited for everyone to talk with each other about the things I'd listed. I was still thinking about that human figure we'd seen yesterday. I just wished I knew for sure if there were people everywhere or just in one place. It would make it so much easier if we had someone to communicate with.

Night put his thoughts out there first. "Well, I think that checking the second site in Texas is a good idea. I think checking on the rest of the world is a good idea. Maybe we can learn something about the other countries' conditions. As for the people asleep, I think we should leave them. And we should hold a trial for Lita and Ryker as soon as possible. That way, whatever the punishment is they can be sentenced to it now."

"I agree," Kilian piped in after Night finished talking.

Zahirah gave her opinion calmly. "I wouldn't mind waking people now just so everyone was awake and aware of what is going on. Yet something still tells me we should wait until we land. The potential for chaos is too high, and we're too close to landing back on Earth."

Savinka added her thoughts to the conversation. "I agree

on not waking people yet. I think we should wait for a trial until we get to Earth. It would just make things easier. I do like the idea of checking out the rest of the countries as best we can. It would be nice to know what some of our home countries are like now."

"I agree with the women," Ronan said. "I also agree with checking on the second site in Texas. None of us want to deal with snownadoes."

Verruca spoke for her group.

"Well, I agree with Night on everything but the trial. I think that should wait until we get to the ground. Jax and Ryo agree with me."

"I think we agree with what everyone is saying too," Juniper said. "It has been hard enough to control who we have awake right now. I mean, look at Lita and Ryker. Oh, and let's not forget Dash and his friends making moonshine. We are too close to getting back to Earth. We don't need anything hindering us from getting there."

"Okay, then it's settled. We will check on the second Texas site. We will check on the rest of the countries. Lita and Ryker will remain in their cabins. The rest of the people will remain asleep. Okay, those were the things I needed to know to plan out the next couple days and start making plans to land. As soon as we have results back from the site, I'll let you know. Hopefully, no later than tomorrow night. We will pick the best site and then make preparations for our descent. Thank you, everyone. We will pick up tomorrow night."

We all left the bridge, and I headed to check in on sample results.

Walking into the lab, I saw Vashanti, Lotus, and Sphynx at the back of the room. "Hey, guys."

Everyone paused in their movements and looked at me. After a second they seemed to snap out of their trains of thought.

"Hi, hello," they said almost at the same time.

I laughed. "Well, y'all were all lost in your own thoughts."

Sphynx laughed. "Yeah, I am singing in my head and focusing on my work."

"It's okay, I was just checking in to see what we had found out so far."

"Well, the fresh water seems to still have some high levels of radiation in it. The bay water is not any better. It has high levels of plutonium as well because of the runoff. I don't think this area will be able to sustain us. We wouldn't be able to filter the water enough to use," Vashanti explained.

"Son of a motherless goat. Well, I guess it is a good thing that we're looking at another site tomorrow. It is probably our last chance for a good landing site. Well, since we know the water is no good, I don't think you need to test everything else. Y'all can take the rest of the afternoon off."

Vashanti smiled wide and said, "I would love to."

Everyone was putting things away and getting ready to leave when I spoke.

"Sphynx, could I see the bunny before you go?"

"Sure," Sphynx said. "The babies are doing good so far. Our little bunny is getting stronger with every meal."

"Aww. Good, he is too cute to not make it."

Sphynx walked to the other side of the lab and opened the box. Inside was our little bunny snuggled down into some torn fabric. His little nose started to wiggle as he tried to figure out what was going on. I looked down at his pink body with white peach fuzz starting to show. Every time I looked at him thriving it amazed me that we had grown him in an artificial womb. He lifted his little head as he continued to sniff the air. When he turned his head, I could see that the right eye was trying to open.

"He is too cute, with his Fu Manchu mustache going on." I reached over and slightly rubbed the fur down on his cheek, so his mustache was not so crazy. "Okay, let me get out of your hair so you can go enjoy some free time."

"I will, as soon as I give the little guy some food. I want to make sure he is full in case I am held up for any reason," Sphynx said as she picked up the little bunny and went to get his bottle.

I waved bye as I walked out the door and headed — well, I didn't know where I was headed. It wasn't quite time for dinner, and I really didn't have much else to do. I got into the elevator and just let it go up. When it stopped I stepped onto the bridge, and it was empty. I was relieved. I just felt like being alone. I pulled up a visual of space on one side of the main screen and Earth on the other side.

I took a seat in the captain's chair and lazily looked back and forth at different portions of the images that caught my attention. When I was younger, I had wondered what it would be like to go into space. I had always loved the stars, but now that I was here, all I could think about was getting back to the ground. It's crazy how you think you wanted something until you got it and then you realized you were happy the way things were.

It was relaxing just sitting here watching the screens and letting my thoughts drift. I am not sure if I fell asleep at some point, or if I was just that lost in staring at the screens, but Kilian startled me when he came in. I wasn't even sure how long I had been on the bridge.

"*Chingoa!* You scared the shit out of me," I yelled at him.

He jumped. "I'm sorry, I didn't know you were in here. I came to look at the map table. I wanted to see what info we had on tomorrow's research site."

I waved my hand toward the table, indicating for him to go about his business. Then I fell back into the chair and resumed my staring at the screens. The cameras focused on a spot that looked like it had a lot of trees or at least green land. It looked like it might have been somewhere about where North Dakota or Montana was located. I watched the camera intently as it zoomed in more. I was trying to ignore the fact that Kilian had moved into my periphery. The more in-focus the land became, the more I could tell the green was some open space with trees lining one side of the meadow. I could also see movement in the green grass, but it was hard to tell what it was. I continued to watch the movement until one of the moving things landed in a dead patch of grass.

My mouth fell open. I was shocked to see a green-furred, rabbit-looking creature sitting there. He looked to be as big as a medium-sized dog. His ears were so long and wide I was sure he could have picked up TV stations with them. His fur was a marbleized mixture of greens. He turned his head sniffing the air. His front teeth looked like two fangs hanging out of his mouth. His whiskers were also extra-long, but his nose still twitched like a normal rabbit. I continued to study him, and I saw each front paw had one very thick, very large claw. They looked like a raptor's front claw.

I slowly looked over at Kilian, and he was staring at the image as well. I walked up to the screen and clicked on the picture. It took a still of the rabbit creature and I sent the image to the map table. I then tapped the screen on the table to enlarge the area where this creature was found and dragged the photo into place. We had a very wild and exotic menagerie on Earth now. Who knew what we were going to find once we were back on the surface.

Kilian looked at me up and down before he spoke. "So, what are you doing in here all alone?"

"Babe, I don't feel like talking right now. I just want some alone time. I'm not trying to be rude, and I'm not mad. I'm just tired. Can I talk to you later?"

Kilian's face fell slightly before he gave me a tight smile and said, "Yes, I'll see you later."

I stood up and pulled him in for a long kiss. Before he could try to take the kiss further I pulled out of it, turned him around, and slapped his ass as I shoved him toward the door. Laughing, Kilian got on the elevator. I plopped down in a chair, content on continuing my staring into space, but then remembered I needed to message Cash. I asked him to contact me on my communicator as soon as the drones were ready tomorrow.

I returned to staring into space, letting everything and nothing take up space in my mind. I was not sure how long I had sat there before I texted Night and asked him if he could bring dinner to the cabin. I just wanted to have a quiet dinner with the three of us. After the text was sent, I stood up and stretched. I left the views of space and the Earth up on the screens and exited the bridge.

CHAPTER TWENTY-NINE: FINDING OUR NEW HOME

All three of us were up early in the morning. We went to breakfast in the dining room, but I was still dragging ass. I went back for a second and third cup of coffee.

The guys left me to my coffee and went to get the drones ready for today's launch. Verruca and Sphynx were waking the new people and then they had to get them acclimatized to our situation as much as possible.

Not truly ready to get my day started, I dragged myself to the bridge. At least there I could pretend I was doing something productive. I stepped onto the bridge, and reports were waiting for us on the screen. I tapped the report, and the weather for this area was ready for me to read up on. I enlarged the information and tapped the speaker icon on the corner of the screen. The soft female voice began reading the reports to me as I made my way to the captain's chair.

She told me that the current weather conditions were mild. The high temp today would be around fifty one degrees, the low would be thirty. No signs of storms, and the wind coming off the ocean was barely moving at around three knots. All and all it was a calm day in Corpus. I sat back in the chair lost in thoughts of the last time I had been in Corpus. I remembered going down to North Beach, which was where we were exploring today, Verruca and I had walked along the beach and looked at the Lex. She had been naming all the jets sitting on the deck of the enormous aircraft carrier. We'd just enjoyed the day laughing and talking.

"Atlantis!"

"Atlantis!"

I jumped startled at the loud noise and looked all around.

"ATLANTIS!" Night's voice came over my communicator.

"Yeah, why are you yelling at me over my holo?"

"Because I have been trying to get a hold of you for like five minutes."

"Okay, I guess I fell asleep for a little bit. I'm on the bridge, what do you need?"

"We are ready to launch."

"Okay, go for it. I'll be on the bridge if any of y'all want to join me."

"Vega, can you pull up the feed of the drone launch?"

"Yes, Ms. Atlantis, where would you like me to display it?"

"Main screen on the bridge."

The live feed appeared on the screen in front of me. I sat up a little more so that I could see things clearly. Just after the feed appeared, my wrist began making noises and vibrating again. I looked at it and it was Verruca.

"Where are you?"

"On the bridge, why?"

"Just want to let you know that we're getting started on waking the new people."

"Oh good. The guys are launching the drones now. Let me know when you're done with the awakees and we can meet up and catch up."

"I will."

I stood up and walked over to the screen. I studied the earth as the drones descended toward it. I was so looking forward to being on the ground and getting a break from always being the leader. Not that I didn't enjoy being in charge, because I didn't know any other way, but I didn't always like being responsible for everyone's lives. It was hard trying to make sure I was thinking of everyone's thoughts, feelings, and needs. I knew it sounded selfish on my part, but I just liked it better when I was only responsible for myself and Verruca.

I was jerked from my thoughts when Night and Kilian walked onto the bridge. They both kissed me just as the drones dropped through the cloud banks, which were hanging low today.

The bay area and land were starting to come into focus. Everything was very overgrown, but there were still remnants of structures peeking out of green mounds that most might mistake for hills or small mountains. Since this was my old stomping grounds I knew better—this land was flat. I watched as the drones flew back and forth letting us get a good overall view of what the area looked like now. Then I saw it. Well, most of it. Some had fallen down. I tapped the screen to open a line to Cash.

"Cash, please fly drone two closer to that bridge?"

"Yes, Iksen."

The drone made its way to the Harbor Bridge. I started crying. It had been one of my favorite things about going to Corpus when I was a kid. I'd made my dad or my grandma drive over it every time. When Verruca was little, I had taken her over it. Our first time back after being away for a while we'd driven into town at night and the bridge had been lit up in rainbow lights. It had been beautiful and a symbol that you were on North Beach.

That meant that those structures were the museums and the aquarium. Verruca stepped up beside me and put an arm around my shoulders. We leaned our heads together and just watched.

"Wait, what are you doing here?"

"I wanted to see for myself. Sphynx can handle things. All she is doing is getting them food and talking over things with them before she shows them the videos."

I looked at her, not sure if she had made the right decision.

"She promised to call me if she needed help."

"Okay, if you believe in her, so will I."

She leaned her head back on my shoulder and we returned to the screen. The drone was just hovering and giving us a good look at the bridge and its surroundings.

"I remember we always had to make sure we came into Corpus from the Calallen side so we could drive over the Harbor Bridge," she said quietly.

I nodded my head. "I loved that bridge. It was the bridge that made me fall in love with bridges. You could see forever out into the water when you were dead center, and everything looked so blue way up there."

"Yeah, that's the bridge that made me not be afraid of bridges. That made me love going over them just to see what was out there." Verruca wiped a tear from her cheek.

Night looked over, saw us, and got worried.

I smiled at him sadly. "We are okay," I said so softly that barely any sound came out. He still stepped closer and took my hand in his.

"Cash, the drones can do what they need to now."

"Copy," Cash answered.

Cash directed them to begin gathering the samples we needed. As he maneuvered one of the drones toward some foliage, I could see remnants of the port area sticking up through the trees. A lot of the area was severely overgrown but some of the silos were still visible poking through. I could not tell which silos they were, but I was sure most of them were petroleum or chemicals of some kind.

"You know what I just thought of?"

"No, what?" Verruca asked nervously.

"There were production plants in this area all the way toward the Robstown area. I don't remember what kind they were."

Verruca and Night both looked at me confused.

I put my finger up to hold them off on asking more questions. I began tapping on the screen. I was giving Vega instructions to run a battery of air control tests through the drones. I also had him try some thermal imaging just in case. He informed me that he didn't have a thermal camera per se, but most of his cameras could detect things on multiple light spectrums. So I instructed him to try that.

"I could not remember if any of them were nuclear plants of any kind. The last thing we need is for us to be all settled and then a reactor melts down. If every sci-fi movie ever has taught me anything it is to check for things like that."

Verruca rolled her eyes. "This is not a movie or TV show."

The drones finished up their sample collecting and began their journey back to the ship. I kept looking at the pictures of the area. It was wild and crazy to me that this was what the majority of the cities looked like now. Even though I was worried about the refineries, I still had a good feeling about this location. I finally turned to the council members that had joined us and asked them if they had any questions or anything they wanted to go over.

Zahirah raised a hand-"Now that we have gathered these samples, what is the next move?"

"Well, Vashanti, Savinka, and Sphynx are going to rush all the testing while we prep the ship to move to the other side of the Earth. I want to start our trip first thing in the morning. It will take about four hours to line us up over Europe and then move over as much as we can in the next three days.

"We may not see everything going on, but maybe we can get an idea of what that side of the Earth looks like. Maybe even send the drones down to look around. On the morning of the fourth day, we will start our four-hour journey back in line with wherever we decide is the best place to land."

Zahirah spoke up again, "Then how long will it be before we land?"

"That is going to depend on what we decide. We can do one of two things. We can just head down blind, or we can send a scouting party to physically check things out."

Verruca looked around the group then asked-"Do we want to waste that kind of time?"

Ryo spoke up. "I don't, but I'll go with what everyone wants to do."

Ronan was nodding in agreement before he spoke- "I know it might be the smarter option, but getting on solid ground is so close I just can't wait. A scouting party will just slow things down."

"No, no scouting party," Jax said adamantly. "Not after last time. I say we just land."

I saw a lot of heads nod in agreement. Then little discussions broke out.

I waved my hands in a settle down gesture-"That is why the council will vote on it. Then we go from there."

Everyone seemed to be happy with this, and slowly but surely, they all left the bridge to go about doing other things. I stayed to review the video from the drones more in depth. I was about five minutes into the first video when my holo began vibrating and chiming.

"Hello."

"Iksen, we have the samples from Cash and are about to start testing. Would you like to join us?" Savinka's smiling face appeared on my screen.

"Yes, I would. I'll be there shortly."

When I arrived at the lab, the girls were already in full swing, each one at a different machine. Sphynx was at the microscope. Vashanti was separating water samples into different vials. Savinka was sifting dirt through a very fine screen, and Lotus was adding the sifted dirt to vials in a large machine.

"Hey, guys."

Savinka waved me in, and we began looking at some of the dirt and the water under the microscope.

"I don't see anything unusual, but I am not sure I would know if I saw anything." I continued to look at the water sample through the scope.

Savinka assured me as she continued to look through the microscope. "The dirt looks healthy. I don't see anything strange in it."

Sphynx blurted, "Same over here with the water."

Vashanti picked up the vials-"Okay, well let's run the chemical tests and see what happens." She had a door open on a large machine and placed the vials in.

"Was that here last time?" I asked.

Sphynx spoke up over the sound of the machine, "Yes, but it was in the storage cabinet that is built into the wall over there." She pointed toward the far wall closet next to one of the embryo cryo tanks.

I raised my eyebrows in surprise and nodded my head. While they were running the tests, I began compiling the air readings on my communicator. I asked Vega to send the videos taken in the different light spectrums so I could analyze them. I used a tablet that was lying on the table to look at the video. I played through the videos, scrutinizing them for anything that might indicate an issue with the refineries that were close by, but I had not seen anything. Each picture had three different versions to look at, but the last set had something that caught my attention. The first version, the regular version, didn't have anything visible. The second version, the ultraviolet version, had a faint human outline. It looked like it was kneeling or crouching. I looked at the next version, the infrared version, and the outline was more prominent.

I wasn't sure if it was someone or something else. I wasn't

really sure what to make of it, but if it was really a person, we would deal with that when we got to the ground.

Savinka too was excited, "These are the best readings that we have gotten from a site so far."

I turned to look at her, and she was smiling widely.

Sphynx's tone was just as giddy as Savinka's, "Yeah, the fresh water is in really good shape and the salt water is almost as good."

Lotus was reviewing a printout from the large machine "The soil has very little traces of nuclear materials in it. The plant samples are perfect. I mean they all have defects, but that is natural."

"So, this is our site then?" I asked hopefully.

"I would say so." Vashanti beamed at me.

"That is great. I was praying that was the case. I am tired of looking for a place to land." I let out a deep sigh. "Now I need to let everyone know. How do y'all feel about this place?" I looked at each of them.

They all looked at each other and then they looked at me for a few seconds before anyone spoke.

Vashanti cleared her throat. "I think it's had the best results so far. The other sites all had an issue with something or another. Water was not clean enough, soil was still in bad shape, or both. I like this one and I am just as ready to get off this ship as the next person."

Sphynx ran a hand across her forehead. "I agree. This site has looked the best. I also wanted to say I am not thrilled about spending an additional week looking at Europe. I know it sounds cruel, but I just want to get on some land."

I looked over at Savinka, and she nodded. I turned to Vashanti and Lotus, and they nodded as well. "Okay, I'll put it to the whole group tonight at dinner. I want to let them know that we have found our site."

Before we said our goodbyes, I checked on the baby bunny.

His fur was starting to come in. It was still white around his ears and nose, but the new fur was gray. He was doing so well and so was the lamb. I asked the girls to keep running tests on the samples and make sure that the initial results were correct. After I was satisfied that the animals were doing well, I headed back to my cabin. I had about an hour before dinner time. I wanted to relax before I stood in front of everyone.

I turned on the hot water and climbed into the shower. I washed my body and then just stood under the water until the water ran cold. I climbed out, found clean clothes, and pulled my hair up. I hauled my ass off the bed after sliding on my boots and made my way to the dining room. On the way I decided to let everyone eat first before I talked to them.

Rogue, Vox, Garrett, and Mercury had made chicken strips with mashed potatoes. It looked really good, and I was ready to try it.

"Mercury, I see you're settling in. I'm Atlantis, the leader of this rag tag group of people."

Mercury smiled shyly, "Nice to meet you. I'm not sure that I'm settling in, but I wanted to come see what I was supposed to be doing while I processed everything I was shown this morning."

"That's a good way to handle it. Keeping busy will help keep you from freaking out."

"She is doing good so far," Vox assured me. "I already told her we're here to help, and if she needs anything, Rogue and I got her."

Garrett just rolled his eyes. He evidently was still on Lita's side.

"Thank you. These three are really great guys. They will do their best to help you with anything. And I am always available if you need me."

"Yes, Mama," Mercury said with another shy smile.

"It's Atlantis or Iksen. You don't have to be so formal

around here."

She smiled again, and Vox handed me a plate of food. I took my plate and sat down next to Verruca. The rest of the group filled in around us. We chatted about the site we'd researched today. Verruca and I reminisced about old times and talked about when we'd visited the aquarium. She remembered when she was real little looking at jellyfish under the bridge. It would be nice being back somewhere we knew, but it was crazy that it didn't look like what we knew.

I took a deep breath and stood up. I called for everyone's attention. "Hello, everyone. I wanted to let you know that we have found our site."

Cheers erupted throughout the room. I had to laugh. It wasn't what I was expecting. I guessed that would teach me to underestimate everyone's willingness to get off this ship.

"The site we researched today seems to be the best. The initial tests show there is minimal radiation in the soil and water. The plants are almost in perfect condition. I can't say we won't run into problems, but it appears to be the best option. Now more tests are being run to make sure that initial results were correct, but I feel good about this site.

"It has been brought to my attention that not everyone would like to check on Europe. I would like to know how many people would like to do this?" I waited to let everyone have a chance to think about the question. "If you would like to check Europe, raise your hand."

Two hands shot into the air. Then slowly about three more hands raised.

"Who would like to get ready to land ASAP?"

Just about every hand in the room shot into the air. Everyone was ready to get on the ground. I nodded in acknowledgment.

"Then let's be clear. Y'all want to land as soon as we can."

"Yes," the majority of the group answered.

"Our site will be the site we investigated today, which is on the bay of what used to be Corpus Christi, Texas."

"Yes," was again the answer.

"Is there anyone that doesn't agree with this?"

Asp raised his hand.

"Yes?"

"I know that it sounds a little selfish, but I would like to see what has happened to Italy. Most of my family was in the US, but I did have grandparents in Italy. I would think that others who had family on that side of the world want to know what happened."

Dash spoke up, "I had friends that were over there. I just wondered how bad it was there."

Camila stood up. "I just want to know."

I looked around the room. "What does everyone else have to say?"

Gage spoke next. "It would be good to know what the rest of the world is like. But I would rather get to the ground." Many other heads nodded in agreement.

Still nodding in agreement, Clover spoke, "I know we should get as much info as we can about the world as a whole, but I just want to be on solid ground. Once we settle, we can find a way to learn about the other side of the Earth."

"Okay, sounds like the majority is in agreement. We will land instead of researching the other side."

The crowd nodded their heads and murmured *yes*. I sat down and went back to talking to the council at the table. "We need to have a meeting in the morning. I want to put this to a vote with y'all before we make a final decision." The group nodded in agreement. We all sat a while longer talking about what we were going to do first once we were back on land. Personally, I could not wait to go to the shore and walk in the surf.

Eventually, the conversations died down and everyone

began to leave.

Night got up and reached his hand out to me. Taking it, I said goodnight to everyone and followed Night out of the dining room. Before the elevator doors could close, Kilian stepped into the elevator with us. He took my free hand. None of us talked until we were lying in bed. All we said was goodnight before we passed out.

CHAPTER THIRTY: THE END IS NEAR

I got up early the next morning and left the boys sleeping. I got dressed quickly and headed off to the dining hall. I grabbed something quick and had Rogue take food to the cabin for the guys. We had a lot to do to get ready for a landing. I stepped on to the bridge, and everything turned on.

"Vega, I want you to monitor the air and weather every minute of every day for the Corpus site until we land."

"Yes, Ms. Atlantis," Vega said as tiny sparks shot off in front of me until his form came into view.

His theatrical entrances were something. I just shook my head as he looked at me waiting for commands. "I want video and pictures of the area too. We need all the info we can get about this area so we have as complete a picture as we can of the site. Also, please scan for the best spot to land the ship and create a living space. I would like it to be as close to the beach as possible."

"Yes, Ms. Atlantis."

"One last thing. I need you to pull up our landing procedures. We need to know how to land this thing. Everyone needs to be prepared in their roles to land this ship in case we need to do it manually."

"Sent, Ms. Atlantis."

"Now let's start a to-do list for pre-landing actions."

"I am ready when you are, Ms. Atlantis."

I ran through the things to do, and Vega made the list. Once it was complete, he put it on the main viewing screen. I was double checking it when people started trickling in. After another five minutes, everyone had made it onto the bridge.

"Morning, everyone. We need to vote on landing first or checking out Europe first. I am good with whatever everyone wants. I just want to make sure that it is what everyone wants or at least what the majority wants."

Jax scooted forward in his seat-"I think landing is the right call, to be honest."

"I have to agree," said Juniper. "I want to know what the rest of the world looks like, but we need to be on the ground. I worry that if we try to make this ship get up to those speeds, something will happen to keep us from landing."

Cash sat down next to Juniper. "I worry that the longer we're up here, the harder it will become to get down, too. Also, there is good weather right now, and we don't know when that might change."

Ronan leaned back and placed his hands behind his head-"Look like it's obvious that everyone just wants to land. We want off this ship."

"Well, that settles that. We will land instead of checking the rest of Earth. Next thing is the checklist. I sent the list to everyone. On this list are things for everyone to do to get ready to land. There is also a copy of the landing procedure. We all need to be familiar with how to land this ship manually in case we have to.

"This ship has been in space over a hundred years, and we just don't know how it will hold up as it enters the Earth's atmosphere. Everyone will need to be prepared for this. Please let me know when you have completed the checklist and read over the landing procedures. Last thing is, when do we want to land? How fast can we get prepared, do you guys think? Am I being optimistic by saying we can do this in five days?"

Jax's tone was eager and excited, "Hell, no. I think if everyone starts right now, we can easily be ready in five days."

"Okay, so this is our new plan?" I asked, meeting every-one's eyes. "Get us ready for landing in five days?"

There were answers of *yes, absolutely,* and nodding heads from the council.

I maneuvered myself in front of the group asking for the finial time, "Anyone have any doubts or any reasons to delay or issues you think might need to be addressed before we start this final adventure of ours?"

Everyone sat there for a minute thinking through every-thing. I waited for their answers as I looked over the to-do list. I was broken out of my thoughts when Verruca spoke.

"I don't think there is anything that needs addressing, but I do think that everyone should go through the landing pro-cedures. Like in a simulation so we can train a little bit in case of issues."

Night stepped forward, "I agree on the training. I think all of the council should train on their assigned jobs. I also think that myself, Jax, Kilian, Ronan, and Ryo need to check all com-ponents of the engines along with the core. We need to make sure everything is running correctly, and nothing pops up in all the diagnostic."

"I agree. I think the agents should be put in charge of se-curing the cargo bays, and as much as they can on each deck. Juniper, can you work with Vega to set up the simulations for any possible issues we could have during landing?"

Juniper nodded sharply. "I'll start right away."

"Cash, can you make sure all equipment is ready for explo-ration when we land and then make sure it is secured for landing? Especially, we need to make sure that the human-sized drone is ready for a flight."

Cash typed notes on his tablet before he said, "I'll run all the preflight checks on all the drones. They will be ready when we land."

"My last thing is for when we land. We will need to set up

a perimeter as soon as we land. We will need some kind of alarm system that will notify us if anything passes a certain point.

"Along with that, I think we need some kind of deterrent for the animals, but for people as well. Juniper, can you assign this to a specific group of people?"

Juniper tapped her finger on her chin for a minute. "Yes, I'll find some people. I think I already know who would be great at this."

"This is also a good time for Ace to start putting his currency plan or some type of plan to pay people together. Ronan, can you let him know to have this complete and ready to go no later than the second week we're on the ground?"

"I will," Ronan answered.

I clapped my hands-"Then let's make this happen."

After the group left, I went back to examine the newest reports for our site. I knew it had only been a few hours, but I wanted to start filling in what we were going to be facing once we were on the ground. Vega had compiled several reports on the weather and air. I looked through them, adding info to our table map. I had been at it for a couple hours when I remembered I needed to check in with the girls in the lab.

"Vega?"

"Yes, Ms. Atlantis."

"Can you do your best to communicate with the satellite this week? I would like to know any and all information that it passes to you. I know it's not reliable in its communication but whatever we can gather might be a help in our plans to land in five days."

"Yes, I'll collect everything I can from it. I'll also do my best to decipher the info and compile it into different groups that will help you understand it better."

"Perfect, I want to head off any and all issues beforehand if possible."

"Yes, Ms. Atlantis."

Vega and I finished just as the elevator made it to the black deck. I wandered my way to the labs, and when I walked in the girls were busy prepping everything for landing. They looked like busy little ants hard at work. They were so busy they didn't even notice me until I spoke.

"I see y'all heard about our plan to land in five days."

They all jumped and turned. "Bloody hell, you scared t'shite out of me," Sphynx said, clutching her chest.

A snort of amusement burst out of me before I could stop it. "Your English side comes out big time when you get scared."

"Sorry, but you really scared me."

"Yes, to answer your question, we know," Savinka said, still slightly breathing hard. "Verruca sent us a message because she knew the lamb was due any day now."

"I'm sorry, guys. I was coming to check to see if the other tests came back with the same results as the first. I didn't mean to give y'all a heart attack."

Savinka smiled widely. "Yes, they did. This is our spot."

Vashanti bounced on her toes. "Oh, and guess what? We are delivering the lamb this afternoon. I want to make sure he is doing well before we land."

"Would it hurt him if we leave him until we land? I mean I am worried about the whole landing and changing gravity effect on him that might hurt him when he's so new."

Vashanti and Savinka said in canon, "I hadn't thought about that being an issue."

Vashanti paused for a moment thinking- "Technically, the lamb is due in six days. It shouldn't hurt him to stay in his bag until we land, but we would have to get him out very shortly afterward."

Sphynx looked at some notes on her tablet. "The other bunny will be due about another five days after we land."

"I think we should leave him until we land, but you guys know better than me. So I need y'all to tell me what's best." I looked between the three women.

Vashanti answered, "We can leave him until we land." The other two nodded their agreement.

"Okay, let me know if anything changes or if y'all need help securing everything before we land."

"We will," they called out in unison.

Not knowing what to do next, since everyone else was doing all the hard stuff, I decided to go get a snack. I wandered my way to the other side of the black deck, but about halfway to the dining hall it hit me — we were about to go back to the ground for real. Not just a quick let-me-see-how-things-are trip, but we-are-staying-for-a-long-time trip. I leaned heavily into the wall, body going slack, allowing myself to slightly slide down it. I felt a little dizzy thinking about it. I took deep breaths as I rested my hands on my knees and leaned my head forward. It was just that finally we were getting to the end. We had reached our goal. We were only five days away from walking on actual grass, breathing real air, hell! Touching sand and ocean. Sighing deeply, I stood up slowly to gain my composure. Once standing, and not feeling like I was going to pass out anymore, I slowly walked the rest of the way to the dining hall.

When I got there, Rogue and Mercury were busy making lunch for everyone. When Rogue saw me, he immediately began making me a plate of food. He was such a good kid. I took the plate from him and let them both know about our plan to land in five days. We also discussed what needed to be done to secure the kitchen for the landing. They assured me they would have things ready by then. I then went out to find a seat.

Sitting at the table by myself. I let my mind drift back to what Earth used to be like. Memories of things we used to do in Corpus flooded my mind.

Verruca's first trip to the aquarium rushed in. Her little face had lit up when she'd seen all the fish. We'd had to find the sharks before we could look at anything else. Once the sharks had been seen for at least a good thirty minutes, it had all been about the sea kitties. That's what she'd called otters. She'd laughed and laughed as they slid down the slides and turned flips in the water.

I was jerked out of my memories when Verruca touched my shoulder.

"Mom, you good?" Verruca tilted her head sideways with a questioning smile on her lips and a quizzical crease between her brows.

"Yeah, I'm good. I was just remembering your first trip to the aquarium. That's all."

"Oh my god. Please keep that to yourself. I don't need anyone knowing how excited I get about animals."

"Ahh, come on, you don't want anyone to know how much you love sea kitties or sharks? Or that you have a shark birth mark on your shoulder? I mean, some people on this ship already know that one." I raised one eyebrow and smiled.

Verruca squinted her eyes at me while puckering her lips in a look of *how dare you call me out like that*.

After a few seconds I shrugged my shoulders, tilted my head slightly and smiled innocently at her.

She walked into the kitchen area to grab some lunch, then came back and sat down with me. As we reminisced, more and more people trickled in to get lunch.

Once our group of people joined us, the conversations turned into story telling. Everyone remembered different things that they used to do. Some talked about their favorite places to go when they were kids. Some talked about just hanging out with family and barbecuing. I sat back and enjoyed listening to everyone's stories. Everyone was laughing, having fun.

They had all begun to relax up here in their roles and were beginning to find their groove in our lives as we knew it. I just hoped that we would find even more of this sense of community and togetherness once we were on the ground.

As each one finished their meal, they began to head back to what they had been doing or headed toward new tasks. As for me, I walked back to the bridge to see what had been going on with our site for the last few hours. I pulled up all the reports and scattered them across the screen. Weather so far had held out as mild, holding steady at fifty five. A little warmer than predicted, but since there was only one half-assed satellite sending out weather info, I doubted it was one hundred percent accurate.

I continued to study our site for several hours trying to learn all that I could from the incoming information. Vega had been able to compile the first round of information from the satellite for me, and that was wild to read through. There was random information about a meeting that was to be held in the capital. The more I read, the more I was convinced that the information was from the past. I moved over to some weather info. I wasn't sure if the first set of info was about our area or more like a bunch of different areas all run together. Moving farther down the page, I came to some relevant weather information about our landing site. I put the information into a chart. Some was previous days' weather and others were upcoming weather. The info gave me a little bit of a look at what had been going on and what was to come. After getting that info sorted and trying again to make heads or tails of the other, I decided I needed a break.

It seemed to be later than I thought, so I checked the time on my holo. It was five thirty which meant dinner would be ready soon, but I didn't feel like going to the dining room. Lifting my wrist, I sent a quick message to Night and Kilian for one of them to bring me food. I went to our cabin and flopped over on the couch. Once comfortable, I gave commands for the projector to play a movie.

I was well into my second movie when the guys came in with dinner. I didn't get off the couch. I just sat up and waited for my plate.

The guys put all the food on the counter and began making plates. After a couple minutes Kilian walked over to the couch and handed me mine. They both took seats on either side of me, and we ate as the movie finished. Then I started a third one. I just wanted a night of relaxation.

Kilian took my plate when I was done and let us know that he was going to take a shower.

Night pulled me over to lie in his lap. He ran his fingers through my hair as we watched the movie.

When Kilian returned, they switched places and Night went to take a shower. Kilian began running his fingers through my hair. By the time the movie was done, not only was Night done with his shower, but I was sleepy. I led them to bed, and we crawled in. I was too tired for anything fun tonight, but it seemed the guys were as well.

Chapter Thirty-One: Rough Landing

The next three days flew by with training on landing procedures, running diagnostics, prepping the ship, and doing a few minor repairs. They guys found a leak in cargo bay B4's door. They thought it had happened during the asteroid storm. Then we had some glitches with black holos and tablets not connecting with the main system. Vega, Kilian, and Ronan, with a little help from Rogue, were able to get the glitches worked out.

Now it was the day before launch, and I could feel the nervous excitement in the air. Everyone was more than ready to get off this ship, me included. I spoke with almost everyone today. I gave last-minute instructions and assured everyone that we had done all we could to make sure we got back to Earth safely.

It was finally dinner time, but I could not spend the night with everyone in the dining room, my nerves were too out of control. I had Rogue bring me food for at least three people. I let the guys know, and I began making dinner. I wasn't even sure if I could eat. I decided to keep it simple and make steak, home fries, and carrots for dinner. I was throwing the last round of potatoes in the skillet when Verruca came in. She came straight over and hugged me.

"What's wrong, baby girl?"

"Just a little worried about tomorrow. I know we have done everything we can. I know the area has been proved to be the best place to land. I'm just still a little nervous about all of it. What are we going to encounter on the ground?" She stood next to me with her head lying on my shoulder. Then she stole a fry from the plate.

"Hey." I smacked her hand out of my fries. "I know. I have been running a number of scenarios in my head all week, but we don't know, so we just have to be prepared for all of it," I said and laid my cheek on top of her head while I continued to flip potatoes.

We stood like that for a little while. Then Verruca asked if all seven of us could do dinner together tonight. I didn't care we just had to get more food. Verruca volunteered to go get more stuff. She said she would inform everyone on her way. Once she got back, we finished making dinner. We added some chicken to the mix so there was enough for everyone.

We had finished the food just before our people came in. Ryo and Night went next door and got two tables and extra chairs. They set it up, and Verruca, Sphynx, and I laid the food out on the tables. Once everyone had a plate made, the chatter died down.

After everyone had taken several bites, the talking began again. The conversation returned to the first thing they were going to do once we landed. When I was asked what I wanted to do first, I let them know I wanted to go to the water.

Ryo agreed with me. He felt the ocean calmed him. Verruca was ready to just see some green land. Night and Kilian agreed with her. Sphynx and Jax wanted blue sky and the river. Jax also wanted to go on a hunt for a motorcycle and see what he could do to make it run.

He had the right idea, and my mind ran off in a tangent on vehicles. We were going to have to find a way to make vehicles run or maybe create some kind of vehicle. Nope, I told myself, stop right there, because that was a problem for after we landed. I rejoined the conversation, and they had moved on to living arrangements. Everyone wanted to make homes off the ship, and they were talking about what they were going to build. That was one thing I had been thinking about a lot. Ryo wanted to build something on the beach so he could wake up every morning to the water. I liked that idea myself. I looked at Kilian and Night, nodding my head and pointing to myself, as Ryo talked about building a house on the beach.

"I think we have our work cut out for us," Night said to Kilian.

"Damn straight you do, but I could work with one on the river."

They laughed, but I wasn't playing, and Verruca told them so. Then we laughed because their faces dropped a little.

"It's okay, boys. Mom will build her own if she has to. Y'all don't know her. Of course, I'll help her, but she will get out there and do it herself."

Sphynx turned to look at her. "Well, I think I want something close to the river as well. Where do you want a house, Verruca?"

"I think closer to the river because I like the greenery more than the sand," Verruca answered her while taking her hand.

"Well, I guess we will see what options we have once we land. We will have to see what's under all those hills."

"That is true," Jax said. "We have to make sure that the ground we build on is stable. Hell, we may find some houses under all that foliage."

"Maybe, but what would be standing after all these years?" Kilian pointed out.

"Well, the bridge was mostly still standing. Pieces of the aquarium were still standing. It looked like some of the holding tanks for the refineries were still standing too. So, we may find something." I shrugged my shoulders.

The conversation now moved into what would still be standing after all this time. We shifted to the living room once everyone had stuffed themselves. We sprawled on the couch, the chairs and some on the floor. The conversation was ongoing and jumped from one subject to another until Sphynx realized it was almost eleven. As hard as it was, we decided to call it a night. We all said our goodbyes and Verruca's quartet left for their cabin.

I went to the kitchen to put up what was left of the food. Then I joined Kilian and Night in bed. When I got there, they were passed out. I, on the other hand, took a little longer to fall asleep. My mind would not shut up for a while. It kept running though all kinds of things.

I guess finally my body won out, because I was woken up by the alarm. I rolled to my left but didn't hit a body. I rolled to the right and didn't hit a body. I forced my eyes to open and saw that I was in bed alone.

I got up, took a shower, got dressed, and was fixing to head out to the dining room when I saw my breakfast was waiting on the table. I sat down at the table and enjoyed it in silence. Honestly, it was just what I needed before we started our landing today.

I had only been sitting for a few minutes when Verruca came in. She was carrying two muffins and a glass of tea. She sat down in the chair across from me and we ate our breakfast. We didn't talk, we just sat there and ate. When we were done, we got up to head to the bridge. Halfway to the elevator she linked our arms together. While in the elevator she leaned her head on my shoulder. Then before the door opened, she hugged me hard.

The door opened, and our game faces were on. Night was standing at the flight control panel. Ryo and Juniper were at the communications panel. Jax, Kilian, and Cash were in the engine room. Sphynx, Vashani, and Savinka were getting everyone to the common area of the blue deck. Zahirah, Onyx,

Camila, and Gage were setting up the nearest cabin in case we had injuries during the landing. All the agents went to escort Lita and Ryker to the common area and were in charge of watching them until we landed, and then they could go back into lockdown.

Verruca took a seat in one of the three seats that would be considered captain and officer chairs. I was too anxious to sit.

"Vega, open a line of communication to everyone."

"It's open, Ms. Atlantis."

"Is everyone ready?"

I received *yeses* from everyone. I took a deep breath.

"Everyone, we are about to make the best and wildest trip of our lives. We are going back home, but it is not the home we left. There are so many unknowns that you might be scared. Please know that I want all of us to make it in one piece and to thrive in this new world. Everything we have done has led us to this point, and I want to say thank you for trusting me enough to get us here. Now, everyone settle in, and let's get this show on the road. Vega, please start our descent."

"Yes, Ms. Atlantis," Vega answered, and the countdown started.

I took a seat next to Verruca. I watched the numbers on the screen count down. When the one disappeared from the screen, the thrusters kicked in and we felt a weight pulling us toward the floor. The ship was vibrating very hard as the thrusters pushed us toward the Earth. I had debated with myself over and over about whether I wanted to see where we were going or not. Finally, I decided I wanted to see, so the main screen was on live view.

The closer we got to the Earth the harder the ship vibrated. It took another thirty minutes before we began to enter the outer portion of the atmosphere and the shaking picked up. The front of the ship was starting to turn red as we entered.

The shaking was so hard I had to adjust myself before I slid out of my chair. I jumped at the sound of an alarm going off from the panel in front of Juniper and Ryo.

"What is going on?" I said loudly over the noise.

Juniper yelled back, "We don't know yet, Iksen."

She and Ryo were frantically typing. Their hands flew across the panel tapping in some places and sliding fingers along other sections. They got the alarm to shut off but had not found the reason why it went off.

"The GPS function is not working," Ryo said as his hands still danced across the panel.

"How will that affect us?"

"Not completely sure yet. We can still navigate the ship. But it will probably cause us not to hit our target right on," he answered.

"Okay, keep working on it. If it's just GPS, and all that happens is we land off course, then we're good."

We were now about midway through the thermosphere. All we were seeing was the ship breaking through the barrier. I was slightly nervous that our ship's thermal protection couldn't handle this heat. We were just entering the next layer when another alarm went off.

"*Chingoa!* What now?" I yelled, gripping my seat arms tightly.

"A main thruster is sputtering. It could just be spitting out the dust. Let's give it a minute to work out the kinks," Night said as he turned to look at me.

"Okay, sorry. It's just we're getting so close I don't want to be derailed."

Night was right. After a few minutes the thruster worked out its issues and began to function correctly.

"Vega, can you pull me up a live feed of the common area where everyone is riding this out."

"Yes, Ms. Atlantis."

A live stream popped up on the far side of the main screen. People were huddled together, but everyone seemed to be handling it well. I was glad they had not heard the alarms go off. I settled back into my seat. We were only a few miles from breaching the last layer of atmosphere. It looked like we were heading in the right direction when another alarm went off.

"That thruster went out completely. Our nose is pointing down too much. I am working on pulling it back up," Night informed us before I could get a word out.

I stood up, but I didn't go to the panel like I wanted to. I let him work, but it took everything I had to not go over and push him out of the way so I could fix it myself. I stood staring at the back of his head willing him to fix the problem. Verruca reached over and grabbed my leg. I looked down at her and raised my eyebrow in a questioning gesture. She looked down at my foot. I guess I had been tapping my foot and didn't realize it.

"I think I got it. I had to pull the nose up a little higher than usual so we stayed flat as we continued to enter the atmosphere. I also have several impulse thrusters working overtime on the left side to help compensate for the malfunction. So for now, we're going in a little butt heavy," Night called out as he constantly maneuvered something on the panel.

I snorted slightly and so did Verruca. Our strange sense of humor always kicked in at the wrong times. We could now see land. It was looking like we were coming in right where we needed to be. Then another damn alarm went off.

Night raised a hand. "Don't ask. We are coming in a little fast, but we should be fine." Then another alarm went off. "It's okay, we lost two of the impulse thrusters, but I am making all the others give me all they have."

The ship was now extremely butt heavy and leaning to the left. I looked over at the live video of our passengers. More groups were huddled together, forming larger groups.

"Vega, patch me through to the other passengers."

"Done, Ms. Atlantis."

"Awakees, this is your Iksen speaking. Please hold on. We are almost on the ground—" I was cut off because my body was jerked forward by the ship hitting something.

I looked up at the screen in time to see something white falling in the wake of our ship. Whatever it was it had been pretty tall for us to hit it this far in the air. The closer to the ground we got, the more things we seemed to be hitting. It was another few minutes before we actually hit solid ground. Well, somewhat solid, It felt like we were listing slightly to one side.

The group of us on the bridge went down to the main cargo bay. We opened the door and let the ramp down. As soon as the ramp fell into place it scraped against something metal. Out of nowhere, a wall of flames shot into the air.

Night snatched me back out of the way and flung his free arm out to stop Verruca who had tried to follow me. He pulled us back into the cargo bay. Kilian slammed his hand on the button to lift the ramp and close the door.

"Son of a motherless goat!"

My hands flew to the front of my hair checking to see if it had been burned. Verruca was clutching her chest and breathing hard. Night's hands were running all over my body and Kilian flew to my side trying to check me for injuries as well.

"Stop it," I said slapping their hands away. "I'm fine. Vega, what the hell happened?"

"I am not sure, Ms. Atlantis. We seem to be about a mile and a half off target. But I am not sure about the rest. I am running the database right now trying to learn as much as I can about what used to be in this area."

"Is the fire still burning?"

"Yes."

"Can you move the ship without us on the bridge?"

"I can try, Ms. Atlantis."

The ship jerked into movement, and I fell forward onto my knees. Verruca fell on her ass and then we all laughed. But our hysterics were over as quickly as they had come. Verruca and I stood up with help from Night and Kilian.

"Vega, speak to me."

"I am maneuvering the ship farther down, closer to where I believe we were supposed to land. We are touching ground now."

Sure enough, we were jostled around some more as the ship touched down.

"Vega, is it safe to open the door?"

"Yes, Ms. Atlantis."

Kilian was about to push the button again to open the door and lower the ramp when Verruca stopped him.

"Vega, call the rest of the awakees so they can see this too."

"Yes, Ms. Verruca."

We waited for several minutes while the rest of the awakees joined us. Kilian then pushed the button again. This time when the ramp lowered, we were looking at nothing but green grass, a barely visible flowing river in the distance, and waves crashing on to the shore. Everyone spilled out of the ship and scattered across the grass.

Night was dragging me by the hand as Kilian walked fast to try and keep up. Verruca, Sphynx, Ryo and Jax stood just ahead of us. Night stopped just behind them and wrapped his arm around my shoulders, tucking me into his side. I leaned my head against Night's chest, and Kilian, who had finally caught up, snaked his arm around my waist.

We stood just taking in the beautiful sight in front of us. I was just so relieved that I took a long deep breath of fresh air and exhaled it.

The guys both looked at me with big smiles on their faces, then squeezed me between them in a hug.

Verruca and her quartet were pointing and talking about the landscape. She was leaning into Ryo with one arm around his waist. Sphynx was leaning her head on Verruca's shoulder and Jax had an arm across both girls' shoulders. Then Verruca turned her head to looked at me. A small smile played at the corner of her lips. She mouthed, "Thank you," and reached out a hand to me. I released my hold on Kilian to take her hand. She held it for several long moments, but we didn't need words to convey what we were both thinking.

We made it was what we were both thinking, and we knew it was because my determination had got us here.

To be continued . . .

ABOUT THE AUTHOR

Michell Burgan's debut novel is a wild ride of surviving in space and finding love. She loves art in all its forms and practices many of them herself. Besides writing fun and steamy novels, she paints, draws, works with acrylic, and does photography. Several of her photos have won awards online.

Michell is a Texan at heart but decided to change her scenery. She and her daughter made a move across the country to Oregon to try something new.

To find some of Michell's other fun stories and blogs, please visit her at rydiankainbooksandart.wordpress.com or see her pictures on Instagram @michellburgan.

Glossary

AGS: Anti-Gravity Suits.

Awakees: What the people on the ship are called because they have to be woken up from cryo sleep.

Bea: (Pronounced Pea) Overly large Polar Bear-looking creature with translucent patches of skin that allow one to see inside their body.

Black Holo Communication Device: AKA: black holo, holo, or communicators: A smart-watch-like device that the awakees on the ship use to communicate with each other.

Coronal Cloud: Often confused with solar winds. Coronal clouds are released when a solar flare becomes a coronal mass ejection. The coronal cloud often contains more radioactive particles than the mass ejection itself.

Drakes: The middle rank of the vampires. Extremely strong but have some healing issues. They are used as the warriors of the vampire ranks.

Drone Cargo Bay: The cargo bay on the Black deck or Deck 5 that holds the human sized drone and the storage crates with the four smaller drones.

Embers: The lowest level of the vampire ranks. They barely made the transition. Their stamina is brief. They are used as the soldiers of the vampire armies because they are expendable due to their health issues.

Fang Wraiths: The humans that did not make the transition into vampires. They are mindless rabid creatures that attack anything. The disease causes their bodies to rapidly deteriorate.

Fuel Tabs: Compressed powder tabs of a low grade jet fuel.

Gila Monster: A large venomous lizard. Usually, they have black and orange stripped skin. Native to the southwestern US and Mexico.

Grimm Dog: Very large black wolf like creature with shaggy black fur.

Iksen: A word for a leader.

Jades: Top rank of vampires. Called Jades because they all have green eyes. Smartest, strongest, and overall healthiest of the vampire ranks.

Launch Bay: The bay located between the drone bay and another cargo bay on the Black deck where the drones are actually launched from. This room will seal off from the other cargo bays before the drones are launched.

MC: Motorcycle Club

Moon Viper: The spaceship that everyone is on.

Prospect: An initiate/pledge for a motorcycle club.

Razor Cat: Overly large black panther-like cat. Furless, black leathery skin with white spine-looking bones that protrude from their tails.

Rot Fang: A fang wraith in the last stages of the disease. One is called a Rot Fang because they lose their fangs first, then slowly but surely other body parts begin to fall off.

Sexcapades: Sexual escapades.

Shaka: The universal surfer hand gesture.

Venom Dog: Overly large hyena looking dog with green toxic drool.

Decks of the Ship

Deck 5 or Black Deck: bottom deck of ship; three pod rooms; dining hall; cargo bay B1 and B2 are drone hangers with flight room between; three cargo bays equipped to hold animals; several large empty rooms; engine room on far end.

Deck 4 or Gold Deck: family cabins located at front of deck; three labs; several empty work rooms.

Deck 3 or Silver Deck: all cabins; family cabins located at back of deck; two-bedroom cabins located at front of deck; communal spaces located at back and front of deck.

Deck 2 or Green Deck: five one-bedroom cabins located at front of deck; two-bedroom cabins take up the rest of deck; communal area located at front and back of deck.

Deck 1 or Blue Deck: all one-bedroom cabins; communal area located at front and back of deck.

Bridge: a circular room located on the very top of the ship; holds all navigation and communication main workstations.

APPENDIX OF CHARACTER NAMES AND FUNCTIONS ON THE SHIP

Vega: ship's AI.

Atlantis Rey: MC of story; Iksen/Leader of the group; former loss prevention manager; mother of Verruca Rey; lover to Night Blue and Kilian Ryan.

Night Blue: Council Member; ship engineer; back up pilot; former airplane mechanic; lover to Atlantis Rey and Kilian Ryan.

Kilian Ryan: Council Member; ship Sargent At Arms; oversees security team; former navy weapons specialist; lover to Atlantis Rey and Night Blue.

Verruca Rey: Vice Iksen; daughter to Atlantis Rey; former hair stylist; lover to Ryo Kekoa, Sphynx Jade, and Jax Kelean.

Ryo Kekoa: Council Member; ship lead pilot; back-up engineer; former pilot; brother to Ronan; lover to Verruca Rey, Sphynx Jade, and Jax Kelean.

Ronan Kekoa: Council Member; security team inspector; former martial arts teacher; brother to Ryo Kekoa; lover to Savinka Azeem and Zahirah Harber.

Jax Kelean: Council Member; lead engineer; former motorcycle mechanic; lover to Sphynx Jade, Verruca Rey, and Ryo Kekoa.

Cash Lee: Council Member; a lead trainer; lead drone

operator; former music teacher; lover to Juniper Lovelace.

Juniper Lovelace: Council Member; a lead trainer; overall helper; former science teacher; lover to Cash Lee.

Savinka Azeem: Council Member; lead researcher and doctor; former oncologist; lover to Ronan Kekoa and Zahirah Harber.

Zahirah Harber: Council Member; former court translator; mom to Talora 5 years old, Kyril 7 years old, and Sefa 13 years old; helps where needed.

Sphynx Jade: research assistant; former research lab tech and tattoo artist; lover to Jax Kelean, Verruca Rey, and Ryo Kekoa.

Lita Quinn: mediation team member; former lawyer; in a simi-relationship with Ryker Devin

Ryker Devin: ship cook; former chef and restaurant owner; in a simi-relationship with Lita Quinn.

Gage Delgado: mediation team member; former construction business owner.

Camela Tack: mediation team member; former lawyer; ex-sister-in-law to Sybella Faden; aunt to Isadora Faden.

Vashanti Tate: research assistant; former ER nurse; wife to Lennox Tate; mom to Ky Tate.

Lennox Tate: clinic assistant; security team agent; former X-ray tech; husband to Vashanti Tate; father to Ky Tate.

Sybella Faden: clinic assistant; former dentist; mom to Isadora 16yrs old.

Shade Griffin: security team agent; back-up pilot; former Navy Seal.

Clover Drum: security team agent; former cop and welder.

Lotus Haze: research assistant; former scientist; lover to Onyx

Drake.

Onyx Drake: clinic assistant; former medicine women/ natural healer; lover to Lotus Haze.

Ace Stokes: security team agent; former banker; twin brother to Vox Stokes.

Vox Stokes: ship cook; former restaurant/bar owner; twin brother to Ace Stokes.

Rogue Nightshade: ship cook; former YouTube star.

Knox Fuller: security team agent; former stockbroker.

Dash Zager: security team agent; former store manager.

Sage Fox: security team agent.

Asp Mabin: security team agent.

Mercury Eagleton: kitchen assistant; former professional surfer.